Broken

K.M. Harding

To Nicola,
Thank you! ♡

Cover design by Andrew Harding
Independently Published.
ISBN: 979-8-7397-4744-0

For Ryan & Rachel,
Andy,
Cathy, Claire,
Ann & Janice.

Chapter One

I'm running. I'm bolting as fast as my feet can carry me. My legs are aching. My ankles are starting to swell, but I refuse to slow. I keep moving forward. Never looking back. I keep running. I need to keep running.

I know he is there. I can hear his footsteps pounding in the distance, echoing my racing heartbeat. I can hear the twigs cracking under his feet and the sound of his deep voice as he calls my name. An involuntary shiver runs down my spine at every "Daniella" he yells, and I can only hope and pray I will come across someone, anyone, before he catches me. I can't let him catch me. I keep running. I need to keep running.

I have nowhere to run to, nowhere to hide, yet I keep going. Staring straight ahead, I weave my way through the vast trees. No matter where I go, he will eventually find me, but I can't let that stop me. He will never stop. He will never tire, never slow, and never give up. I keep running. I need to keep running.

My ankle gives way, sending me crashing to the ground with a thud. I cling to my ankle, wincing from the searing pain shooting up my leg. The tears are stinging my eyes. I need to get up. I need to move. I'm wasting time. I climb to my feet, but I fall straight back down, the fatigue overwhelming me. I can hear him growing closer. I need to run. I need to keep running.

I drag myself to my feet, limping as I desperately try to regain my speed. It's no good. I've slowed down. His footsteps are louder now, and the sound is deafening. Fuck! I can hear his harsh, penetrating breaths as he nears. My legs feel weak. My ankle is screaming in agony. The tiredness is creeping into my bones. My body is failing me. The tiny sliver of hope is draining away and evaporating into thin air. I try to keep running. I need to keep running.

A hand yanks my hair. My head snaps backwards, and my back lands hard on the ground. I hear something crack, and I involuntarily let out an almighty, ear-piercing scream.

"You can run but you can't hide," he taunts cockily, towering over me. "I will always find you."

I can't move. He's on top of me now, pinning me to the ground. I want to get up, to use any morsel of remaining strength to throw him off me, but I'm too weak, and he's too strong. He's smirking, and the sight sickens me. I spit in his face in one last attempt… Crack. *He punches me in the chest, and the pain is excruciating. The tears I've been fighting so hard to hold back come streaming out like endless waterfalls down my cheeks. I shouldn't cry. He likes it when I cry. He gets off on it. Crying only makes things worse.*

He stands. I try to take the opportunity to move but he slams his foot against my chest, knocking the wind out of me. I cough, gasping for air as he allows me to roll onto my side. My head is starting to spin. The nausea is burning the back of my throat. My chest is writhing in agony, and I cling to it, wrapping my arms around my body, preparing for what's to come.

Slam. *His foot collides with my stomach.* Slam. Slam.

I wake up screaming, jolting upright, in a pool of sweat. I instinctively scan my surroundings, my bed, my bedside table and empty magnolia walls. I take a deep breath. I'm safe.

My alarm clock rings. I groan, slamming my hand against it, and the silence that follows is blissful. It's half-six in the morning. Despite my usual, nasty wake-up call, getting up still isn't easy. I want to stay in the comforts of my bed, wrapped in my duvet where it's warm and cosy, but unfortunately, I need to get my backside to work.

The sun is shining far too brightly through the useless cream curtains I keep meaning to replace as I drag myself out of bed and head over to my free-standing mirror. I scan my reflection and sigh. I'm starting to think I'll never get used to the twenty-five-year-old face staring back at me, yet despite my lack of sleep, I don't look completely awful. My long blonde hair is loosely curled, falling around my shoulders, and the circles under my hazel eyes are not too obvious. I'm pale, but that's just my unfortunate natural skin colour – there is no colour – and I'd make a bloody good vampire at Halloween, no make-up required.

It doesn't take me long to get ready – it never does – and I quickly wash before heading back into my bedroom. From the suitcases I've yet to unpack sitting on the floor, I grab my clean clothes and throw on my usual long-sleeved black top that falls neatly to just below my hips, making sure the holes at the bottom of the sleeves are fastened securely around my thumbs, my matching hip-length cardigan and my work-only jeans. I take another glance in the mirror – sigh-free this time – and run a brush through my hair. I'll do.

I make my way into my open-plan living room slash kitchen, heading straight for the kettle. Just like most mornings and every second of the day thereafter, I'm craving a caffeine fix and a nice, hot cup of coffee is calling my name. I glance at the empty dishes sitting pretty next to the sink as I wait for the kettle to boil, reminding me of the company I kept last night. And no, before your dirty mind kicks in, it wasn't a man. Well, technically, there was a man, but not in the way you're thinking. It was my neighbours.

I live in a two-bedroomed basement flat in a rather large block of flats in a place called Stanton, a town on the outskirts of Manchester. The perk of being in the basement is that I share a communal entrance with only one other flat, but the downside is it's shared by two people, two *relentless* people who, despite my best efforts, have practically forced themselves into my life.

I moved in roughly a year ago with every intention of keeping myself to myself and for the most part, I still do, but no matter how much I tried, I could not keep my neighbours, particularly Jess, at bay. It took a week before the pair of them were inviting me out or in for a brew and at first, I respectfully declined. But like I said, they are relentless and before long, I resigned myself to an easy life by opting for the lesser of two evils, staying home rather than going out, but with company rather than alone.

I don't do going out, apart from work and my weekly food shop, and no matter how relentless my neighbours are, that is not going to change any time soon. So, to keep the peace, my neighbours clog up my living room once a week for a movie night. I also cook, providing my neighbours with probably the only home-cooked meal they eat, but as a non-drinker, they bring their own booze. As much as I want a life of solitude, I'm a realist and I know it's impossible to avoid people completely. And despite my many, many issues, I don't mind hanging out with my neighbours, provided it involves the safety and comfort of my own home.

Jess, whom I briefly mentioned, is not bad company despite being the complete opposite to me, both in looks and personality. She's an attractive lass, with long, dirty-blonde hair that falls to her waist, bigger than average boobs, a provocative dress sense that leaves nothing to the imagination and no filter whatsoever, constantly talking about boys and sex like she's stuck in high school despite being twenty-two years old. She enjoys lapping up the male attention though, and from what I've seen, which granted isn't much outside my four walls, she likes to be the centre of attention in all things, and as an aspiring model, she knows how to flaunt it. Yet underneath the partying and blonde bimbo persona, she has a sweetness about her that I like, and I genuinely believe her heart is in the right place.

But with Jess comes her flatmate, James, the buff fitness instructor with an ego the size of China. He's the kind of guy who sleeps with anything that walks and talks provided they are female. He calls it the exploration of all things sexual. I call it having a dick for a brain, but we agree to disagree. He's six foot tall, blonde, tanned and has muscles that bulge out of his T-shirt, on the days he bothers to put a T-shirt on in the first place. Our paths cross in the hallway quite regularly and nine times out of ten, winter, spring or summer, he's topless. Looks-wise, he's every girl's dream guy and he knows it.

Just for the record, James is not *my* dream guy before you start getting any crazy ideas. James is *too* good-looking, and he's got an arrogance about him that grates. Saying that, if James has got one good thing going for him it's his sense of humour. He's a funny guy and he rarely fails to make me laugh.

I've gotten to know quite a bit about both James and Jess, especially since Jess likes to invite herself over a little more regularly than our weekly movie night, usually when James is at it in the bedroom with his latest conquest, and Jess likes to talk. Gossip is probably more accurate, and she's filled me in on every single bad habit James owns, whether I wanted to know about them or not, which is also why the conversation is typically one-sided. I like my privacy, and something tells me Jess would splatter my personal life across every wall in Manchester if I shared, so my silence is something I'm clinging to. James is a little nosier and keener to learn about the mysterious Daniella as he sometimes calls me, but I tend to keep things vague.

I'm about halfway through my brew when I hear my phone ringing from the coffee table in the middle of my basic living room, and when I say basic, I really mean it. There are two brown leather sofas in an L shape, one against the back wall facing the outdated fireplace, and the other with its back towards the kitchen. The walls are magnolia and pictureless, but I am blessed with laminate flooring, and there's a mirror above the white, empty fire surround, but only because it was there when I moved in. In the far-left corner is my telly, and in the right-hand corner is my prized possession, my music set-up, including a large keyboard, two guitars, speakers, a mixer and everything else I need for my songwriting. You'll learn very quickly that music is my one and only passion.

I move to answer my phone and groan at my boss's name flashing across the screen. After a quick hello, I listen to Lloyd asking if I could stay on an extra hour due to a colleague phoning in sick, and although I'm silently cursing, I'm agreeing. Lloyd thanks me then hangs up and resigning myself to a mere hour between my two jobs today, I head into my bedroom to grab job number two's embroidered T-shirt to take with me. There's not much point in returning home in between given both of my jobs are about a half hour's drive away from my flat.

Job number one is as a waitress at Lloyd's, and number two is at Dave's Music Shop, both part-time, but you can guess which one I prefer. Tuesdays, Wednesdays and Thursdays are spent at Lloyd's working eleven in the morning until six in the afternoon, along with a Friday morning, seven-thirty until eleven-thirty, or in today's case, until twelve-thirty. Friday afternoon, half-one until half-five, and a full half-eight until half-five on a Saturday are spent at Dave's. Between them, they give me roughly the equivalent of full-time hours and they pay the bills. Are either of them a career? No. But then my dream career would involve putting myself out there and the likelihood of that happening is slim-to-nothing, so I'm happy to settle with what I've got. Plus, I have a Sunday and a Monday each week to spend working on my music.

I finish my coffee, diminishing my caffeine cravings for the time being, and grab my bag, flinging it over my shoulder so it's sitting across my body before dragging my feet out to the communal entrance. My neighbour's door swings open just as I step out, and I catch a glimpse of James standing in the doorway wearing nothing but his Calvin Klein boxers with a short, blurry-eyed woman beside him. I notice the lass attempting, and failing miserably, to pull down her tacky leopard-print dress that barely covers her backside as I move to retrieve yesterday's post from the locked basket hanging at the back of the main door, and I can't help but smirk. She's a typical example of the many women who share James's bed, a little trashy but drop-dead gorgeous. She stands facing James as if she's waiting for something, but if it's a goodbye kiss, there's nothing but disappointment coming her way. I've played witness to this scene a little too often.

"I had fun," James says in between yawns. "I'll text you."

Liar. I have never seen the same girl twice. I move back towards my flat as the bewildered woman is ushered out of the main door, James shutting it firmly behind her.

"Good morning, Dani," he says, smiling brightly.

"Morning, Jay," I reply, not quite so bright. "Good night?"

"Not everyone is a party pooper like you," James taunts. "And as you can see," he adds, gesturing towards the door and the exited woman, "it turned out to be a very good night."

"Your idea of a good night and mine are two very different things," I say, sifting through my post to check for anything important.

"You need to lighten up and have some fun for a change," James declares, hovering in his doorway again. "All work and no play make Dani an impossible lay." I roll my eyes. It's all about sex for James.

"There's more to life than getting laid."

James laughs, leaning one arm up against the doorframe near his head as though he's posing for a photoshoot. "Yeah, 'cause staying home playing that bloody keyboard all the time is such an exciting life."

I wisely choose to ignore that comment. James will never understand and that's fine by me. Music is my sanctuary. It's the one thing that helps me escape the craziness in my head, and trust me, I need the escape.

"One of these days, Dani," James continues, "I will get you out, and I *will* show you a good time."

"Keep dreaming."

"You don't know what you're missing," he teases, and after chucking my unopened mail inside my flat and locking the door, I purposefully look him up and down.

"There's not much else to miss."

James laughs, flashing me his cheeky boy grin, a grin I can imagine goes down very well with the ladies. "Only the best part," he says, almost seductive in his tone, and I instinctively feel the urge to heave.

We both know exactly what he's referring to, as I'm sure you do too, and I shake my head. I can't fault James for his banter. He doesn't offend easy, and as a sarcastic person myself, most of the time unknowingly, I can pretty much call him every name under the sun or take the absolute mick out of him and he just takes it, giving as good as he gets.

"Seriously," James says, "you should let me take you out sometime. Maybe dinner or the cinema. I promise there will be fun to be had."

If I didn't know any better, I'd say that's an invitation to a date. Nah, no way. James can have any woman he wants, and I highly doubt a scarred freak like me fits the bill. And what James doesn't know is I'm scarred on so many levels, but the one which I am referring to at this moment is the knife wound on my face; it runs from the top right of my forehead, across my nose and to the bottom of my left cheek. My face is not my best feature, something which I pretend not to be self-conscious about, but even I can't deny it affects my confidence. Let's face it, even if James is asking me on a date, it's only out of pity, and the last thing I want is pity.

"Never gonna happen," I say bluntly.

"We'll see," James replies, smiling that cheeky boy grin again, and with that, I exit the building.

The roads are quiet as I drive my good old Nissan Micra towards work. So far, the traffic is light, which is typical of Stanton town, but it'll busy up once I hit Manchester city centre. I call Stanton a town but given its small size, it reminds me more of a large village, with just one supermarket, one bank and one post office occupying its so-called high street. Although there are a lot of pubs for such a small place, not that I've ever stepped inside any of them. I'd rather chew off my own arm.

I arrive at work fifteen minutes early, typical of me being an early bird type who cannot abide being late, and park my car around back before walking down the little side alley to Lloyd's café. Unlocking the door, I prepare myself for the quiet day ahead. Unfortunately, the café is set off down a side street and doesn't get much by way of footfall, and with the increasing number of coffee shops and restaurants popping up, Lloyd's is struggling. It's declined quick too. When I first started here about ten months ago, the place was steady enough and I was kept going, but not so much nowadays. There have been days when I've served maybe only two or three customers in a seven-hour shift. It's dire.

As a result, apart from the two staff members who came and went of their own accord, last month Lloyd was forced to make cuts and lay two people off. Luckily, I wasn't one of them. The pot washer and one of the waitresses were both sent packing because Lloyd couldn't justify paying them anymore. It does mean the remaining waitresses pitch in with the pot washing and food prep from time to time, during those increasingly rare moments the café is busier, but it doesn't bother me. I like to keep busy at work anyway.

Lloyd employs only three people now. His son, Dan, the chef, if you can call him that – it's a café, not a Michelin star restaurant, and we serve pie and chips, not fillet steak or beef wellington – me, of course, and Pamela, a fellow waitress. Lloyd fills in the gaps by working himself, and it tends to be only Dan, or Lloyd on Dan's days off, in the kitchen and one waitress working at any one time. It's become a solitary job – Dan tends to skive off out the back for a fag or on his phone every five minutes – but it works for me. As you've probably gathered, I'm a loner type.

I dump my bag in the tiny staff room and grab my thigh-length, belly-button-high white apron and name badge. Popping them on, I head for the office to retrieve the till money before carrying it out onto the café floor to count the float. It's an archaic method, counting the money before shift and manually, as in handwritten, logging it on the daily record sheet. In fact, everything about Lloyd's is archaic, from the old-fashioned pad and paper ordering system, the out-of-date patterned wallpaper, the basic plastic tables and chairs, and ultimately, the general feel of the place. It's in a desperate need of an upgrade, but Lloyd is stuck in his ways and I won't be the one making any kind of suggestion; it's not my place.

Once the money is counted and the tray popped into the till, I switch on all the necessary machinery before helping myself to a coffee. One of the perks of working in a café is free coffee on and off shift, and I never say no to a coffee. I take a welcome sip and glance at the clock on the wall. It's five minutes to opening. I might as well unlock the door now. It's not like we've got customers queuing down the street, although our only regular customers will be arriving soon.

Ten minutes later, five minutes after Dan's not-a-second-early arrival and his usual hello in the form of a grunt, I hear the annoying bell ding as the door swings open and Black with One Sugar and his wife, Latte with Extra Cream, arrive. I should know their names, but I'm rubbish at names, so I tend to nickname customers based on their drink of choice. Sad, I know, but what's sadder is just how often people order the exact same drink, and they say variety is the spice of life.

"Morning, Daniella." Latte with Extra Cream, an older woman in her sixties I'd say, beams.

"Morning," I reply, my customer service voice in place. "The usual?"

"Yes, please," Black with One Sugar, whom I'm assuming is a similar age to his wife, replies.

"Grab a seat. I'll bring it over."

I think it's obvious what their usual drink order is, but added to that is a full fry-up for the Mr and scrambled egg on toast for the Mrs. The married couple are here every morning like clockwork Monday to Friday, and every single time they have the exact same order, which cannot be good for the Mr's cholesterol, just by the by. I have wondered though, if their visits are a daily ritual or an excuse to get out of the house because surely it would be easier and cheaper to eat at home. Not that I'm complaining. Their custom pays my wages.

I tend to their order, popping their drinks down on the table before writing out their food order and ringing the bell that sits on the open hatch in the middle of the back wall three times to let Dan know an order has come in. I try to hide my scowl as Dan appears from out the back door and proceeds to wash his hands. I'm not Dan's biggest fan. He's an arrogant, lazy twat who skives at any opportunity, hence why I need to ring the bell, and it does nothing but annoy me. I have a decent work ethic, and I'm a firm believer I'm paid to work, not to sit around doing nothing. I can't abide lazy workers, but I guess getting away with murder is a perk of being the boss's son.

Whilst I wait for Dan to complete the order, I pick up a cloth and start wiping down tables. There's not much point as no one's sat at them yet, but as I said, I like to keep busy. I get through seven of the eleven tables when the bell rings again, my head groaning at the sound. I wish Lloyd would take that god-forsaken thing down as it is without a doubt the most annoying sound on the planet, but on a brighter note, I have another customer to serve. Simple things, I know.

"Hi there," I say and as I look up, I'm met with a beautiful smile staring back at me.

The smile belongs to a guy. I'm guessing mid-twenties with natural dark brown hair styled in a military buzz cut and a youthful glow in his lightly tanned face, highlighting his square jawline. He stands at the counter as I make my way back around to the employee side, and it's only then, once I'm a little more up close, that I notice the blue of his eyes. It's a gorgeous blue, like a cloudless sky on a bright day and for a second, I'm mesmerised. Until I remember I'm not some stupid lovesick damsel in a romance novel and I give myself a mental slap.

"What can I get for you?" I ask.

The almost six-foot-tall customer scans the menu on the back wall for a minute and that's when I spot the dog tags hanging around his neck, falling on top of his figure-hugging white T-shirt. I guess that explains the clean buzz cut and the well-built, yet subtle, muscular frame. He's an Army boy.

"I'll have an Americano, please," he says politely, in a masculine, slightly Irish twang.

"Take away or staying in?"

"I think I'll stay and eat," he says, looking around at the almost empty café, possibly questioning his decision. "What's the soup of the day?"

"Chicken," I answer, but Americano – I bet it's his usual choice – doesn't look impressed, and he has another look at the menu.

"What's good?"

I fight back the urge to laugh. There's not all that much to choose from and every meal, apart from the all-day breakfast selection, comes with chips, whether you want them or not.

"Personally, I love the breakfast bap," I offer. "But I've never had a complaint about any of our food options."

Americano flashes me that beautiful smile again, all white teeth and pale lips, and I'm wondering if a little sarcasm slipped into my sentence unknowingly. He looks a tad amused. "Breakfast bap it is," he says.

"You have a choice of sausage, bacon or egg," I explain. "Or if you're feeling daring, you can have all three."

"Do I look like the daring type?"

13

"I should imagine you have to be a little daring to join the Army." I'm being uncharacteristically over-friendly. I'm not usually the type to ask questions or make assumptions, and I mentally shake my head at myself.

"What makes you think I'm in the Army?" he asks, a mixture of confusion and surprise etched into his face.

I point to his chest. "The dog tags."

He peers down at his tags, lifts them and tucks them beneath his T-shirt. I merely watch as his face fills with a touch of sadness and maybe a hint of disappointment thrown in there too; I can't say for sure. Whichever way, I've overstepped the mark, and it's time to move the conversation along.

"So, what's it to be?"

"I'll take all three."

I write out his order and turn to start preparing his Americano. I glance back and he's still standing at the counter. "Take a seat. I'll bring it over."

"Thanks."

Americano quietly takes a seat at the nearest table, which is unusual. Most customers prefer to be as far away as possible. I'm convinced they think the staff here have nothing better to do than listen in on private conversations, hence the tendency to create as much distance as possible. Although as a small café, it is difficult not to overhear things, but I let whatever I hear go through one ear and out the other. I don't care enough to purposefully earwig.

I give Americano's drink a quick stir before moving around the counter and placing it down in front of him. He's busy messing with his phone, but he quickly puts it down as I arrive at his table.

"There you go," I say politely.

"Thanks."

"Your food won't be long."

Speak of the devil. The bell rings and I move to retrieve Black with One Sugar and Latte with Extra Cream's food. I deposit Americano's order through the hatch first before carrying the two plates of food to the couple's table.

"Fry-up," I say, setting the plates down. "And scrambled egg."

"Thank you, Daniella," Black with One Sugar says. "Oh, and I've been meaning to ask, how's the songwriting going?"

It takes me a minute to remember how exactly he knows I write songs until my naturally shitty memory kicks in. A couple of weeks ago, he and his wife were having a random debate about music, something along the lines of which is harder to write, melody or lyrics, and I was dragged into the conversation. I vaguely remember mentioning I write both.

"Always a work in progress," I answer truthfully. There's always room for improvement.

"The mantra of a true perfectionist," Latte with Extra Cream jokes.

"That's me." And it is, only I don't believe in perfection.

"I look forward to hearing a song on the radio one day," Black with One Sugar adds, and I bite back a laugh. There's a slim-to-nothing chance of that happening, but out of politeness, I keep shtum.

I swiftly return to my cleaning until the hatch bell dings, and I move to pop Americano's breakfast bap down in front of him.

"Smells great," he says, slipping out of his khaki jacket and placing it on the back of his chair.

My eyes are drawn to a tattoo on his right arm; it's a rifle in an Army boot, an Army helmet sitting on top with a ribbon curving from top to bottom and the words *Brother in Arms* written within the ribbon. I smile. It's a nice tattoo.

"Enjoy your food," I say, all customer service like, keeping the tattoo admiration to myself.

Once back behind the counter, I start cleaning out the coffee machine, and I'm soon lost in thought. It's only when Black with One Sugar and his wife approach the counter, I realise almost half an hour has gone by, and I'm forced to pay attention. I ring up their bill in an efficient manner using the older than old, work-out-the-change-for-yourself till.

"See you next week, Daniella," Latte with Extra Cream says, reminding me today is my last Lloyd's shift of the week.

"Have a nice weekend," I reply brightly.

The couple nod and leave, waving as they pass by the window, a gesture I return before collecting the couple's empty plates, depositing them on the hatch shelf for Dan to take to the back for washing – when he resurfaces, of course. I take a quick glance at Americano. He's still eating, so I resign myself to my pointless cleaning.

"So, you're a songwriter?" Americano asks, forcing me to turn my head to look at him.

Small talk. I hate small talk, but I've come to learn it's an expectation in the customer service industry, and I've been forced to get used to it.

"Do you make a habit of listening in on other people's conversations?" I ask, adding a smile to indicate I'm not actually offended. The couple and I weren't exactly talking in private.

Americano smirks. "I couldn't help overhearing."

"Yes, I am," I answer.

Americano, I notice, has finally finished his bap, and I'm about to move to collect his empty plate, but he beats me to it, standing up and bringing it over to the counter before I have a chance.

"I'll be out of a job if you carry on," I joke.

"Just being courteous," he says casually.

"Now there's a word you don't hear every day," I say, taking his plate and adding it to the pile sitting on the hatch shelf.

"You any good?" he asks, retaking his seat.

"At what?" I'm lost.

"The songwriting," he says with amusement, probably at my inability to follow a basic conversation.

I lean my palms against the counter, contemplating my answer. "I suppose that depends on the listener."

Americano smiles. "That's a very diplomatic answer." Yes, but I've never played my songs to the public. The only place I write and perform is in the comforts of my flat. "Do you have an instrument of choice?" he asks, before swigging the rest of his drink.

"Keyboard mostly," I answer, moving to collect Americano's now-empty glass before he decides to be courteous again. "You wanting a refill?" I ask, hearing the beeping of his phone still sitting on the table.

"I'd love one, thanks."

It doesn't take me long to make his second beverage and place it down in front of him. He's tapping away on his phone, but he flashes me his beautiful smile as I set down his drink, and I can't help but smile back. His smile is bloody infectious, and it awakens an unfamiliar feeling in the pit of my stomach. Is that butterflies? I quickly slap them down. Not going to happen, not in a month of Sundays. I swiftly retake my place behind the counter.

"What kind of songs do you write?" Americano asks, his

phone disappearing into his pocket.

"All kinds," I reply. "Depends on my mood at the time. I do have a soft spot for musical-style songs though."

"A theatre fan," he states.

"You can't beat a good musical."

"That depends on your definition of a *good* musical."

I laugh. "Not a fan, then?"

"I don't mind musicals," he says, not overly convincingly. "But I'd rather go see a concert or a festival myself."

"Let me guess," I tease. "You're more of a DMA's, Coldplay kind of guy?"

Americano appears impressed. "What gave me away?"

"You're a guy," I mock.

"So, being female," he bites back, "I'm assuming you're a massive girl band fan?"

I grimace. "God, no. I'd rather listen to bloody 'Yakety Yak' than a girl band, no offence to girl bands like."

"'Yakety Yak'," Americano says deadpan, yet his eyes tell me he's desperate to burst out laughing. I'm impressed he knows the song, to be honest.

"It's a classic," I insist, shrugging. Americano's laughter erupts, and just like his smile, it's infectious. I'm soon laughing along with him.

Americano's phone beeps again, and I watch him almost growl at it, shaking his head before practically downing his drink in one go. Phone still in hand, he smoothly glides his khaki jacket over his broad shoulders before being courteous again and bringing his empty glass to the counter.

"Stop doing my job," I insist before swiftly ringing up the till. "That'll be seven-fifty, please."

Americano hands me a ten-pound note, and I return the

gesture with his change. He hovers at the counter, sliding his phone, change and receipt into his pocket before heading towards the door. He stops shy of leaving, turning back to look at me, flashing that beautiful smile.

"You got space for a new regular?" he asks.

I scan the empty room a touch too dramatically. "I think we can make room."

"It's nice to meet you, Daniella."

And before I can insist that he calls me Dani or remind myself for the thousandth time to change my name badge, or even ask him his name, he's gone. I stand for a minute watching him walk past the window, and it's then I realise I'm wearing a ridiculous grin, the kind of smile a teenage girl gets when she's just met a cute boy, and I quickly wipe it from my face. We'll be having none of that, thank you.

Chapter Two

It's Saturday and I've just walked through job number two's door – Dave's Music Shop. It's a quaint little shop just up the road from Lloyd's. Surrounded by instruments and all things music, it's nothing much, but there's a practice space on the shop floor consisting of two bar stools and a resident amp, and a practice room in the back where Dave teaches guitar Monday through Thursday, typically from four in the afternoon onwards. His clientele tends to be kids rather than adults.

"Hiya, Dani," Dave calls, scaring the absolute shit out of me as he wanders into the main part of the shop from the back.

I hadn't even noticed the alarm didn't go off when I unlocked the door, nor that all the lights were on, though I should have. I wisely decide not to tell Dave that fact.

"Bloody hell, Dave," I say, ignoring the major league headache groaning in response to my loud protest and extra pissed off at not having any painkillers on me – I took my last two this morning – but Dave merely snickers. "What the hell are you doing here?" I ask. A little rude considering I'm talking to the guy who owns the place, but I hate it when people make me jump, and my heart is beating like a samba drum.

"Sorry," he says.

"Are you wearing pyjamas?" I ask, glancing down at his red-and-white-checked bottoms.

"I may have pissed Emily off," he says, shrugging as though it's a regular occurrence. Emily is Dave's wife, a lovely lady by all accounts. "But don't worry. I plan on heading home before opening to grovel for forgiveness."

"You couldn't have done that last night?" I jest, but Dave

20

merely shrugs again, disappearing off into the back as I go through my usual opening-up routine.

Dave reappears minutes later still wearing his pyjamas but with a rucksack slung over his shoulder.

"Anything special need doing today?" I might as well ask as he's here.

Dave shakes his head. "Just the usual."

"Cool."

As bosses go, Dave is awesome – laid-back and easy-going. He's a stereotypical rocker type and a fantastic guitar player who once had a recording contract back in the eighties, until it all went a little south. You know what they say, sex, drugs and rock and roll, and Dave took it a tad too seriously. It's a far cry from the dad-of-three music shop owner and guitar teacher he is now mind, although the rocker dress sense is still ever so present, today being the exception, and on a normal day, he insists on wearing ripped-at-the-knee skinny jeans and big black boots with his branded T-shirt.

Dave hired me to give him free time to spend with his family. Before me, he was working every day bar Sunday, the only day of the week the shop closes, but I think Emily was getting a little fed up with Dave never being home, which is understandable with three kids under seven. With me around he's free Friday afternoon through to the end of play Sunday, and although he had a few issues letting go of the reins for a while, he's getting there and his trust and confidence in me is growing; he no longer pops in to check on me on a Saturday anymore. Unless the misunderstanding with his wife is a ploy and he's secretly checking I locked the place up properly last night. Now there's food for thought.

I do think being a musician myself and a quick learner has

helped Dave relax as far as passing the baton is concerned though. I spent the first month on the job reading and learning as much as I possibly could about every instrument and piece of equipment the shop has to offer. That way, I can answer anything a customer should ask, and Dave was impressed by my dedication and progression knowledge-wise. My entire life, apart from work, revolves around music so apart from performing or songwriting as a profession, a music shop is about as good as I'm going to get and if swotting up is what it takes to keep my job, then I'm going to do it. I pride myself on being a hard worker in any job that I do.

Dave leaves, and I set about cleaning the guitars, which are aligned closest to the shop window. I handle each one with care, as any instrument should be handled, and I'm about five guitars in, standing on Dave's rickety old stepladder when I hear the doorbell sound. Dave's doorbell is a much better sound than Lloyd's, a simple *ding-dong*, and I turn to look towards the door. I'm highly surprised to see Americano wandering in looking as gorgeous as he did yesterday in that khaki jacket, a black, figure-hugging T-shirt and dark denim jeans that cling to his muscular thighs.

"Daniella?" Americano sounds equally surprised.

"Americano." Did I *really* just say that out loud? I subconsciously groan. That's not embarrassing at all.

"I'd love one," he teases.

"Sorry," I say, the blood rushing to my cheeks. "I nickname Lloyd's customers based on their choice of drink." I'm not sure why I'm explaining myself as it's doing nothing to ease my embarrassment. In fact, I think I'm just digging a bigger hole. "I just wasn't meant to say it out loud."

"So, in your head, you call me Americano?" he asks, his eyes amused.

"Yep," I admit, climbing down the ladder. "Sad, I know."

"That's your cue to ask my name." He smirks.

"I'll only forget it," I say, shrugging. "But go on then, what's your name?"

"Damien."

Damien. It's not got the same finesse as Americano, but it's a nice name. Although… "Is that not the name of some devil kid in…" I cannot for the life of me remember the film's title.

"*The Omen*," Damien answers my unfinished question, and I can tell from his indifferent expression it's not the first time someone has made that reference.

"Sorry," I say again. "You probably get that a lot."

"Only sometimes," he admits, and I can appreciate his sarcasm.

"So, what can I do for you?"

"I'm looking to try out a Gibson Les Paul," he states. "The Studio if you stock it?"

Direct and to the point, I like it. Amer – I mean, Damien obviously knows his guitars, and it only makes the fluttering in my stomach heighten. Gorgeous *and* a guitar player. I'm growing increasingly aware that, under different circumstances – if I thought I was open to intimacy – Damien is looking like my kind of guy.

"Okey-doke," I say, grabbing and moving the stepladder to the opposite side of the room. "Can I ask why the Studio?"

"It came recommended."

"I only ask because you're a fairly tall guy," I explain. "The Studio's slim frame might look a little lost on you. It's a great-sounding guitar though, and a good all-rounder. Is it an all-rounder you're looking for?" Damien nods. "If it's a Gibson you want, you might be better with a Standard rather than the Studio, but if you're not picky about brand, you might want to consider the Fender American Performer Stratocaster. It's what I'd describe as a jack-of-all-sounds. With the HSS model, you get a bridge humbucker that you can split into two single coils, and it gives so much versatility. You still get the traditional Strat sound, but it's great for experimenting with genres. I'd say the only downside is the large headstock ain't to everyone's taste."

Damien eyes me inquisitively, and I fight the resurfacing blush embellishing my cheeks. "I thought you were a keyboard player."

"I play the guitar too," I admit, shrugging.

I refrain from stating the obvious and reminding him I work in a music shop. Irrelevant of whether I can play an instrument or not, I'm paid to have musical knowledge. It's my job.

"Multitalented," Damien praises.

I climb the stepladder, acutely aware Damien is watching my every move, and retrieve the guitar he requested. I gesture for Damien to take a seat on one of the two bar-stool-style chairs.

"Do you want headphones?" We offer headphones as a form of privacy. Not everyone wants to be heard playing, something I can one-hundred-percent respect.

"Nah, I'm good, thanks."

Fair enough. I swiftly plug the guitar into the resident amp and carefully hand the guitar to Damien. He smiles that beautiful smile, and I mentally shake my head at the grin inching across my lips as I move to polish the guitars on the lower, no-stepladder-required level. Damien starts to play a melancholy tune, and although I had planned to keep busy, I find myself staring at him. It's a beautiful tune, and its unfamiliarity is causing me to wonder if maybe he wrote it. My uncharacteristic over-friendly nosiness is making another appearance.

"Did you write that?"

"Yeah," he answers, pausing playing. "Back when I was in college."

"It's nice," I offer.

I'm distracted by the bell and in walks our only familiar face, an older, stuck in the eighties, right down to his quiff hairstyle, guy in his fifties. He's an avid vinyl collector, and he pops in roughly once a week to see what Dave has to offer.

"Good afternoon, Daniella," he says in his deep Scottish accent.

"All right, Brian," I reply. "You're gonna be disappointed, I'm afraid. Dave didn't manage to nab much this week."

"Slim pickings everywhere lately," he says with a hint of dejection.

"Ever thought of getting yourself a smartphone?" I ask. "Or an iPod?"

Brian cackles. "Over my dead body."

He proceeds to have a quick look through the records as Damien continues to play, albeit a little quieter. I'm not sure if he's turned the volume down out of politeness or to earwig.

"You're right," Brian suddenly says. "I'm disappointed."

"Sorry," I offer.

Brian turns his attention to Damien. "I see you're trying out the Gibson Studio." Damien nods politely. "I prefer a Yamaha personally, but I'm sure Daniella would disagree with me, and you'd be wise to listen to what she has to say."

"Yes, sir," Damien says, continuing his politeness.

"From what Dave tells me she's a bit of a know-it-all when it comes to instruments." Sounds like Dave.

"Know-it-all, huh?" I say, faking offence. "I prefer the term *knowledgeable* if you don't mind."

"My apologies," Brian offers, fully aware my offence is merely playful banter. "The point was, you're definitely more than a pretty face, lass."

It's a compliment, and I should take it, but all Brian has done is put the emphasis on my scarred face, and I'm conscious of Damien's eyes on me. The blush is redecorating my cheeks.

Brian continues to nosey for a few moments longer before admitting defeat and saying his goodbyes. It's then I notice Damien has stopped playing completely and is on his feet, eying up the Fender guitar I mentioned earlier.

"You want to give it a whirl?" I ask him.

"Why not?" Damien replies brightly.

I move, lifting the guitar from its stand, handing it to Damien, and return to my polishing.

Unfortunately, working in a music shop is not the most glamorous of jobs. Yes, I get to spend the day with instruments, but the majority of my time is spent polishing rather than playing. To be fair to Dave though, if I get all the required tasks completed before the end of shift, I am more than welcome to have a little recreational time, and I tend to do just that. Like I said, Dave is an awesome boss.

"So," Damien asks, now sitting and casually playing a little tune. "You got any more jobs up your sleeve?"

"Just the two."

"This one makes the most sense," he muses. "As a musician."

"I'd work here full-time if I could."

Damien starts to play a familiar melody, and I can't help but quietly sing along. In fact, I'm so lost in polishing and singing, it takes me a minute to register Damien is playing a lot quieter than he was. I turn to look at him, and he's smiling that beautiful smile, his eyes playful.

"You have a nice voice," he compliments. "You do anything with it?"

"Like what?" I ask, turning away and keeping my back to him.

"Performing."

"Nope," I answer bluntly.

"Can I ask why not?"

"You can ask," I say. "Doesn't mean I'll tell."

I hear Damien laugh, but I don't look at him. I would've thought the reason behind my unwillingness to perform was obvious.

"Humour me," he says, and I can picture him shrugging whilst speaking.

I sigh. Damien's curiosity is unnerving, and frankly, it's none of his business, yet my mouth is opening, and I'm sticking to the less complicated answer. "There's not much point playing for a bunch of people who will be so busy wondering what happened to my face, they won't even hear my music."

"Is there something wrong with your face?" Damien asks, and I force myself to turn and look at him, throwing him a what-do-you-take-me-for glance. "Music isn't about appearances last time I checked."

"Bollocks." Excuse my French. "And so easy for you to say. You walk down the street and people think *Hey, he's a good-looking guy*…"

"You think I'm good-looking?" he asks, his tone mischievous.

I sigh. "Not really the point."

"So, it's a confidence thing," Damien says, or asks, I'm not entirely sure which.

"Something like that," I admit, resuming my polishing and

turning my back to Damien once more.

Chronic anxiety is probably more accurate. I don't do people or crowds, and I cannot abide being the centre of attention, all thanks to a past I can't forget. Unfortunately, my scars run much deeper than the one on my face, and even though the stranger in the room appears to be effortlessly dragging a little honesty out of me – the last time that happened was with my former therapist – I've discovered if I keep the focus on the scar I can't hide, it tends to stop people from delving deeper.

"And what about the songwriting?" Damien continues to probe.

"That usually involves showcasing your songs," I say. "But you already know that."

"What makes you say that?"

"Army boy or no Army boy," I say, "you're obviously a musician."

"*Ex*-Army boy," Damien corrects, and I'm back to looking him in the eye. "Medically discharged."

"Sorry to hear that," I offer.

"Thank you," he says. "I got off lucky compared to some though." My stomach churns at the sadness in Damien's voice. I can empathise. I understand how hard it is to lose people. "And I wouldn't go back now even if I could."

"Really?" I ask, surprised. Stereotypically, Army boys are gluttons for punishment.

"The Army was the family business."

"Music is the passion then?"

"Unfortunately, music doesn't pay my bills," he says, and I get that. The music industry is a bitch. "But I'm in a band. We do gigs, pubs and events, that kind of thing."

Interesting. I had Damien pegged for a solo artist. I don't

know why, it's not like I know the guy, but he gave off a solo vibe. "You're in a band?"

"Yeah," he says. "But I'm a self-employed personal trainer by day." I grimace and Damien laughs. "Not the fitness type?"

"Definitely not," I answer a little too quickly, shaking my head for dramatic effect. "A personal trainer would be a personal hell for me."

"Maybe you just haven't found the right trainer." Was that a flirtatious comment? If it was, I walked right into it.

"If that's an attempt to gain business," I say. "I'm afraid I'm a challenge you will never conquer."

"Is that right?" Damien eyes me menacingly, as though I've awoken a dangerous competitive side.

"Trust me, you'd be wasting your time."

"I doubt spending time with a fellow musician would be a waste," he says. I walked right into that one too.

"Anyway," I say awkwardly, steering the conversation back where it belongs. "You decided on which guitar you prefer?"

Damien plays a few more notes. "I can't decide which one I like the feel of."

"Personally, I think the Fender suits you better," I offer. "And it comes in black, aubergine, three-colour burst, or if you're feeling funky, satin surf green."

Damien smirks. "Not sure satin surf green is my style."

"Oh, I don't know," I jest. "I totally see you rocking a green guitar, maybe add in some neon blue skinny jeans." I start to sing "Wake Me Up Before You Go-Go", and Damien laughs.

"You really do have a beautiful voice," he compliments. "It's a shame such a talent is wasted."

All right, yes, I can sing. I am a musician in every sense of the word, but that will not get me on a stage any time soon, wasted talent or not.

"You sound like a bloody talent rep," I joke.

"Sorry," he says, sounding sincere. I'm not sure he heard the humour in my tone.

I take the opportunity to steer the bizarrely effortless conversation back to the guitars once again, amazed at how quickly Damien and I keep veering off course.

"Personally, I think the Gibson is too slim," I say. "Both have a great sound, but I think the quality of the Fender for the cheaper price is a good deal. What kind of amp do you use?"

"Marshall DSL20CR."

"Do you like it?" I ask. "I'm thinking of the gigging. I have the VOX AC15C1 at home. It's smaller but it doesn't compromise on sound quality."

Damien flashes me that beautiful smile again, reawakening the butterflies and my frustration simultaneously. A simple smile should not have such an effect on me, yet it does.

"You know your stuff," he praises.

"I do work in a music shop," I say, the obvious unavoidable.

"Fair point," he agrees. "Do you stock the VOX?"

"We do."

"Can I try it out?"

"Sure."

I move towards the back of the shop, opposite the guitar section, and retrieve the requested amp. I carefully place it between the two stools and allow Damien to plug in the guitar.

"Do me a favour," he starts, just as I'm about to leave him to it. "It'd be good to hear the two guitars together. Would you mind?"

He gestures to the guitar not currently in his hand, asking me to play without uttering the words, and it's the first time a customer has asked me to play *with* them. I'm wondering if I have the right to refuse, but in the spirit of good customer service, I reluctantly take a seat on the empty stool and pick up the guitar.

"You want to do the tune you were just playing?" I ask, slowly making my way through the notes I think I heard him play.

"How did you do that?" he asks, baffled.

"Do what?"

"You just played my *original* melody almost note for note."

"*Almost* being the key word there," I say. "What came after B?"

"G," he answers.

I replay the notes in order until I'm happy I've just about got it. "Okay," I say. "Ready?"

Damien is staring at me, and I shuffle uncomfortably in my seat. Although Damien is just one person, I suddenly feel like I'm standing on a stage in front of a thousand people, all eyes on me. My anxiety is screaming at me to get our little playing session over and done with as quickly as humanly possible.

"Earth to Damien," I say, a slight irritation in my tone. I also get cranky when I'm uncomfortable.

"Sorry," he says, snapping out of his solo staring contest. "I just, I mean, I'm a quick learner, but you…"

I shrug. "I have a way with music."

Damien wisely decides to leave it at that, and we play the melody simultaneously. I can feel Damien's eyes on me, and even though the butterflies are dancing in delight, I avoid eye contact completely. I feel self-conscious enough as it is. As far as the guitars are concerned, for me there's no contest; the guitar being happily plucked by Damien wins hands down. Our session is gratefully cut short by the sound of Damien's phone ringing.

"What's up?" Damien's mobile hits his ear, although his tone is less how-you-doing and more leave-me-alone, and I can't help but smirk. "Okay… What's with the worry? She's a teenager… Yeah, all right… Chill… Although if she isn't answering to you, I don't see why she'd pick up to me, mate… All right, I'll try her."

Oh, dear. I can't exactly help overhearing, and it sounds as though this "she" either hasn't come home and isn't answering her phone or is purposefully ignoring – I'm going to guess a parent. Damien ends the call and proceeds to dial another number, mouthing a *sorry* in my direction, a sorry that is not needed. I'm grateful for the distraction. I lean the guitar against the stool I'm now vacating and head to sit behind the counter, putting a little space between Damien and me. His never-waning eye contact has left me a little flustered.

Damien almost growls when whomever he's calling doesn't answer. "Bloody teenagers."

I chuckle, yet I'm suddenly wondering if the teenager in question is *his* kid. I'd put Damien in his mid-twenties, but I could be wrong, and he may just have a youthful face. It's a stretch, but it is possible he could wear the dad title. In fact, the caller could well be his wife – there's no ring, I notice – or his girlfriend, or at the very least the kid's mum.

"Yours?"

"Hell no," he laughs, standing and popping his guitar on the stand I retrieved it from earlier. "Wait, how old do you think I am?"

"I don't know, do I?" I ask, laughing. "For all I know you could've knocked some lass up at thirteen."

"So, I'm not old, I'm an idiot," Damien says, moving towards the counter, his playful tone signalling a lack of actual offence.

"Not your kid, then," I say, holding my hands up in surrender, and on that note, I decide to steer the conversation back in the right direction. How many times have I had to do that so far? "So, you made a decision?"

Damien shrugs. "I'm gonna sleep on it."

Uh-huh. You have no idea how many times I've heard that. Sometimes I think people wander in here to get a free play of a decent instrument rather than to make an actual purchase. If it wasn't for Dave's reputation in the music industry, leading in sales to professionals, he'd never make any money relying on the general public. I've made only a handful of instrument sales to non-professionals in the ten months I've worked here, yet I'm forever selling replacement guitar strings and music scores, the smaller stuff.

"It was really good to see you again, Daniella," Damien breaks my inward ramble.

"Dani, please," I correct. The only people I let get away with using my full name are the older generation, mostly because they refuse to do anything but. Customer Brian is one example.

"Dani," he reiterates. "I'll maybe see you tomorrow."

"We're closed tomorrow," I point out. "We don't open Sundays, but Dave will be here Monday."

"You don't work Mondays?"

"Day off Monday," I say, acutely aware that most customers don't particularly care who's behind the counter when they walk through the door, and it's a question I've never been asked before. "I only work here Friday afternoons and Saturdays."

Damien nods, silently musing to himself before heading for

the door. He stops shy of leaving, just like he did yesterday at Lloyd's, and turns back to look at me, a mischievous smile playing at the corner of his lips.

"Maybe I'll get to hear one of *your* songs next time."

I scoff. "Keep dreaming."

"Something tells me I will."

And with that, he walks out the door and leaves me hanging, wondering what the hell he meant by that. Did he mean dream about me or about hearing one of my songs? I don't want to know. There's something about Damien that makes me feel both comfortable and *un*comfortable at the same time, and it's a bizarre feeling. It doesn't help that the conversation between us flows so easily despite meeting only yesterday. In fact, it's a little scary. When I talk to him, it feels like I'm talking to an old friend.

I try to shake my jumbled thoughts, but I'm hit by another stark revelation, a revelation that should have hit as soon as my scarred face weaved its way into the conversation. Damien didn't give me what I can only describe as "the look". Most people see my face and "the look" naturally follows – a mixture of surprise and curiosity with the occasional stab of disgust thrown in. The pity in their eyes soon follows, and it irks me every time. I don't need or want pity. Damien though, he looked at me like he would anyone else, like my scar doesn't exist, even brushing over it in conversation as if it is insignificant, and it's oddly comforting. The annoying butterflies are fluttering with a vengeance at my thoughts, and I guess I can't deny I'm attracted to him.

I allow myself a second to wonder what it would be like to have a romantic relationship, but it does nothing but send shivers shooting down my spine in horror. I sigh. I have to be realistic. The scar on my face is easier to overlook, but the scars that lie underneath are much scarier. One look below the surface and even the politest, non-judgemental person in the universe won't be able to hide *their* horror.

Chapter Three

"Crap," I whisper, my latest nightmare abruptly interrupting my sleep.

I glance at my bedside clock; it's five in the morning. With a pounding head, I swiftly abandon the idea of going back to sleep and resign myself to spending the morning drinking a mountain of coffee and getting dressed for work.

Mountain drank, half-seven hits, and I head out into the communal hallway. Locking up, I'm met by an amusing sight. James is sitting on the floor, his head buried in his hands, and it doesn't take a rocket scientist to figure out he's been out all night partying and has either forgotten or lost his keys. My money is on lost.

"You all right down there?" I ask, and he lifts his head to look at me.

"Locked out," he states. "I'm guessing Jess is either passed out or not home. I've lost my keys, and my wallet, though my phone survived." Told you.

"Lucky phone," I mock.

"I did knock on yours too," he adds, eying me with suspicion, and I respond with a casual shrug.

I'm not surprised I didn't hear him. I tend to play my music with my headphones in out of respect to my neighbours, something James understands nothing about, and come to think of it, I'm surprised his regular loud music hasn't gotten him evicted yet. No, wait, the landlord is his uncle. Dan's face invades my mind, and I'm realising I'm surrounded by idiots who take advantage of their family members.

"My parents are arriving today too," he says in a totally

pissed-off attitude I can't help but smirk at. "I'm gonna have to have the locks changed, tell my uncle…"

I would love to feel sympathy, but I don't. Cold, yes. Too cold, maybe, but he's a grown man, and it's not like he accidentally left them somewhere. He got pie-eyed and probably dropped them in the bloody street. If that's not an advert for avoiding binge drinking to the point that all control or common sense leaves the building, I don't know what is.

"Luckily for you," I say, after contemplating prolonging James's torture and deciding against it, "Jess is not as dumb as she acts, and she gave me a spare for emergencies."

James practically jumps to his feet, moving as though he's about to hug me, and I instinctively take a step back. "I don't do hugs," I remind him, putting a hand up in front of me for dramatic effect.

"Hug you?" he says. "I could kiss you."

"I don't do that either," I say, lowering my hand to pull the spare key from my keyring. "Here."

"Thank you so much, Dani." James beams, genuinely grateful, and I think it's the first time I've ever seen a softer, less cocky side to James. "I owe you one, seriously."

"Yeah, yeah."

I leave James to it and make the journey to Dave's. I open up in the same manner as I do Lloyd's, albeit Dave's till is a little more sophisticated – all the money logs are electronic, which is ten times easier than manually writing everything down – and I have a little glance into the practice room to make sure Dave isn't about to surprise me again like last week. I'm grateful to find myself alone.

Once the shop is set up, I hover behind the counter and await my first customer. I let out a yawn, fully aware I had maybe three hours' sleep in total last night, which is not unusual for me, but not particularly good for me either. I spend half my life tired and weary, thanks to my at least once a night – sometimes twice if I'm extra unlucky – nightmares, and every time I wake up with a start, sometimes screaming, sometimes not. Each one as bad as the one before, reminding me of the shitstorm I call my past and the reason why my future isn't overly bright. I'd give anything to make the nightmares stop, to forget, but if therapy didn't help me – it did in so many ways, but not in the nightmare department – I'm not sure there's anything else out there that will.

I'm lost in thought when my first customer arrives, and I can't help the wide smile that worms its way across my lips. Amer – damn it, Damien is wandering inside.

I had expected to see him in Lloyd's after his "regular" comment, but since he never surfaced, I figured I'd probably never see him again. There was an element of disappointment at that fact, I won't lie, especially as Damien's songs and the elegant way he handles a guitar have been swirling around the back of my mind for the past week, which is a nice distraction from my nightmares yet infuriatingly annoying at the same time.

I quickly notice he's sporting a different look today. I'm guessing he's walking in straight from a run or an early personal training session – the tight, navy blue tank top and grey joggers are a dead giveaway – and as much as I hate to say it, sweaty Damien is somehow even more attractive. If I didn't have my head screwed on straight, I'd be drooling at the sight.

"Morning," I say, my customer service voice in full swing. "An *energetic* morning by the looks of it."

"Early PT session," he explains, moving towards the counter. "Been absolutely swamped this week," he adds with a hint of irritation that has a smirk forming at the corner of my mouth. I guess that explains his absence from the café.

"Ain't being swamped good for business?" I ask, a teasing tone to my voice. "Being self-employed."

"Yes," he admits. "But I would like to have a life too."

"Fair enough." I shrug. "I take it you've finally made a decision?"

"I'm gonna give them both one more shot, then decide."

"Okey-doke," I say brightly, moving around the counter and retrieving the relevant guitars.

Damien takes a seat and within minutes, he's playing away and delighting my ears with another unknown melody.

"These tunes you keep playing," I say as I polish a flute behind the counter. "Did you write all of them?"

"Yeah," he answers, continuing to play yet his eyes finding mine. "The melodies at least. I can't write lyrics."

"Really?" I raise an eyebrow. "I find lyrics easier than melodies."

"Care to share?" Damien asks, grinning away complacently.

"Ha-ha," I say sarcastically. "Nice try."

"Worth a shot." He shrugs.

My gaze trails to the Army tattoo as he flexes his arm in rhythm to his melody. Unfortunately, Damien notices, and I force myself to look away, a familiar blush embellishing my cheeks. I don't need to look at him to know he's smirking, assumingly amused by my slight embarrassment. I give myself another mental shake. I can't remember the last time I blushed, yet I've blushed more times than I can count since Damien came along. I need to get a grip.

"You got any tips for writing lyrics?" Damien breaks the uncomfortable silence, for which I am immensely grateful.

"Not especially." I shrug. "I tend to write what I know or feel or *imagine* feeling."

"You must have a writer's genes," he says in humour, I think.

"I think my mum was a writer," I say out loud, though I hadn't intended to. I'm not sure where my sudden outbursts of sharing keep coming from.

"You think?" Damien asks, and I let out a small, yet sad, laugh. That is why I don't share. Questions lead to questions, and curiosity fuels curiosity.

"You don't miss a thing, do you?" I counter a question with a question, a typical deflection tactic. Damien merely smiles, not cockily like I'd expected, but sweetly, almost apologetically. "Long story," I offer, and Damien nods in understanding. He obviously knows how to take a hint.

The doorbell is a more than welcome distraction. Oh, crap. I take it back. Jess moseying in is *not* a welcome distraction at all. I like Jess, but if she's here, which she never is, it can mean only one thing: she wants something.

"Hey, Dani," she says, sashaying towards the counter in her trademark provocative attire – a low-cut, way too tight, green strap top under a light denim jacket, a pair of extra skinny jeans, and her usual six-inch stiletto heels.

"What on earth are you doing here?" I ask.

"Well, hello to you too," she responds crabbily. "I thought I'd pop in and say hi."

"Not buying it," I say frankly as Jess plants her forearms against the counter, giving me an unnecessary view of her cleavage. "What do you want?"

"Can't a neighbour say hi without wanting something?" she asks, her innocence as fake as her eyelashes.

"A neighbour can," I state. "*You* can't."

Jess childishly sticks her tongue out at me, gaining her a slight curve at the corner of my mouth in amusement. "Okay fine," she relents. "I need a favour."

"There it is," I mock.

Jess stands up straight as I plonk myself on the stool behind the counter, suddenly wondering why I'd been standing and wasting unnecessary energy.

"James's parents are coming to stay for a couple of nights," Jess explains, not looking overly impressed by that fact. "I was hoping I could crash in your spare room while they're here. I really don't want to have to sleep on the couch, and James won't even fit on the couch..."

I want to say no. There's a reason I live alone. I can handle James and Jess popping round knowing I can kick them out whenever the hell I want, but overnight is another kettle of fish. Jess is throwing me her best puppy-dog eyes.

"Don't you have like a thousand mates you can crash with?" I ask, baffled as to why she is asking me. Unless it's merely for the convenience of being across the hall.

"Not really," she answers, a hint of dejection in her voice. "The people I party with aren't people I'd call mates." I didn't realise she calls me *mate*, if I'm honest. "I know you like your space, but it's only a couple of nights, and I'm desperate."

There's those puppy-dog eyes again. Out of the corner of my eye, I notice Damien smirking, although Jess appears oblivious to his presence.

"Please," Jess begs. "I really don't want to be stuck with James's parents. Have you met them?"

I'm assuming there's an ulterior motive behind Jess's question as she is fully aware I have indeed *not* met James's parents before, nor have I met hers. I merely respond with a shake of my head.

"They're all Godly and shit," she says, the bile oozing from her words. "And they disapprove of James sharing a flat with a woman he's not married to. They'll totally come at me and I don't —"

"All right, all right," I cave. "Save the melodramatics."

Jess squeals, piercing my ears as she jumps up and down on the spot like a giddy child. My head groans in response, and I make a mental note to fish out some painkillers at the first opportunity.

"I have ground rules." Jess stops jumping and wipes the smile from her face. "No overnight guests."

"Yes, Mum," she belittles, but my unyielding gaze tells her I'm deadly serious. "As if I would."

"I wouldn't put anything past you."

"Thank you, Dani," she says gratefully, electing to ignore my sarcastic remark.

At that moment, Jess cocks her head and notices Damien. I stand and watch as her entire demeanour changes from casual to full-on seductress. I still don't know how she didn't spot him as soon as she walked in the door considering he's been quietly playing and earwigging throughout our conversation, but then I've always gotten the feeling Jess only sees what she wants to see.

"Why hello," she purrs, and I fight the urge to gag. "Dani." She's addressing me, but her eyes are fixed firmly on Damien. "You never mentioned how hot the music clientele is." The sexual confidence Jess oozes is staggering.

"Hi," Damien offers.

"Hi yourself."

God help me. I resign myself to my daily polishing. Whether

42

Damien wanted company or not, Jess is helping herself to the empty stool facing him. I notice Damien shuffle uncomfortably in his seat, and I can't help but smirk. Is it possible the gorgeous Army boy is a little intimidated by Jess's brazen tactics? Interesting.

Jess breaks my thoughts by introducing herself. "I'm Jess."

"Damien."

"Do you live around here?" Jess asks.

"Not too far," Damien answers, playing it close to his chest. "I take it you're a friend of Dani's?"

"*Friend* is a bit of a stretch," I pipe up, hearing Jess scoff and Damien chuckle.

"Good to know," Jess says sarcastically. "I'm Dani's neighbour. Although I guess you could call me her flatmate for the next couple of nights." Yay for me. I keep my silent, sarcastic thoughts to myself. "And *you* are a guitar player," Jess states the obvious, and I resist the urge to say "No shit, Sherlock" out loud.

"I am," Damien confirms.

"You any good?"

"I suppose that depends on the listener," he says.

Is it possible to have an inside joke with a guy you met only a week ago? If so, two can play at that game. "That's a very diplomatic answer."

Damien flashes me that beautiful smile, but I'm conscious Jess is eying me with curiosity, and the last thing I need is Jess winding me up about my attraction to Damien. Did I mention she's relentless? I'd never live it down.

"He's good," I tell Jess, keeping the conversation on track as casually as possible.

"Now, that *is* a compliment coming from you," Jess mocks,

a suggestive glint in her eye I wisely decide to ignore, before turning her attention back to Damien. "Dani plays the guitar too."

"Yeah, I know," he says. "Dani's the reason I can't decide which guitar I want."

"Isn't that the opposite of your job description?" Jess cocks her head to look at me. "Aren't you supposed to *help* people find an instrument?"

Damien laughs, and I shake my head in response. "I merely offer my recommendations. It's up to the customer to make the final decision."

"Oh, how very professional," Jess mocks before once again focusing on Damien. "Play me something. Maybe I can help you decide." I let out an involuntary laugh. Jess is tone deaf, but she opts to ignore me.

"What did you have in mind?" Damien asks Jess.

"'Barbie Girl'," I pitch in, unable to stop myself, though I probably should rein it in before Jess decides to make the next two nights a living hell, and trust me, she could. "Sorry, couldn't help myself."

"I'll tell you what," Damien says. "How about you both come to the Duke Bar in Stanton tomorrow night, and you can hear me play then. My band is doing a gig, starts at seven."

"Oh, I'm in." Jess beams. "But only if you dedicate one of your songs to me."

Damien laughs. "I'll see what I can do."

"Dani?" Jess asks. "Do I bother asking?"

"Not when you already know the answer," I say, keeping my back to them both.

"Sorry," Jess says to Damien. "But getting Dani out of the house is like pulling blood from a stone." I refrain from commenting. "But I'll be there." Jess's seductive voice is in full swing. "I'll even let you buy me a drink."

I turn just in time to see Jess flash Damien a sexy wink, walking backwards towards the door. She's about as brazen as they come, yet sometimes, I wish I had a tiny ounce of her confidence.

"She seems like an interesting woman," Damien says the second the door closes, signalling Jess's exit.

"She's a pain in the backside."

"But you love her really," he kids, I think.

"*Love* is a strong word," I state. "Occasionally, I like her."

"You wouldn't offer up a spare bed for someone you *occasionally* like," he says, a little too deep and serious in his tone for my liking.

"You would if you're a mug."

"Mug, nice person." He tilts his head from side to side in contemplation. "Toe-may-toe, toe-mar-toe."

I think there's a compliment in there somewhere, but as the uncomfortable atmosphere is starting to feel a little claustrophobic, I believe it's time to move the conversation along.

"So, you decided yet?" I ask him, referring back to the guitars.

"I have," he replies, rising to his feet with my recommendation in his hand. "I'm gonna go with the Fender."

"Wise choice," I say, a smug smile forming upon my face as I log onto the till. "The only problem is I ain't gonna be able to get it here until Monday at the earliest."

"No worries," he says, carrying both guitars back to their respective stands, once again doing my job for me.

"Satin surf green, was it?" Damien laughs, moving to stand at the customer-side of the counter as I unsuccessfully hide my smile.

"I think black is more my style."

"Okey-doke," I nod. "It comes with a case and a strap. Do you want any spare guitar strings?"

"Going full saleswoman on me now?" he asks playfully.

I shrug. "I have to ask."

"Nah, I'm good."

"In that case," I say, "that'll be one thousand five hundred and fifty pounds, please."

Damien pulls his wallet from the back pocket of his joggers and slides out his bank card. I swivel the card machine to face him and turn my head away as he enters his pin. The transaction goes through smoothly, and I hand him his receipt. It's an expensive purchase, but I keep shtum on the matter. Damien's finances are none of my business.

"You can pick it up any time after noon on Monday," I explain. "Bring your receipt as proof of purchase, and Dave will sort you out."

"That's right," he says, sliding his card and receipt into his wallet. "You don't work Mondays." Well remembered. "Back in the café Tuesday?" he asks, popping his wallet back in his pocket, and I nod, conscious he's once again hovering a lot longer than a typical customer. "Well, thanks for your help, Dani."

"That's what I'm here for."

After eying me for what feels like forever, Damien finally turns to leave. I can't help but watch him go, and there's a teeny tiny part of me that doesn't want him to.

"I hope to see you tomorrow," he says, and the invitation to his gig I'd almost forgotten about comes flooding back, causing me to sigh gloomily. "And for the record. That face you're so worried about, don't be. Personally, I think it's nothing short of beautiful."

And without giving me a chance to argue, Damien leaves. I stand watching him as he walks past the shop window, shell-shocked. I should be flattered, and the butterflies are certainly happy, but all I feel is sadness. A gorgeous, music-loving guy has just called me beautiful, and if I was anywhere close to normal, I'd be throwing myself at him. I sigh. Damien has fallen victim to my happy, banter-filled, chatty shop worker charade, and yes, it *is* a charade. Or at least, it usually is.

And there's the crux. My encounters with Damien haven't felt like a charade. I've been mostly honest and open, which is a rarity for me, and I have this weird longing to know more about him, again a rarity. I don't usually ask questions or partake in any conversation outside of the generic, yet I happily spilled my confidence issues, not to mention dropping the "think" regarding my mum into the conversation. I don't usually make mistakes like that. I keep things close to the chest, mostly because I don't want to introduce anyone to the anxiety-riddled mess underneath my sarcasm-as-a-defence-mechanism persona, but beyond that, for safety.

Alongside confidence issues, anxiety and my never-ending nightmares, I'm also a little paranoid, and my paranoid side is screaming at me that settling down and staying in one place is not only dangerous for me, but for anyone around me. Realistically, if I ignore the paranoid voice in my head, there's a slim-to-nothing chance of my past coming back to haunt me any time soon, but I can't help the nagging doubt that if I let people get close to me, I'd be putting them at risk, and the truth is, I can't face losing anyone else.

You need to let go of the past. My former therapist's words echo in my mind. *You are safe, Daniella.*

I moved to Stanton to start a new life, to let go of everything I've been through and focus on the future, but my nightmares are proof that moving on is not as easy as it sounds. The thought of getting close to someone and bearing my scars, both physically and emotionally, is terrifying. I'm not ready, and to be honest, I'm not sure I ever will be.

Chapter Four

"Dani… Dani… Dani!"

The sound of Jess's voice rings in my ears, and I wake up with a jolt, my heart pounding so hard against my chest, I think it might break free, or at the very least break a rib.

I'm on the couch, Jess's hands are on my arms as if she's been shaking me, though I didn't feel it, and I quickly wriggle free from her grip to move into a sitting position. Jess, in her slinky, leaves-nothing-to-the-imagination pyjamas, remains sitting by my feet, her worried-slash-shocked expression an unusual sight. I'm not sure when exactly I fell asleep on the couch, but I obviously conked out at some point, and I certainly didn't hear Jess come in.

"You were screaming," she says. "Are you okay?"

I wipe the sweat from my brow using my sleeve as I desperately try to control my ragged breath. *I'm safe*, I silently tell myself. *I'm safe.*

"Dani?" Jess forcefully calls for a response.

"Yeah, Jess," I lie. "I'm okay."

"You scared the shit out of me," Jess scolds, lightly slapping my leg to show her disdain for that fact. "I thought there was a madman in the flat. You sounded like you were being tortured."

I hold back a nervous laugh. Mentally, I *am* being tortured. Repeatedly.

"Sorry," I offer weakly. "I get nightmares. There's a reason why I live alone."

I slide that in there for the sake of it. I don't usually have to worry about waking anyone up with my screaming, and technically, I don't need to apologise for it either. I can't exactly control my nightmares, though I wish I could. I really, really do.

"You want to talk about it?" she asks.

I shake my head. "Not especially."

I force myself to look at the time on my phone lying on the coffee table. It's four in the morning. I rub my hands over my face before rising to my feet and heading to the kitchen. I set the kettle to boil and pull out a fresh cup. I need coffee to keep me awake. I'm fed up with sleeping only to be disturbed by the bastard in my dreams. Jess coughs, and I'm quickly reminded she's still hovering on the couch, watching my every move.

"You head back to bed," I tell her. "I'm good."

"Are you sure?" she asks, and I guess I should be touched by her concern.

"Yeah, I'm sure."

I plaster on my best smile, and Jess reluctantly relents, her need for beauty sleep kicking in presumably. She disappears back into the spare bedroom, and I wait for the door to close before letting the tears flow, silently yet endlessly. I shouldn't allow myself to cry, but despite almost three years passing, every time I have a nightmare, I can still feel his hands on my skin and the intense heat from his breath on my face like it was only yesterday, and it's unbearable.

A mountain of tears later, my coffee now in hand, I resign myself to my keyboard, plugging in my headphones and losing myself in my music. I need it. Putting my thoughts and feelings down on paper is my way of coping, and the only way to take a morsel of power back from the control my nightmares hold over me. I let inspiration take over and immerse myself into my escape, my sanctuary.

I spend the entire day in front of my keyboard, occasionally switching to my guitars, and although Jess has opted for a day in too, she's had the telly for company. I've stopped for a natter a couple of times to keep her sated, but I'm suddenly realising I haven't eaten anything all day, and my stomach is rebelling by growling. Reluctantly, I remove my headphones and switch off my equipment.

"Fancy a takeaway?" I ask Jess, who's lying on the couch, still in her pyjamas, messing on her phone.

"No time," she says, moving to sit up. "We need to start getting ready."

"Getting ready for what?" I ask, remaining seated on the little stool that sits in front of the keyboard, totally oblivious.

"Damien's gig," Jess says in a "duh" tone.

Oh right, that. "Yeah, I ain't going."

"Yes, you are," Jess insists, rising to her feet.

"No, I'm not," I insist harder. "You go. Have a good time."

"Come on, Dani," Jess pleads, standing in front of me. "It's not healthy sitting around your flat all the time. You need to get out and have some bloody fun."

I sigh. "Going to a crowded pub full of drunk twats is not my idea of fun."

Jess places her hands on her hips, pulling her stern face, and I fight the urge to giggle.

"I'm sick of you moping about," she says. "A gorgeous guy has asked you to go see his band play a gig. *You* are the most music-obsessed person I know. You have no excuse whatsoever not to go."

I have a thousand excuses, thank you very much. It's a silent answer, but I can feel my frustration growing. "Just leave it, Jess."

"Do I need to get on my knees and beg?" she asks. "'Cause I will."

"Don't be ridiculous."

Jess decides ridiculous is exactly what she wants to be, and before I can blink, she's on her knees, her hands clasped together in front of her as though she's praying. "Please, Dani," she pleads. "I don't want to go alone."

"You have loads of mates you could take."

"No, actually, I don't," she says with an uncharacteristic sadness to her voice. "I know you think I'm a socialite or whatever, and yes, I have the people I party with, but like I said, they're not *real* friends. I couldn't pop round for a brew or whatever like I do with you. In fact, the only person who listens to me talk and moan about men or work, even though I know you don't want to, is you. Why do you think I keep trying to get you out and spend more time with you?"

I stare at Jess in surprise. I didn't see that coming, and it's probably the most heartfelt thing I've ever heard escape Jess's mouth. I feel like I'm seeing Jess in a completely different light. I always knew her heart was in the right place, but I guess I hadn't realised listening to her moan meant quite so much to her. When Jess insinuated I was a mate, she clearly meant it, and despite my constant insistence that I'm a loner type, it's oddly comforting.

"Besides, the only person Damien wants there is you," she states, and I can't help the roll of my eyes that follows.

"I'm sure Damien doesn't give a shit if I go or not," I argue weakly, but I can barely convince myself, let alone Jess.

"Are you kidding?" Jess scoffs. "He invited *me* out of politeness. It's *you* he wants to see there. Stop pretending you don't know that he's totally into you."

His "beautiful" comment didn't go unnoticed, no.

"Not exactly sure why," I mutter.

"That's 'cause you think the only thing people see is your scar," Jess says rather intuitively. "What you don't see is how hot you are underneath it. It isn't half as bad as you think it is."

It is to me. Okay, so if I really stop and think about it, it could be a lot worse. It's difficult to describe but imagine having a dented line running across your face, like the tread in a slightly worn tyre, and running a two-pence piece through it with a pale pink marker. That's pretty much what it looks like, and you're probably agreeing with Jess, but how other people see my scar and how I see it are two very different things. Jess didn't have the pleasure of seeing my face pre-scar, I did, and I miss that face. Not to mention my scar is a constant visual reminder of everything I've been through.

"Besides," Jess adds, "there's way more to you than your face. You're actually a really likeable person."

I think that's probably the nicest thing anyone's ever said to me. Although Damien's "beautiful" comment is high in the rankings too.

"When did you get all insightful and wise?" I ask.

"Hey," Jess protests. "I'm way more than just a pretty face." I laugh. "So, how's about we get ourselves dolled up," she says, rubbing her hands together excitedly, "and go see if this Damien guy's band is any good?"

I take a deep breath. My pulse is already climbing, and I haven't even made it out of the door yet. Even my palms are starting to sweat, yet Jess's puppy-dog eyes are tugging at the tiny part of me that really wants to see Damien in action.

"Okay," I finally say. "But I don't do getting dolled up." I have one style, jeans, and my trademark figure-hugging, long-sleeved top with thumbholes at the end of each sleeve, that's it.

"Well, I do," she says brightly. "I'm gonna need a good half hour."

Jess sets to work, disappearing off into the spare bedroom as I sit for a minute, second-guessing my decision. I force myself into my bedroom to change out of my pyjamas into my trademark clothing, but I opt to swap out my Converse trainers for my only pair of low-heeled grey boots. It's about as dressy as I get. I even give my dust-covered straighteners a whirl, mostly to kill the time whilst Jess plasters on her ten layers of make-up and squeezes into the sexiest outfit she can find, no doubt. Satisfied I don't look a total mess, I head out into the kitchen to down another much-needed cup of coffee.

Three coffees later, Jess finally appears, and boy has she gone to town. The ten layers of make-up are firmly in place with bright red lipstick to boot, and the little black dress she's sporting is skintight, although longer than I was expecting, falling to the middle of her thighs. Her greatest asset, her precious cleavage, is perfectly highlighted, and once again, I fight the urge to roll my eyes.

"You ready?" she asks, looking me up and down.

"Keep your opinions to yourself," I order. "Not all of us want attention."

"Yet you'll get it," she teases, referring to Damien, and this time, I let the roll of my eyes happen extra dramatically.

I grab my denim jacket from one of the two stools sitting at the breakfast bar and slide it on. Jess foregoes a jacket completely, grabbing her matching clutch bag from the counter and tucking it under her bare arm.

"Let's go have some fun," Jess says.

Jess leads the way to Duke Bar, which, as it turns out, is our local, not that I would have known, and it's only a ten-minute walk away. I won't tell Jess, but my heart rate is smashing through the roof with extra force, and it's taking all my strength to keep my jelly legs from failing me. My entire body is as stiff as a board, and my brain is screaming, ordering me to turn on my heel and run back home. I steal glances at the passers-by as we walk, almost cowering if they pass a little too close like a scared, lonely child. I stop walking, feeling abruptly breathless, and it takes Jess a minute to realise I'm no longer beside her.

"Dani?" She walks back to me. "You okay?"

"This is a bad idea."

"No, it's not," she argues, taking my hand and dragging me along with her.

I reluctantly don't fight Jess's grip, but as we grow closer, I can see through the extra-large window that the pub is already busy, and the nausea hits the back of my throat like acid burning me from the inside out. I almost let out a yelp in surprise when we're stopped in our tracks about six feet from the pub's entrance by an alcohol-fuelled guy smoking a cigarette.

"Hey there, ladies," he says, blowing smoke into my face, making the nausea even more unbearable. "Can I buy you both a drink?"

"No, thanks," Jess says with an enviable confidence as she barges past him.

Unfortunately for me, the guy's drunken state is making him less than rational, and he grabs my shoulder, dragging me, and consequently Jess, back towards him. I hold back a scream as the feel of *his* hands overwhelms me with a sickening vengeance, his rough skin rubbing against mine like sandpaper. I can feel the pain as vividly as I can see *his* eyes burning into me. I shake my head, but the flashbacks refuse to dissolve.

"That's not very nice," the drunk guy groans as I regain enough composure to force myself free of his grip, my entire body shaking like a leaf blowing in a gale force wind.

"Back off, jackass." Jess shoves him backwards.

"Hey," the drunk guy scoffs, but to be honest, I'm not really listening. I'm too busy trying to shake the never-ending flashbacks plaguing my eyes.

"I'm gonna be sick," I suddenly say, and before I can stop myself, I throw up.

"My trainers," the drunk guy yells. "You dumb bitch."

"Hey," Jess yells as I force myself upright. "Don't you dare talk to her like that."

"Is there a problem here?" I hear a voice say.

I turn to look behind me, conscious that my dignity is in the toilet, to see Damien standing a couple of inches away. I hadn't noticed his approach and if Jess had, she opted not to mention it.

"Just a drunk dick," Jess tells Damien.

"The bitch threw up on my trainers," the drunk guy protests.

Damien moves to square up to the drunk guy as I lean myself against the pub window, my breath caught in my throat, and my chest fighting for oxygen. Jess stands beside me, her arms folded across her chest, clearly pissed off.

"Watch your mouth," Damien warns.

"She needs to give me some money," the drunk guy insists. "My trainers are fucked."

"There's a speck of sick on one shoe," Jess points out. "And they'll wash, dickhead."

"Maybe I'll rub her face in it," the drunk guy bites out, referring to me. "She can lick it up."

In a flash, Damien grabs him by the shirt and pushes him up against the pub window, his other arm resting against the drunk guy's neck. Oh, shit. I instinctively shuffle, putting a comfortable

– not my best choice of word – distance between myself and the scuffle.

"Threaten her again, and I'll have you eating your own shit, mate," Damien says calmly, yet forcefully. "Apologise. Now."

The drunk guy sneers, but Damien's resolve doesn't dissipate, and I stand watching as Damien raises a fist. I don't know if Damien intends on hitting the guy, I hope not, but the suggestion is enough to dampen the guy's cockiness, and he turns his head to look at me, fear encompassing his face.

"I'm sorry," he says quietly.

"I'm not sure they heard that," Damien says sternly.

"I'm sorry," he says loudly. "I'm sorry, okay?"

Damien lets go of the drunk dude's shirt, and he scampers off down the street as fast as his wobbling legs can carry him. Damien immediately turns his attention to me.

"Are you okay?" he asks, yet all I can do is sniff back an escaping sob. "Dani?"

"I'm fine," I lie, wiping away a stray tear. "I'm just gonna go home." I start to walk away, but Jess opts to follow, and I quickly stop. "No, Jess, you stay. You enjoy your night."

"I can't leave you alone like this," she insists, taking a hold of my hand.

"Alone is exactly what I need right now."

"Dani," she argues.

"Please," I beg, and thankfully, but reluctantly, Jess doesn't argue further, releasing my hand. Before I walk away, I force myself to look at Damien. "Thanks for the rescue."

"Are you sure being alone –"

"I'm sure," I cut him off. "Have a good gig."

I walk away and let the tears flow, powerless to stop them. Deflated, disappointed... I should have known better. I'm an absolute idiot to think my fucked-up bullshit wouldn't get the better of me. Even if the drunk guy hadn't come along, something would have triggered the flashbacks; something always does.

His image is still front and centre. I can't shake him. I can never shake him. Even though I know he's locked away and can't hurt me anymore, he *is* hurting me. He's torturing me, in my dreams, and in my memories. He is the reason why I live my life in fear, and I will never be free from him no matter how hard I try.

It's not the drunk guy's attitude or comments that bothers me, it's the fact he lay his hand on my shoulder that's got my anxiety working overtime. Thanks to a little thing called post-traumatic stress disorder, and my seriously screwed-up brain, I can't stand to be touched. I can handle hands, even my arms, but my torso, including my shoulders, is a different story.

When a person touches my torso, I'm hit with flashbacks, memories of the bastard that ruined me in so many uncountable ways, and it's too much. I feel actual pain, like he's right here, physically hurting me, and I tend to spiral from there, sometimes into full-blown panic attacks, but more commonly, I vomit. That's why I avoid crowds. I'm terrified someone will act in an unpredictable manner and put a hand on me because that's all it takes. It's ridiculous and pathetic, but I am the way I am, and not even therapy could cure me.

Most of the time, whilst I understand my experiences, I don't understand my anxiety. The way it manifests is bonkers. I have a fear of letting people in, and of crowds, yet I was utterly and completely alone when *he* found me. My family were dead, and any friends or colleagues or anyone else had been forgotten. All apart from my uncle's police force partner, Ray, who took it upon himself to take care of me in the wake of my family's demise and is the reason I'm alive to tell the tale. Taking that into account, you would think I would crave company to feel safe if nothing else, yet I choose to live a life of solitude, keeping the people who have wormed their way in at arm's-length. Ridiculous and pathetic is an understatement.

That's fear all over though. I can try to rationalise my fear all I want, but all fear is irrational. Justified in some cases, arguably mine, but irrational nonetheless.

After what feels like forever, I finally make it back home only to find James sitting on the steps that lead down to the communal entrance. I sigh. I'm not really in the mood to entertain James right now, but there's no way to slip past him unnoticed.

"Hey, Dani," he says as I wander towards the steps. My eyes must be red from crying because he asks, "Are you okay?"

"I'm fine," I lie, unlocking the main door and heading inside, James following close behind.

"No, you're not," he says, and I stop at my door, turning to face him.

"Jay," I say, "I've had a really shitty night, so if you don't mind, I want to go inside and drown my sorrows in music."

"Did he hurt you?" James asks, taking me by surprise.

"Did who hurt me?"

"That guy you met at Dave's," James clarifies. "What's his name? Damien."

I stand, momentarily surprised, until my brain kicks in and reminds me that Jess, despite today's touching admission, has a mouth like a foghorn. "Don't be ridiculous. Damien's got nothing to do with nothing."

"Yeah, right," James scoffs.

"Okay," I say slowly, a little thrown by James's sudden

change in attitude. "I have no idea what's going on with you right now, but I really don't care. Good night, Jay."

I unlock my door and step inside, but before I have a chance to shut it, James is entering uninvited, gaining him a heavy, unimpressed sigh from me.

"I want to know what it is about this guy," James says. "I've known you for almost a year, and you've never once taken me up on going out somewhere, yet this Damien shows up and you practically jump out the door."

"Okay, no offence, Jay," I snap, "but what I do or don't do is none of your damn business."

"You barely know the guy," James continues regardless, but I've had about as much as I can handle tonight.

"Get the hell out of my flat, Jay," I yell. "Now."

Thankfully, James relents without further argument, and I slam the door closed behind him. In a flash of rage, enhanced by James, I pick up the closest thing to me, the telly remote sitting on the breakfast bar, and throw it across the room. I move into the kitchen, feeling an urge to let every ounce of anger seep out in a violent and destructive manner, and start smashing anything I can find until the tiled floor is covered in broken pieces. I lay my back against the cupboards and slide to the ground, letting the tears consume me.

I'm so ashamed, I hate myself. I hate what I've become, a beaten down, broken shell of a woman. I hate that I can't move on and get on with my life. I hate that I keep telling myself I'm better off alone, that I'm happy living my life of solitary confinement. Hell, I've told myself so many times I've almost convinced myself it's true, but it's not. Who the hell wants to be alone?

I know what you're thinking – make your mind up. One minute I want to be alone, the next I don't. Welcome to the minefield that is my screwed-up brain. I have no idea what I want. No, that's a lie. I want to be normal. I want my past to be some horror story that belongs to someone else. I want to go back in time before my entire world got turned upside down. I want my life back. Only I can't have that, and tonight proved it. My old life, a life I don't even remember, is dead, and all that's left is the shell I call Daniella.

I need fucking help, that's what I need.

Chapter Five

I wake up on the couch feeling groggy. I have no idea how long I've been asleep, and it's the sound of my intercom buzzing that's waking me up. I force myself to sit up and look at the time on my phone; it's almost midnight. I look over at the kitchen, suddenly realising I've yet to clean up my mess, which is a massive mistake as Jess is probably going to freak. Too late now. I drag my backside to the telephone-style intercom and pick it up.

"If you've lost my spare key," I say sternly. "I'm gonna kill you."

"Bollocks. Why didn't it occur to me Jess would have a key?" a male voice responds, throwing me completely off balance.

"Who…?" Light bulb. "Damien?"

"Hi," Damien replies, and my mouth dries up in response. "I'm really sorry to wake you, but I've got Jess with me, only she's erm…"

"Bladdered?" The obvious assumption.

"I thought it was best to bring her home," he says, and I take a second to appreciate his gentlemanly style.

I press the buzzer, and after placing my intercom back on its receiver, I open the door. I'm about to step out into the hallway when my eyes drift to my kitchen. I freeze. Oh, crap. It's one thing for Jess to walk in on the smashed chaos that is the kitchen, but Damien… Yep, too late. He's already in my doorway, practically carrying Jess inside. Her arm is wrapped around his broad shoulders, but her feet are barely touching the ground. I fear if Damien was to loosen his grip for even a second, Jess would hit the ground face first. She's totally out of it, yet she smiles upon seeing me.

"Spare room," I tell Damien, but he looks at me blankly, and it takes me a minute to register that he has no idea where the spare room is located.

I jump into action, leading Damien through my living room and into the spare bedroom. I pull the covers down, and Damien carefully drops Jess to the bed. She mutters something inaudible as I cover her up with the quilt. I notice Damien slip back out into the living room, and after a quick nip to my tattered kitchen to retrieve a bucket, I pop it next to Jess, who's now dead to the world, and make my exit, closing the door behind me.

I glance at Damien, standing between the back of the couch and the breakfast bar. "Thank you for bringing Jess home."

"Yeah, course," he replies. "Better that than someone taking advantage."

How very chivalrous. I sound like I'm mocking him, but I'm genuinely not. It's been my experience there are one too many men out there willing to take advantage of women, especially when they are unable to defend themselves. Chivalrous men are hard to come by, if that's what Damien truly is. At the end of the day, one brushstroke does not make a finished painting, and I don't know Damien well enough to tell the difference between a charade and reality. Although, there's something inside me that's telling me Damien is one of the good guys. A gut feeling, maybe?

"Although, I'll confess," he says, and I'm instantly doubting my gut, "I'm glad it gave me a reason to see you."

I eye him with curiosity. Even though a practical stranger is standing in my flat at such a late hour, which is a godawful idea given my history, seeing the ex-Army boy shuffle uncomfortably is an endearing sight. I sigh when his gaze moves to my kitchen.

"I wanted to make sure you were okay," he says. "Are you? Okay?"

That's sweet, I guess, and I don't blame the extra need for clarification at the end of his sentence there since my kitchen is nothing but a fragmented sheet of porcelain and glass.

"I'm fine," I lie. "I took my frustration out on my plates."

Damien chuckles nervously. "I can see that."

"You really didn't need to check in on me," I point out. I'm not Damien's responsibility.

"I know," he agrees, fiddling his keys between his fingers. "But I *wanted* to. You seemed a little shaken."

"Nothing I'm not used to." I try to shrug off my embarrassment and my vulnerability, probably unsuccessfully. I'm lying, of course. I don't leave the house enough to be used to vomiting in public, but it's not the first time it's happened, and I doubt it will be the last either. "But thanks for checking in *and* for helping me out earlier."

Damien smiles softly. "Anytime."

"How did the gig go?" I'm a little gutted I missed it, despite my justified reluctance to leave the house.

"It was good, yeah," Damien replies. "Jess seemed to enjoy herself. Maybe a little too much."

"She usually does."

There's an awkward silence as Damien continues to fiddle with his keys. I'm not sure what else there is to say. I can barely look Damien in the eye, my cheeks reddening, yet he's not showing any signs of leaving. That's when he clocks something in the far corner of my room, and his face lights up like Blackpool Illuminations.

"Is that what I think it is?" he asks, wandering over to my guitar.

I smile. "If you're thinking it's a 1958 Gibson Explorer, then yeah."

"Where the hell did you get one of those?" he asks, stopping short of picking it up to ask permission first. "Can I?"

"Go for it," I say. "It was my dad's. I don't know where he got it."

"You do know they only ever made like nineteen of these, right?" he asks, taking a seat on the couch against the back wall, cradling the guitar as if it were a baby. I can't help but giggle.

"I didn't know that, no," I admit. "I knew it was a fairly rare guitar, but that's about it."

"It'll be worth a fortune," he declares, running his fingers along the framework. "It feels like bloody new. The condition is amazing."

"Do you want me to leave the room or…" Damien smirks, and I refrain from finishing my sentence.

Completely transfixed by the guitar, he starts to play a few notes, amp-less given the late hour, and I appreciate his respect for my neighbours. Jess too, I suppose.

"Listen to that," Damien says in a dreamy, I-want-one kind of tone that has my giggles resurfacing. "I'd love to know how your dad managed to get his hands on one."

I sigh, sitting down on the opposite sofa. "I'd ask him," I say with a lump in my throat, "but he died a while back."

"I'm sorry," Damien says, throwing me a sympathetic glance. I nod, desperately trying to ignore the grief creeping into my heart and mind.

Damien starts to play another one of his melancholy songs, oblivious to my wandering parent-related thoughts, thankfully, and I sit, watching and listening. I find myself getting lost in the sound, totally mesmerised by the elegant way Damien's fingers glide over the guitar strings, and the way he closes his eyes like he's lost in his own world. That's what music does. It lets you forget all the shit and drama in your life. It's a sanctuary from reality, and Damien clearly gets that.

Feeling brave, or hypnotised by Damien's music, I stand and walk over to my keyboard. I can feel Damien watching me, but he doesn't stop playing. I take a deep breath and start to copy his melody. As is my way, I pick it up fairly quick, and Damien and I are soon playing in perfect unison.

"Why can't you write lyrics?" I suddenly ask.

Damien shrugs. "I don't know."

"Have you tried?"

"Oh, I've tried," Damien says. "But I can never quite get the right words. I can't seem to get them to flow."

"You got any new melodies?"

Excitement oozes from Damien in waves as he smiles that beautiful smile and moves to take a seat on the neighbouring stool. I don't know why I have two, it's not like I need two, but hey ho.

"Loads," he answers.

"Mind if I have a go at the lyrics?"

I'm feeling an urge to delve into my music zone, my *comfort* zone. Usually, it's a lonely experience, but I guess I'm making an exception tonight. I blame the whirlwind of emotions my brief nap has failed to expel from my system, and a strange desire to *not* be alone for a change.

"That would be great," Damien says, beaming. "Are you thinking slow song or a more upbeat sound?"

"Let's go slow." Me and depressing go hand in hand, funnily enough.

I grab my pen and paper from the little side table that sits next to my keyboard. As Damien plays his melody, I spend a few minutes mimicking the notes until I get into the swing and grasp the melody fully.

"And what do you think about when you play?" I ask him, trying to get a feel of the motives behind his melody.

"Erm…" He thinks for a minute, strumming away. "I tend to think about the friends I lost in the Army."

"I'm sorry," I offer, my heart melting a little. "Can't have been easy."

"It's the risk you take." He shrugs, but I can see the sorrow in his eyes. I don't prod any further. I know what it's like to face loss and pain, I can empathise, but I also know what it's like to *not* want to talk about it. "The Army was like a second family." I obviously misread the situation as Damien appears content to keep sharing. "And the guys I served with were my brothers."

"That explains the tattoo," I muse aloud.

"I thought I clocked you checking it out," Damien says, taking me back to Damien's second visit to Dave's.

"It's a nice tattoo." I shrug.

"So's yours."

I instinctively bring a hand to my neck. I keep forgetting I have a tattoo of my own, mostly because it's usually hidden by my hair, but it's nothing like the size of Damien's. Sitting on the side of my neck, between my ear and my shoulder, is a detailed design of a heart, not a love heart, but an actual scientific depiction, wearing headphones. It's only about as big as a tangerine, but I like it. Not entirely sure *when* I got it, but that's a story for another day.

"The tattoo's my way of paying tribute," Damien shares.

"Writing is a good way to do that too," I state. "But since you claim to be unable to write, I'll try my best to pay tribute on your behalf."

I let inspiration take over, flitting between scribbling and playing, pulling some funny concentration faces along the way, no doubt. Patience is obviously Damien's strong suit as he merely sits and watches without saying a word.

"Okay," I eventually say. "Let's give this a whirl."

I play my keyboard and sing the lyrics I've created. I don't look at Damien, but I can feel his lingering gaze. Interestingly though, I don't feel self-conscious. Funny how music has a way of making the tension disappear. Or maybe it's the company I'm keeping. Either way, I feel strangely at ease.

I fiddle around with a few words, replaying and re-singing a few times over until I'm satisfied enough to ask for Damien's opinion. "What do you think?"

Damien is staring at me, and if I was a little more confident, I'd go as far as to say he's staring in awe. His gorgeous sky-blue eyes are wide, and his pale lips are parted slightly. He looks a little dumbfounded, and I shuffle uncomfortably at his prolonged silence.

"I think," he starts, finding his voice, "that you're amazing." The blood rushes directly to my cheeks, and I tear my gaze away. "Your voice really is beautiful," he praises.

"I meant," I say, chuckling, "what do you think of the lyrics?"

"Right, those," Damien says, fake coughing for dramatic effect, drawing a smile to my face. "I think you've hit the nail on the head."

"Okay," I say. "Polite ain't gonna cut it here. There's no way you ain't got one single criticism."

"I have no right to criticise. I can't write."

"It's still *your* melody," I remind him. "You're entitled to an opinion." Damien looks at me warily. "I promise I won't be offended."

"You sure about that?"

"I'm a big girl."

"Okay," he says with a tinge of caution. "The only part I'm not feeling is the 'take me by the hand'. It feels a little girly."

I laugh. "Girly?"

Damien fails to hide his smile. "It doesn't quite fit with the Army vibe."

"You are aware that *girls* can join the Army, right?" I tease, gaining me a slight smirk from my guest.

"They're usually women," he corrects, purely in jest. "But you said it was my melody, and it just so happens I'm a guy."

"No," I say overdramatically and with a sarcastic emphasis. "I hadn't realised."

"It's the hair, right?" he jokes.

I burst out laughing. "Yeah, 'cause a buzz cut is totally the new trend."

The image of Jess sporting a buzz cut pops in my head, and it only makes me laugh harder. I take a minute to compose myself, turning my attention back to the lyrics at hand, and my concentration returns.

"Okay, so..." I stop to think. "Instead of 'take me by the hand', how about 'follow my command'?"

Damien's eyes light up. "I like it."

I grab the paper and replace the lyric. As soon as I pop the paper back on the stand in front of my keyboard, Damien starts to strum the melody, and I'm taken aback when he opens his mouth to sing. A gorgeous, husky Kings of Leon sound delights my ears, enveloping me like a warm blanket on a cold winter's night, comforting and soothing. Holy hell, Damien's voice is mesmerising.

"I did *not* see that coming," I state once Damien wraps the song up.

"You're not the only one who's multitalented around here," Damien jokes.

"Your voice is gorgeous," I tell him, a little delirious from the hypnotising effect he's just had on me.

"Pot kettle black," he states.

"I'm obviously not the only one who can't take compliments."

"Oh, no." He grins. "Please, keep them coming. What've we had so far? Good-looking, good guitarist, gorgeous…"

"I said your *voice* was gorgeous," I remind him, but he merely laughs. I try to hide the ridiculous grin on my face by turning away from him, but I have no doubt Damien is fully aware of the effect he's having on me. My blushing cheeks tend to be a bit of a giveaway. "You ain't gonna be able to fit through my door if your head gets any bigger."

Damien laughs again, and it's such a beautiful laugh, almost like a childish giggle but with a deep, manly tone to it. Like his singing voice, it's such an infectious sound.

Damien and I continue to play for a while, chiming in with sarcastic comments along the way and laughing harder than I've ever laughed. Unfortunately, our playing is halted by the sound of the spare bedroom's door creaking open and Jess bolting out of it in the direction of the bathroom. I notice Damien reluctantly replacing my guitar in its stand with a frown. Something tells me he's going to miss spending so much time with my Gibson. It's a little adorable, but as an avid guitarist, it's understandable. It's a bloody good guitar.

Jess returns to the living room moments later, groaning, yet upon seeing Damien, she manages an extra bright smile. "I think I should be thanking you."

"It's all right," Damien says casually. "Are *you* all right?"

Jess suddenly heaves, and in a flash, she's back in the bathroom. I sigh. Something tells me Jess might be at that for a while, and the chances of me sleeping through it are slim-to-nothing. I'm suddenly wishing Damien wasn't planning on making his exit. As it turns out, I've thoroughly enjoyed making music together. Damien's good company, not that I shall be telling Jess that should she decide to interrogate me, which we all know she will.

"Does she usually drink herself into oblivion?" Damien asks.

"Yep," I answer bluntly. "It's just not usually my problem. Remind me again why I thanked you for bringing Jess home?"

Damien shakes his head. "That's cold."

"I'm kidding," I insist. "Well, half kidding."

"You two have an interesting relationship."

I shrug. "That's one way to describe it."

"She thinks a lot of you," Damien tells me.

"I'm going to assume you two did some talking before you showed up here."

"Your name may have dropped into conversation."

"Whatever she said," I urge, "do not believe a word of it."

Damien laughs. "Give her a little more credit. She said some really nice things. Threw in a few other less complimentary details too."

Jess barely knows any details, although I'm sure my continuous antisocial behaviour was a hot topic of conversation with a few choice words from dear Jess too.

"Such as?" I ask.

Damien glances at his watch. "Look at the time. I should be

getting going. I've got an early PT session."

Nicely played, leaving me hanging in anticipation. I guess karma does exist since I plan on doing the exact same thing to Jess when she initiates her interrogation. Unlike Jess though, it won't eat away at me. Nothing Jess could say about me is a cause for worry or concern; she doesn't know enough.

Damien smiles and heads for the door, and I'll admit, I can feel a pang of disappointment. Ignoring the drunk guy fiasco and my brief encounter with James, tonight has turned out to be one of the most relaxed and fun nights I've had in, well, as far as I know, forever. Damien's got a great sense of humour, and my cheeks are stinging a little from all the laughing. I started the night tense and on edge, but now I feel relaxed to the point where I almost feel normal. My issues, scars and anxieties exited the building tonight, and it's exactly what I didn't know I needed.

"I had a lot of fun tonight," Damien says, stopping to stand by the front door.

"Yeah, me too," I admit.

"We make a good songwriting team," he adds. "We should do it again sometime."

And in true Damien fashion, he doesn't give me a chance to respond, probably out of fear of what I'll say, and he's out the door. He closes it for me, and I allow myself to sink into the sofa, a mixture of emotions taking me under.

Talk about sending mixed signals. What the hell am I doing? Nothing's changed. I'm still me, and I can kid myself all I want, but deep down, I already know that Damien and I are dead in the water before we've even jumped.

Now, if someone could tell that to the ruthless, fluttering butterflies, I'd much appreciate it.

Chapter Six

My shift is dragging like hell. It's Wednesday, and I'm about six hours into my seven-hour shift at Lloyd's, on countdown as I'm on holiday from both Lloyd's and Dave's for the rest of the week. I've had maybe four customers all day, and with Dan ringing in sick and Lloyd busy, I'm manning the place solo.

So far, the only meal I've cooked is Black with One Sugar and Latte with Extra Cream's breakfast. The other two customers, another couple, merely ordered drinks and a cake. I've pretty much spent the rest of the shift cleaning, but even a busy bee like me is running out of jobs to do at this point. I've cleaned everything I can think of, so I'm resigning myself to a coffee. Screw it. If Dan can get away with bogging off all day, I can get away with hovering behind the counter for a while. I sincerely doubt Pamela, the other waitress, does as much as I do anyway.

I make my coffee and just as I'm about to take my first sip, that godforsaken bell rings and in walks the only person I seem to talk or think about lately. Annoyingly, he looks as good as ever, and upon seeing me, his beautiful smile awakens. It's a smile I return just as brightly.

"Hey, Dani," Damien greets me, approaching the counter.

"Hi," I reply. "Americano?"

Damien chuckles. "Are you calling me that or offering me the drink?" Ha-ha, very funny.

"Offering the drink."

"Please."

Damien takes a seat at the nearest table, his future *regular* spot, I'm thinking, as I quickly make his drink and move around to place it in front of him.

73

"Nice day off?" he asks as I retake my position behind the counter, reminding me it's the first time I've seen Damien since Sunday.

"A day in front of my keyboard is always a good day," I reply. "Although I unfortunately encountered my neighbour's parents in the hallway."

I chose the wrong moment to head out for my weekly shop, running into Mr and Mrs Holding. Interestingly though, I managed to learn that James is a barefaced liar since his parents believe he attends church every Sunday, which he doesn't, and that he's apparently saving himself for marriage. How I kept my face straight, I'll never know, but when Mr Holding proceeded to give me a lecture on the benefits of devoting your life to the Lord, I made as swift an exit as possible.

"Interesting people?"

"Religious." I grimace, and I probably should have checked if Damien is religious before revealing my contempt. "Not that I have anything against religious people, just the ones who try to force their beliefs on others."

It's not a lie. Despite being an atheist, I'm not against religion. In fact, I personally think it must be such a nice way to live, being able to attribute everything to God's master plan, but I'm just not wired that way.

"Not religious then?" he asks, and I shake my head. "Me neither." Good to know. "It's James, right? Jess's flatmate?" I nod, assuming Jess filled Damien in at the gig. "Good-looking guy?"

"If arrogant, egotistical, and a womaniser is a good-looking guy, then yeah." I'm a little too blunt in my choice of words. "I sound like a right bitch." Damien laughs but says nothing. "He's not all bad. He's down-to-earth and funny, but he's not the kind of guy I could see myself with."

"And what kind of guy *do* you see yourself with?" Damien asks, and I instinctively sigh at my idiocy. I just keep walking right on in.

"I don't," I say, although I'm pretty sure that isn't the answer Damien is looking for. "I would love to find the right guy, settle down and all that jazz, but I don't see that happening. I'm too…"

"Complicated?" Damien finishes my sentence. "Some guys like complicated."

"I get what you're doing," I say. I'm not blind. "But if I was you —" I opt to casually let him down gently, knowing it has to be done "— I'd find yourself a nice lass who doesn't have skeletons the size of China in her closet."

"Everyone's got skeletons." He doesn't back down. "Doesn't mean we should end up alone because of them."

"Some people like being alone." I shrug.

"Do you?"

Damien's hit the million-dollar question on the head. Do I? Or don't I? I'm still not one-hundred percent certain of the answer.

Our conversation is interrupted by the sound of the bell and a young guy, I'd guess early twenties, looking very stylish in black skinny jeans, a flowery print silk shirt that falls to his thighs, and sporting one of those modern-day, fringe-across-the-face hairstyles that probably took hours to perfect, sashays his way in.

"There you are," he says to Damien. "You do know what a phone is meant to be used for, right?"

He bypasses the counter completely and takes a seat facing Damien, who pulls out his phone from his jacket pocket.

"Silent." Damien shrugs, holding his phone up in the air for dramatic effect, I'm assuming, before slipping it back into his pocket. "What's up?"

I sip away at my coffee, contemplating looking busy, but I literally have nothing to do, so I resign myself to merely standing and trying not to earwig. I already know it's impossible, and even though I said I let anything I hear go in one ear and out the other, it's Damien, and let's face it, Damien makes me curious.

"Nothing," Damien's friend says casually. "Just felt like making a dramatic entrance."

I try not to laugh as I watch Damien slowly shake his head, an amused smirk sitting upon his lips. "You're definitely dramatic, mate."

"But since you chose to ignore my calls," the friend says, "you can buy me a latte as an apology."

Damien laughs at his mate's cheekiness, but he turns his head in my direction, and I quickly pop down my brew, plastering on my customer service face. "Dani, could you get my mate here a latte, please?"

"Coming right up."

"Dani?" The friend repeats my name with a hint of intrigue. "So, you're Dani."

I refrain from answering until I've made the latte, moving around the counter and setting it down in front of Damien's friend. "That's me, and you are?"

"Raif," he says, holding out his hand.

I shake it politely. "Nice to meet you."

"You have an amazing figure," Raif compliments.

Not the typical first-meet conversation, but I manage an, "Erm, thanks."

"Raif is our bass player," Damien explains. "Hairdresser and beautician by day."

The latter makes more sense than the former given Raif's flair, and I can't quite picture him standing behind a bass. I'm thinking he's gay too, not that his sexuality is overly relevant. Although, you should never judge a book by its cover, and I could be way off the mark, so who knows?

"I would love to give you a makeover," Raif adds as I shimmy back behind the counter. "You have beautiful hair. Do you style it?"

"I straighten it very occasionally," I answer openly. "But mostly, I let it dry naturally."

"I know so many women who would kill to be able to do that," he admits.

The easier the better in my book. Some would say I don't take pride in my appearance, but I am what I am, and I don't see any point in trying to be something I'm not. That, and I could not be bothered to take the time to style my hair every single day. That's far too much effort.

"I have a foundation that would work wonders for you," he continues. "It'd hide the…" Raif waves his hand in front of his face, and it doesn't take a rocket scientist to figure out what he's referring to.

"Raif," Damien scolds, and I'm thinking, thanks to the "ow" escaping Raif's mouth, Damien's booted Raif under the table. "Tact, mate."

"I didn't mean anything by it," Raif defends, rubbing his shin. "You know I have no filter."

"Don't worry," I say. "I'm not offended."

At least Raif was polite about it. In so many ways, wearing make-up would probably be great for my confidence, but I'd still know it was there, and I'd always be wondering if people would change their mind about talking to me or whatever if they knew what was underneath. That, and I cannot be bothered with the hassle of piling make-up on any more than I can styling my hair every morning. I'd rather spend my time drinking coffee.

"But I'm not a make-up kind of lass either," I add.

"What kind of woman are you?" Raif mocks.

"Not everyone needs to be knee deep in layers to look good," Damien says, and I can't control the roll that overcomes my eyes.

Despite being an obvious compliment aimed in my direction, I think Damien is also having a little dig at Raif, who clearly loves his make-up. Raif's face is tastefully decorated though, his foundation matching his skin tone, his black eyeliner complementing his blue eyes, and the slight tint of blush on each cheek highlighting his high cheekbones. He's obviously got artistic talent and an eye for detail.

"And you do know thumbholes are so nineties, right?" Raif asks, almost as if he's out to prove his no filter statement.

"I like the nineties." I shrug. "And I like my style."

Raif chuckles. "No offence, honey, but to call a thumbhole top with jeans and a cardigan style is a crime against fashion."

"Mate," Damien scolds again, but I merely laugh.

"I did say no offence." Raif shrugs.

"He's not wrong in his assessment," I agree.

"Thank you, Dani." Raif beams.

"You really shouldn't encourage him," Damien tells me, causing Raif to roll his eyes.

"So, everything set for Saturday?" Raif asks Damien, changing the subject.

"Good to go," Damien answers. "I'm gonna get there early

with Paul and get everything set up."

"What's Saturday?" I ask nosily.

"Charity gig," Damien responds. "A dementia charity is holding a ticket-only event, and we're the entertainment. Supposedly there's gonna be tombola, a cake stall, and a bunch of other usual fundraising stuff." Interesting choice of talent for a charity event, but if it brings the crowd, it brings the money.

"Damien here tells me you're a musical talent yourself," Raif says.

"Damien gives me too much credit."

"You sell yourself short," Damien pipes up.

"Do you always have to have the last word?"

"Oh, you have no idea, honey," Raif is the one to answer. "Stubborn as a mule this one."

"I feel sorry for you all," I joke.

Damien throws me a playful scowl. "Trust me," he says. "A few hours with Raif and Paul, and it'll be *me* you're feeling sorry for."

"What's that supposed to mean?" Raif asks, but there's not a single hint of seriousness to his voice. I'm thinking banter is a common occurrence amongst these two, Paul as well, whoever Paul is.

"Imagine Jess times ten," Damien tells me.

"I think you just sent a shiver down my spine," I joke. "In pure horror."

"Jess is adorable," Raif defends, and I blink, momentarily confused. "I met her at the gig," he explains for my benefit, I'm assuming. "We went out partying last night. She's such a laugh."

She wasn't such a laugh early Monday morning. I had been correct in my assessment, and Jess kept me up with her never-ending waves of vomit that threatened to stain my toilet. Luckily, she was too groggy to interrogate me, but that didn't stop her from popping round after work on Monday for the gossip. True to form, despite our growth, I left her hanging, but other than the annoying effect Damien continues to have on me, there's not all that much to tell.

"That part's true," I admit, returning to Raif's "good laugh" comment and wiping Monday morning from my mind. "Jess knows how to have a good time." Not that I've experienced it first-hand.

Thankfully, talk turns back to music with Raif probing me on my songwriting skills until he makes his exit, leaving Damien and me alone again.

"Come to the charity gig," Damien blurts out.

I sigh heavily, leaning my palms against the counter. "My last outing wasn't exactly a positive experience."

"All the more reason you should come," he reasons. "It's at a town hall, not a pub."

"I don't know," I say honestly, forever confused as to the best course of action in anything I do.

"Tell you what," he says. "You got your phone?"

I eye him suspiciously, but I oblige to his request, nipping into the back and returning with my phone. I pop in the passcode and hand it to Damien.

"Here's my number," he says, typing away on my phone. I soon hear a beep coming from his pocket. "And now I have yours."

"Is there a point to that?" I ask as he hands me back my phone.

"Think about the gig," he explains. "I'll text you Saturday and if you're up for it, I'll give you a lift to the venue. You can bring Jess too if you want. I got a couple of tickets going spare."

I'm about to say something when the bell rings, and I suddenly want to run and hide. It's James, whom I have been avoiding since his weirdness Sunday night. I swiftly retake my stance behind the counter, sliding my phone onto the shelf underneath.

"Hey, Dani," James says, moving to the counter.

"Hey."

"Any chance of a lift home?"

I keep forgetting the gym James works at isn't all that far from Lloyd's. It's not the first time I've driven James home after work.

"Erm, yeah," I answer. "I still got half an hour until the end of shift though."

James shrugs a shoulder. "I can wait."

At that moment, Damien rises from his seat and carries his empty cup to the counter. I can't help but smile at his politeness, nor can I help but witness James's expression changing from friendly to fierce in the blink of an eye as his gaze trails from Damien's feet to his face. What the hell is that about?

"You're Damien, aren't you?" James asks icily.

"That's me," Damien answers politely, holding out his hand. James hesitates for a little longer than necessary before relenting and shaking Damien's hand. "James, right?"

"You been talking about me, Dani?" James asks with a proud smirk, and I wisely choose to ignore him.

"I should be heading off," Damien says, instigating the ringing up of his bill. "Let me know about Saturday."

"What's Saturday?" James asks.

"None of your business," I tell him.

"Are you two going on a date?" he asks in surprise, his eyes landing on Damien's smirk, which isn't about to help the situation any. "Seriously?"

"It's not a date, Jay," I bark.

"You do know he's just trying to get into your pants, right?" James asks me, ignoring my comment completely and instantly sparking a wave of anger that makes me want to slap him across his cocky little mouth for making a bloody scene. I'm suddenly grateful for a lack of staff and customers. I glance at Damien, but his expression is deadpan, giving nothing away.

"You would think that," I scoff, "seeing as though you go through women like they're going out of fashion."

I really shouldn't be rising to James's shit, especially not at work, and definitely not in front of Damien, but his attitude lately is royally pissing me off.

"And you think he doesn't?" James spits.

I glance back at Damien again. Despite being rudely talked about as if he isn't even there, he looks super calm and unfazed by the confrontation erupting before him. James may have a slight point. Damien could have a vibrant sex life for all I know, but at this moment in time, it's irrelevant.

"You're saying you two are just friends?" James adds.

"That's right," Damien says, deciding to speak.

"Bullshit," James spits. "You don't want to be her friend, and don't even think about denying it."

Damien chuckles, obviously amused, though I can't imagine which part he's finding funny.

"I wasn't going to." Damien shrugs, and if I'm brutally honest, I'm not surprised. I'm starting to realise Damien is a what-you-see-is-what-you-get kind of guy, and he's not afraid to say what's on his mind.

"See," James scoffs in my direction. "He only wants one thing, and you know it."

"You're way off base, mate," Damien states.

"I'm not your mate," James hisses. "But please, enlighten me."

"I like Dani," Damien obliges, though I'm not sure why he feels the need to. "But I'm not looking to fuck her then fuck her off." That's a vulgar way to put it, but it makes the point. "That's not my style. All I want is to get to know Dani better, and if something comes of it, great, if not, then fair enough. I'd settle for friends over nothing because believe it or not, and you won't, I'm a decent guy."

James's fists clench, and if the bulging vein in his forehead is anything to go by, I'd say his temper is rising. Damien, meanwhile, is still as cool as a bloody cucumber. Me, I'm tempted to pour hot coffee over James's head. It's just a snippet of what he deserves right now.

"You do know you didn't need to justify yourself to James," I point out.

"I know," Damien replies, his eyes locking with mine. "I didn't do it for him."

He did it for me, I'm assuming, to clarify his intentions, and it's appreciated. James's behaviour, however, not so much.

"Are you falling for this shit?" James asks me.

"That's enough," I snap, sending a wave of pain shooting through my already aching head. "I have no idea what the hell is going on with you, but you need to pack the whole protective big brother shit in, right now."

"Protective…" James scoffs in disbelief. "You know, I had you pegged for a lot of things, but stupid wasn't one of them."

Damien inches closer to James, his cool demeanour replaced with a flash of disgust. I reach over the counter and put a hand on his arm to stop him. He looks at me and shakes his head, but he doesn't make a second attempt to move. The last thing I want is a fight breaking out, although I appreciate Damien's desire to defend me. I'm guessing it was the "stupid" part that irked him.

"I like you, Dani," James clarifies without being asked, and my breath hitches.

I'm floored, eyes wide and jaw dropped. James is staring at me, but what's terrifying is the indisputable honesty with a hint of vulnerability and fear in his eyes; he means every word. I don't think I've ever seen James look… I don't even know how to describe it. Nervous? Intense? Desperate?

"And not in a neighbourly, big brother way, but in a –"

"Do not finish that sentence," I cut him off, the realisation hitting me like a hammer to the head. Out of the corner of my eye, I spy Damien retaking his seat.

"What did you think the invitation to dinner was?"

Last week in the hallway, the same day he shamelessly sent his latest conquest packing, James *was* asking me out. I don't know where to look or put myself, but I sure as hell do *not* want to go on a date with James. No offence to the guy, but he's not my kettle of fish.

"But…" I'm gobsmacked. "Jay… You can't."

"Why not?" James asks. "He does." He wafts a hand in Damien's direction for dramatic effect, and I officially can't argue.

"No offence, Jay," I say instead. "You're a nice enough guy, and I like you as a neighbour, but I don't see you in that way at all." I emphasise the "at all" a little too much. "And I can tell you right now that it ain't ever gonna happen."

"Are you gonna stand there and tell me you're not attracted to me in the slightest?" he asks, and I scoff.

"Arrogant much?" I mock, but James is deadly serious, and he's awaiting an answer. "I'm really not. I'm sorry."

"But you are to him?" James is determined to keep dragging Damien into this, and I really am getting a little sick of it.

"It doesn't matter," I state calmly. "Doesn't change anything."

"You really are stupid."

Okay, that's the last straw. "You know what, Jay? I've tried to be nice, but since you're determined to piss me off, you can walk home. In fact, I think it's best you stay away from me for a while."

James laughs, not a happy kind of laugh, but more of a pissed-off snigger. Thankfully, he doesn't argue and storms out of the café. I stand, shaking my head in sheer bewilderment.

What the hell just happened?

Chapter Seven

So, what's the verdict?

It's the text message from Damien I've been dreading all day, and as I stare at it, I honestly don't know the answer. Saturday is here, and he's referring to the charity gig he invited me to. I want to find the courage to go, knowing I will probably enjoy myself or at the very least, I'll enjoy the music, but the thought of being in a crowded room has me crumbling at the seams. That, and I haven't – or should I say I *deliberately* haven't – talked to Jess about it and being a Saturday, there's every chance she already has plans. The thought of going alone only makes me feel worse.

I don't – delete – *I just* – delete.

I slam my phone down on the breakfast bar and bury my face in my hands. What the hell is wrong with me? It's just a charity event. It's just people. No one there wants to hurt me. No one there gives a crap about me, except Damien. And there's the real issue right there: Damien. If I go, I might as well be holding up a sign saying "I'm yours". Okay, so I'm overexaggerating, but I can't seem to get a handle on the way Damien makes me feel.

My phone beeps again, only this time it's Jess.

You got twenty minutes to get ready x
What are you talking about? x

I already know the answer. She and Damien are in cahoots, and they're planning on ganging up on me. I suppose I should appreciate the effort and determination, even if it is an ambush.

You know what x

I sigh. Deciding to go compliantly and avoid being dragged

kicking and screaming, I resign myself to changing into my trademark clothing, and my grey ankle boots. Not feeling my denim jacket, I dig deep into my suitcase and pull out a casual cotton blazer-style jacket I'd almost forgotten I had, sliding it on. It'll do for tonight, and although it's nothing like a school blazer with shoulder pads and more like a collared cardigan, it's enough to appear dressier than normal.

Twenty minutes fly by, and there's a knock at my door. I take a much-needed deep breath before sliding my phone, keys and money into my jacket's zipped pockets, forgoing a bag, and opening the door.

"Nice jacket," Jess says. "Damien's waiting outside in his car."

"When did you two get so pally?"

"When we discovered we have a mutual acquaintance that needs to get a life."

"Acquaintance," I repeat, chuckling. "That's a big word."

"Bog off," she says, grabbing my hand and dragging me into the hallway.

I lock up and we head outside. Through the car window, Damien smiles that beautiful smile, and I return the gesture unknowingly. Jess jumps into the back seat, leaving me to plonk myself into the passenger side. Damien doesn't say a word, but the smugness in his face is as clear as day.

"Just drive," I order.

"Yes, ma'am."

Damien drives us through Manchester and to a neighbouring town, pulling up at a large town hall I'm assuming has a large function room, a bar and kitchen facilities. Jess jumps out first, Damien next, but I'm hesitating a little. Damien walks around the car and opens the passenger door, smiling that bloody smile again. I reluctantly climb out, desperately ignoring my quickening pulse and clammy palms. You don't need to tell me I'm being ridiculous. I'm fully aware.

"You do know we're an hour early," I point out. "You can go in, but –"

"It's fine," Damien cuts me off. "If anyone asks, I'll tell them you're here to help set up."

"That I can do, actually," I say, entirely aware of how a musical set-up works. "Jess, on the other hand…"

"I can lift shit." Jess shrugs. "Or stand around looking pretty."

"Where's your gear?" I ask.

"Paul's on his way in his van," Damien explains.

Damien leads us inside, and the room's already set up, ready to go. It's large, as I expected, with circular tables laid out around the edge of the open space I'm assuming will be used as a dance floor. The kitchen is to the left with a large hatch, and the stage is to the right, set back against the same wall as the entrance. I notice double doors leading off to the side of the stage, on floor level, with a poster advertising tombola and various other fundraising games, finished off with an arrow pointing up and the words "This Way" signalling the presence of another room. There's no real decoration other than bunting lining the walls advertising the charity's name and ways to donate. I will say though, with the number of tables and chairs laid out, they must be expecting a decent number of people to show up.

A rough-around-the-edges bloke with a bald head and yesterday's stubble enters the room, making a beeline for Damien. "Van's outside, mate."

"Paul," Damien says, instigating the introductions, "this is Dani, and you remember her mate, Jess."

"Is that what I'm reduced to?" Jess scowls playfully. "*Her* mate." Damien merely laughs as Paul shakes each of our hands.

"It's nice to finally meet you," Paul speaks directly to me in a Mancunian accent, the hint of suggestion in his tone unmissable. There's a weird glint in his eye too. "I've heard a lot about you."

I opt to ignore his comment, hoping Damien's only had nothing but nice things to say, flashing him a polite smile instead. I'm going to go out on a limb and say Paul's the drummer. It's a vibe I'm getting. He looks older than Damien, maybe early-to-mid-thirties with a bit of a dad vibe too, and his dress sense, made up of a Led Zeppelin T-shirt and ripped-at-the-knee jeans, reminds me of Dave. In fact, he looks like the kind of guy you'd find screaming at a football match on the telly down at the pub after one too many ciders, only with a slightly rockier, athletic edge to him. His tattoo-covered arms scream former bad boy, yet there's one tattoo that looks rather familiar.

"You two have the same tattoo," I point out, not caring which one of them answers.

"We served together." It's Paul who enlightens me. "No one knows Damien here better than me, lass, so if you're ever looking for the low-down." I smile. "Or a good laugh at Damien's expense."

I can imagine Paul's got plenty of embarrassing stories hidden up his sleeve, and I'll admit, a part of me is brimming with curiosity. I eye Damien, but his gaze is on Paul, shaking his head and silently warning his mate to keep his mouth shut, I presume.

"Paul's our drummer," Damien explains, and I mentally pat myself on the back. "And a jackass." I notice Paul shrug in complacent agreement and laugh. Yep, definitely a banter-filled group.

"Can I give you a hand bringing stuff in?" I ask Paul.

"Sure," he says. "Follow me."

Damien, Paul and I carry the equipment and instruments from the van to the stage bit by bit whilst Jess does what she does best, and exactly what she said she would do: stand looking pretty, or should I say, *sit* looking pretty. I start to help set up, plugging stuff in and whatnot, when – crap, what's his name? – Raif, I think, and another guy I haven't met wander inside. Raif makes a beeline for me, whilst the other guy greets Damien and Paul.

"Hello again, Dani," Raif says, beaming. "Damien got you doing slave labour?"

I laugh. "I offered."

"Jessica." Raif spots Jess at a nearby table, sashaying towards her, and the two of them embrace in a kiss-on-each-cheek hug. They've obviously hit it off fast.

Damien and the last remaining band member, a punk rocker styled lad with multicoloured, short hair, a nose ring, eyebrow ring, and I think I count seven ear piercings, head my way for another introduction, I'm assuming.

"Dani," Damien says. "Meet Danny."

"Nice name," he jokes.

"Right back at you."

Up close Danny looks ridiculously young in the face, and I'd put him around eighteen years old. He's as thin as a rake, even thinner than Raif, and his skinnier than skinny jeans make his little legs – he's quite small in height, maybe an inch taller than me – look like twigs. His skull and crossbones T-shirt, and the several festival bands around his wrists scream teenager and immaturity too. Damien's band is certainly made up of a wide age range, and I'm suddenly realising I've never asked Damien how old *he* is, or anything overly personal, come to think of it, but given my history, it would be wise to do that at some point. But I digress. The point I'm making is that the band is made up of an interesting set of characters, and I wouldn't have put them together at all.

Before long, guests start to arrive. Jess and I grab a seat at the nearest table next to the double doors to the right of the stage – there are no reservations as far as we can see. That's the first time I spot the woman who I'm assuming is running things, wearing a charity branded T-shirt and the brightest smile I have ever seen, making her way around the room. I also meet our tablemates, if you will, all six of them: a family consisting of mum and dad, two kids, one around thirteen years old messing on his phone, and a girl around six, and a young, professional-looking couple. I say hello out of politeness, but I don't plan on making much conversation.

After a quick ramble from the woman in charge, highlighting tonight's events, Damien and his crew take to the stage. Damien partakes in a little introduction before the band get down to business and get the night started. I almost melt into the sound of the gorgeous, husky tone to Damien's voice, sending the best kind of shivers down my spine. The urge to close my eyes and block everything out to focus solely on Damien's voice consumes me, but I wisely resist, quickly remembering I'm in public.

Damien's band has a pop-rock edge, and I'm finding myself wondering who the lyricist is. I've already discovered Damien's lyrical skills, and they are somewhat lacking, but I'm assuming the melodies are all his. I like the songs, mostly upbeat so far, and in all honestly, I'm itching to write myself. I'm feeling inspired, and I wish I had a pen and paper to hand.

After roughly six songs, the band cease playing, and the kitchen opens for food. I'm in no rush, not feeling overly hungry, but Jess is one of the first to head over, claiming starvation. I roll my eyes at her before turning my attention to Damien, who's heading my way and nabbing Jess's seat from under her.

"So," Damien says. "What do you think?"

"You guys sound good," I compliment, nodding. "I like your style."

"I'm glad to hear it," he says, beaming.

"Who writes the songs?"

"Most of the melodies are mine," Damien answers. "But they're songs I wrote with an old friend a lifetime ago."

"What are you gonna do when you're in need of new material?" Damien smiles that beautiful smile. I walked right into that one too, although willingly this time. I had a feeling he might look to me. "And who says I want to share my lyrical talents?"

"At least you'd be getting your songs out there," he points out, and I guess I can't argue with that. "Besides, I really loved writing with you."

"Yeah, me too," I admit.

"I'm glad you came tonight," he adds, popping a hand over mine, and although I revel in the warmth of his touch, the guilt kicks in with a vengeance. I knew coming here tonight would send the wrong kind of signal.

Jess returns with as much food as she can possibly balance on one plate, and Damien exits her seat, heading over to the kitchen himself. The sound of the six-year-old sitting next to me is a slight distraction, and I instantly feel for the obviously stressed-out mum sitting next to her. The little lass is not overly impressed with the selection of food her mum has provided her with, complaining that she wants a burger. The mum is attempting to explain that the kitchen doesn't serve burgers, but the kid's having none of it.

"Hey," I say to the kid. "Watch this."

I grab a cocktail sausage from the kid's plate, followed by a bap. I leave the sliced cheese on the bun whilst I cut out a small circular shape from the bap, making a second mini bap, if you will. I chop the sausage into mini slices and pop them on the bottom of the bap in a circular pattern, the cheese sitting on top.

"Mini burger," I say, and the lass practically beams at me in delight. "But if I let you have this mini burger, you need to be a good girl and eat the food your mum's given you, right?"

The lass nods enthusiastically, instantly tucking into one of the two mini sausage rolls on her plate. I quickly notice the mum is looking at me.

"I'm sorry," I suddenly say, realising that I may have just stepped on the mum's toes or completely undermined her parenting. "I didn't mean to –"

"Thank you," she cuts me off with a heavy breath of gratitude.

"You're welcome." I turn my head, and Jess is looking at me in a weird, indescribable way that instantly makes me feel uneasy. "What?"

"You're just full of surprises," Jess says. "Where did that come from?"

"I have no idea." I shrug, and it's the God's honest truth.

I instantly wonder if I've maybe had experience with kids in the past, but knowing I'll probably never know the answer, I resign myself to being grateful it worked. It would have been embarrassing if it hadn't. I could have quite easily made the poor mum's life ten times harder.

Damien makes his way back, Raif and Paul in tow but Danny nowhere to be seen. They hover behind Jess and me, leaning their backs against the windowsills as they eat. Jess is mid-conversation about her latest conquest when I spot a familiar face amongst the crowd.

"Oh…" I stop short of finishing that sentence, acutely aware a child is sitting next to me.

"What?" Damien asks, never missing a beat, and I point to the person in question.

"Oh, crap," Jess suddenly says. "I totally didn't think. James told me ages ago he was going to some charity event with his uncle…" I think Jess is having a light bulb moment. "Whose wife has dementia."

"Do you think I can sneak out without being seen?" I ask half-heartedly, but Jess dramatically shakes her head.

"You're going nowhere," she insists sharply. "You're not gonna let James ruin your night."

"Who's the hunk?" I hear Raif ask Damien, confirming my irrelevant gay theory.

"My neighbour," I answer before Damien has a chance. "And Jess's flatmate."

"Oh, him," Raif says knowingly, and I'm not sure if it's Jess who's mentioned James, or Damien.

"He's got a thing for Dani," Jess tells Raif. "Problem is, it's not mutual, and James isn't all that happy about it."

I filled Jess in on my run-in with James. Thursday night, the day after James's bullshit at Lloyd's is usually movie night, and not wanting to see James, I cancelled. As you can imagine Jess was having none of that, demanding an explanation, and once filled in, she insisted movie night could continue minus James in the future. I can live with that. Jess is on her way to being called a friend, and she assured me she gave James what for too, about as impressed as I am with his attitude. I'm oddly touched Jess is in my corner considering she's known James for a lot longer, but since she called me her only *real* friend, I'm not too surprised.

"That the one who kicked off on you?" Paul asks Damien, and although I want to be annoyed with Damien for sharing, Damien talking to Paul is no different than me talking to Jess, so I haven't got a leg to stand on there.

"That's the one," Damien replies in an indifferent, uninterested tone.

It's only a matter of time until James spots me, but I'm hoping the company I'm keeping will deter him from heading my way.

"Looks like a bit of a pussy prick if you ask me," Paul adds, and I find myself instinctively looking to the kid and her mum, cringing at Paul's rude description, but luckily, they are deep in conversation and not paying attention.

"I think he's hot," Raif comments.

"You would," Paul mocks.

The woman in charge takes the stage, silencing the room, and I spot James taking a seat at the opposite end of the dance floor, near the kitchen. His gaze catches mine, but I tear my eyes away, refusing to give him the satisfaction.

The charity staff steam ahead with the auction element of tonight's events, and it turns out the charity is auctioning off short breaks, caravan holidays, trips to Blackpool and whatnot, that have kindly been donated. The charity obviously has a few connections to gain the generous donations, but I'm more surprised, as the bidding starts, at how much the guests are willing to pay. I keep my hand firmly lowered, but I reluctantly notice James making a bid on the trip to Blackpool, which is just another surprise to add to the mix. He's soon outbid though, and the auction passes by quickly.

Damien's band are soon back to playing, and now the drinks have been flowing for a while, people start to make their presence known on the dance floor – Jess, the young couple, and the mum and six-year-old included. No surprises the dad and teenage boy remain on their backsides engrossed in their phones.

I merely enjoy the music, happy enough to be left to my own devices. But as the evening starts to draw to a close, unfortunately for me, James, who's tipsy, borderline drunk, if his glazed-over eyes and a sluggishness about the way he's walking is anything to go by, takes the opportunity to snag Jess's seat. I fold my arms across my chest, keeping my eyes on the band, or should I say, Damien.

"Hi," James says.

"I'm pretty sure I asked you to stay away from me," I state, refusing to make eye contact.

"I'm sorry."

"I don't want to hear it."

"Dani, please," James begs, but before I have a chance to respond, Damien's speaking voice commands the attention of the room.

"I'm going to dedicate this last song to the beautiful woman who helped me write it," he says, and I suddenly don't know where to put myself, my cheeks reddening. "It's called 'My Brothers in Arms'."

I smile, but secretly I'm calling Damien a cheeky bastard for playing a *co*-written song *without* my permission – the Army-related song we wrote almost a week ago. That being said, I'm a little intrigued to hear what it sounds like being performed by a band rather than quietly on my keyboard or amp-less guitar.

"I take it that's you," James sniggers before downing his alcoholic drink in one gulp and disappearing into the crowd.

I mentally shrug, happy to be left alone again as I let the music wash away the unease James has left behind. I keep my focus on Damien, his eyes burning into me with an undeniable intensity as my lyrics flow effortlessly out of his mouth. The vibrations of Damien's husky voice continue to be hypnotising, and when the chorus hits, I well and truly consider myself lost.

You are mine, my past echoes in my head. The sickening sound of *his* voice rings in my ears, and I instantly break eye contact with Damien. *You will always be mine.*

I give myself a shake, determined to ignore the invasion, but it's too late – *he's* there, and he's forcing my anxieties back to the surface. I suddenly feel a little claustrophobic and light-headed. I need air. I don't look at Damien as I head outside, but I can feel his eyes on me. Jess has probably got one beady eye on me too and will no doubt make a beeline to follow me unless she's already drunk beyond recollection or eying up some late-night company.

Once outside, I lean against the wall for support, taking long, deep breaths. I'm a little sweaty, and tears are pricking the backs of my eyes. No matter what I do or where I go, *he* is always there, and now more than ever, when the chance at a new life is staring me in the face, I hate him with every fibre of my being. Sometimes I think I must have been a mass murderer or something in a past life and living with the memory of *him* is the universe's idea of karma.

"Dani?" I hear James's voice and bite back the urge to scream.

"Just piss off, Jay," I snap, probably harsher than intended, but I'm in the middle of a mini anxiety meltdown over here.

"Are you okay?" he asks, ignoring my request and moving to stand beside me.

"Please," I almost beg. "Leave me alone."

"I can't," he says, and I force myself to look at him in disbelief. "I can't get you out of my head."

"Not my problem."

"Just hear me out," he pleads. "I have slept with countless women." I resist the urge to stick my fingers down my throat in dramatic disgust. "And I have never wanted to take the time to get to know any of them. The sooner they were out the better."

"I'm well aware of your womanising ways, Jay."

"But not you," he says, or should I say slurs. "You, I want to wine and dine. I want to get to know you and believe me, it's as much a shock to me as it is you." I highly doubt that. "I think…I have feelings for you."

I scoff. "No, you don't. You're only interested in me out of pity or because you can't have me. One or the other. I'm just another conquest to you."

"That's not true." He shakes his head.

"You know what," I say, thoroughly fed up, "it really doesn't matter. It's not gonna happen."

"Please," he begs. "All I want is a chance, Dani. One dinner or a movie, that's all I'm asking."

I refrain from bursting out laughing at the ridiculousness of that suggestion. "Jay, I've already made it clear I don't want to be with you, so please, back the hell off and stop pushing."

"But you want to be with him?" James snaps, his demeanour transforming from gentle to aggressive in the blink of an eye.

Oh, my God. How has James gone from playboy neighbour to jealous prick on a rampage in such a short space of time? I had always thought of James as level-headed, but I'm starting to see he's utterly delusional.

"I'm not doing this again," I insist, walking past him with the intention of going back inside, but James grabs my arm to stop me from leaving. "Let go of me."

I try to wriggle free from his grip, but he's holding on too tight. My heart rate skyrockets. He grips me tighter and throws me against the wall, pushing his body up against mine. I scream. James silences me with his lips.

"James, don't," I beg. "Please, don't."

I try to fend him off, but it's useless; he's too big and too strong. I'm pinned as James's lips invade my mouth and neck. His hand slides across my breast, and the flashbacks hit me like a bolt of lightning. I bite my lip to hide the pain.

His hands are trailing up and down my naked body.

I can't breathe.

I stifle a scream as the cold leather hits my back.

It hurts.

He begs me to scream as the lashes come thick and fast, tearing into my delicate flesh. The blood starts to trickle down my skin.

Make it stop. Please make it stop.

He throws me onto the bed face down. I don't move as he climbs on top of me. I close my eyes and try to picture myself in a happier place. I hear the sound of his zip lowering as I fight back the tears. The weight of his body on mine is crushing as he leans down and forces…

Help me.

Chapter Eight

I hear yelling and a loud crack. I fall to the floor in a heap as I vaguely, through blurry eyes, see James thrown down onto the concrete.

"Damien, don't," I think I hear Paul say, followed by a struggle. "Damien!"

I'm straining to catch my breath, my heart racing like a cheetah on speed. I start to cry. I wrap my arms around my body, longing to feel safe. All I can see is James, *him*, James, *him*, like a never-ending movie reel I can't switch off. I want to scream, but no sound leaves my mouth. The pain of *his* endless assaults stings as if I'm still there, locked in that basement and at the mercy of his compulsion.

I can hear Jess saying my name, but I can't seem to respond. My head is spinning, and black speckles are tarnishing my vision. I feel sick and dirty, blinded by *his* face and the sheer pleasure he took in breaking me.

"Walk away," I hear, and I think it's Paul again, followed by a moment's silence. "Don't push it, kid. Or I'll be the one helping him bury your body after he beats you to death."

"Dani?" I think that's Damien, and he's close. "Dani, look at me."

I try, but everything is too blurry. I feel the warmth of Damien's hands as he takes a hold of mine, holding them out in front of me. I feel him slide something cold between them, a phone maybe, before he slowly guides my right hand, holding the phone, outwards and then back into the centre again, all the while keeping my left hand dead centre in front of me. He repeats the process with my left hand, out then in, and then my right again, and so on.

"Focus on your hands," he tells me. "Just keep taking deep breaths and focus on moving your hands."

Damien lets go, and I find the strength to keep up the rhythmic hand motions. I don't know how long I partake in the exercise, a good while I suspect, but eventually, I feel my heart rate slowing. I continue until Damien's face comes into view, and my breathing is no longer ragged. It's then I realise I have an audience. Paul and Raif are standing behind Damien, and Jess is kneeling beside me. The concern on Jess's face is both strange and touching. I've never seen such worry sit upon her face before.

The nausea hits me, and I force myself to my feet, my jelly legs threatening to drag me back down. Running around the side of the building, I vomit violently and profusely all over the path. A touch grazes my neck, causing me to flinch.

"Hair," Damien merely says, and I relax a little, allowing him to gently pull my hair to safety from the nonstop vomit ejecting from my mouth.

Eventually, my nausea subsides, and I lean upright against the wall as Damien lets go of my hair. I wipe my mouth on the back of my sleeve, very unladylike. It's safe to say any dignity I had left, if any at all, has well and truly vanished, never to be seen again.

"Are you okay?" Damien asks, and I laugh nervously. "Stupid question."

Jess runs around the corner, swooping in for a hug, but I cut her off. "Please, don't touch me," I beg, leaving Jess standing in a puddle of confusion. "It won't help me." Hugging me now, and ergo, touching my torso, will only make the flashbacks resurface, and I'm not sure how much more I can take.

101

"Okay," she says, her eyes betraying her, revealing her disappointment. "Are you okay?"

"I'm fine."

"You are *not* fine," she argues. "You were attacked –"

"Please," I beg again. "Just –"

"Let me drive you both home," Damien offers, but I shake my head.

"I can't go home."

James lives across the hall, and there's every chance he will be waiting for me; to apologise or attempt round two of his unwanted advances. I can't handle either.

"Do you want me to call someone?" Jess asks. "A family member…"

"There's no one to call," I say, a little blunter than intended, suddenly realising just how little Jess knows about me despite our growing friendship.

"You can stay with me," Damien says.

I can count a thousand ways that's a bad idea, but I've already established I have nowhere else to go.

"I can stay too," Jess adds, and Damien nods his head in agreement.

"No," I tell Jess. "It's fine. *I'll* be fine."

"I left you alone once," Jess says. "I'm not doing it again, not after this."

"Please," I plead. "Damien will be there. There's no point both of us having our night ruined, and I really don't want a fuss."

Jess hesitates for a minute, appearing not at all impressed with her arms indignantly folded across her chest. "You'll take care of her?" she asks Damien.

"Of course," he answers. "Although I'm not sure you going

back to your flat is the best idea either, what with James…"

"Oh, I can handle James," Jess spits, the bitterness spilling from her mouth like a waterfall of pure bile. "Trust me."

"Damien has a point," I suddenly say, my sensible side waking up. "James is obviously unstable."

"That's putting it mildly," Damien mutters, emitting the same bitterness Jess did only moments ago.

"Maybe you *should* stay at Damien's," I add.

"I'll happily crash on the couch," Damien says.

"Or you can stay with me," Raif pipes up, popping his head around the corner. "My housemate is out of town for a few nights, and it'll save Damien kipping on the couch."

I can tell by the fierceness in Jess's eyes that she *wants* to have a confrontation with James, but when she opens her mouth to protest, I cut her off. "I'll sleep better." Reluctantly, she relents by nodding.

After driving me to his home, Damien potters about, leaving me to my thoughts, and I sit, contemplating the universe and its hatred towards me. The memory of James's hands, his mouth, his… An involuntary shiver runs down my spine. I force myself to take deep breaths as Damien appears, handing me a cup of steaming hot chocolate, and my lips curl into a small, grateful smile.

"Are you okay?" he asks, sitting beside me, the concern etched into his face a heart-warming sight.

"Honestly," I sigh. "No."

"I should have gotten there sooner," Damien says with obvious regret.

"It's not your job to protect me," I remind him.

Damien looks at me, a sadness in his eyes that tugs on my heartstrings. "I wanted to cave his head in right there and then.

If Paul hadn't stopped me…"

I sigh. I'm the last person to condone violence, but I can understand Damien's reaction. He cares about me, it's as plain as day, and if someone hurt somebody I cared about, I'd react the same way.

"He would've deserved it," I say. "But I'm glad you didn't. He'd only have gotten you done for assault."

"I'm sorry."

"You've got nothing to be sorry for," I tell him. "I'm grateful you got there when you did. Even more grateful you managed to drag me out of a panic attack. Where did you learn that hand thing?"

"In the Army," Damien explains. "Most guys won't admit it, but panic attacks are pretty common out there."

It's one thing to train for battle, but to be in the thick of it is something else entirely, and I can imagine it's overwhelming at times. I can understand it. It's the same as hearing horror stories about people being held captive. Unfortunately, I can say from first-hand experience it's not the same as living it. Nothing can prepare you for that.

"Well, thank you."

"Anytime," Damien says softly. "Have you thought about what you're gonna do?"

"About James?" I ask, and Damien nods. "I want to forget it ever happened."

Ha! That's hypocritical considering I can't seem to forget *him* and the shitstorm he put me through, constantly letting it hold me back even though I know I should be moving on. Maybe it's because of *him* what James has done pales in comparison. Oh, I'm pissed off, and I never want to see his face again, but I've been through worse.

"You should go to the police," Damien tells me.

Going to the police hadn't even crossed my mind, though it probably should have. I shake my head regardless. "It's he-said-she-said. He was drunk and stupid."

"Please don't defend what he did," Damien pleads, moving to stand. "You don't know how far he would have gone if —"

"Don't," I tell him, sitting up straighter. "Don't go there. There's no point dwelling on what-ifs. I'm fine."

"He assaulted you," Damien spits, lifting his hands behind his head, pacing the room. He's pissed off, and I don't blame him.

"I've got enough shit to deal with," I say. "I don't have the energy to add James to the list."

Damien instantly softens, ceasing pacing and dropping his hands to his waist. He stares at me for a minute before sighing heavily and retaking his seat on the couch.

"It's up to you, but I'll back you up whatever you decide." There's a moment's pause, yet it's not an uncomfortable silence.

"You know what," I say dramatically. "I don't get it."

"Get what?"

"The attraction," I admit. "I mean, look at me. I see my face in the mirror every single day, and nine times out of ten I still cringe."

"You're asking the wrong person," Damien answers.

"No, I'm not," I insist, my eyes meeting his. Damien is exactly the person I should be asking because he sees whatever James sees too.

"Well," he sighs. "For starters, that scar isn't half as bad as you think it is." Déjà vu much? "And you are beautiful whether you see it or not, but you seem to forget there's more to you than your face." Double déjà vu. "I've known you for two weeks

105

and in that ridiculously short space of time, I've laughed more than I probably ever have. I've seen passion, a passion for music even *I* can't compete with, plus *com*passion – you let Jess into your home even though you didn't want to. Strength…" That draws out a laugh. "That's your problem right there," he changes tact. "Negativity."

"It's just standard with me, I'm afraid."

"That's because you don't see what's right in front of you," he argues. "It doesn't take a genius to see you've been through some shit, that you've got a few issues, confidence being one of them. I'm guessing anxiety is in there too."

"A panic attack is a bit of a giveaway," I half joke.

"Just a little," he agrees. "But what you don't seem to get is the strength it takes to even attempt to put the past behind you. I saw some seriously screwed-up shit in the Army, things I can never un-see, and when I got back, I didn't cope with it all that well. I have demons and emotional scars that will never heal, and when I look at you, I see the same pain in your eyes."

Damien can see right through me. It's a little unnerving yet comforting. I'm finding myself longing to know more about him, to know what he's been through and how he managed to overcome it. I want nothing more than to do the same, but it took serious professional help to get me to the nervous wreck I am now, so in all honestly, I'm not sure I'll ever be able to let my demons go.

"I've been where you are," he says.

"Where's that?"

"Lost," he says softly, reading me like a book. "Caught up in the past and ignoring the future."

"And tell me again how that's a sign of strength?" I ask, confused. "Last time I checked, strength ain't running away and hiding."

"Strength is putting one foot in front of the other and taking one day at a time," he says. "Which, whether you believe it or not, you're doing just by getting out of bed every morning."

"If you say so." I'm not entirely convinced by Damien's definition of strength.

"I do," he states, playfully smug. "I'd say the only thing you need to realise is that you don't have to do everything on your own. You have people around you, and if you want my advice, lean on them. Don't shut yourself off. You'll be surprised how much letting people in helps."

"I'm not so good at the talking thing."

"Doesn't have to be talking." Damien shrugs. "Sometimes all you need is a shoulder to cry on and be willing to use it. And for God's sake, wake up and realise that you *are* beautiful."

I laugh, utterly amazed at Damien's ability to make me feel instantly comfortable, despite the uncomfortable situation we've just experienced. He's got a gift, that's for sure.

"Why is it…" I stare at Damien in awe. "That I feel like I've known you for years?"

My paranoid side stirs, but I swiftly slap it down. I can't spend the rest of my life thinking badly of people, especially not someone who has done nothing but be nice to me. Let's face it, if Damien was connected to *him*, I'd be dead in a ditch or at the very least, tied up in the middle of nowhere.

"I think I'd remember your face," Damien teases, and I gasp dramatically in fake offence. "Although can I ask you something?" I nod. "And I'm not looking for an explanation as to why. I just want to know so I don't overstep the mark." Another nod. "When Jess came towards you…"

I sigh. Damien is clearly always paying attention, even when

I don't realise it. "I don't like to be touched," I explain. "Or more specifically, I don't like people touching my torso. Hands, arms, I can handle, but it's a PTSD thing, or so my former therapist told me. It stirs up memories I'd rather forget." I omit the feeling pain part to avoid Damien's curiosity growing.

"I get that," he says, nodding. "I'm the same with sudden, loud noises. Takes me right back to Afghanistan."

"Afghanistan," I repeat. "You were posted overseas?"

"Yeah," he says. "It was rough. Almost died once after our truck was ambushed. At some point in the firefight, a bomb went off. I landed some shrapnel close to my spine, needed surgery to get it out, plus a nice bout of physio."

"You're lucky to be alive."

"Didn't feel that way at the time," he says sadly, and I'm touched by his honesty. "Survivor's guilt is a bitch."

I know how that goes. I feel the same about my family. To lose everyone you care about and survive despite the odds being dramatically stacked against you is a lot to contend with. The combination of grief and a gruelling recovery is overwhelming.

"Is that why you were medically discharged?" I ask, putting the pieces together.

"My back is weakened," he explains, nodding. "But the PTSD diagnosis didn't help things."

"PTSD is a bitch too," I state.

"You know what you need?" Damien suddenly says.

"What's that?"

"A drama-free day," he answers. "A day of nothing but fun."

"I'm pretty sure your idea of fun and mine are two very different things."

I shake off the invading déjà vu, quickly reminded the last time I used that sentence was in a conversation with James, and

James is the last person I want to think about right now. In fact, I want to burn his image to smithereens.

"Maybe a walk in someone else's shoes is exactly what you need," Damien argues. "Let me treat you the way you should be treated."

And with that, my heart sinks and the guilt soars. My time is running out. Damien has made his intentions clear, and his feelings are growing deeper, his reaction to James is proof of that, but I can't keep stringing him along. Yet I want to. I want to pretend we aren't going to end the way I know we will because the beautiful man sitting across from me is the only person in the world who has a sliver of understanding as to what being mentally screwed up feels like. For the first time, I don't feel completely alone, and there's a newly introduced shred of hope pleading with me to cling to Damien for as long as possible.

Against my better judgement, I find myself saying, "Okay."

"Okay?" Damien repeats, probably wondering if he'd misheard me.

"Okay."

The sparkle in Damien's eye tells me there's every chance I may live to regret my decision.

Chapter Nine

He's losing control. The towels are wrapped around my wrists, slowing the bleeding. I want to rip them off. I want the blood to flow until there's nothing left. He's not supposed to be back yet. I fight the urge to scream in frustration. This was my way out. My chance at freedom. My only chance at finally finding peace.

He's angry. He's screaming at me. There's a scalpel in his hand. He's waving it about like a rag. I flinch repeatedly, my eyes fixed firmly on the blade. I've never seen him like this. He's usually so calm. Even when he's hurting me, he's collected. Relaxed, even. He's never paced the room like a madman before.

I blink, and before I can register what's happening, the cold blade penetrates my skin. The towels fall to the floor as I bring my hands up to my face. The blood seeps through my fingers, blinding my vision. I drop to the floor in shock, and I can't stop the tears from falling.

"Fuck!" he yells.

I scream, bolting upright and soaking in sweat as yet another bastard nightmare plagues me. The bedroom door swings open, and it only makes me scream louder as I jump from the bed in shock.

"Woah," Damien says. "It's just me."

Shit. Damien switches on the light, and after blinking my eyes into adjusting, I quickly scan my surroundings. I'm not at home. Why am I not at home? It takes me a minute, but then last night's events come flooding back like a tsunami, overwhelming me and taking me under. I force myself to sit back on the bed, leaning my back against the headboard for support and pulling my knees up to my chest as a form of comfort. Damien tentatively sits down on the edge of the bed near my feet.

The tears start to fall. The sting of both assaults is lingering, and I cannot stop my fragile body from shaking. I notice Damien move slightly, and I don't stop him from taking my hand, squeezing it tight. It's all he can do comfort-wise, and he knows it.

"Nightmare?" he asks.

"Sorry."

"Don't worry about me," he insists. "As long as you're okay. That's all that matters."

What a wonderful night tonight is turning out to be. Or is it morning now? I don't know without looking at my phone, and it doesn't feel like a priority right now. First the James shit, and now I'm waking Damien up, screaming. I think Damien is being introduced to the broken mess that is me a little too quickly, and I'm suddenly wondering why he isn't running in the opposite direction. Probably because we're in *his* house.

"I'm sorry I woke you," I apologise again.

"You didn't. I've been awake for hours," he says softly. "You want to talk about it?" I shake my head. "In that case, I'm making breakfast, if you fancy some?"

I suddenly realise I haven't eaten since breakfast yesterday, and I'm freaking starving. I throw Damien a quick nod, and he disappears out of the room with a soft smile. I wallow for a little longer before climbing out of Damien's bed, still dressed in yesterday's clothes, and heading out into Damien's warehouse home. I'd been in such a state last night I didn't really take in my surroundings, but as I wander out of the walled-off section that houses Damien's bedroom and the spare bedroom next door, I can't quite believe the sheer size of the place.

It's exactly the size you'd expect from a first-floor warehouse flat with ridiculously high ceilings and almost floor-to-ceiling windows with noughts and crosses frames. Decoration-wise, it's nothing like what you'd expect from a warehouse with crisp white painted walls, dark natural wood flooring polished to perfection and rows of spotlights lining the ceiling. And apart from the separated bedrooms at the far end facing the front door, the rest of the room is open-plan.

I look at the room as if I've walked through the front door, and the living area is to the left, made up of a large, dark brown L-shaped sofa and matching cuddle chair pointed at the ultra-modern fire, a dark brown coffee table between them. Stereotypically, Damien has a humongous telly hanging above the fireplace complemented by surround sound, and I have no doubt the lights and heating are all electronically controlled too.

To the right of the front door is the kitchen. It's dark brown, obviously Damien's theme, with black marble worktops and one of those fancy islands playing home to four bar stools. Damien's red utensils and kitchenware are an interesting colour choice, but they complement the brown nicely, and the spotlight theme continues under the upper-level cupboards, shining down on the worktops. I'm suddenly wondering where the bathroom is, but I quickly spot a door leading off the kitchen and I'm assuming it's in there. I'll admit, I'm intrigued to see how big the bathroom is.

The best part of Damien's home, however, sits in the large space between the living area and the bedrooms, and it's his impressive music set-up. There's everything a band could need, from instruments to mixers, to amps and microphones; you name it, he's got it. The only thing Damien's lacking is a stage.

"This place is awesome," I say in amazement. "How do you even afford a place like this?"

"I'm good with money." Damien shrugs, cooking away in

the kitchen. "And it's probably not as much as you think. My landlord happens to be a close, personal friend."

"Paul?" It's the first name to pop into my head.

Damien chuckles. "Yeah, his dad was a property developer, but when his health started taking a downhill turn, he signed two properties over to Paul and sold the rest."

"Generous."

"Very."

"How old are you?" I suddenly ask, gaining me a laugh.

"Where did that come from?" I shrug. "Twenty-six. You?"

"Twenty-five."

I had figured Damien was close to my age, but it's a relief to have confirmation. I'm not sure how I'd feel if he was like ten years older, or worse, younger than me. Although, I guess age is just a number. Listen to me, talking like Damien and I are going to happen, when we've already established several thousand times over it's not. I mentally give myself yet another stern slap.

"Breakfast?" Damien changes the subject.

"It smells amazing," I admit, walking over and taking a seat at the end of the island. Damien plonks a plate full of food down in front of me, and although I'm starving, I still doubt I will eat it all. I have a small stomach.

"Full English breakfast is served, my lady," Damien says in a fake posh voice. "And how would you like your coffee?"

I chuckle. "Lots of milk, three sugars."

"Three?" Damien drops his posh voice in favour of an over-dramatic tone.

"Yes, three," I repeat. "Save me the health lecture, please."

I can imagine as a personal trainer, Damien is a healthy eater, but healthy eating isn't really my bag. Eating in general tends to slip my mind, if I'm honest. Damien wisely doesn't comment any further, kindly making my brew using a fancy coffee machine, I notice, and sliding it in my direction. He takes a seat next to me so we're sitting at a right angle from one another, and we tuck into our breakfast. Damien has opted for scrambled egg on toast, saving the fattening food for me, and I wonder if that's a hint of some kind. I consider making a snide comment, but I decide to shrug it off.

"This…tastes…" I say between bites. "Divine. Thank you."

"You're welcome." Damien beams.

"You can cook."

"I used to cook with my mum when I was a kid," Damien explains, and I realise this is the first time Damien's mentioned his family. Probably because I've never asked. "Then when I moved to England with my dad, he was always busy with the Army, so I used to help my step mum, Tina, cook too."

"Step mum?" I allow my curiosity to run free. "Where was your mum?"

"Back in Belfast," Damien answers. "My parents divorced when I was two. My mum was an alcoholic, a violent one, and when social services got involved, my dad took me in. I was eight."

"And how's your mum now?"

"She's clean and sober," he says with a hint of pride. "Ten years this summer."

"That's great," I offer. "You go back and see her?"

"Not as much as I should," he admits. "My relationship with my mum is a little estranged."

I nod in understanding, though I have no reason to. From what I've been told, I had a loving family. The violence came later, and it wasn't at the hands of my family.

"What about your dad?" I ask. "Where's he now?"

"Stationed down in Kent."

"Still in the Army, then."

"Oh, yeah," Damien chuckles. "Till the day he dies. What about you? Where are your family? I'm assuming not around here since you told Jess there was no one to call."

I know I've said it so many times now, but Damien's got the art of observation down to an absolute tee, and I would kill for his recall. Something tells me he's an elephant in disguise.

"Erm," I say with hesitation. "There's no one to call because there's no one left."

"I'm sorry," Damien says softly. "Can I ask what happened?"

"That depends." I shrug. "You got a violin?"

Damien throws me a not-funny kind of glance, but if I'm not crying, I'm making light of a situation to make me feel better. Why do you think I rely on my sarcastic sense of humour and banter to survive? I contemplate giving Damien the short answer, but he shared his Afghanistan story last night and let me stay in his home, so it's only fair I give him an inch. That, and if anyone is going to understand loss, it's Damien.

I guess this part of my story is called *bullshit memory loss*, and *the death of my family*.

"God's honest truth," I say. "I don't remember."

"You don't remember?"

"I only know what I was told," I continue. "My uncle John was a copper working on a drugs case. One night, a group of men came into our home and shot my entire family. I was just shy of turning twenty-three. I lost my parents, my aunt and uncle, my cousin Seth, and my pops that day. Not one of them survived."

115

"I'm so sorry." Damien's voice oozes sympathy.

"I got shot too," I add. "Fell from the first-floor balcony. I'm assuming I was trying to escape or something. I broke my arm and collarbone, suffered severe blood loss, and a lack of oxygen to my brain, but I hit my head so hard I had a subdermal hematoma, a brain bleed."

"Jesus, Dani," Damien says.

"I had surgery for that," I state. "I got lucky really. If there hadn't been the porch roof directly below me to break my fall, I'd probably be dead. I have side effects though, constant, nagging headaches, which probably ain't helped by the amount of caffeine I drink, and a slight weakness in my left arm. But the worst side effect, the biggie, is what the doctors called retrograde amnesia."

"Amnesia?"

"I woke up a few days after the shooting, drowsy as hell from the surgery, in a hospital bed without a single memory past the age of seven or eight, I reckon, which ain't much," I explain. "I don't know many people who can recall their childhood in detail even on the best of days. I can remember what my parents looked like, but nothing concrete beyond faces and a few experiences. I don't remember what my parents did for a living or anything other than the few happy memories I cling to."

I fight back the imminent tears. It's a strange kind of grief I feel when I think about my family. I grieve for my lost memories, yet I can't truly grieve for my family's deaths because I can't remember enough to truly feel the pain of losing them. I *understand* the pain of losing people, yet I've been robbed of my opportunity to accept it. I will never get closure until my memories return, and after three years, I'm not expecting that to happen.

"I know my dad played the guitar," I state. "And I *think* my mum was a writer."

"That's what the 'I think' at Dave's was all about," Damien says, nodding, and I smirk at his elephant likeness once more.

"But you have pictures? Stuff like that?"

"Nope," I say sadly. "After the twats gunned us all down, they burned down my house and everything in it. That guitar is the only thing I have left, only because my old car survived, and it was in the boot."

"That's awful," Damien says, but I merely shrug.

"It is what it is," I state, a little coldly, but the more I think about what happened, the angrier I get. My family didn't deserve to die the way they did, no one does. "The doctors were sure my memories would return over time, but apart from a few flashes here and there, they've continued to elude me so far. It doesn't help there's no one left to fill in the blanks in any real detail."

"No grandparents? Siblings?"

I shake my head. "My mum's parents died before I was born, and my dad's mum died of cancer when I was little, or so the police told me. Pops was the only grandparent I had left. Mum was an only child, as was Aunt Sharon, and my dad and uncle didn't have any other siblings." Damien smiles sympathetically. "I had hoped my uncle's police partner could shed some light, but they'd only been working together for a couple of months, and apparently, my uncle was a bit of a closed book."

"What about your aunt's family?"

"Her mum's dead," I state, probably too bluntly. "And her dad is serving a life sentence in prison. According to records, Aunt Sharon never visited, and he never rang, so even if I reached out, he wouldn't know anything." I sigh. "There's probably a great-uncle or somebody out there, but things were…complicated."

"I'm sorry," Damien says, and I offer him a nod of appreciation for his lack of further prying. *Why* things were complicated is not something I want to share.

"But I do know I was loved," I add. "And that brings me comfort."

"Is that a positive spin coming out of your mouth?" Damien asks cheekily.

"Don't get used to it," I urge him. "But that survivor's guilt you were talking about, I get that." Damien puts a hand over mine as a form of comfort. "The craziest part though? Falling from that balcony took a massive part of my life, yet it saved it too."

"If you hadn't fallen from the balcony…"

"I'd have burned in the fire."

Damien squeezes my hand a little tighter, and I'm grateful for the comfort and understanding. If only that was the end of my violin-inducing story and not the beginning of my shitstorm life. You know, when I really think about it, I wasn't a mass murderer in a past life, I was something much, much worse.

"Actually," I say, removing my hand from Damien's grip and attempting to lighten the mood a little, "what's even crazier is despite all the memories I lost, I never forgot how to play or read music."

"Really?" Damien asks, and I nod.

"It's safe to say that the brain works in mysterious ways scientists can only dream of understanding."

The brain is sadistic if you ask me, but I don't say that part out loud. Ironic too, I think – I never could grasp the concept of irony – because I would give anything to regain the memories I've lost, yet the only part of my life I wish I could forget, the nightmare-inducing, torturous flashback part, refuses to fade into my already established black hole. I always thought the brain was supposed to protect you from trauma, not the happy times, but I guess that bump to the head screwed me up more than I thought.

"Music has a way of sticking around," Damien says, moving to clear away my half-eaten plate, dragging me back into the conversation.

"Very true," I agree, before opting for a swift change of subject. "But anyway, dare I ask what exactly it is you have in mind for today?"

Damien smiles. "Time will tell."

"I need to pop home first," I remind him. "For a shower, some fresh clothes, and some ridiculously strong painkillers." My head is pounding.

"Yeah, course," he says, and that's when I notice he's already fully dressed in his usual denim jeans and a figure-hugging T-shirt. "I'll drive and help myself to that guitar of yours while I wait."

"Any excuse."

"It's a gorgeous guitar," he coos.

Damien chucks the dishes in the sink whilst I grab my phone and jacket. We head outside to Damien's car, and he drives the short journey to my flat. I'm silently holding back my dread, hoping and praying we can sneak in without waking the neighbour. I cannot handle an encounter with James. It will send me over the edge, and I'm pretty sure if Damien sees him again, he might just follow through and, as Damien put it, cave his head in.

We manage to get into my flat disturbance-free, and I quickly shower and change my clothes whilst Damien plays away in the living room. I give my hair a quick blow dry, allowing my natural loose curls to fall before heading out to find Damien.

"All set," I tell him, but he hesitates, sitting and clinging to my guitar.

"I've changed my mind," he says, deadpan. "I think I'd rather just stay here with his beauty all day."

"Sounds good to me." I shrug.

Damien shakes his head. He was obviously joking, but a day at home playing music is exactly how I like to spend my days, we all know this, and if recent dramas are anything to go by, staying home is the better and safer option.

"Sorry," he says, popping the guitar back on its stand. "I promised fun."

"Music *is* fun," I remind him. "And you know, I'll let you have as much quality time with my guitar as you want, not to mention free coffee, free food…"

"Nice try."

It was worth a shot. Actually, I think it might be worth another shot. My stomach is in knots. "Erm," I start. "I know I agreed to this, but…"

Damien moves to stand in front of me, his expression sympathetic. "If at any point, anything gets too much or you get overwhelmed, we can call it quits, but…"

"Don't think." I flash back to one of the many, many catchphrases my therapist drilled into my head. "Just do, right?"

Damien chuckles. "I was gonna go with don't give up and try, try and try again, but that works too." I sigh. "You're not alone, Dani," he points out. "I'm right here, and I'm not going anywhere."

Such a simple sentence, yet it holds so much promise. Problem is that promises are fragile and easily broken. In fact,

Damien shouldn't be promising me anything, and I sure as hell shouldn't be expecting him to. Yet I'm relenting, and Damien's flashing me that beautiful smile.

One day of fun can't hurt, right?

Chapter Ten

Paintballing. Bloody paintballing. That's Damien's idea of fun. I'm sceptical, mostly because I'm up against an ex-Army boy who's trained in stealth. What chance do I have? None. Absolutely none, and when the events draw to close, I can safely say my arse is well and truly kicked. Although I will admit, despite my reservations, it was fun. The set-up was great, very authentic, made up of various zones, including a London apocalypse zone with overturned buses and half-burnt outbuildings. I even managed to get a few hits in, of which I am extremely proud, and I laughed – a lot.

Paintballing, which hurts I might add, despite the kit we were geared up in, is followed by lunch at a café in Manchester, not Lloyd's, and I treat myself to a pain au chocolat afterwards. Paintballing may have been predictable for Damien, active and adventurous, but when Damien pulls up outside AMF bowling, I'm surprised. I hadn't pegged Damien for a bowling fan, and even though I have no idea if I've ever bowled before, I hold my own and manage to win one of the two games. Damien even pays for the VIP lane, which means we're separated by a partition, keeping us apart from other players. Distance from people is always a bonus in my eyes, and he gets brownie points for that.

We're now sitting on a bench in a park in Manchester, sipping takeaway coffees, and I'm marvelling in feeling relaxed. It's becoming a common occurrence in Damien's presence, and I'm clinging to this feeling for dear life. I don't want today to end.

Our quiet time is interrupted by the sound of my phone beeping, and I'm forced to pull it from my jacket pocket.

Where are you? x

"That Jess?" Damien asks, and I respond with a nod.

Out with Damien, why? x

Just wanted to make sure you were okay. I haven't been home yet, still at Raif's. You staying at Damien's again? x

Wasn't planning to x

I'll pop round later x

I suddenly realise I've been texting away whilst Damien's sitting in silence. Rude much? I slide my phone back into my jacket pocket.

"Sorry," I say. "She was just checking up on me."

"She's a good friend," Damien compliments.

"Yeah, she is," I admit. "She hasn't been home yet. She's still at Raif's."

"Raif probably won't let her leave," Damien jokes.

"Those two have definitely hit it off." Two peas in a pod, I reckon. "How'd you and Raif meet? I get Paul…"

"Raif's Paul's cousin," Damien explains.

"You three seem tight. Danny not so much."

"Danny's a kid. He's like nineteen. He only joined the band to get some gigging experience."

"Paul's older though, right?"

Damien nods. "Thirty-four." He chuckles. "I remember a couple of newbies on the unit. It was Paul's last tour, so he was the daddy, you know." I smile. "The arrogant twats thought Paul's age was a disadvantage and made the grave mistake of challenging him."

"What happened?"

"Let's just say they never did it again." I laugh. "Paul got a warning, mind, and a stern reminder we were supposed to be fighting the enemy, not each other, but Paul's not the type to back down. Man's my brother in every way bar blood, but even I wouldn't want to get on his bad side."

"Noted," I joke, before sighing. "Pretty sure my cousin and me were like that, as close as siblings, but we had a weird family set-up."

"How so?"

"We all lived together," I say. "As in parents, aunt, uncle…"

"In one house?" Damien asks, surprised.

I nod. "A *big* house, but yeah."

"You must have had a really close family."

"Yeah, I guess so," I agree, ignoring the sting in my heart.

"Do you remember the house?" Damien asks.

"Not really," I answer. "But I went back after the fire to see if being there would trigger any memories…"

"That can't have been easy."

"It wasn't."

Silence falls, the conversation turning a little too heavy, but as Damien takes my hand in his, a wave of comfort washes over me, and I manage a weak smile.

"You're amazing, you know that?" Damien says.

"How'd you work that one out?" I ask, taken aback.

"You got shot," Damien replies bluntly. "Suffered a brain bleed, lost *almost* all your memories, yet here you are, sipping on coffee and smiling that gorgeous smile."

I sigh. I guess I'm being dragged back to reality a little quicker than I had hoped, and the inevitable awkward conversation I've been avoiding is growing closer. I can either face it or I can cut and run.

"On that note," I say, rising to my feet. "I should probably be heading home."

Damien sighs. "I didn't mean to make things awkward."

"I know," I say calmly. "I'm just trying to avoid the conversation."

"So, there's a conversation to be had?"

I retake my seat, sighing. "We both know there is."

"Do I want to know how it's gonna go?"

"Probably not."

Damien sighs, tugging on my heartstrings. I don't want to hurt him, I really don't, but the reality is hand-holding is one thing, being intimate is another thing entirely.

"I don't care, Dani," Damien says, a hint of desperation in his voice. "About your past or your anxiety issues."

"Except my issues run a shitload deeper than anxiety," I state. "I can't be touched without my past flashing before my eyes for crying out loud, and…"

"And what?"

I force myself to meet his gaze. "It *hurts*."

"Hurts?"

"I can feel the pain," I tell him. "Like it's physically happening even though it ain't, which is why I can't be…" I choke on a breath. "Intimate. I can't physically be with someone."

"I don't care," he repeats, glazing over my pain admission as if I never spoke it.

"You say that now," I argue. "But further down the line, you'll need more. You'll *deserve* more. I can't give you what you need."

"How do you know if you don't try?" he asks, and reluctantly, I silently admit he has a point.

Damien moves a little closer and lifts his hand, his eyes asking for permission. For some undefined reason – curiosity or hope, perhaps – I find myself nodding. He gently runs a finger down my cheek, tucking my hair behind my ear, and my breath quickens. I lower my head, my body hardening in anticipation, but with a single finger under my chin, Damien raises my head back up again. Our eyes meet, and his sky-blues burn into mine, awakening a fire in the pit of my stomach. I should walk away, but as he leans in closer, the smell of his aftershave or deodorant or whatever intoxicating me, I find myself helpless and unable to move. Damien trails his finger down from my chin, onto my neck… I pull away, my breath caught in my throat.

"I can't do this," I say, my voice trembling as I rise to my feet. "I'm sorry."

"Dani," Damien pleads, standing up. He knows I'm going to run, and *I* know he wants to follow or stop me altogether.

"No," I snap. "Please, just don't."

I take off running, fully aware that if he wanted to, Damien could easily catch up to me, but I'm hoping he decides to listen and leave me be. I keep running until I reach the furthest edge of the park. Out of breath and feeling a little weak at the knees, I crumble onto the nearest bench and let the tears of self-pity and regret flow. I never should've let things with Damien get this far. Stupid, selfish, and everything in between.

I sit on the bench for a while, watching the many dog walkers and runners pass me by until I force myself to drag my arse to the nearest train station. The journey home is short and sweet, but as I walk up to the communal entrance, the nausea hits. I hadn't thought about the possibility of seeing James again, and now that I'm alone, any confidence I had has dissipated. Luckily, I manage to get inside without incident, and I could not be more grateful. I am considering finding a new place to live though, as the thought of bumping into James on a regular basis makes me cringe. I will never forgive him, so there's no chance of being polite or civil either.

Once inside, I sink into my couch, wrapping my arms around my body, and I let myself cry, hopelessly and endlessly. Unfortunately, there's a knock on my door. I contemplate ignoring it, but Jess's voice begs my attention, and I reluctantly let her in.

"What's wrong?" she asks as I throw myself back onto the couch, Jess moving to sit beside me. "Dani?"

"Things came to a head between Damien and me." I can't believe I'm saying this, but I need someone to talk to. There's a first time for everything, I suppose, and other than Damien, Jess is my only other option.

"What are you talking about?" Jess asks.

"I can't be with him, Jess," I sob.

"Why not?"

I sigh. "Because my past is more fucked up than you can imagine, and as much as I want to move on, I can't. I can't let it go. Every time I close my eyes…"

"But surely Damien understands that," Jess says softly. "He doesn't seem like the type to push."

"He's not," I agree. "But I don't know if I'll ever be able to…" I don't even want to say the words. "Be *intimate*."

"Oh, Dani." Jess suddenly looks as if she might cry. I can imagine she's got a few theories about what I've been through running through her head. None of them good.

"But I knew this," I say. "I knew it would come to this, and I let it because I was selfish and stupid and −"

"It'll be okay," Jess soothes, taking my hand in hers.

"How?" I ask, a little louder than intended.

"Because I'm here for you," she says. "In any way you need me, and eventually, it *will* be okay."

I manage a weak smile. "Thank you."

"That's what friends are for."

And that's exactly what Jess is – a friend. The *only* friend I have right now, for which I'm grateful. Damien was right about one thing, my therapist too if I think about it: I can't deal with my shit on my own. Don't get me wrong, I'm not planning on sharing the ins and outs of my colourful past just yet, but I need someone to cry on, someone with no strings, non-romantic strings at least, attached.

My issues are psychological, I know. My therapist always said I have the power to overcome my fears if I'm willing to try, and in so many ways, I already have. I moved to a new town, got two jobs, and I've socialised in the indoors-only sense. That's a far cry from the non-verbal mess I was two years ago, believe me, but when it comes to relationships, I don't know where to start. I want to believe Damien's touch would bring me nothing but comfort, and that he would still want me despite my fucked-up-ness. I even want to believe I can eventually learn to let go of the past and finally move on, but then I flashback to *him*, and my hopes and dreams shrivel into nothing.

But then the rollercoaster that is my mind crawls back up from the dip it just dived into, reminding me I have nothing else to lose, so why not take the leap? I could throw all caution to the wind. I could tell my cannon-armed guards to stand down and bare all, right here, right now. If I stand any chance of taking the risk and embarking on a relationship with Damien, he needs to know what lurks beneath, so why not now? That way, he will have the full picture and... I sigh. I can barely look myself in the mirror, so there's little chance Damien will be able to hide his disgust and seeing it on his face will destroy me. I'm going around and around in circles, and I'm starting to feel dizzy.

I don't know how long Jess and I sit in silence before she opts to make us both a brew, leaving me to curl up on the couch with my thoughts. It's short-lived though, and just as Jess is about to hand me my cup, the sound of my intercom buzzing pierces my eardrums. It doesn't take a genius to figure out who is on the other side.

"Leave it," I tell Jess. My phone rings, but I ignore that too.

"Dani," Jess says softly. "It's not fair to leave him hanging."

With a heavy sigh, I force myself to my feet. Without saying a word, I press the door release and open the front door. In seconds, Damien tentatively wanders in, looking, I don't know, relieved, maybe.

"I'll give you guys some privacy," Jess says, heading for the door. "Just knock if you need me."

I nod, sitting back down on the couch, and Jess leaves. Damien continues his tentative movements to sit on the opposite couch, twiddling his keys in his hands, and it only makes me feel guiltier. I didn't want this. I didn't want Damien to have to deal with my crap.

"I tried looking for you," he says. "I should've run straight after you."

"I told you not to," I remind him. "And I shouldn't have taken off in the first place." I should've handled the situation like a grown-up.

Damien sighs. "I didn't mean to push."

"You didn't push." I shrug. "Things were going the way they were going."

"I don't want things between us to change," he says, that hint of desperation making a second appearance. "I liked the way things were going."

"Except they can't keep going that way."

"Yes, they can," Damien insists. "I honestly don't give a

damn about your baggage, Dani. I don't want to give up on whatever it is between us. Not when I think we could be great together."

"You have to," I state, trying to hide my emotion. "I can't put my baggage on you. I *won't* put it on you."

"I can handle anything you throw at me."

"You shouldn't have to."

"I want to," he almost pleads, leaning forward to sit on the very edge of the couch. "I want you to let me in. Let me share your pain. Hell, I'd take it away if I could. You don't have to deal with everything alone."

"I know that," I say with a slightly raised voice. "But it doesn't change anything. I'm too fucked up."

"We're all fucked up one way or another," he says, raising his voice to mirror mine. "Your problem is you're closed off in your bubble of self-pity and negativity, pushing away anyone that cares to know you, too afraid to let anyone in because if you did, if you let the walls you've built around yourself break down, you wouldn't have an excuse to hide anymore. You might actually have to live your life, and to you, that's scarier than any of the shit that goes on in your head."

Seriously? He's not wrong, to an extent, but it does nothing but piss me off. I stand and move around the back of the couch, folding my arms across my chest.

"That's not fair," I snap. "You have no idea what I've been through, and you have no right to judge me. In case you ain't noticed, I *have* been trying, yet every time I do, bad shit happens. Look at all the shit that's happened with James, for God's sake. Bad shit follows me around, and I don't want to drag you down with me."

"Drag me down," he begs, clambering to his feet and moving

to stand facing me. "Please, drag me down to hell for all I care. If it means I get to be with you."

"Why me?" I suddenly ask. "You can have any girl you want, and you pick the most complicated lass around. Why?"

My paranoid side is reawakening. Damien's determination to be with me is unnerving. I'm being ridiculous, I know, but what if Damien's kind and caring personality is all an act? What if he's manipulating me into getting close to him in some sick and twisted game *he* wants to play? I mentally shake my head. No. I don't believe that. I can't, I *won't* believe that.

"Because there's something about you," Damien says softly. "I knew it from the first time I saw you, as cheesy as that sounds. I can't explain it and yeah, we've only known each other for two seconds, but it doesn't feel that way to me. All I know is when I'm with you, I don't want to be without you."

I shake my head, the tears starting to fall, but at least my paranoid side has dampened a little, my rational side taking over. If *he* was playing a game, it wouldn't involve letting me develop feelings for someone else; he's too possessive for that.

"I am begging you," he pleads. "Don't push me away."

"You don't know what you're asking," I say. "One look underneath, and that attraction you feel will turn to disgust."

"That could never happen."

"Damien, please –"

"Just let me in," he begs, cutting me off. "And if you're right, if I don't like what I see, I'll walk away, but I already know that nothing you could tell me will send me packing. Give me the chance to prove that." I stand, staring into his sincere sky-blues. "Please."

"You really want me to let you in?" I ask.

"Yes."

It's now or never. Before I have time to change my mind, I lift my top and pull it over my head, leaving me standing half-naked with just my bra for coverage. Damien's face drops to the floor as he takes in the sight of the whip lashes, the deep bite marks, and the knife wounds that cover my torso front to back. It's not a pretty sight, and my torso makes my scar on my face look like a freckle, but Damien wanted me to let him in, so here I am in all my disfigured glory.

Let's see how Damien likes this part of my never-ending, multilayered sob story, shall we?

Chapter Eleven

"This is why I don't like to be touched," I state, still standing half-naked in front of Damien. "Because every time I feel someone's hand on me, it reminds me the only touch I have ever felt is one of mind-numbing, searing pain. Every time I look in the mirror, I'm reminded of what I've been through, what *he* did to me. I don't have the luxury of moving on from the past because the bastard carved it into me. *Adrian* –" I quiver at the use of his name "– made sure I would never, *ever* forget."

"Dani," Damien says softly, but I shake my head, quickly putting my top back on and wiping the tears from my eyes. "What…"

"I was kidnapped, beaten –" I pause for breath, not wanting to say the next part out loud "– and raped." Damien's eyes widen. "Over and over, for months. *Adrian* ruined me, and there's no coming back from that."

Damien merely stands staring at me. For the first time since I met him, Mr Always-Has-an-Answer-for-Everything is speechless. He looks angry too, furious even, but I'm assuming it's at Adrian and not me.

"It's a long story," I offer.

"I got time," he says in a weird, biting-back-his-anger kind of tone, and I sigh deeply. I guess I've opened the floodgate, so there's not much point in trying to close it now. I drag myself back to the couch and sit. Hesitating, I take a few deep breaths before speaking again.

"After I got shot," I start, knowing I've already explained that part. "I needed surgery for the brain bleed. I was taken to the hospital, but as far as the media was concerned, I died along with my family. It was for my protection. The men my uncle was targeting were powerful drug dealers, the kind of guys willing to commit murder to protect their business, and if they knew I was alive…"

"They'd have finished what they started," Damien finishes my sentence, sitting down beside me.

"But…" I say, laughing nervously. "And this is gonna sound stark raving bonkers, but I swear to you, I ain't bullshitting. I actually lived this shit."

"Tell me," he urges.

"Turns out," I say, "one of the most respected doctors at Royal London Hospital was behind one of the most sophisticated drug syndicates in London. God, saying it out loud, it sounds so ridiculous."

Damien shakes his head in disagreement as I brush my hands over my face and sigh.

"Doctor Adrian Harris," I say spitefully. "He was my surgeon. He could have killed me whilst I was under, but he didn't. Funny, since I was supposed to die with my family, a murder *he* orchestrated, but unfortunately for me, he saw my face for the first time and liked what he saw." Or at least, that's what he told me. "On the day before I was due to be discharged, I was taken for an X-ray to make sure my broken bones had reset properly, only I never made it to X-ray."

"The police?"

"They fucked up," I state bluntly. "They were supposed to be posted outside my door, day and night, but the guy on duty wasn't there. I later found out he'd asked one of the nurses to keep an eye whilst he went to the toilet."

"That's convenient," Damien utters, suspicious.

"The perfect opportunity," I say through gritted teeth. "A

porter came with a wheelchair to take me to X-ray, which, of course, the nurse didn't think to question, and at some point, I felt a pinprick in my neck. The rest is a blur, and the next thing I know I'm waking up on a bed in a locked basement." I'll never forget the terror I felt at that moment. "And then I saw Adrian."

"The porter was working for Adrian."

I nod. "All part of his grand scheme."

"He knew what he was doing," Damien says as a hint of rage flashing across his eyes.

"He always knew what he was doing," I seethe. "I've never met anyone as smart or calculating as him. He had this charm about him too. Up until the kidnapping, he was my favourite doctor, and he always brought me a Costa coffee before he started his shift. He knew how much I hated the hospital coffee." I feel Damien tense beside me. "He made me like him."

"Were you attracted to him?" Damien asks, and I turn to look at him, a little taken aback by the relevance.

"No," I admit. "Adrian was a decent-looking bloke, and yes, I appreciated the coffee, but for me, he was a little *too* charming. A little like James, I guess, arrogant and overconfident. That, and I'd just woken up with amnesia, so funnily enough, attraction was the last thing on my mind."

"Sorry," Damien offers, but I shake my head.

"Don't be. It's a hard thing to grasp." I shrug. "People expect evil from certain types of people. It's difficult to think of a good-looking, successful doctor who's nice enough to bring a patient coffee as the bad guy, I know. If I hadn't lived it, I wouldn't believe it either."

"I believe you, Dani," Damien assures. "That's not what I meant —"

"I know," I cut him off. "But it doesn't stop me from knowing how hard it is to take in. I can stop…"

"Only if it's too much for you," he says softly. "Don't stop because of me."

I nod. I could stop, and a massive part of me wants to, but it's not fair to Damien. He needs to understand why I'm pushing him away, why I can't be what he wants or needs. He deserves to know the truth.

"The next twelve or so weeks were a living nightmare," I continue. "I honestly thought he was going to tie up loose ends and kill me, but no, he decided to hold me captive instead." I wipe a stray tear from my eye as every detail of the hell I endured plagues my every thought. "He beat me repeatedly, cut into me like a piece of meat, but he didn't do it to punish me because I'd done something wrong. It was a compulsion, almost like medication he needed to function. He took so much pleasure in carving his way through my body. He got off on hurting me, the way a junkie does on heroin."

"That's sick," Damien says, stating the obvious.

"I tried to get away," I insist. "I even made it out once, but I didn't get very far before Adrian dragged me back kicking and screaming."

"No one heard?" Damien asks.

"He lived in the middle of nowhere," I say. "Nearest neighbour was miles away. I screamed and screamed, until one day I just stopped, knowing I was wasting my breath."

It took me a while to figure out how far from civilisation I was being held given Adrian rarely let me out of his basement. I can't remember why he let me into the main house the night I made a run for it, but it was a mistake he never made twice. I even got an extra bolt added to my unbreakable door for my troubles, along with an added dose of violence, of course.

I should have known from the start Adrian would live in the middle of nowhere. I was living in a horror movie, and the bad guys always have plenty of distance between their property and the next. I might as well have run up the stairs instead of out the front door like a stereotypical soon-to-be-dead character. Wait, I may have already done that once. I'd love to know what the hell possessed me to try to escape from the *upstairs* balcony the day my family were murdered, but I've come to learn panic destroys any rational thinking, and maybe the horror movies have got it right after all.

"But…" I stifle a sob. "It wasn't the beatings that broke me." The tears fall again, and I don't hold them back. I can tell it's taking all of Damien's strength not to pull me into his arms and comfort me. He chooses to take my hand in his instead, squeezing it tight, and I let him, allowing his warmth to soothe me a little. "He raped me, Damien," I sob. "After every beating, he dragged me onto that bed, and he raped me." I feel Damien's body harden through the tension in his hand. "I thought it would never end," I say, wiping away the tears once more and letting go of Damien's hand to roll up a sleeve. "So, I tried to end it myself."

Damien stares down at the faded scar running across my wrist, there's a matching one on my other wrist too, and Damien looks about ready to join me in the tears department.

"The thumbholes," Damien says, nodding as he puts two and two together. I nod alongside him as a means of confirmation.

The scars on my wrists are pale and almost unnoticeable, but I'd rather not take the risk of a sleeve rolling up and someone seeing them. It would only gain me a look of sympathetic pity or questions I'd prefer not to answer.

"In a rare moment of stupidity, Adrian left his scalpel lying around one night," I explain. "I slit my wrists without hesitation. I had nothing to live for. My family were dead, and if there was anyone else who mattered, I couldn't remember them. So much time had passed, I figured any chance of being rescued had already gone, so I decided I would rather be dead than have his hands on me one more time."

I hit bottom. My life was ruined. My dignity, self-respect, and hope were non-existent. The night I slit my wrists, I smiled as the life drained out of me, finally feeling a semblance of peace. The thought of death brought me solace and freedom. Adrian wouldn't be able to hurt me anymore, and I'd be with my family. Or so I thought anyway. I should have known that even then the universe would never grant me an easy escape.

"Only Adrian came home earlier than expected," I continue, unable to hide my disappointment. "And in his rage at finding me bleeding to death, he took the scalpel and slashed my face. It was the one of only two times I saw him lose control, 'cause that's the most sickening part, he was *always* in control. He avoided causing damage anywhere but my torso because he always thought ten steps ahead. He used it in his defence, claiming it was a mutual BDSM relationship, blah, blah. He even went as far as to say I *asked* him to cut my face."

Damien shakes his head. "Sick bastard."

"He patched me up anyway," I sigh. "He had the skills, and I suppose I should be grateful. The scar on my face would look a shitload worse if my kidnapper *wasn't* a doctor."

I let out a nervous laugh, but it only makes Damien retake my hand. At this rate, he's squeezing so tight he's going to bruise my fingers, but I don't stop him.

"How did you escape?" Damien asks, hauling me back into

the conversation.

"My uncle's partner, Ray, never gave up," I answer. "Two days after my suicide attempt, Adrian's home was raided by the police. The fake porter he paid to kidnap me found himself up on a murder charge. Turns out he was in the drug business, the same syndicate my uncle was targeting, so Ray did a little probing, and after a little persuasion, the guy offered information for a lesser sentence. That's probably the only mistake Adrian ever made."

"The police got lucky," Damien says, but there's no hope or joy to his words, only anger and frustration. "At least tell me they threw away the key?"

"Not exactly," I say sadly, feeling a familiar pang of disappointment. "Adrian was charged with several offences, and it went to court. I testified by video link, but with the porter's testimony, Adrian was smart enough to know he was screwed. In the end, he wrangled himself a deal. He was tight with a lot of key players in the drug business, bigger fish and all that, and the police couldn't ignore valuable information. He sold everyone out to save his own skin."

Perks of being the boss, I guess. I can imagine he had a nice little black book of every dodgy bastard he did dealings with just in case his time ran out.

"No wonder people don't trust the justice system," Damien states, unable to shake his abhorrence. "How long did he get?"

"Twenty years," I answer. "He'll be a grand total of fifty-eight years old when he gets out, if he even serves the whole sentence."

My paranoid side is screaming again, calling me an idiot for even considering the idea of building a normal life, and the word *boyfriend* is so far beyond foreign to me, it's idiotic to believe it's something I can truly have. I can't allow someone to get close to me with the risk of Adrian returning. I don't even want to think of the things he would do to the people I care about. And that's the problem, isn't it? Having people I care about is having people to lose, and I can't lose anyone else.

You deserve the chance to live. My former therapist's words invade my ears again, and I force my paranoia back into its hole. It's bad enough Adrian controls ninety percent of every move I make, I will not beat myself up for wanting a little company, to not be completely alone. Ray will let me know the second Adrian is released, and I will go from there. Until then, I will keep doing what I'm doing. Besides, Damien will soon move on, once it finally sinks in our relationship can't go the way we both want it to, and Jess will eventually pursue her modelling career, so I'll soon be back to my bubble of solitude.

"You're lucky you survived," Damien says.

"I didn't *feel* lucky." I shrug. "I was a shell, broken, beaten, and terrified of Adrian finding another way to get to me. The police managed to keep my identity out of the papers though, so as far as the world was concerned, I was still dead. I was sectioned, but when that ended, I stayed voluntarily, terrified of the outside world. I lost count of how many therapy sessions I had."

"Did it help?"

"It did," I admit. "I mean, I can function now. I could barely blink without panicking back then. I was a wreck. Traumatised, they called it. I didn't utter a single word for the first three months, and even when I did, I never talked as much as I should have. I tend to struggle in that department."

"I hadn't noticed," Damien jokes, and even though it's a tad inappropriate for such a heavy conversation, I manage a weak laugh.

"I eventually discharged myself," I say. "Ray put me up for a while, but London held nothing but misery and pain, so with Ray's help I changed my name —"

"You changed your name?" Damien asks, raising an eyebrow.

"My surname," I clarify. "I kept the Daniella, just because I didn't think I'd be able to get used to another first name. It'd be one of those ditsy moments when someone's saying my new name over and over, and I don't even look at them because I don't register it as being me. I couldn't be bothered with that."

"Makes sense," Damien agrees.

"Ray found me a new flat too," I add. "And I landed in Stanton." I pause, sighing sadly. "Doesn't matter where I am though. I'll never be free."

"That's not true," Damien argues.

"Yes, it is," I insist. "Adrian may be behind bars, but he's still here." I point to my head. "Every night, torturing me in my sleep. I mean, look at my life. Yes, I'm functioning, but I've spent the best part of three years hiding."

"*Best part* being the operative words there," he points out.

"I'll always be hiding, one way or another," I utter. "And you should be running for the hills."

"Only if you run with me."

I rise to my feet in protest. "Have you even been listening?"

"Of course I have," he says. "You were a *victim*, Dani. None of what happened to you is your fault. And every tiny step you take towards moving on, whether it's as little as taking one step out the front door or hanging with Jess, it doesn't matter. Just the fact you're here, trying to make the most of your life whatever way you can, is an achievement to be proud of."

"Making friends, putting on a smile," I argue. "None of that should be a big deal."

"Dani, don't you realise that after everything you've been through, it's okay to *not* be okay?" he asks. "And those things *are* a big deal because they matter to you, not to me or Jess, or anyone, *you*, and that's all that matters. *You* matter, Dani. You matter to *me*."

"Just stop," I yell. "Stop trying to fix me."

"I'm not trying to fix you," he yells back. "I'm trying to show you that you're *not* broken." He sighs, lowering his voice. "I'm trying to tell you I don't want to give up on us because I care about you too much."

"And what if Adrian comes back?" I shout. "What if he hurts you to get to me? I couldn't live with myself."

"I can handle myself," Damien states.

I let out a nervous laugh. "You don't know Adrian."

"And you don't know he will come back." Damien argues. "At the very least you've got twenty years. Do you really want to waste your life on a what-if? You can't keep living in fear, Dani."

"Yes, I can!" I'm boiling over, my body starting to shake. "Living in fear is the only way I know how to live!"

"But it doesn't have to be," Damien says softly. "You deserve more than that. You deserve to be happy, and if you'll let me, I want to be the one who makes you happy."

Damien's reawakening that tiny shred of hope, but I force myself to slap it down. Moving on could take a lifetime, and I won't ask him to wait. I refuse to.

"Please," I beg. "Just go."

"That's it? You think I'm just gonna walk away?" he asks. "Dani, none of what you've told me changes the way I feel about you."

Damien takes a step closer but staying strong in my resolve, I take a step back, increasing the distance between us. Ignoring the heartbreaking disappointment written upon Damien's beautiful face, I turn my back to him.

"Dani…"

"Go!" I yell.

Chapter Twelve

His hands are in my hair, tugging gently as his tongue moves in perfect unison with my own. The feel of his soft lips against mine is tantalisingly good, and he tastes of cinnamon. I can feel the passion scorching inside me. I want him, right here, right now, more than I've ever wanted anyone.

My heart is racing, the blood is rushing to my head. I slide my fingers along every inch of his torso, his entire body responding to my touch. He skims his fingers down the back of my neck and it tickles. I giggle, pulling my mouth from his. I step back, overwhelmed with heat, and fan my face with my hand. I stare at him, taking in every detail of his hair-free chest and every feature on his delicate face. I lean in close, planting sweet kisses up and down his torso, my eyes not once leaving his. The intensity in those gorgeous sky-blues is enough to make me yearn for him. He's begging me with his eyes, and I like it. He kisses my mouth, hard and fast.

"Damien," I moan as his lips trail my neck.

He grips me tight, forcing my arms together, my entire body tensing in response. I look into his eyes. They're no longer blue, but brown. His hair is no longer a buzz cut, but longer and curlier. His soft, lightly tanned skin is now pale. I blink. I blink again in the hopes my eyes have deceived me.

"Adrian," I whisper, the fear engulfing me like a blanket of nails.

Damien is gone. His soft, sensual touch replaced with a penetrating grip that stings, and I let out an involuntary yelp. I start to shake. I desperately try to wriggle free, but his grip is too strong, and he's refusing to let go.

"If I can't have you," he whispers, his lips grazing my ear, "no one can."

I wake up on the couch in my usual pool of sweat, only for a change, it wasn't a memory, it was fiction, and it's not the Adrian part that's the cause of my tears, it's the vivid image of Damien kissing and caressing me.

It's been twelve days since Damien walked out of my flat without looking back and yet, I can't get him out of my head. I don't blame him for walking away – I did ask him to leave – but it doesn't stop it from hurting. Knowing I will never see Damien's beautiful smile or feel the warmth of his hand is a new form of mind-numbing torture, and the pain is unbearable.

I've slunk back into my old routine, home and work, home and work. Jess has popped round every day, and I stuck to our movie night without James, who has disappeared, just by the by. According to Jess, James packed up and took off without a word, and it was only when his uncle contacted Jess to see if she still planned on renting the place, Jess realised he wasn't coming back. Fine by me. At least I won't have to face bumping into him in the hallway. The downside is though, Jess's soon-to-be – within the next week, I believe – new flatmate just happens to be one of Damien's closest friends, and a constant reminder of what I've lost: Raif. Fabulous. Just bloody fabulous.

I drag my backside into the shower, dress, down a few painkillers to settle my nagging head and drag myself to work. The café is quiet as usual, but with the lack of sleep I'm getting, quiet is exactly what I need. I've barely slept for the past twelve days, catching maybe one or two hours a night if I'm lucky. I can't get my mind to settle. Between my usual Adrian crap and now Damien, I can't get a minute's peace. I'm exhausted and drained, and the last place I want to be is at work, but I got to pay the bills somehow.

I open the café to a note from Lloyd, telling me I'm flying solo again this morning, but Lloyd will be in for Pamela's shift later to do the cooking. Of course, good old, reliable Dani can manage on her own, and I'm realising sometimes being a hard worker doesn't pay off. Not that it matters. I doubt I'll be doing much cooking or anything, today or any day. In fact, given the café's dire state, I'm seriously thinking it might be time to start looking for a new job.

I set about cleaning, but as lunchtime hits, the sound of that godforsaken bell is like a hammer to my head. Serving customers feels like a chore, but that's my crappy mood talking. I almost groan when I see Paul wandering in for the first time, and I'm hoping he isn't here to make Damien's case because I have not got the energy to hear it.

"Hey, Dani," he says, approaching the counter.

"Hiya," I reply. I would say brightly, but I don't think I quite pull it off. "What can I get you?"

"A favour," he answers, and I resist the urge to roll my eyes. I've met Paul once. I'm not sure I qualify as enough of an acquaintance to be asked for a favour, but he's asking, so I guess I'm listening.

"Depends on what it is."

"My daughter Kayleigh has this assignment at school." I told you he gave off a dad vibe. "She needs to write and produce a song. I'd help but I'm no good with tech, and Damien mentioned you have an Apple Mac Pro with some fancy software at home."

Audio interface, a DAW – digital audio workstation – microphones, headphones, studio monitors… I'll stop there. I think Paul's referring to the less complicated software built into my computer that doesn't require the home studio materials anyway.

"Yeah, I do."

"I was hoping you'd help me out," he utters. "Help Kayleigh out anyway. She's a keyboard player and Damien…"

"Mentioned I'm a keyboard player?" I finish his sentence,

146

gaining me a smirk.

"Kayleigh's a great player," he praises. "But she's new to tech, and she could use a tutorial."

"Why don't you ask Damien?" The obvious choice. "He's got the same system as I have, and he's way better with tech than I am."

Paul looks at me, confused, then his expression changes, telling me something, I'm not sure what, has just sunk in. "You don't know?"

"Don't know what?"

"Damien's in Kent," Paul explains. "His dad had a heart attack. Damien left a week ago Monday."

The day after Damien walked out of my flat. Holy shit. I've been assuming Damien has broken off contact because he's given up, despite what he said about my bullshit not changing anything, but now... I give myself a sharp mental slap, so hard my metaphorical cheek is stinging. Damien walking away is the right thing for everyone, so that tiny shred of hope can fuck right off.

"Is his dad okay?" I ask.

"Yeah, he's on the mend," Paul says. "Damien's staying down there until he's fulfilled his sonly duties. I take it he hasn't been in touch?"

I sigh. "Damien and me ain't on the best terms at the minute."

"He may have mentioned it." Paul nods.

He did what? No wait, I'm not going to jump to conclusions. This is Damien we're talking about. He's not about to go and parade my deepest darkest secrets, not even to his closest friends, surely. He's more respectful than that. Right?

"Don't panic," Paul chuckles. "He didn't go into detail." I

rapidly realise I've been holding my breath, and I let it out as a massive sigh of relief. "He just told me you put a hold on things, but we both know that's the last thing he wants."

"Yeah, well," I say. "The last thing I want is to hurt him." I don't have to justify myself to Paul, yet I am.

"Then don't."

"If only things were that simple."

"Look," Paul says, a dad-like seriousness to his tone. "Damien's a great guy. They don't get much better than him."

I know that. I don't believe in perfect, but Damien's as close to perfect as anyone can get, and he's been nothing but respectful and understanding and… Oh, for God's sake. I can't keep going around in circles. I've made my decision, and I need to shut up and deal with it. I am sick of being a broken record.

"I don't need you to tell me that."

"You should text him," Paul suggests, unoffended.

"I'm probably the last person he wants to hear from."

"You can't actually believe that?" Paul scoffs. "Damien worships the bloody ground you walk on. It's nauseating."

I sigh, and I think, from the understanding look in his eye, Paul is sensing my reluctance to discuss Damien further.

"All I'm saying is," he concludes, I hope, "I'd think long and hard before you let him walk away 'cause guys like Damien don't come around too often."

Paul is not helping my desire to stop being a broken record at all. I'm starting to think I'll never be able to get away from all things Damien. My mind casts back to my soon-to-be new neighbour; nope, never going to get away.

"But anyway," Paul says. "Kayleigh."

I don't owe Paul anything, yet I'm starting to realise maybe underneath all the tattered brokenness, I'm not a bad person.

"When and where?"

"What time do you finish?"

"What makes you think I don't have plans tonight?"

"'Cause I've heard you're a hermit," he says, and I can hear Jess's voice in his words.

"My God, Jess is making friends fast," I say dramatically.

"She's our first groupie," Paul jokes.

"She's got a big mouth too."

"Half-six work for you?"

"Works for me."

"Give us your phone," he says, and I oblige, pulling it from under the counter, unlocking it and handing it over.

Paul types in his number and his phone rings, telling me he now has my number too. Even that takes me right back to Damien, and I internally shake my head. Paul hands me back my phone.

"I'll text you my address," he states, typing away, my phone soon beeping in acknowledgement.

My heart rate spikes a little. I'm acutely aware, bar one brief meeting, I don't know Paul from Adam.

"Actually," I say. "Could we do this at my place?"

The thought of going to Paul's alone is a little anxiety-inducing, and at the very least, I can manipulate Jess into staying next door on high alert, just in case Paul turns out to be a psychopath in disguise.

"Erm, yeah," Paul agrees. "In that case, text me *your* address." I oblige. "I appreciate this, Dani. Kayleigh needs to nail music to get into the college she's looking at for September."

"She's young." I shrug. "She'll pick it up in no time. It's not hard once you know how."

"Is that a dig against my age?" Paul asks, chuckling.

"Well, you know what they say," I tease. "Can't teach an old dog new tricks."

"Now, there's something Damien *didn't* mention," Paul mocks. "That you're a cheeky bitch."

"I try."

Paul smirks and heads for the door, but like most people in my life, he's as just as dramatic, and he stops short of leaving, turning back to look at me.

"Oh," he says. "And if you do decide to come to your senses about Damien, text him. You're the *only* person he wants to hear from right now."

I shake my head as Paul leaves, throwing him a wave as he passes the window, and as soon as he's out of sight, I bury my face in my hands. I have never felt so confused. That's a lie, waking up and having no memories was pretty confusing, but in a matter of mere seconds, I'm right back to square one. I have no idea what I want or what to do.

I miss him. If I'm brutally honest, I really, really miss him. I miss his smile and his laugh, and his amazing sense of humour. I miss the way he always knows the exact right thing to say at the exact right time. I miss listening to the sound of his sexy, husky singing voice and watching the way his fingers elegantly tame a guitar. I miss the feel of his hand entwined with mine. Damien's absence has left a hole, and I'm quickly realising nothing I say or do is going to fill that void.

I scroll through my contacts until I reach Damien's name. Despite everything, Damien has been there for me, and I need him to know I'm still here if he needs me, or if he needs someone to lean on or talk to. It's the least I can do after everything Damien's done for me. I may have kyboshed our relationship, but that doesn't mean I've switched my feelings off. I still care about him.

Hi. I know things are awkward between us right now, but I've just heard about your dad. I hope he's okay, and just know I'm here for you if you need anything x

I hover my finger over the send button, not entirely convinced I'm making the right decision, but hoping and praying Paul is right. I take a deep breath, and before I have another second to talk myself out of it, I hit send. All I need to do now is wait for a reply. If I get one.

The rest of my day drags by in a depressing haze of quiet, and after heading home and downing a few coffees, I find myself opening my door to Paul.

"Brew?" I ask as he takes a seat on the couch against the back wall.

"Coffee, milk, one sugar," he answers, his eyes surveying my living space, I notice.

"Where's Kayleigh?" I ask, tending to the drinks in the kitchen.

"She's running late," he says. "She has a keyboard lesson until six."

I nod. Great. More awkward alone time with Paul. I wonder how long it will take before D –

"Did you text him?" Barely even a minute, apparently.

"Does every conversation we have need to revolve around Damien?"

"He *is* our common denominator."

"Erm, music," I say in a "duh" tone.

"Talking about Damien is much more fun."

I roll my eyes, but Paul's eagerly awaiting an answer to his original question. "Yes, I texted him."

"Wise choice." Paul's smugness is a little irritating, but I'm starting to think it's just standard with him.

"He ain't replied," I state, attempting to dampen said smugness.

"He will."

"Overconfident much?"

Paul laughs, but thankfully, after handing him his brew and sitting down on the opposite couch, talk turns to Kayleigh. Turns out, Paul was a mere eighteen when his now fifteen-year-old daughter was born, but he didn't know she existed until roughly two and a half years ago. Kayleigh was her mum's best-kept secret, and the only reason the truth surfaced was because Kayleigh's mum was on her deathbed.

Poor kid. That couldn't have been easy, but Paul didn't hesitate in stepping up to the plate, resigning from the Army and taking Kayleigh in. They've slowly been building a relationship ever since, and he obviously adores the bones off her. Paul's voice is full of pride every time he says his daughter's name, and although the Army was his dream and he'll be forever grateful to get to live it, he regrets not knowing about his daughter sooner.

Okay, so I'll admit, Paul is growing on me a little. I'm not wrong when I call him overconfident, but he's a down-to-earth, laid-back kind of guy, and he says it like it is, which is the best way to be. I can see why Damien and he hit it off in the Army; Damien's honest and direct to a fault too, something I could probably take a lesson or two from. Although, when Paul tells me his day job is as an electrician, I must admit I didn't see that coming.

"What did you think I did?" he asks.

"I don't know," I admit. "But it wasn't an electrician."

Paul's phone rings, signalling Kayleigh's arrival, and I buzz her entry. A few seconds later, in waltzes a pretty lass with long, very straight, brown hair. She's slim and tall, at least five foot nine, I reckon, dressed in her school uniform paired off with a khaki jacket. It's just Damien, Damien, Damien everywhere I turn.

"Sorry I'm late," she says. "The bloody bus missed."

"Don't worry about it, kid," Paul says. "This is Dani."

I offer Kayleigh a slight wave, popping my now empty cup on the coffee table. "Hiya."

Kayleigh and I waste no time setting to work. Kayleigh's a fast learner as I expected, and she picks up the computer's workings in no time. Paul surprises me by ordering a pizza, and I can't resist looking at the time on my phone; it's almost half-eight. The almost hour and a half since Kayleigh wandered in has flown by, not that I mind. It's not like I've got anything else to do.

"So, can you plug a mic right in?" Kayleigh asks me. "For recording vocals?"

"Yeah," I answer. "Although it'd have to be one with a USB if you want it direct to the computer."

"That's awesome." She beams.

"Do you write?"

"I try," she admits. "But I take after my dad in the lyrical department."

"Dani's good with lyrics," Paul pipes up from the couch he's made himself at home on.

"Let me guess," I joke, "Damien said so."

"He played your song at the charity gig, remember?" he says, and I'll admit, I'd forgotten about that, blocking the entire night out completely for good reason.

"Oh," Kayleigh says slowly and dramatically. A light bulb

153

moment, I'm assuming. "You're the girl Damien's got a thing for."

I eye Kayleigh with curiosity and surprise. "Either you're scarily close to your dad or…"

"I tend to overhear things," Kayleigh admits. "Dad's not so good at keeping his voice down."

"Now *that* I don't doubt," I tease. Paul throws something at me, and I look down at the floor, grateful I managed to duck my head out of the way, avoiding any actual contact, to find my television remote lying beside me. "I got enough face damage, thank you. I don't need a black eye added to the mix."

I'd love to know what compelled me to drag my face into the conversation, and as Kayleigh smiles weakly with a sympathetic glint in her eyes, I instantly regret my choice of words. There's a slight tension seeping into the room, and even Paul's cockiness has exited the building, replaced with an equally sympathetic glance in my direction.

"Anyway," I say slowly, turning my focus back to Kayleigh. "You can hold on to my computer for a while if you want?"

"Seriously?" Kayleigh can't hide her sudden burst of giddiness.

I'm as surprised as she is by my offer, but I like Kayleigh. She's talented and passionate about music, and something tells me she'll treat my computer with respect. So far, Paul's not giving me any psycho vibes either, and he is Damien's mate, which has to count for something. Besides, if worst came to worst, Jess has obviously gotten pally with Paul and Raif, so I could always send her to hunt Paul and ergo, Kayleigh, down if needs be.

"Yeah," I assure her. "It's not exactly a cheap computer, and I doubt your dad over there plans on forking out." I hide my face with my hands, pretending to protect myself from another flying object, and while Kayleigh laughs, Paul merely sits looking unimpressed.

"My assignment's due in about a month," Kayleigh says.

"I can survive for a month." I shrug. "And if you need any more help with it, just give me a shout."

"That's awesome, thanks," Kayleigh says brightly. "Although…" I have a feeling I know what's coming next. "I could use a hand with some lyrics." Kayleigh doesn't disappoint my suspicions. "Not to steal. I'm allowed to co-write as long as I cite you as a source."

"You don't need to cite me," I chuckle. "I'm not one for taking credit."

"Is that a yes?" Kayleigh asks, her hope evident.

"You don't ask for much, do you?" I joke.

"Like father like daughter," Paul pipes up.

"I have one condition," I say, addressing them both.

"Name it," Kayleigh responds.

"If either one of you mentions Damien," I say sternly, "I'm kicking you out."

"Deal," Kayleigh doesn't hesitate.

"Nicely played," Paul compliments. "You're smarter than you look."

"I'll try to not be offended by that," I state, unimpressed.

I hear my phone beep from my jacket pocket, and my stomach does a little backflip. Paul's back to smirking smugly a little too quickly for my liking as he watches me move into the kitchen to retrieve my phone from my jacket pocket. I glance at the screen and smile.

Damien.

Chapter Thirteen

I decide to wait until Paul and Kayleigh leave to properly read Damien's text. Kayleigh and I play until almost ten, time flying, and after an exchange of numbers and a promise to keep my line open should Kayleigh require my assistance, I'm on my couch, staring at my phone.

Thanks for texting. I needed something to put a smile on my face – So smooth, even in a crisis. – *I'm sorry I haven't texted. Things have been crazy down here, and I figured you might want some space x*

I contemplate texting Damien back, but there's every chance he's sleeping, and sleep is something he probably needs right now. I take myself off to bed instead, and after two nightmares plaguing my sleep, it's now six in the morning, and I'm back on the couch, nursing a cup of coffee.

My phone is in my hand, ready to reply. Damien will be awake, most likely out on a run as I'm pretty sure a lie-in is an alien concept to him, no matter how stressed he is.

You don't need to explain. I'm not totally conceited, and I do know the world doesn't revolve around me :) You've got bigger things to think about. Glad to be of help though – *the smile part. How is your dad? x*

I resign myself to getting showered and dressed, knowing it will most likely take Damien a while to reply, and as I chuck on my embroidered Dave's Music Shop T-shirt, tying my hair back in a ponytail for a change, I hear the beep of my phone coming from the living room.

He's okay. Being a stubborn bastard and insisting he needs to go back to work. How are you? x

Stubborn, huh? I guess I know where Damien gets it from.

I'm okay. How are you doing? x

156

I head into the kitchen to make my third cup of the day, and it takes as long as the kettle does to boil for Damien to reply.

Stressed. My dad drives me crazy at the best of times. I just wish we could talk. I'm really happy you texted x

I sigh. I was hoping to avoid the awkward conversation about how we left things, hoping to keep our exchanges light, but I guess it's inevitable, and I've opened the door by messaging him.

You've got enough on your plate. How about we talk about – Us? It? What happened? – *things when you get back. I wasn't sure you'd want me to text x*

The good thing about text is not having to look Damien in the eye, and somehow, it's easier to be a little more honest.

I meant what I said. Nothing's changed for me x

Let's just talk about it when you get back x

I need time to think, not that it gets me anywhere, and I guess now is as good a time as any since Damien isn't here to cloud my judgement. A knock on my door distracts me, and I open it to find Jess smiling brightly.

"Rather early for a social call," I tease.

"I wanted to catch you before work," Jess says, wandering inside and helping herself to a cup from the cupboard. She's gotten good at making herself at home.

"Do I want to know why?"

"It's Kayleigh's birthday today," Jess enlightens me.

"Huh," I retort. "She never mentioned anything. I met her yesterday."

"Paul is throwing her a surprise party, and he's left the planning to me," Jess says, smiling. Planning a party is right up Jess's street. "He mentioned it last week, but being a bloke, he hadn't gotten around to planning anything. I offered to sort it for him."

"Of course you did." I smirk. "But well done for pulling off whatever you've got planned in a week."

"It wasn't hard." She shrugs. "Once I got a venue, which is the same one the charity gig was at, it was just a case of buying some decorations, sorting the food and entertainment, making sure Paul gave me names and addresses for invites."

"Sounds like a lot to me," I comment. "A little too much to do out of the goodness of your heart."

Jess rolls her eyes. "Are you suggesting what I think you're suggesting?" I nod. "I am *not* into Paul," she argues, and even though I'm not overly convinced, I let it go. "It's tonight at seven, and you're invited."

"Thanks for giving me time to get a gift," I point out, although I do work in a music shop, and Kayleigh *is* a keyboard player, so I'm sure I can figure something out.

"Sorry." Jess is in a repetitive shrugging mood today. "I didn't want to give you a chance to think about it too much and back out."

I'd protest, but I can't argue with her logic. I've taken the hermit label to the extreme since Damien... Speaking of, my phone is beeping.

"How are things between you and Damien?" Jess asks, making assumptions as to who is on the other side of my text; correct assumptions, but still...

"Did you know about his dad?" Jess has been spending quite a bit of time with Raif and Paul since the charity gig, so it's not a stretch to think one of them might have mentioned it to her.

"I did," she admits.

"And you didn't tell me because?"

"I was hoping you'd reach out without being guilted into it," Jess states. "Or that Damien would reach out first."

"So, for once," I say, unable to hide my disbelief, "you were keeping your nose *out* of something?"

"First and *last* time!" Jess exclaims. "You two need your heads banged together."

"Damien's not the problem."

"I already know that," she scoffs. "I was trying to be polite."

"Since when are you polite?"

Jess sticks her tongue out at me before nodding towards my phone, reminding me I've yet to read Damien's message. I guess I'm making assumptions too, but the only other person who ever texts me is standing in front of me, so it's not an assumption at all really.

I miss you x

I don't know whether to cry or burst with happiness. I stare at my phone, contemplating my reply. *Honesty*, I silently tell myself. Honesty is the best policy.

I miss you too x

Jess and I natter away for a little while before I drag my backside to work. My shift passes by uneventful, but steady enough to keep my mind from wandering to Damien, and it's not long before I'm showering and getting redressed for Kayleigh's birthday party. I opt for the casual black blazer I wore to the charity gig, and my boots rather than my trainers, but you should know by now I don't do dressing up.

It's almost seven when I pull up outside the hall. Carrying a birthday card with a fifty-pound Dave Music's Shop voucher inside – the best I could do at such short notice – I take a deep breath and head inside, all the while repeating *It's fine, I'm fine, everything's fine* over and over in my head.

I'm not entirely sure why I'm here, but I think maybe I'm trying to prove to myself I can take baby steps without Damien, literally and metaphorically, holding my hand. Here's hoping I don't regret the inch of confidence I'm feeling, and I manage to get through tonight unscathed. Although, if James magically appears, I'm out of here.

I let the main door close behind me, and the first thing I notice is the massive "16" balloon at the far end. It's almost floor to ceiling in height and bright pink – eye-catching and dramatic to say the least.

I take a minute to marvel at the difference between the charity gig's decoration and the effort Jess has gone to. The ceiling is lined with "16" bunting, and the walls are covered in poster-sized photographs of Kayleigh, covering the span of her entire sixteen years by the looks of things. Lining the perimeter, there are tables nestled underneath crisp white tablecloths, and each chair has a small "16" balloon attached. The food is already set up on a long table near the kitchen hatch, which I'm assuming will be serving alcohol, albeit not for the birthday girl unless Paul is feeling generous, and a DJ is setting up on stage in front of the massive "Happy Birthday Kayleigh" banner hanging behind him. It's then I spot the photo booth next to the stage, near the double doors, with various accessories, such as hand-held moustaches, sunglasses, and other bits that go along with a standard photo booth. Jess has gone all out.

I glance at my phone to look at the time, and it's three minutes to seven. I'm assuming Kayleigh will be arriving at seven or just after to make sure all the guests have arrived first. Yet, as I scan the room, there's not an overly huge number of people here, and a lack of school-aged kids, which is surprising. There are two full tables of six occupied, made up of Kayleigh's family, I reckon – most of them are older looking – and there's roughly fifteen more people dotted about. I don't know, maybe it's the size of the hall making the numbers seem small. I guess I just figured the floor would be filled with schoolkids.

I wander towards Jess, who's talking to the DJ, and she smiles upon seeing me. "Hey Dani," she says, abandoning the DJ.

"Hey," I reply. "The place looks good."

"Thanks," Jess says proudly. "Paul's gonna text me when he's five minutes out with Kayleigh."

Jess and I are soon joined by an excitable Raif, whom I'd yet to notice in his trademark curved edge shirt, a black one today, and his skinnier than skinny black jeans. "Hey Dani," he says warmly. "How you doing, honey?"

"I'm good, thanks," I reply. "You?"

"Fabulous," he replies, beaming. "Looking forward to becoming your new neighbour." I smile through gritted teeth. "And if you're feeling charitable, I wouldn't say no to a little help moving in."

"Surely, you can't have that much crap?"

"Have you met me?"

Our conversation is cut short by Jess rapidly gathering the guests on the floor, repeatedly shushing us and switching off the lights. We wait in silence until the door opens, and Paul leads a blindfolded Kayleigh inside. Jess switches on the lights as Paul removes the blindfold, and we all shout a merry "Surprise!" in unison.

"Oh, my…" Yep, Kayleigh's surprised, and from the blush spreading across her cheeks, I'd say a little embarrassed.

"Happy birthday, kid," Paul says, wrapping an arm around her shoulder and giving her a peck on the forehead.

Kayleigh mingles amongst the crowd – there's an awful lot of hugging – as the DJ starts the party. I take a seat at a vacant table, and Raif decides to join me, popping two drinks down on the table.

"Get that down you," he says, but as I pick it up and give it a sniff, I quickly put it back down again.

"I don't drink."

"Come again?" Raif states dramatically.

"I don't drink," I repeat, though I know he heard me the first time.

"And why the hell not?"

"I prefer to keep my wits about me."

With alcohol, inhibitions, common sense and dignity exit the building, and since I have perhaps only a scrap of dignity remaining, I'd like to hold on to it. That, and I hate the idea of being vulnerable, particularly in public, open to manipulation or anything else untoward, which, you know, has a habit of happening regardless. So, no thank you, no alcohol for me.

I'm distracted by the sound of my phone beeping.

How's the party? x

Jess is in her element. Kayleigh and Paul are mingling. Raif is trying to get me to drink booze. I guess I'll label it interesting x

Less than fifteen minutes in, the dance floor is filled with tip-tapping feet, including Raif, and I'm left to my own devices. I'm quite happy people-watching, but I'm still finding it hard to comprehend the majority of the guests are not Kayleigh's age. There's one or two, but if the guest list is anything to go by, Kayleigh clearly doesn't share her dad's sociable genes.

My people-watching is soon interrupted by an announcement from the DJ that karaoke is now open, and I can't help but chuckle. I would pin it on Jess, but since Paul is the first to walk on stage, I'm wondering if Paul's harbouring a guilty pleasure.

Paul opts to sing Stevie Wonder's "Isn't She Lovely",

162

dedicating it to his daughter, and I'm surprised to find Paul has a decent voice. It's more of a Frank Sinatra sound than the pop-rock sound his band spurts, but yeah, he's got a powerful set of pipes.

Paul's song ends with a round of applause, including a clap from me, and it seems a love of karaoke runs in the family. The DJ is being bombarded with names and requests, but I'm quickly distracted by my phone again.

I'm gutted I'm missing it. You don't drink?? x

I'm pretty sure you'll come up in conversation more times than I can count, so you're never far away. Why is not drinking such a surprise to everyone? x

I put my phone in my pocket and mosey on over to the buffet table. I grab a few bits to keep me tied over, and a non-alcoholic drink, all the while enjoying the questionable vocal talents gracing the stage. Jess and Raif are dancing away. Paul is sitting nattering with a couple of older gentlemen and Kayleigh... I can't see Kayleigh. Maybe she's popped to the loo or something. I retake my seat and tuck into my mini sausage rolls.

I can only apologise for my mates. And I'm not surprised at all x

It's not just your mates. Mine's just as bad. Hold up, why ain't you surprised? x

"Wait, what?" I say quietly, doing a double take at the sound of the DJ's voice.

Did he just say my name? Paul is walking towards me, smirking away. Oh, shit, the DJ *did* say my name, and Paul's name in the same sentence. I shake my head in an overdramatic, not-a-chance-in-hell manner, but it doesn't deter Paul in the slightest.

"Come on," he says.

"Not happening," I insist. "I don't sing in public."

"It's barely public," he argues, grabbing me by the hand and dragging me up to my feet. Wow, he's strong.

Paul practically hauls me onto the stage, so much so I almost trip over my own feet. The DJ hands me a microphone, and I avoid eye contact with the guests, my heart jumping to my throat. I can hear Jess and Raif cheering as I glance at the karaoke screen. I roll my eyes at the sight of Elton John ft. Kiki Dee, "Don't Go Breaking My Heart". Paul merely laughs at the I'm-so-not-impressed face I'm using to hide the rising panic.

My stomach churns. It's all eyes on me, and I can feel my legs turning to jelly beneath me. *Keep it together, Dani*, I silently tell myself. I cannot pass out or have a panic attack at Kayleigh's birthday party. I refuse to have another embarrassment added to my newly formed list. I take a deep breath and picture the only thing I can think of to help me stay calm: sitting in my flat with Damien, just him and me, making music and having a laugh.

I open my mouth and start to sing. I allow myself to glance out at the audience and spot Jess and Raif staring at me in awe. Turns out, they're not the only ones. The shocked expressions are hard to ignore, and music aside, it's eerily quiet, as though the guests have been rendered speechless. I know I can sing, but I wasn't expecting such a warm reaction. It does absolutely nothing to stop my racing heart or the sweat pouring from my brow though.

Thankfully, I keep my anxiety in check long enough to make it through the song, and once it's finished, I couldn't get off that stage quicker if I tried. I race back over to my seat, burying my face in my hands and taking long, deep breaths. Once again, my irrational fear irks me. It was singing karaoke on a stage at a party, not live at Wembley Stadium, yet I'm shaking, and my heart is pounding. When I look back up, Paul is sitting beside me.

"You're a dick," I state bluntly.

"I know." He shrugs, not at all bothered.

"And I suppose Damien mentioned I'm scared of performing?" Damien's mentioned almost everything else.

Paul appears surprised by my admission. "Stage fright?"

"Something like that," I mutter. It's a simple and fitting description, I guess.

"I wouldn't have known," Paul says, possibly as an attempt at comfort. "If I had, I'd have asked you to perform at a gig, just for the fun of it."

Not a chance in freaking hell. Performing at a gig is a dead-firm no, and Paul could attempt to drag me all he wants. I'd dig my heels in on that one.

"Definitely a dick," I reiterate, and Paul laughs. "And you didn't *ask*."

"You can sing, lass."

"So, can you," I compliment through gritted teeth.

"Seriously, you should consider gigging," he says, and I stifle a laugh. "Are you gonna sit there and tell me you didn't enjoy that?" I nod enthusiastically. "Liar."

Okay, so maybe it wasn't as bad as I thought it was going to be, now I've calmed down a little, but gigging is another world, open to scrutiny and heckling, and I'd rather not put myself through that, thank you. It's a stress I don't need.

"Kayleigh's just like you," Paul declares.

I furrow my brow in confusion. "How so?"

"Talented," he says, praising us both, "but lacking in confidence. In Kayleigh's defence, she's still a kid. What's your excuse?"

I point to my face. "Please don't act stupid, when we both

know you ain't."

"How could you possibly know that?" he asks, clearly enjoying himself. "You don't know me."

"Point and case exactly," I say. "*You* don't know *me* either."

"I know you better than you think." What the hell is he chatting on about? Oh, hello, paranoia. "Or your type anyway."

Silent sigh of relief. "You don't know shit." Paul laughs, and I'm assuming it's in agreeance. "*But* it doesn't take a genius to figure out a scar like mine ain't a common occurrence, and something bad obviously went down. So, yeah, my *type* is complicated."

"How bad?" he asks, and I sigh. I don't even know why I'm still talking.

"Bad enough to keep me far, far away from the limelight for the rest of my life," I state bluntly.

Oh, and did I forget to mention I'm paranoid? The limelight opens the possibility of photographs, attention, and the dreaded world of social media, and the last thing I need is my face plastered everywhere. I'll never be convinced Ray managed to take down *all* of Adrian's acquaintances, or that Adrian doesn't still hold some power in the outside world. And there I go again, being ridiculous and justifying my lack of confidence with irrational excuses. My paranoid side needs to get a bloody hobby.

"Sorry," he offers, and I nod, accepting his apology.

Jess strolling over is a welcome distraction from the unexpected and slightly tense conversation. "Have you seen Kayleigh?" she asks, stopping to stand next to Paul. "It's time for the cake."

"Last time I saw her she was talking to my niece," Paul answers, scanning the room.

"I ain't seen her in a while," I admit.

"I'll check the toilet," Jess says, shrugging.

"I'll have a look outside," I offer. "Maybe she went for some air."

We go our separate ways, but as I step outside, Kayleigh is nowhere to be seen. I do a walk around the building to double-check, but no joy. I head back inside, over to Jess and Paul standing near the double doors.

"She's not in the toilets," Jess tells me.

"I've asked around." Raif's joined the search now too. "Kayleigh told your niece she needed some air, but no one's seen her since."

"She's not answering her phone," Paul growls.

"Why would she leave her own party?" Raif asks.

"I don't know," Paul admits. "But it's not like Kayleigh to just take off."

"We'll track her down." I try to sound reassuring, but I'm not sure I pull it off. "Where does she like to go? Hang out?"

"She doesn't," Paul states. "She's not the social type. She spends most of her time at home. Almost everyone here is family or friends of family." I guess my unsociable assessment was correct, though right now, I wish it wasn't. "But I've already called the neighbours. No one's seen her come home, and trust me, Mrs Grains is a permanent curtain twitcher."

"Don't panic," I tell Paul.

"How can I not panic?" he almost yells. "I have no freaking idea where my kid is."

I have a way to find out, but it's not ideal. Kayleigh taking off is probably something or nothing. She is a teenager after all. Paul is freaking though, possibly overreacting, and it's making me suspicious.

"Is there something going on?" I ask him, and although he

acts put out, his eyes tell a different story. "Paul?"

I flash back to the phone call Damien received at Dave's when I mistook him for a possible parent, and I'm now wondering if it was Paul on the other end of that line.

"Kayleigh's not been herself lately," Paul says. "Locking herself in her room. Not talking. I've tried to get to the bottom of it, but she won't talk to me. She even skived school a few weeks back. That's why I got you to help with the school thing. I was hoping someone other than me that loves music the way she does would perk her up, and it did, so it's got to be school-related."

"Bullying?" Raif asks, and Paul nods.

"That's what I've been thinking," Paul admits. "I wanted to throw the birthday party to show her she has plenty of people who care about her, that she isn't alone." He sighs. "But what if it's more than bullying? What if…"

"She's depressed?" I finish his sentence, and the desperation in his eyes is all the confirmation I need.

Okay, extreme measures it is. First, I need privacy. The last thing I want is twenty questions. Do I think an interrogation will materialise as soon as the drama is over? Hell yeah, but I'll cross that bridge when I come to it.

"Let me make a call," I tell the group.

"How will that help?" Paul asks.

"Just trust me and don't ask questions," I plead.

Jess and Raif eye me with curiosity, but neither protest. With a quick nod from Paul, I turn on my heel and head outside, leaving the noise and prying ears behind. Ignoring the message I didn't know I had from Damien, I scroll through my contacts and hold my phone up to my ear as it rings.

"Dani?"

"Hey, Ray," I say.

"What's wrong?" he doesn't hesitate in asking, the concern evident in his voice. Ray and I ring each every few months to check in, but since I'm ringing unscheduled, I don't blame him for worrying.

"Nothing," I reassure him. "But I do need a favour."

"What kind of favour?"

"A friend of mine's kid has disappeared," I explain. "She's suffering from depression, and her dad's worried she's going to do something stupid. I know I'm taking the piss by asking, but she's a kid…"

"What's her number?" Ray obliges without argument, and after a quick scroll through my phone, I reel off the number Kayleigh gave me yesterday. "I see you're keeping yourself out of trouble."

Ray's tone reeks of sarcasm, and I chuff in response. "Trouble follows me around."

"But you're okay?" That's genuine unease.

"Yeah, course," I reassure a second time. "I'm doing exactly what you told me to and building a support network of friends."

"Good."

"Yeah, until my friend's problems become my problems," I say, sighing.

"Just be glad you got me to help," he teases.

"What would I do without you?"

It sounds like humour, but it's not. Without Ray, I don't know where I would be. I didn't even remember who he was the day he walked into the hospital, but that didn't stop him from taking care of me and trying to keep me safe. He's a good man, and the only person from my past life who knows how to contact me. I owe him, and his wife for that matter, more than

I could ever repay.

"How are things –" Adrian flashes before my eyes.

"Nothing to worry about here," Ray cuts me off. "You'd be the first person I'd call if there was."

I wait patiently until Ray tells me Kayleigh's location within the nearest kilometre. I thank him profusely before hanging up and racing inside to grab Paul. Jess and Raif move to come with us, but Paul politely asks them to hang back in case Kayleigh returns, and they reluctantly agree. Paul and I jump into my car, and I drive off.

We arrive at Gulliver's Park and start to scour the area. My heart stops. Kayleigh's standing on the edge of the tall bridge that runs over the park. I tap Paul on the shoulder. The two of us leg it as fast as we can in her direction. Paul arrives first, but I hear a "don't" come from Kayleigh's mouth. Paul stops in his tracks a few metres away, allowing me the chance to catch up.

"Don't come near me," Kayleigh says, sobbing.

"Kayleigh," Paul says. "What the hell are you doing? Come down, yeah? Let's talk about this."

"I don't want to talk!" she screams. "I just want it to end."

"Want what to end?" Paul asks.

"Everything," she says a little too calmly.

"Don't be stupid," Paul yells. "Get down from there now!"

I grab Paul's arm, shaking my head. That's not the way to get through to her, and although he frees himself from my grip, he stays quiet.

"You can't talk me out of this," she argues, and I instinctively hold my hands up in a don't-shoot fashion. "You don't understand."

"What don't we understand?" I ask.

"He took everything from me," she sobs. A boy. Of course

it's a boy. There's always a bloody boy.

"You're gonna throw yourself off a bridge because of a boy?" Paul scoffs, and I have never wanted to hit someone so badly for being so insensitive. "You know what. Screw this…"

Paul starts to walk closer to Kayleigh, but when she screams "No!" at the top of her lungs, I grab his arm again.

"Paul," I scold, gaining me a grunt of exasperation as he snaps his arm from my grip.

"I'm not having it," Paul snaps at me. "I'm dragging her off that bridge."

"I'll jump first," Kayleigh says.

Paul's expression instantly transforms from angry to heart-broken. "But why?" he pleads for an answer. "What the hell did this kid do that's worth killing yourself for?"

"He raped me," Kayleigh screams.

Holy shit. My entire body has just turned to stone. The flash-backs surface, but I shake them away as best I can, forcing my-self to look at Paul. His fists are already clenched, and he's got a murderous look in his eye. There might as well be steam com-ing from his ears, not that I blame him in the slightest. I have no doubt the rage is a mask to hide his pain.

"I begged him to stop," Kayleigh says, but I think it's more to herself than anyone else. "But he was too strong. I couldn't… I froze." Kayleigh shakes her head as if she's trying to shake the image from her mind. "I can't forget. I can't."

"Come down from the bridge, Kayleigh," Paul says. "Tell me who the hell did that to you, and I'll bloody well throw him over instead."

"That won't help me," Kayleigh spits, and although Paul's reaction is expected, Kayleigh's right, it's not helping. "I told you, you don't understand."

"I do," I interject, ignoring the shocked expression Paul's throwing my way.

"Yeah, right," Kayleigh scoffs. "You're just saying that to make me feel better."

"Believe me," I assure her. "I wish I was."

"I don't believe you."

"You want proof?" I ask, and Kayleigh tentatively nods. I reach down a hand to lift just enough of my top to reveal the scars covering my stomach, and Kayleigh's eyes widen with intrigue. Paul's too since he's also having a gander, and it's enough to keep me talking. I hadn't banked on Paul hearing any of this, mind.

"I was kidnapped," I explain. "I was beaten, cut into *and* raped repeatedly for months. I'm on a first-name basis with the king of hell, believe me. I know exactly what it's like to hit rock bottom and feel so alone you feel like there's nothing left to live for." I roll up my sleeve and Kayleigh's eyes travel to the faded scar running across my wrist. "And I didn't have anyone to talk me down from the ledge."

"You tried to kill yourself?"

"Yes, I did," I admit. "But you don't have to."

"Yes, I do," she sobs. "I can't take it anymore. I've tried to ignore it, tried to forget… He's ruined my life."

"Only if you let him," I tell her. "I get it. He's violated you, destroyed your confidence and self-belief to the point you feel worthless, and it hurts like hell. And the more you think about it, the more you close yourself off, embarrassed, ashamed, and afraid to talk about it because you think talking is a sign of weakness. You blame yourself for what happened, convincing yourself that somehow you deserved everything he did to you. You feel like there's no one else in the world who understands what you're going through, or what it feels like to sink into an oblivion of pain and self-hatred, but I'm telling you now, *I* understand. I get it, Kayleigh, because I've been there."

I take a couple of steps closer, and Paul moves along slightly behind me, following my lead.

"And I don't blame you for shutting yourself off, I did exactly the same," I admit. "Hell, I've spent the past three years hiding, keeping everyone at arm's-length because I couldn't bear the thought of people knowing the real me, the broken me, but I'm here now, and I'm taking one day at a time because that's all I can do. It's all *anyone* can do."

Kayleigh's eyes are locked on mine, the tears streaming down her cheeks, and I'm clinging to the hope she's hearing me.

"And it's all because of one person," I continue. "And apparently —" although I'm only just realising it now "— that's all it takes, just *one* person who has the tiniest shred of understanding as to what real pain feels like to remind you that you're the *victim* in all this. What's happening to you, what happened to me, it's not *our* fault."

Kayleigh's eyes shift back to the river, and my heart jumps to my throat. I inch closer, continuing to take tentative steps. I hear Paul's breath hitch, and I'm amazed he's holding back as well as he is.

"People who hurt other people," I prattle on. "They do it because they are alone and afraid. But you and me, we're *not* alone. *You* are *not* alone. We —" I shake a finger between Kayleigh and me "— are survivors. We don't need to be afraid because we're better than the men that hurt us. Life has dealt us a shitty hand, but I promise you, we *can* move past it." Hypocritical, but necessary, I feel. "You want to hurt the boy who hurt you? The best way to do that is to live your life with your head held high. Show him he is nothing. Show him what he did does not define you and won't stop you from becoming whoever it is you're meant to be. You have the power to take back control, Kayleigh, because you are *not* weak. You are strong, and you know why?"

"Why?" she asks, and I'm taking a response as a good sign.

"Because strength is coming out the other side." Sound familiar? "Strength is taking one day at a time and putting one foot in front of another. Strength is knowing you have people around you that you can count on to help you through this and knowing you *will* get through it, because I promise you, you will. You just need to believe it. But if you throw yourself off that bridge, he wins." Kayleigh looks back down at the river, and I take the opportunity to move to just a metre away from her. "Let me be that one person for you," I plead, holding out my hand. "Don't let him win."

Kayleigh slowly takes my hand, and once I have a grip, I practically yank her down from the bridge into Paul's arms. I turn my back to them for a minute, leaning my palms against the wall, looking down at the ground. I take long, deep breaths as the relief washes over me. I had no idea if talking would work, and Kayleigh could have jumped at any second. Holy mother of hell. That was without a doubt the scariest thing I have ever done, and that's saying something.

"Thank you," I hear Paul say, and I lift my head to look at him. The tears are threatening to fall from his eyes as he holds his daughter tight, but all I can bring myself to do is nod. "You're welcome" doesn't seem like the right response, and I can't think of anything else that doesn't sound patronising or insensitive. A nod will just have to do for now.

After a few minutes of watching Paul and Kayleigh embrace,

I offer to take them home. Walking to the car, I decide to shoot Jess a text to let her know the score, minus the attempted suicide out of respect for Kayleigh's privacy, but when I unlock my phone, I spot the text message from Damien I've yet to read.

Because alcohol can make you vulnerable, and after everything you've told me, I figure that's the last thing you want x

It takes just one person who understands.

Chapter Fourteen

I'm sitting outside Damien's dad's house, staring at the door through my car window. Yes, on complete and utter impulse, I dropped Paul and Kayleigh off and drove to Kent. I am aware of how ridiculous that is, but after getting Damien's dad's address from Paul, I spent the entire almost five-hour journey down questioning my decision. And now that I'm here, my nerves are kicking in with a fierce vengeance, begging me to turn the engine back on and drive straight back home.

I look at the time on my phone; it's almost three in the morning and not exactly a sociable hour. I didn't think this through at all. I run the risk of not only waking a sleeping Damien but his dad too, who, after suffering a heart attack, needs his rest. Any and every excuse I can think of to chicken out is running through my mind, and it's taking all my strength not to act on them.

Are you awake? x

I opt for a less house-rousing option by sending Damien a text, but I'm suddenly realising if he's sleeping, my chances of a reply are zero, and I'm not sure I can handle sitting in my car until a more reasonable hour. Patience is not my friend at this moment in time.

Can't sleep. Can't stop thinking about Paul and Kayleigh. I'm glad you were there. Are you okay? x

News travels fast. *I'm* assuming *he's* assuming I'm awake for the same reason or because of a nightmare, and I'm touched by his concern. He's got no idea how wrong he is, but if I was looking for the element of surprise, I've certainly got it.

Open your front door x

Have you forgotten where I am? x
Okay, open your DAD'S front door x

I climb out of the car and wait at the door. Less than a minute passes before it opens, and as Damien stands in the doorway dressed only in his pyjama bottoms, blessing me with the glorious sight of his smooth as hell, lean torso, I almost forget why I'm here.

"What the hell are you doing here?" Damien asks, stepping outside but leaving the door ajar. I'm assuming he's not inviting me in to prevent waking his dad, which is understandable.

"I'm sorry," I say nervously. "I couldn't wait."

"Couldn't wait for what?"

"To see you."

"Okay," he says slowly, obviously confused, or so I'm assuming from his slightly knitted brow. "Are you okay? I can imagine Kayleigh stirred up some unwanted memories."

Definitely, but... "That's not why I'm here."

"Then what?"

I take a deep breath, trying to find the right words to convey how I'm feeling, but as you know, words are not my strong suit. Unless I'm writing a song. Maybe I should've written Damien a song rather than driving a ridiculously long journey just to make an idiot of myself, and yes, I'm probably going to make an idiot of myself here.

"I need you to listen." The words stumble out. "And to let me get this out."

Damien nods, sliding his hands into his pyjama pockets. "Okay."

"Okay," I say, taking one more deep breath. "I've been an idiot. I've been an unbelievably stupid idiot, but I don't want to be an idiot anymore."

177

"What are you –"

"Please," I cut him off, and taking a leaf out of my book, he rolls his eyes but shuts his mouth. "You are probably the most amazing, sweetest, funniest, hot as hell guy I have ever met. You make me feel alive again, normal even, and…" I let out a nervous giggle. "I talked Kayleigh down from a freaking ledge tonight, and yes, it's because of what I've been through, but the confidence to actually do it, to share my horror story to help someone else, that's because of you."

"You're giving me too much credit," Damien argues.

"No, I'm not," I insist. "You get me. I spent eighteen months getting psychiatric help, yet it's taken *you* to finally give me, I don't know, a reason to want to live a life that's more than just sitting in my flat and going through the motions. I don't know how the hell you've done it, and sometimes I feel like you know me better than I know myself, which is ridiculous because we've known each other for like four weeks. Yet, you always know what to say, what to do, and because of you, I've done more, laughed more, *relaxed* more than I have in well, forever, and it's amazing."

I take a much-needed deep breath, reminding myself to be honest and open. I don't want to hold anything back.

"But it's terrifying too," I admit. "I've spent so long living in a bubble surrounded by walls and armed guards because I'm scared, and that's why I've pushed you away. I'm scared if I let you in, I'll only let you down. I'm scared of not being able to move on and give you what you need because as much as I like you, the thought of being physical still has shivers running down my spine. And because of that, I'm scared you'll get fed up with waiting, that you'll give up on me, and I'm scared if you did, it would break me, and I've been broken too much already."

"Dani," Damien says softly, taking a step closer.

"But then I realised," I say, "if I let you walk away now then I've lost you for good, and that's what scares me the most: losing you."

Damien takes another step closer until he's just inches away. He reaches a hand up to my cheek and wipes away a stray tear with his thumb.

"And I'm not saying we're destined to work out." I downplay my desperation a little. "Relationships, from what I've heard – " I wouldn't know "– are hard work, but I want to try. I want to give *us* a shot at least."

I'm about to say something else, but Damien slides his finger over my lips to silence me. My heart pounding with anticipation, he leans in close, but I'm distracted by the sound of a woman's voice.

"Damien?"

I push open the door to see a beautiful brunette standing halfway down the stairs wearing what looks like Damien's T-shirt and not much else. Damien turns his head to look at her too, and I don't hesitate, turning on my heel and racing back to my car. Damien is calling my name, but I'm already climbing into the driver's seat. Without putting on my seat belt – irresponsible and stupid, I know – I start the engine and zoom off.

I keep driving, my seat belt now on, until I reach the first service stop on the motorway, and after parking up and switching off the engine, I let the tears flow like never-ending waterfalls of pain and heartache. I feel like my entire world has just come crashing down around me and I'm buried in the rubble, unable to breathe. After everything I've been through, I didn't think anything could hurt me the way Adrian did, but I was wrong.

I had my shot, and I blew it. I pushed Damien away, and he

found solace in the arms of another, who is no doubt able to give herself to him in ways I can't. I don't blame him, but the reality that I will never be with Damien is like a bullet to the brain. It's excruciating.

You know what, I take that back. I *do* blame Damien, at least half as much as I blame myself. He's not innocent in all this. Less than twenty-four hours ago, he was texting me telling me he missed me and that nothing had changed regarding his feelings for me. Was all that just a lie?

Maybe I'm old-fashioned. Technically, we're not a couple. Damien has every right to sleep with whoever the hell he wants, so I have no right to feel betrayed, yet I do. I feel like I'm just another conquest Damien's failed to actually conquer, and it hurts like hell. I sigh. Maybe all men are the same, and Damien isn't the diamond in the rough I thought he was.

My phone starts to ring, and one glance at the screen tells me it's Damien. I don't answer it. I don't want to hear his excuses or his apologies or whatever he has to say. All I want to do is go home and lock myself away in my bubble of solitude where I belong.

I let myself wallow for a while longer before making the gruelling journey home. I'm not sure how I manage to stay awake after an almost non-stop ten-hour round trip, but as I lock up my car, my sluggish shoulders and aching limbs tell me the fatigue is kicking in. Thank God it's Sunday – no work – and I have the freedom to go inside and crash.

I head inside through the communal door, and the sight of Jess appearing in the hallway, almost as if she's been waiting for me, is not at all welcome. I sigh at the worry encompassing her face, failing to hide the anger lying underneath, and I instinctively brace myself for some form of lecture or interrogation. I open the door to my flat and let Jess follow me inside. She remains eerily silent, her hands firmly on her hips like a mother about to scold her child, and I revel in the calm before the storm. I throw myself onto the couch against the back wall, and Jess soon breaks her silence.

"What the hell is going on?" She raises her voice a little too loudly, awakening a shooting pain in my forehead. "I've had Damien on the phone, freaking out, wanting me to text him the second you got home."

"Have you?"

"Not yet," Jess states, sitting down on the opposite couch. "I'm not done being pissed off at you for taking off to Kent in the middle of the night and not telling me."

"Last time I checked," I say unnecessarily, but as you can imagine, my tiredness is making me crabby, "you ain't my mother."

"No," Jess says, remarkably calm, though I can see a hint a frustration in her eyes. "But I am supposed to be your friend, and after the Kayleigh shit last night, I'm a little on edge. The least you could have done was send a text or leave a note on your door."

As much as I hate to admit it, she has a valid point. I instantly soften, guilt replacing my crabbiness. "I'm sorry. I didn't think."

"Apology accepted," Jess says far too quickly. "Now, are you gonna tell me what the hell is going on? Damien was vague."

"Yeah, I bet he was," I say spitefully.

"What's that supposed to mean?"

"Damien's sleeping with someone else," I answer flatly. No wonder he didn't let me inside, I suddenly realise. Absolutely naff all to do with his dad.

"No," she says in a ridiculously over-the-top manner. "Do

you have proof?"

I sigh. "A woman on the stairs in one of his T-shirts."

"So, you didn't actually catch them in the act?" Jess asks, and I shake my head. "So, technically, you don't know for sure they're sleeping together."

I scowl. "Whose side are you on?"

"Yours," Jess insists. "And I get I don't know Damien all that well, but he's like infatuated with you, and after everything Paul and Raif have told me about him, he doesn't seem the type to throw in the towel and jump into bed with someone else."

"If you were in my shoes," I state, "what would you think?"

Jess mulls it over. "The same, but I'd have stuck around to give him what for."

"I run and hide." I shrug. "It's what I do."

"Was she really wearing one of Damien's T-shirts?"

"It was definitely a bloke's," I say. "But I'm not on a first-name basis with Damien's wardrobe."

"I'm gonna kill him," Jess suddenly spits, rolling over to my side of thinking.

"No, you're not," I order. "Damien's done nothing wrong." Technically.

"Are you kidding?" Jess raises her voice far too loud for my nagging head. "You may not have been officially a couple –"

"My doing."

"It's irrelevant," Jess maintains. "You can't come on as strong as he did and then move on to some slapper."

I allow myself to let out a laugh. "You don't know she's a slapper."

"Yes, I do," Jess affirms. "Because *I'm* a slapper, and only slappers put out on the first date."

I shake my head. "You don't know that either. For all we

know she could be an old flame or a friend with benefits he hooks up with when he goes to visit his dad."

"Whichever way," Jess states. "What Damien's done is not on, and I'm not gonna let him get away with it scot-free."

Again, I shake my head. "He's a guy. It's what guys do."

"Not an excuse." Jess's serious voice is refusing to fade, and in a way, I'm comforted to know she has my back.

"It's my own fault, Jess," I say sadly. "I let my bullshit get in the way, and when I finally opened my eyes, it was too late."

Jess sighs. "I'm sorry."

"Not your fault I'm fucked up." I shrug, fighting back the impending tears, but either the tears are welling up in my eyes anyway or Jess is reading my mind because she moves to sit next to me.

"You're not fucked up," she says softly.

"Yes, I am," I state, the tears starting to fall. Jess moves to put an arm around me, but I stop her in her tracks by sliding over a little. "Don't, please."

Jess sighs. "What is that about, Dani?" she asks, obviously fed up with being in the dark. "That's the second time you've stopped me from comforting you." She's referring to the night of James's attack, and her words only make me weep more.

"It's a really long story," I tell her.

"I got time." She shrugs. "And you do know it's hard to give advice without the whole story, right?"

Damien knows. Paul and Kayleigh know the gist. I guess there's no point holding it back from the person I'm starting to think of as my closest friend anymore, especially when in truth, with Damien about to be history, Jess is the only person I've got left.

"You're gonna want a drink," I tell her. "Or several."

Jess merely urges me to start talking, and after a long, deep breath, I oblige. I fill her in on everything, from getting shot, to my amnesia, Adrian, and everything else that makes up my bloody sob story. Jess barely says a word throughout, listening with her usual scary intensity, and now that I've finished, a miracle is occurring right before my eyes: Jessica Baines is speechless.

I'm now on my feet, making myself a brew. Jess is still sitting on the couch, gob-smacked and attempting to process everything, I think.

"You want a brew?" I ask her, but she shakes her head. I make my coffee in silence before moving back into the living room, taking my previous position next to Jess on the couch. "Are you gonna say something?" I ask, attempting to break the awkward silence.

"I don't…" she starts. "I don't know what to say. I mean, oh my God, Dani. It's…"

"Unbelievable."

"Except you lived it."

Remarkably, talking to Jess has brought on a calmness I didn't expect. I think I've told my story a few too many times in the past week, I'm getting used to it. That, and I know Jess cares about me. If anything, the truth can only allow our friendship to grow. Secrets and friendship, or a relationship for that matter, I realise, are not a good mix, and I'm glad Jess knows. It almost feels like a weight has been lifted from my shoulders. I have nothing to hide anymore, from anyone, and after the night I've had, it's a welcome relief.

"So, you don't like to be touched because you actually feel the pain?" Jess asks.

"I get flashbacks," I explain. "And it's like I'm there all over again, and yeah, the pain feels real too. Not as strong, obviously, but it's there."

"That's…" Jess shakes her head in disbelief. "So much makes sense to me now."

"Yeah, I bet."

"I'm so sorry I gave you a hard time about not going out," she says. "If I'd have known…"

"Don't be sorry," I say, shaking my head. "I'm glad you did. I mean, Damien can't take all the credit. You've been here from day one. If you hadn't forced your way into my life –" Jess playfully scowls "– I'd be alone right now. Believe it or not, but you are the only constant I've had since I moved here, and you're the one person I can always rely on. You've been there for me the entire time. It just took me a while to see it."

Jess grabs my non-coffee-cup-wielding hand and squeezes it tight, the brightest smile encompassing her face. "You really mean that?"

"I really do."

If I was a hugger, this would be a perfect hug moment, but I'm not, so I settle for squeezing Jess's hand just as tight.

"Well, as long as we're confessing," she says, instantly intriguing me, "I need to thank you too."

"What the hell for?"

"For being there for me too," she says. "If you put aside the fact you let me prattle on for hours about meaningless shit without complaint, which is a sure-fire sign of a good friend right there, you aren't the only one who's felt lonely."

Jess and *lonely* are not two words I would have ever contemplated putting in the same sentence, but I should know by now, especially after Kayleigh, what you see on the surface is not always a reflection of what lies underneath.

"I've told you before I have no real friends," Jess continues. "And I really don't. Most of the people I partied with were James's mates, who I've cut all ties with." She didn't need to say or do that, but I appreciate her loyalty. "I'm not great at the making-friends thing. Girls tend to hate me."

"Jealousy," I state.

"I don't know," she says, shrugging, but I do. Jess is gorgeous, and I can imagine a lot of women find her intimidating. "But you were different. Antisocial as hell, but I guess I saw something in you I saw in myself, and that's why I never stopped asking you over for a brew even when you used to say no. And you've never once judged me for sleeping around."

"Yes, I have," I tease. "I tell you all the time you're a sex fiend."

Jess laughs. "Yeah, but you don't *really* judge me. You wind me up, and you're bloody brilliant at that, but I always know it's in jest. You don't judge anybody, and that's what I love about you. You accept people for the way they are, and the more time I spent with you, the more I realised I didn't need a massive group of friends like James to stop the loneliness. I just needed *one* friend who liked me for me, and that's you."

"I used to think you only made the effort with me out of pity," I admit.

"Self-pity, maybe," she says, and I give her hand another squeeze. "I used to be fat. All through high school. I was bullied relentlessly, but I lost a shitload of weight in college, and I told myself I'd spend the rest of my life flaunting it. That's why I sleep around, to prove I can. It's sad."

"No, it's not," I reassure her. "We all deal with shit in different ways, and just because society says sleeping around is a bad thing, doesn't mean it is. Hell, men do it, and they get a pat on the back."

The woman on Damien's stairs burns the backs of my eyes, and I silently seethe. Men don't give a shit, so why should women?

"Don't they just," Jess scoffs, and there's a moment's silence before she speaks again. "The bullying affected me more than I like to admit, but thanks to you, I've gained a couple of extra friends too." Raif and Paul, I'm assuming. "But the most important one is sitting right here."

"Ditto," I say brightly, and Jess smiles.

"Just promise me you will lean on me when you need to," she adds. "It's what friends are for."

"I promise," I say without hesitation.

"Now," she says, letting go of my hand, "what are we gonna do about Damien?"

I sigh, the warmth of our conversation replaced with a sadness I can't begin to describe. I had hoped with all the soppiness in the room, Jess would let the Damien conversation go, but her relentlessness is never far away.

"There's nothing to do." I shrug. "It's done."

"We could key his car," Jess suggests, and I can't help but laugh. "Or hijack a gig with a banner that says 'Cheating Bastard' on it."

"I appreciate what you're doing," I assure her. "But I think I need to take the high road."

"Spoilsport," she teases, but I can see the sympathy in her eyes. "I'm sorry, Dani."

"Yeah, me too," I admit. "I really liked him."

"You know he's not gonna just go away, right?"

"He might." I shrug. "I mean, if he's found someone else, he's got no reason to bother with me anymore."

Jess sighs. "You know I've always got your back…"

"But?" There's a definite *but* coming.

"Maybe you got the wrong end of the stick," she says, and I sigh heavily.

"Maybe," I say, though I don't believe my words.

"I think you should hear him out," Jess tells me. "Has he tried ringing you?"

"Yeah," I say. "But I put my phone on silent after the second time."

"You should answer it," Jess instructs. "If nothing else, an explanation might at least bring you some closure."

I nod, knowing deep down Jess is right, but there's something inside me already accepting that maybe Damien isn't the one for me. I'd give anything to go back in time and do things differently, but hindsight is a wonderful thing, and now it's too late.

"Or maybe," I say softly, "I need to let him go."

Chapter Fifteen

Blurry-eyed and in desperate need of some bloody sleep, I let my head hit the pillow as soon as Jess leaves. The next time I open my eyes, it's to the sound of banging on my door. I groan, glancing at the time, groaning louder when I realise it's only half-two in the afternoon. I've only managed a two-hour kip, and I'm contemplating rolling back over and ignoring my door completely.

I force myself out of bed, my entire body aching from the lack of sleep, silently cursing Jess underneath my breath. The banging is relentless, mirroring the banging in my head. Jess is obviously in desperate need of my attention.

"All right," I scold the noise.

I open the door and immediately shut it again, slamming it in Damien's face. I should know by now never to assume Jess is the only one with access to my front door. Shit. I don't want to deal with Damien, not when the image of the woman on his stairs is so fresh in my mind. I was hoping I'd get a chance to calm down and process things rationally. Ha! Since when do I process anything rationally?

"Dani," he says with a tone that tells me he's not at all impressed by my actions. I guess that makes two of us, although I'm referring to Damien's actions, not mine.

"Leave me alone," I call, wondering if Jess betrayed me, or if my new neighbour moved in early.

"I'm not going anywhere until you let me explain," Damien insists. "I will stand outside your door all day if I have to."

Stubborn to the core. I relent, opening the door and allowing Damien to enter my living room.

"What the hell are you doing here?" I ask. "Don't you have your dad to take care of?"

"I did," he says harshly. "But you took off and left me no choice but to come after you."

"You didn't need to come after me," I argue, forcing myself to look at him. I'm pleased to say he's ditched the pyjamas and is now fully dressed in his usual T-shirt and jeans combo, just by the by. "I got the message loud and clear."

"Do you honestly think I'm sleeping with someone else?" he asks, leaning his palms on the back of my sofa.

"The half-naked woman on the stairs is a bit of a giveaway." My spiteful voice is back.

"Half-naked is a stretch, Dani," he points out, and I suppose he has a point. Jess wears far more revealing clothes than Damien's mistress to go out in, let alone sleep in.

"What do you want, Damien?" I ask. "I don't need the details or an explanation. I don't *want* an explanation." Damien sighs. "I pushed you away, and you responded by doing what every other guy in the universe does and got yourself laid to make yourself feel better. And I already know it's all my own doing, I don't need you to tell me that, and I also know I have no right to be pissed off, but I am. I'm pissed off at myself. I'm pissed off at you. I'm even pissed off at the woman on your stairs." I pause for breath. "But if you've come here to ease your guilt, there's really no need."

"I didn't come here to ease my guilt because there's nothing to feel guilty for," he states.

Anger boils inside me like a tidal wave of fury, and it takes all I have not to slap him across the face. *Arrogant* and *Damien* are two words I never thought I'd use in the same sentence, yet I am, and Damien's arrogance is insulting.

"I came here to tell you you're a bloody idiot," he says.

"Yes, I am," I yell, my anger unleashing. "I'm an idiot for thinking you were different. I'm an idiot for sharing my godforsaken sob story. I'm an idiot for pouring my heart and soul out, and I'm an even bigger idiot to think I could ever make a relationship work in the first place, and –"

"That's not why you're an idiot," he cuts me off.

I can't do this anymore. I cover my face with my hands, the anger short-lived and replaced with anguish. I can't hide my pain, but I don't want Damien to see me cry over him. I let myself develop feelings for Damien, but I never should have listened to that shred of hope or anything other than my anxiety-riddled instincts. I knew it would end in heartbreak. Everything always ends in heartbreak.

"I need you to go," I tell him. "Please. I can't…"

"No," he cuts me off, flatly. "Because I'm an idiot too. I should never have walked out that door, and I'm not making the same mistake twice."

Damien moves in close, gently grabbing my face. My heart skips a beat as he hesitates, staring deep into my eyes as though he's waiting for something, and when the realisation of his intentions hits me, I choke on a gasp.

My stomach fluttering, his scent engulfing my senses, he leans in and kisses me. The warmth of his soft, coffee tasting lips is almost addictive, and the rush is like nothing I've ever felt before. My hands find his biceps as my temperature soars to dangerous heights, and my knees feel weak. It's like time is standing still, capturing the perfect moment, and it feels so…right.

I'm so caught up in Damien's lips, it takes me far too long to remember the woman on the stairs, but when I do, I pull away. I'm about to say something, but Damien beats me to it.

"She's my sister," he says, a smirk forming across his lips.

"What?" I yell, taking a step back.

"She's my little sister," he says, slower this time. "My half-sister, actually."

I take another step back, utterly embarrassed and humiliated. There's a touch of fury in there too, and I'm back to wanting to slap him. "Why the hell didn't you say that at the beginning?"

"Because it's insulting you automatically think the worst of me," he says bluntly, and again, he has a point. "And it pissed me off. After everything I've said and done, do you really think I'd jump into bed with someone else when things got rough?"

I shrug. Obviously, I did. I probably shouldn't have thought the worst, but in my defence, Damien has never mentioned a sister, and I'm naturally paranoid and suspicious. That, and… "If it was the other way around, if there was a guy in his boxers standing in my doorway right now, how would you react?"

Damien tilts his head from side to side, mulling my question over, before taking my hands in his. "I see your point."

"Thank you," I say, a little narky in my tone, but I think it's the embarrassment causing my irritation.

Damien leans in a second time, planting another heart-melting kiss on my lips, and I welcome it with open arms – not literally – my embarrassment fading somewhat.

"I would never hurt you like that, Dani," he says softly. "And I don't care what it takes, or how long it takes, I'm gonna be right here. *You* are all I want."

"You sure that's what you want?" I ask, my insecurities infuriatingly ever-so-present. "I've still got hurdles to jump, and I don't know –"

"Was the dramatic, passionate kiss not enough?" he cuts me

off, laughing a little. "Or the fact I dropped everything to chase you home?"

I want to laugh, but my insecurities, like I say, know no bounds, and just because I've taken the first step towards a relationship, it doesn't mean my anxiety is going to just disappear.

"I've never been so sure," he comforts, and without another word, he kisses me, and I'm lost in his lips.

Damien pulls away to bend down as if he's going to lift me before straightening back up again as though he's remembered something. "Legs?" he asks, and I nod in understanding. I don't have an issue with him touching my legs.

Damien hoists me up, forcing me to wrap my arms around his neck to stop from falling backwards. Without touching my torso, not even with his own, he carries me over to the kitchen and sits me down on the breakfast bar. He places a hand on my thigh and reaches up with the other to touch my cheek. I'm graced with another, albeit softer, kiss.

"I honestly thought I'd never be able to do this," he admits.

"I never thought I'd *want* to do this."

"I'm just gonna keep doing it," he says, and I allow him to embrace my lips once more.

I'm distracted by quiet giggling coming from the hallway, ruining the moment. Jess's curiosity has clearly gotten the better of her, although by the sounds of it, she's not alone, and I think I know who her accomplice is. I put a finger to my lips, signalling Damien to keep quiet as I jump down from the breakfast bar and tiptoe up to my front door. I quickly open it, and Jess and Raif fall through, knocking into one another until they hit the floor.

"Ow," Jess squeals, but all I can do is laugh.

"Serves you right for earwigging," I mock as Jess and Raif

clumsily clamber back up to their feet. "Ain't you two got anything better to do?"

"Are you kidding?" Jess scoffs. "You two are better than a bloody soap opera."

"Hi honey," Raif says to Damien. "Didn't expect to see you back so soon."

"Neither did I," Damien admits. "But Dani had other ideas."

"Don't blame me," I argue, snapping my head around to look at him. "You didn't have to chase me home."

"Aww," Jess coos, followed by an over-the-top, sulky pout. "I wish someone would chase me home."

"They don't need to," I state, returning my gaze to my nosey neighbour. "You invite them with open legs."

"Cheeky bitch," she says, slapping me on the arm.

"True though," Raif agrees, and he too gets a slap on the arm for his troubles.

"Anyway," I say, grabbing the door handle and using my free hand to gesture the exit of the terrible twosome.

"Right, yeah," Jess says. "We'll leave you two lovebirds to it."

"Don't do anything I wouldn't do," Raif teases.

"That doesn't leave much," Damien jokes.

"I know," Raif gushes suggestively.

I practically shove them out of my flat with the door, closing it firmly behind them and sighing. I turn back to Damien to see him smiling that beautiful smile with a hint of cheekiness thrown in.

"What?" I ask.

"Do you plan on telling them *why* I had to chase you home?" And that's what the cheekiness in his grin is about. I guess I have one more embarrassing story to add to my growing novel.

"Jess already knows," I state, and Damien can't hide his surprise. "We hit a milestone in our friendship."

"Your mutual hatred for me?"

"Something like that." I smirk. "But if it helps, Jess was convinced I got it wrong, and I'm probably gonna hear about how right she was for the rest of my life."

"I think they call that karma," Damien jokes, and I laugh, moving past him into the kitchen, setting the kettle to boil.

"Karma's a bitch," I retort as Damien appears beside me, taking my hand in his and pressing it to his lips. "Although, if Jess knows, Raif will know, and you'll tell Paul, if you haven't already, so I think karma is handing out an unfair punishment."

Damien laughs. "What makes you think I'd have already told Paul?"

"Paul and I have done a bit of bonding whilst you were away," I tease. "And from what I've heard, you tell him everything."

"Not everything," Damien argues.

"True," I agree, knowing fine well he's referring to my sob story. "Not that it would matter now. There's only Raif left to tell."

"You told Jess?"

"Milestone."

"You *have* come a long way."

"Paul wasn't exactly an intended recipient," I state, and Damien nods in understanding. "How is he?"

"Devastated," Damien answers. "Beating himself into the ground, but I'd be doing the same if I was him. I can't imagine what he's going through right now. Kayleigh too."

"They'll get through it," I say confidently. "They have each other."

"And you," Damien says, brushing his thumb over my knuckles. "If anyone can help them through this, it's you."

"Don't do that," I state, letting go of Damien's hand to pull out a cup from a cupboard.

"Don't do what?"

"Big me up and praise me," I answer flatly. "I got *lucky*, and every time I think about what *could* have happened, it makes me sick to my stomach. In fact, I want to find the boy responsible for making Kayleigh's life a living hell and show him what hell feels like."

Damien grabs both of my hands, and I force the rising anger back beneath the surface. I will never understand why people feel the need to be so cruel. Kayleigh's a kid, and she doesn't deserve to be pushed to the edge, no one does. The worst part is, Adrian is paying for what he did to me, but the chances are the boy who hurt Kayleigh won't. I can only hope karma will eventually bite the bastard in the arse.

"Kayleigh's okay," he soothes. "And whether you want to hear it or not, it's because of you."

"I just waffled," I argue, refusing to take any credit. "Kayleigh made the decision not to jump, not me."

Damien sighs, shaking his head at me. "Sometimes, you are the most infuriating woman on the planet."

Preaching to the choir. I didn't need Damien to tell me that. I do live inside my head, and infuriating is putting it politely.

"Can we change the subject now?" I ask. "Like to when you're going back to Kent."

Damien smiles, reaching up into my cupboard, reminding me I forgot my manners, and plonking a cup on the counter next to mine. "I'm not going back," he states, flashing me that beautiful smile.

I can't hide my surprise, but I'm hoping I'm hiding how happy that makes me feel. I don't want to come across as completely selfish. "What about your dad?"

"I was already planning on coming home tomorrow anyway," he tells me as I go about making our coffees. "My uncle's going to take over babysitting duties."

"You can't abandon your dad," I scoff. "He's just had a heart attack."

"My dad doesn't want me there any more than I want to be there," Damien argues. "He's more likely to listen to my uncle anyway, and it's not like I could stay down there forever. I'm self-employed, remember? Which means I'm making zero income each day I'm not working."

"Still," I say. "If I hadn't taken off, you wouldn't be here a day early, leaving your dad in the lurch."

"Blessing in disguise," Damien jokes, but I don't find it funny, and I'm pretty sure the guilt is written all over my face. "I've not left my dad on his own. My uncle arrived last night. I was only staying a day longer to give him a chance to settle in. Trust me, my dad doesn't give a shit I'm not there. You've got nothing to feel guilty for."

Not going to stop me. I hand Damien his brew, and carrying mine, I make my way over to the couch nearest the breakfast bar. Damien's phone beeps, and he pulls it from his pocket before sitting down next to me.

"It's Amy," he tells me.

"Who's…" Light bulb moment. "That'll be the sister you never mentioned."

Damien laughs. "She wants to know if I plan on being at home tonight."

"Your sister's *here*?" I ask, a little higher pitched than

intended.

"Yeah," Damien says, amused. "She's scouting university campuses, and the University of Manchester is one of her choices. She was planning on staying with me for a few weeks anyway. She just didn't expect to have to pack so quickly."

Great. So, not only does Amy undoubtedly think I'm a complete nutcase, I'm also the reason why she's probably forgotten half the things she needed to bring. Not exactly the first impression I would have liked to make.

"And why exactly wouldn't you plan on being home tonight?" I ask, popping my brew on the coffee table.

"Because someone has finally come to their senses," he says light-heartedly. "And I want to spend every minute I can with her."

"Is that right?" I say, unable to hide my smile. "And what if this 'her' likes her space?"

"Then she'll get it," Damien says, shrugging. "There's two couches and two bedrooms."

"You really do have an answer for everything."

"In all seriousness," he says softly, abandoning his brew to the floor and turning his body to face me, "I'm never gonna push. You set the pace. I got all the time in the world."

I sigh. "There might be times when you need to give me a little bit of a push. Or a pep talk, at least."

Damien laughs. "That I can do."

"Just don't give up on me," I pathetically plead.

Damien rests a hand on my cheek and leans in for a long, sensual kiss.

"I'm not going anywhere," he says softly as he pulls away, those sky-blue eyes holding my gaze. "I'm all in, Dani, no matter what."

I stare at him, searching for any flicker of doubt but coming up empty. "Even if —"

"No matter what," he repeats, interrupting my nagging insecurities, and reluctantly, I nod. "Besides, we can focus on what we *can* do."

"And what's that?"

Damien answers by kissing me again, only when he moves to pull away, I pull him back in, my hand resting at the base of his neck whilst his fingers caress my cheek, our free hands entwining. I revel in his taste, feeling my pulse quickening and the heat in the room rising. For the first time in a long time, I feel like there's a chance at something more than a life of pain and suffering lurking on the horizon, and all I have to do now is take one step at a time to reach it. Fingers crossed I can get there.

Chapter Sixteen

My clothes are on the floor. My hands bound to the bed frame. The blood from my wounds pooling underneath me. He's towering over me, his pupils dilated. He slowly unbuckles his belt.

"Please," I beg. "Please don't."

He laughs, and another piece of my soul shatters. He abandons his jeans to the concrete and slowly climbs onto the bed. He hovers over me, his fingers sliding along the breadth of my skin. I turn my face away from him, but he grabs my chin, forcing me to meet his penetrating gaze.

"You belong to me," he growls. "Forever."

My eyes shoot open, and the tears waste no time in descending. A hand brushes my arm, and I scream in shock.

"Easy," Damien says softly. "It's just me."

Damien continues to stroke my arm, and it's a welcome comfort. A little surreal, but definitely welcome.

After a brief spat about Damien taking the spare room, my counterpoint being even if Damien's hands did find their way to my torso during the night, I'd be asleep and unaware, Damien caved and joined me in my bed. My stomach was in knots, I can't lie, but it's my way of proving, not to Damien, but to myself, I can take baby steps in the right direction, and after falling asleep with my fingers interlocked with Damien's only to be repeatedly disturbed by nightmares, I know I made the right call. It's nice having Damien here to verbally, if not fully physically, comfort me.

"Four nightmares in one night," he says. "Is that usual?" I shake my head, and Damien's face softens. "It's because of Kayleigh, isn't it?"

I nod. "It's triggered a few extra memories."

Damien nods in understanding. "What can I do?"

"Talk to me," I say, entwining my fingers with his. "Keep my head out of the crazy."

"Okay," he says. "You have a topic in mind?"

"Why don't you tell me about the sister you never mentioned?"

Being the good guy and loyal friend he is, about an hour after showing up at mine, Damien nipped off to check in on Paul and Kayleigh, and when he returned, we spent the rest of the evening kissing and making music. I was too caught up in the romance to ask questions, but that doesn't mean I don't want to know.

"Where do you want me to start?" Damien asks.

I shrug. "I don't know." I chuckle. "Age, where she lives…"

"Amy's nineteen," Damien says. "She's been back in England and living with my dad for about a year, but before that, she was in Australia with her mum and nan."

"Australia?"

Damien nods. "My dad and Tina divorced when I was fifteen. It was messy as hell, and Tina decided to take Amy out to Sydney."

"Did you go and visit?"

"I wish," he declares. "But Tina cut all contact. Last year was the first time I'd spoken to or seen Amy in ten years."

"Ten years?" I say dramatically. "What the hell did your dad do?"

Damien chuckles. "It's more a case of what he *didn't* do. The Army comes first." Ouch.

"But Amy's planning on staying?" Damien nods. "And going to university?" Another nod. "Do you have any other family over here?" I ask, fully aware Damien hails from Northern

Ireland.

"Just my dad's brother, Ted, and his son, Phil," he answers. "Everyone else is back in Belfast."

I smile softly. "Do you miss them?"

"I do, yeah," he admits. "I have a big family. My mum's the youngest of seven, my dad the oldest of five, and most of them are married with kids. Some of the kids even have kids."

"Wow," I say. "Your family get-togethers must take some doing."

Damien laughs. "Oh, yeah," he exclaims. "It's crazy."

"You ever thought of going back?"

Damien briefly presses his lips to mine. "I have reasons to stay."

I roll my eyes, but I'm smiling. "Cute."

"Belfast hasn't been home for a long time."

I nod in understanding. "Plus, Amy's here, and your dad."

Damien laughs. "I love my dad," he declares. "But it's best for everyone if we don't spend more than a couple of hours in the same room."

"That bad?"

"You should hear his opinions on music."

"Not a fan?"

Damien shakes his head. "You'll never amount to anything playing the guitar," he says in an imitation voice of, I'm assuming, his dad. "The Army is your only career."

I laugh. "He wasn't wrong though."

"No, he wasn't," Damien admits. "I always knew I'd join the Army. Not just for my dad but because I wanted to, for the experience. Difference was, my dad wanted a son who'd move up through the ranks like he did, but that was never my plan. He was seriously disappointed when I was medically discharged."

I smile weakly. I'd like to think his dad's disappointment is trumped by gratitude and happiness that his son managed to make it out alive, but if not, Damien's dad is not someone I look forward to meeting.

"I highly doubt you're a disappointment," I say instead. "You're too bloody perfect."

Damien chuckles. "That's one hell of a pedestal you got me on."

I shrug. "Prove me wrong."

"You want me to highlight my flaws?" I nod. "All right…" He mulls it over. "I can imagine you heard my snoring."

"I did," I admit. "But that's not a flaw."

"Okay," he says slowly. "I'm a fitness fanatic."

"Well, duh."

"Oh, no, I'm serious," he says. "Those fifty push-ups I did before bed, if I skipped them, I wouldn't sleep. And you ask Paul what I'm like if I miss my morning run. I'm basically a dick, stuck in a foul mood for the rest of the day. It's not a pretty sight." I laugh. "And…" He takes a deep breath. "Your clothes lying on the floor in the corner are driving me insane."

I lean up to spy my discarded clothes. I lack a washing basket, but I do make the effort to pick them up in the morning and pop them in the washer.

"Your music set-up too," he adds.

I furrow my brow in confusion. "What the hell is wrong with my music set-up?"

"The wires, babe," Damien clarifies, and for some weird reason, his use of *babe* awakens the butterflies. I've never, lost memories withstanding, been called babe before. "At least three of them were tangled, the microphone wire was trailing the floor like a bloody snake, *and* you put your guitar lopsided in its stand."

I let out a laugh, until I realise… "Wait, was? Past tense?"

Damien chuckles. "I sorted that shit whilst you were in the bathroom getting ready for bed."

I smile brightly. "Are you saying you've got OCD?"

"I wouldn't go as far as to say OCD," he says. "But yeah, I'm a neat freak, and I can't handle mess or clutter. It took all my strength not to clean up the smashed plates in your kitchen that night."

I burst out laughing before leaning in and planting a kiss of pure relief upon his lips. I pull away, and Damien shakes his head at me.

"You're far too happy about that," he comments.

"Sorry." I shrug. "But it's nice to know you're, you know, as human as the rest of us."

Damien and I continue to natter until exhaustion wins, and I fall back asleep. When six o'clock in the morning hits, Damien goes out for his unmissable run, and not an hour later, I'm honoured with another early morning visit from Jess, her desperation to get all the gory details taking over. She, of course, laughs far too hard upon the discovery Damien's suspected mistress is his sister, but when she then gives Damien the "if you hurt Dani, I'll kill you" speech upon his return, before heading off to work, all is forgiven.

Damien, unfortunately, goes right back to work too, and the rest of my day is spent helping Raif move in next door. He has a shitload of crap for one person, including a life-size mannequin, several framed pictures of Dolly Parton, and enough clothes to fill a shop. I'm not entirely sure where he's planning on putting it all given the flat is already full of Jess's stuff, but something tells me Raif will enjoy the unpacking part.

It's nice to spend some solo time with Raif, having not yet had the opportunity, and despite the hauling and heavy lifting, it's turning out to be a fun afternoon. Raif is hilarious, and his dramatic sense of humour is infectious. He loves to talk too, but I already knew that, and he's thoroughly enjoying filling me in on the ins and outs of all things Raif.

I'm already aware he's a born and bred Mancunian, learning from Damien he's Paul's cousin, and it's their dads who are the brothers. Although while we're on that subject, it is a little weird to think Paul was twelve when Raif was born, mostly because they are so close, and with such a large age gap, I wouldn't have expected it. I air my thoughts, and Raif goes on to tell me he and Paul have only gotten close in the past couple of years, ever since Paul's dad's dementia started to kick in, but before that, they really only saw each other at family get-togethers. Apparently, Raif never even met Damien before he uprooted to Manchester, which is remarkable considering how close Paul and Damien are, but anyway, I digress.

What I didn't realise though is Raif's mum is Italian. She moved to England with her parents when she was seven, and she met Raif's dad, a mechanic by trade, at university. Raif can speak fluent Italian too, demonstrating his ability with his usual flair, and he has family that still live over there, whom he visits when he can. His grandparents are still in Manchester though, and he sees them quite regularly.

I'm not surprised, however, to learn Raif's ultimate dream is to move to London to become a fashion designer, which explains the mannequin. Nor am I surprised Raif's love life is much like Jess's: a never-ending string of one-night stands. Rather him than me on both counts.

Raif does unfortunately ask me about my family, but for a

change, I don't hesitate on filling him in. I leave out the Adrian part, but I happily share my memory loss and my family's unfortunate deaths. He's shocked, as expected, but I merely shrug it off. I think, finally, I'm starting to come around to the whole talking malarkey, and although it's always painful to talk about my family, I don't feel uncomfortable or embarrassed. I feel oddly at ease, but that's probably Raif's naturally easing nature; he has a remarkable ability to take a shit situation or story and make it light-hearted. Some may find it offensive, but I find it endearing. I really like Raif, but then he's practically Jess's double, so how could I not?

My back killing me from all the lifting, I'm now sitting on my couch nursing a cup of coffee, conscious it's nearly half-five. Damien will be here at six for our official first date. When Damien mentioned taking me on a date before he left for work this morning, I did make a jibe about being a little past a first date, which Damien agreed with, but he's determined to take me out. I have no idea what he has in store, but I'm thinking I need at least a morsel of clarification because for the first time ever, I'm wondering what to wear.

I know you won't tell me what you've got planned, even though I hate surprises, but can you at least tell me if I need to attempt to pull something half decent from my suitcase to wear? xx

It takes a few minutes, about as long as it takes for me to finish my brew, for Damien to reply.

You don't need to dress up if that's what you're asking. I'm fully aware fancy, crowded places are not your scene. Plus, you're gorgeous the way you are xx

Forever smooth. My phone beeps an unexpected second time.

But while we're on the subject. Do you plan on unpacking those suitcases or should I be worried about you taking off in the night? xx

I can't help but laugh. I'm so used to living out of my suit-cases, but I can see how it would be weird to someone looking in from the outside.

You don't need to worry xx
Good to know. I'll see you soon xx

I potter about, deciding to stay dressed as I am in my usual style, and my door soon buzzes. I don't bother letting Damien in, chucking on my denim jacket, grabbing my phone and keys and heading straight outside. Damien is standing outside the main entrance dressed about as casual as I am in dark denim jeans and his usual figure-hugging T-shirt, a white one tonight, topped off with his trademark khaki jacket.

"Hey," he says, tilting in for a virtuous kiss.

"Hey," I reply. "We taking your car or mine?"

Damien looks at me like I've just asked him to strip naked in the middle of the car park, or something equally ridiculous.

"No offence," he says. "But your car is shit."

"Don't diss my car." I gently slap him on the arm. "Not all of us can afford a fancy BMW, Mr Self-Employed, and my car is as reliable as they come, thank you very much."

"You're cute when you're pissed," he says, and I bite back a smile.

"I figured you might want a drink," I state.

"There's no booze where we're going," he says, taking my hand and leading me to this car.

I slide into the passenger seat, and as Damien starts the en-gine, the speakers are filled with the sound of Oasis. Damien quickly turns the volume down.

"Oasis, huh?"

"Not a fan?" Damien asks, driving off.

"A little outdated, don't you think?"

"Oasis will *never* be outdated," he argues. "Connect your Bluetooth," he suggests, subtly reminding me just how fancy his car is, with its built-in Bluetooth, satnav, and hands-free phone calling. I'd be jealous but a car is what gets you from A to B as far as I'm concerned, and as long as it drives, I don't care about fancy gadgets. "Play whatever you want."

"Ooh," I tease. "You're gonna regret saying that."

Damien has opened a door, and I take the opportunity to wind him up a little, just for the fun of it. Damien cringes as I turn up the volume and loudly sing along to the sound of "Barbie Girl".

"My favourite," he says sarcastically, yet he's smiling.

"Or how about this one," I say, changing the song to "Yakety Yak", and Damien laughs.

"At least that one has some sentimental value," he says, and I smile at the memory of one of our earliest conversations.

"Classic." I shrug, but I've made my point, so I put Damien out of his misery and turn it off.

I quickly search for a decent playlist, press play, and happily sing along. I lose count of how many songs we get through, roughly a couple of hours' worth, before Damien pulls up in a large car park in a place called Keswick, somewhere I've heard of but never visited, and I resist the urge to groan. Keswick is in the Lake District, and what is the Lake District infamous for? Bloody walking. I shouldn't be surprised. Damien is an active guy, and as relationships are a two-way street, I guess I'm about to take a trip in Damien's shoes. Not literally, of course. I've got my trusty Converse trainers to keep my feet from aching.

I wait in the car whilst Damien gets out to pay for a ticket. When he returns, he rummages in the boot and pulls out a hiker-style backpack, slinging it over his shoulders, obviously well prepared for whatever I'm about to endure. Closing the boot, he swings around, opens the passenger door and holds out his hand. Smirking at his never-waning gentlemanly style, I take his hand, and we start to walk.

I let Damien lead me, keeping my hand entwined with his, capturing the breathtaking views of the neighbouring fields, and the beautiful large lake in the centre shimmering in the fading sunlight. That's a point, it's going to be dark soon. I'm not sure walking in the countryside in the dark is the best idea. I'm not scared, Damien is with me, but the countryside is not typically known for well-lit streets, and I'm wondering how the hell we're going to see where we're going.

"I hope you're up for walking," Damien says, pointing to a nearby hill that looks more like a mountain to me, and I stop dead, letting go of Damien's hand.

"You've got to be kidding me," I say. "I can't walk up that."

I stare at the hill. I'm the leisurely strolling type, you know, down the flat streets of Stanton that involve little to no effort. Actually, I don't walk anywhere, so I'm not sure what I'm talking about, but I'm definitely not the uphill struggle type. I suppress a laugh. If only I could say the same about the rest of my life.

"Yes, you can," Damien insists, retaking my hand and dragging me along.

"It's getting dark," I remind him. "How are we gonna…?" Damien opens his rucksack and pulls out two torches, one of which he thrusts in my direction.

I reluctantly let Damien lead me, focusing on putting one foot in front of the other and not falling flat on my face, but as I lift my head to look at the height, I'm hit with a sudden wave of nausea. I've never been afraid of heights, but considering the slope I'm climbing, today's as good as any to add a new phobia to my already long list.

I take note of the excitement radiating from Damien, like a kid in a sweet shop, but I don't see the appeal. It's a hill. It's walking. It's not like we're climbing Everest, although it feels like it to me. I stumble my way up, a little breathless as I try to keep up with Damien's effortless speed. I stop for a minute, around halfway up, I reckon, before practically falling to the path in a desperate need of a rest. Damien doesn't notice at first, continuing to walk ahead, but it finally clicks, and he turns back, sitting down next to me.

"You hanging in there?"

May I point out that Damien has an unfair advantage here? He's physically fit. Although I'll admit, I didn't realise just how unfit I am until right now, and I'm wondering if inserting a little exercise in my life isn't such a bad idea if only to build up a little stamina. I'm going to need it if I plan on keeping up with Damien.

"Please tell me," I say, catching my breath, "that there's a point to all this and we ain't just walking for the hell of it."

Damien chuckles. "I promise it will be worth it when we get to the top."

"I'm not sure I can make it to the top."

Damien climbs to his feet, grabbing my hands and dragging me up with him. "Do you think you can handle a piggyback?" he asks, referring to my no-touching deal.

I look at him, mulling it over. I guess I could give it a shot. It won't be his hands touching me, just me leaning against his back. Surely, that won't bring Adrian flashing to the surface. Except it's completely irrelevant.

"You can't piggyback me up there," I state. "I'll break your back."

"I've carried heavier weights than you, trust me," he argues. "Besides, you're as light as a feather, but then you don't eat enough." I roll my eyes at that. "So, are you hopping on or not?"

I sigh, but as I glance up at the height still left to climb, the decision is made for me. I nod, and Damien slides the backpack around his body, wearing it across his front before bending down a little to let me hop onto his back. I wrap my arms around his neck, and I can't help but plant a few kisses as he starts our ascent.

"That's a little distracting," he admits, though I can tell without looking he's smiling.

"Sorry," I say, though I'm not. "Couldn't resist."

Damien decides to show off, practically running the rest of the height, and I'm grateful for the lift. We reach the top within minutes, far quicker than if I had walked, and as I jump down from Damien's back, that's when I see exactly what Damien wanted me to see: the view.

"Wow," I mutter.

The thousands of lights below make the scenery look like a black canvas covered in stars, reflecting in the lake as it glistens in the newly formed moonlight. I feel like I'm standing in the middle of a glitterball and it's oddly beautiful.

"What a view," I say.

"Worth it?" he asks, and I turn to see him pulling a blanket from his backpack and laying it on the ground.

"Almost."

Damien sits on the blanket, standing his torch next to him, the light pointed towards the sky, and I join him, watching as he pulls several Tupperware boxes from the endless pit that is his backpack.

"You gonna pull a lamp from that bag too?" I joke.

"I was thinking more along the lines of a hat stand," he says, confirming he understood my Mary Poppins reference.

I glance down at the food Damien's prepared, noticing there's far too much: sandwiches, sausage rolls, vegetable sticks, what looks like mini chicken bites or maybe cheese bites, fruit and breadsticks with a selection of dips.

"You expecting company?" I ask.

"Just tuck in."

I oblige, picking up a breadstick and opting for the pink-coloured dip, though I'm not totally sure what flavour it is. Even when I taste it, I'm still not sure, other than it's a little spicy. Damien picks up a sandwich, taking a healthy bite, and a comfortable silence falls as we eat and take in the view that little bit more.

"It's so peaceful," I say, a little dreamily. "Can I ask why tonight though? I mean, I know the stars are gorgeous and that, but it must be just as peaceful during the day."

Damien smirks knowingly. "You'll see."

"Okay," I say, opting not to protest or pry, moving to sit in a cross-legged position facing him. "So, while we're waiting for whatever, I have a question to ask."

"Shoot."

"What's your favourite colour?"

Damien laughs. "My favourite colour, really? That's your question?"

"Yes," I say sternly. "I think we've had one too many heavy conversations to last a lifetime."

"Blue," he answers. "Yours?"

"Black," I reply. "Favourite film?"

"*Die Hard*."

"*Mary Poppins*," I answer his silent nod.

"Why am I not surprised?"

"Yeah, 'cause *Die Hard* is such an outrageous choice for an ex-Army boy," I say sarcastically. "Or a bloke, for that matter."

"Fair point," he agrees. "All right, I got one for you. Favourite song?" Now, that's a hard question.

"I honestly don't know," I admit. "There's too many to choose from. What about you?"

"'Your Song', Elton John."

"Really?" I ask, surprised.

"Hey," he protests. "I'm a sophisticated guy."

I laugh a little too loudly, and Damien pretends to be offended by my outburst by scowling at me. I can see a twinge of amusement though, and I apologise by leaning in and kissing him. Funnily enough, he accepts my apology without resistance, and his smile returns.

"What about favourite artist?" he asks, and the biggest grin creeps across my face.

"Oh, that's easy," I state. "You."

"Me?" He laughs.

"I could listen to your music all day every day."

"It's only half my music," he reminds me.

"In that case," I tease, "I have two favourites. You, and the mysterious lyricist from a long time ago."

Damien laughs at my theatrics. "Aren't you going to ask me who my favourite artist is?"

"Depends on if you're planning on being smooth," I mock.

"It would only be the truth."

"Come off it," I state. "My music ain't your style. My stuff's depressing."

"It's meaningful," he argues. "And it comes from the heart."

"Still not your style."

Damien sighs. "I like anything that's real. Music is tainted by what sells, and it shouldn't be about money. Music helped me through some of the darkest times in my life because it's an escape from the bullshit life throws at you. Music should be raw and meaningful, otherwise what's the point?"

I stare at Damien with fresh eyes, truly appreciating the man sitting in front of me. I said before that Damien understands the power of music but hearing him say it out loud is heart-warming. He's right in everything he says. Music is an outlet of pain and used in just the right way, it can help battle the demons. It's not a cure, but it's a comfort. I feel incredibly lucky to find someone who sees music the way I do.

"What?" he asks, breaking my trance.

"I just…" I'm searching for the words. "You amaze me."

Damien laughs. "How's that?"

"Because you always know what to say," I tell him. "And how to say it."

"I doubt that somehow," he chortles.

I reach over to take his hand in mine. "Well, don't doubt it," I insist. "And don't ever doubt how amazing you are either."

"Pot kettle black," he jokes, and I smile.

"I'm glad I came to my senses."

"Me too," he replies, kissing the back of my hand. "Although can I ask what it was that changed your mind?"

"Kayleigh," I answer honestly. "I told her that it takes one person to understand to drag you out of the bottomless pit of negativity…"

"You said that?"

I nod. "Because it's true. I don't know what kind of spell you've cast over me, but you got through to me." I sigh. "Seeing Kayleigh on that bridge… It reminded me that I was her once, but it also made me realise how far I'd come since then, and after going round and round in circles for the past three years, I finally figured out what I want."

"And what do you want?"

"Duh," I mock. "You." Damien smiles. "But for the record," I state, just in case, "I ain't with you because you've helped me. It's not some kind of weird I-owe-you thing."

Damien laughs. "The thought never even crossed my mind."

"I liked you from the second I saw you," I tell him. "And I hated the effect you had on me just by smiling." Damien flaunts that beautiful smile, and although I return it, I add in a shake of my head for dramatic effect. "Still do," I add, and Damien surprises me by not laughing, but leaning in close, pressing his forehead to mine.

"You have no idea the effect you have on me," he breathes heavily, stirring my heart into beating faster. "I have never wanted anyone as badly as I do you."

I sigh, the guilt setting in. "I wish I could…"

"Don't," he whispers. "I didn't mean it like that. I mean, I did, as in, I *do* want you, but I didn't mean it in that way. I just meant I'd have done anything to be with you, as crazy as that sounds. I just wanted to *know* you."

"And now you do," I say softly. "In all my fucked-up glory."

Damien sighs, unimpressed, yet smirking at my attempt at humour. He's about to say something, but he stops, opting to look at his watch instead. "Shit," he says. "You might want to look up at the sky 'cause the reason why I brought you here is about to happen."

I lie back on the blanket and stare up at the sky, the anticipation a little exciting. Damien lies beside me, leaning on one arm so he's slightly propped up, and that's when my eyes are drawn to what looks like a shooting star zipping through the sky, followed by an array of fireworks coming from the local town.

"Make a wish," Damien whispers in my ear.

"I don't need to," I say quietly as my eyes lock with his. "I have everything I could have wished for right here."

Damien leans in and kisses me with a longing that has my nerves standing on end. I wrap my arm around his neck, brushing my fingers through the back of his hair, pulling him closer. I feel the urge to melt into him, but when he slides a hand down my cheek, onto my neck towards my shoulder, I flinch. I hadn't wanted to, but I did, and the moment is gone quicker than a shooting star.

Chapter Seventeen

I manage to go all week without meeting the sister, spending my evenings with Damien, which can only be described as heaven. I've never been a fan of the American phrase *making out* – I hate the word *snogging* too – but since that's pretty much the best description to sum up this week's activities, I'll go with it. My songbook has doubled in size mind, albeit the second half is now titled collaborations, and I have no doubt a few of them will meander their way into Damien's band's set list.

The only downside is the lack of progress, touching wise, and Damien, being the patient gentleman he is, refuses to push. The first date flinch didn't help, but Damien continues to assure me he isn't going anywhere. He even apologised for forgetting himself, which was sweet, but should it be necessary? Hell no. He's got zilch to apologise for.

I know I'm being ridiculous. Damien would never hurt me, yet I'm still terrified one touch will make the flashbacks kick in with a determined vengeance, and the last thing I want to feel right now is pain. Thing is, as much as I feel guilty, I don't want to take the step for Damien. He's an important factor, obviously, but I want to do it for *me*. I want some tiny morsel of closure, to know Adrian's hold over me is at the very least dwindling. But more than anything, I want to be able to have a physical relationship with cuddling and touching. I want to be intimate in the basic sense at least.

The only night I don't spend with Damien is Thursday, and it's back to a three-person endeavour. Raif has decided, as my new neighbour, he qualifies to tag along, but since I like Raif, I don't mind. We spent far more time nattering and laughing than we did paying attention to the film though, and the more I watched Jess and Raif together, the more I smiled. They really are two peas in a pod, and after Jess's lack-of-friends admission, I'm glad she has Raif. I'm all for the friendship thing, now anyway, but even if my confidence grows, my disdain for shopping and partying never will, so I'm glad Raif is around to fill my shoes in those areas.

Despite her claim to be incapable of making friends, Jess is obviously improving since she's spent today with Amy, which isn't helping my nerves any. I know Jess wouldn't spill my personal horrors – there was a time I thought she would, which is a sign of just how far Jess and I have come – but I do know she will have spent the entire day talking about Damien and me, and I can imagine she hasn't hesitated in calling me an idiot more than I would like.

To top things off, as if my brain wasn't enough to contend with, I'm even more restless thanks to a phone call I received this morning. I knew it was coming, though I didn't expect it to be today, and the worst has officially happened. Lloyd's has closed its doors for good. I'm now down a job, leaving me with the thirteen hours I work for Dave, which is nowhere near enough to pay the bills.

Just the thought of starting a new job and learning the ropes all over again makes me want to throw up. Lloyd's wasn't much, but it was comfortable, and I knew what to expect. Add in the added complication of finding a job that fits around Dave's – I'm not giving up Dave's – in an already strapped working economy, I'm dreading what I'm going to end up taking for the sake of making money. So yeah, meeting Amy right now is just one more stress to add to my day.

After a full day's work at Dave's and a quick nip home for a change of clothes, I'm parking my car and heading inside Damien's, on edge and fully aware my stress levels are doomed to increase. I'm expecting a grilling because let's face it, Amy's going to have questions for the woman in her brother's life, and even though every part of me wants to turn and run for the hills, out of nothing more than pure embarrassment, I know I can't. Amy is Damien's sister and meeting the family is standard in any relationship, and I *do* want to meet Amy. I just wish I hadn't made such a shitty first impression.

Walking through Damien's door, I'm not at all surprised to find Jess here. Nor am I surprised there are two empty bottles of wine sitting between her and who I'm assuming is Amy. Although Damien is nowhere to be seen.

"Damien not back from work yet?" I ask.

Jess shakes her head. "Must be running late." She shrugs. "No text?"

"No," I answer, swiftly pulling out my phone and sending Damien a message asking where he is.

"Well, while we're waiting," Jess says, "Dani, meet Damien's sister, Amy."

"It's nice to meet you," she says as I nab a seat at the opposite side of the island, facing her. "I've heard a lot about you."

"Oh, I bet," I reply, turning my attention to a grinning Jess.

"I promise," Amy says, "Jess has had nothing but nice things to say."

"You and Damien make a great topic of conversation," Jess teases. "So, how's your day been?"

I sigh. "Shit." I'm met with a round of confused faces. "Dave's was fine, but Lloyd phoned to say he's shut up shop for good."

"Lloyd's is a café, right?" Amy asks, and I nod.

BROKEN

"Not overly glamorous, I know."

"I'm a part-time cleaner," Amy says, and I laugh – equally unglamorous.

"I'm sure you'll find something else," Jess reassures.

"Preferably before I run out of money."

I'm so full of shit. I have plenty of money. I just don't like to share that fact, nor do I like dipping into it either. It's my emergency money, the money I was left by my family, and it's a safety net. My paranoid side hates the thought of using it in case the shit hits the fan, whatever the shit may be, and I need it to start a new life again. I mentally punch my paranoid side hard. How the hell can I even think about such a ridiculous thing when I've just started a relationship with Damien? If he knew what I was thinking, he'd not only be insulted, he'd be hurt. My paranoia needs to fuck right off.

"So," Amy says, changing the subject, "I hear you're the musical type."

"I take it you're not?"

"I haven't got a musical bone in my body," she says, shaking her head.

"Me neither," Jess concurs.

"I like *listening* to music if that counts," Amy says, and I laugh. It's not quite the same thing. "I'm a math geek."

If I were writing a book on stereotypes, Amy would not fall into the "math geek" bracket. The good-looking American-style cheerleader, and the most popular girl at school is a better fit. She's a really pretty lass, with short brown hair falling to just above her shoulders, and a subtle dress sense if today's outfit is anything to go by: a simple light blue vest top and black skinny jeans paired with a pair of stilettos even Jess will be envious of. Her make-up is very understated too, very natural and tastefully done.

"An academic type," I say, impressed.

"Damien tells me you have an amazing singing voice," Amy adds. "I'd love to hear you sing." There's a plea behind Amy's statement.

"Ha-ha," I fake laugh. "I don't sing for people."

"That's a barefaced lie," Jess scoffs.

It takes me a minute to realise what the hell she's talking about, but when I do, I cringe. "Bollocks," I say. "I'd forgotten about that."

"About what?" Amy asks.

"Paul dragged Dani on stage for karaoke at his daughter's birthday party," Jess explains, before chuckling. "I still can't believe you did it."

"I had no choice," I argue. "I couldn't freak out at Kayleigh's party, could I?"

"Why would you freak out?" Amy asks, and I promptly regret my choice of words.

"Stage fright," Jess answers for me. "Not that she's got anything to be afraid of. It was the first time I'd heard Dani sing, and she was amazing."

"Oh, come on," Amy pleads. "Sing us something."

"Damien's the performer," I argue. "Get him to sing something." If he ever gets here.

"Speaking of Damien," Jess says, almost seductively. "How are things going?"

"I sincerely doubt Amy wants to hear the gory details."

Amy nods in eager agreement. "That's right, I don't, especially when you're all he can talk about." I smile. "He's definitely smitten. You sure you've only been his girlfriend for a week?"

Girlfriend. The word hits me like a ton of bricks. Damien and I have yet to put a label on our relationship, but the thought of being called Damien's girlfriend is a little terrifying, yet exciting. Slightly dampened by a glance at my phone, and the lack of a reply from said "boyfriend".

"They've been falling for each other for over a month," Jess pitches in.

"You've been paying *way* too much attention," I tease Jess. "Next you'll be telling me the exact date Damien first walked into Lloyd's."

"Do you even know?" Jess asks.

"No," I admit. "But I bet Damien does."

"He is a stickler for detail," Amy agrees. "And routine, and tidiness. You know he's borderline OCD, right?" I smile and nod.

"Isn't that backwards?" Jess asks. "Isn't it typically the women who remember dates?"

"At least he'll never forget an anniversary."

"One week, and she's talking about anniversaries," Jess teases, and in the midst of my laughter, I notice Amy eying Jess and me with amusement.

"What?" I ask.

"You two are kind of cute," she replies.

"That's because she's my best mate," I tell her.

"Did you just call me your best friend?" Jess asks smugly. Yes, I did. Out loud as well. What on earth was I thinking?

"Don't make a big deal out of it," I say, attempting to play it down. "Unless it's not true?"

"Oh, I don't know." She's enjoying this far too much. "I have so many to choose from." Except we all know she doesn't, unless Raif is pipping me to the post. I pull a sarcastic ha-ha face at her and she laughs, ending her charade. "It's true."

The sound of Damien's door opening is a distraction for all of us, but my excitement is dulled when I realise it's not Damien. It's Raif.

"Oh, God help me," I say sarcastically.

"Well, hello to you too, honey," Raif says, taking the last remaining stool between Jess and me.

"I wonder who invited you," I say.

"Technically," Jess defends, "I didn't invite him. Raif texted asking where I was, the rest is all him."

"I'm assuming you've met Raif," I say to Amy, and she nods. "Lucky you."

"I'm going to choose to ignore the sarcasm," Raif declares, "and take that as a compliment." I smirk. "Where is lover boy anyway?"

On cue, my phone rings, only I'm left disappointed a second time. It's Paul.

"Dani." Paul's voice sounds deeper on the phone somehow. "Damien's in the hospital."

My heart stops. "What?"

"He's been in some sort of attack," Paul explains.

"An attack?" I practically squeal, the colour draining from my face.

"I don't know the details," Paul says. "I'll meet you at the hospital." Paul hangs up, and I drop my phone to the counter in a daze.

"Dani?" Jess asks.

"Damien's been attacked."

I head for the door. I can hear Amy panicking, and Jess and Raif muttering. With shaky legs, I race to my car with my friends hot on my heels. My mind is whirling like a tornado,

Paul's words echoing relentlessly like a bad song on repeat. Starting the engine, I speed through the busy streets as best I can, grateful it's Saturday, and the teatime rush isn't as bad as normal.

It's taking everything in me not to spiral into a panic attack right now. Damien's been attacked, and I have no idea how bad. A thousand thoughts are running through my mind, not one of them good, and my heart is threatening to break through my rib cage it's pounding that hard. Damien has to be okay. I *need* him to be okay. I almost lost him once, I can't lose him for real. Not before I…

I let a stray tear fall. I've wasted so much time panicking about being touched, about my past and everything else that goes on in my warped mind, and now there's a chance I'm too late. I may never feel the warmth of Damien's embrace or the feel of his skin against mine. Damien has given me a reason to live again, dragging me from the darkness until I'm bathing in light, and I've been so wrapped up in my own selfish bullshit to show him just how much he means to me. What if…

No! Damien is going to be fine. I'm going to walk into that hospital and find him sitting on a bed alive and in one piece. Now's as good a time as any to start thinking positive, and I'm praying to a god I don't believe in that it pays off, just this once.

A lifetime of driving passes. I arrive at the hospital and park my car. I quick realise Paul didn't clarify Damien's whereabouts, so I hedge my bets and head for the accident and emergency department. Wiping my sweaty palms on my jeans, I spot Paul talking to what looks like a nurse over by the double doors that lead to the ward. I rush to his side just as the nurse takes her leave.

"Paul," I say. "Is he okay?"

"He's okay," he says gently. Oh, thank God. I cannot tell you how much I needed to hear that.

"Can we see him?" I ask.

"Not all at once," Paul explains, and both he and I look to Amy. "I can hang back," he offers.

"It's okay," Amy says. "You two go first."

"Thank you," I say gratefully.

Paul leads me through the double doors and down a corridor. I let Paul do the talking, but when a nurse points to a bed in the far corner, the relief that sweeps over me is indescribable.

Damien's sitting on the edge of the bed as a nurse takes his blood pressure. I hang back for a minute, fighting back the tears forcing their way to the backs of my eyes as I wait for the nurse to leave. Damien's eye is black, his lip swollen and his cheek red, and there are a few bruises appearing on his bare arm. There's a bloodstained gauze on the side of his head, but he's alive and breathing, and that's all that matters.

The nurse finally leaves, and as I move, Damien spots me. The tears are refusing to be fought and are now flowing steadily down my cheeks; tears of relief, I think. Leaving all my fears and anxieties in the wind along with Paul, I race over to his bed and practically throw myself at him. I almost knock him backwards onto the bed, but he manages to keep his balance as I wrap my arms around his neck. I hear his breath hitch, but his hesitation soon evaporates, and he wraps his arms around me. I instinctively tense, but my tears of relief turn to tears of happiness when all I feel is warmth and comfort, flashback and pain-free. I bury my head into his shoulder, letting myself cry into his blood-stained T-shirt.

"Dani," he says softly.

Lifting my head, Damien stares into my tearful eyes, a

mixture of elation and surprise etched into his battered and bruised face. I kiss him. He kisses me back with a longing mirroring my own – if his swollen lip is hurting, he's not letting on – until my emotion-fuelled anger kicks in.

"You don't get to do that," I say harshly. "You don't get to scare me like that."

"Hey," he says softly. "I'm okay."

"What the hell happened?"

"Two guys came out of nowhere and attacked me from behind with a bat," Damien explains. "I put up a fight, but…" His voice trails off.

"They could've killed you," I screech.

"Hey," he says gently, wiping away my tears. "I've got a few cuts and bruises. I'd say I got off lucky." He has a valid point. Things could have played out much, much worse, but I'm far too emotional to think straight. "Besides, if I knew getting battered would have you throwing your arms around me, I'd have done it sooner."

I lower my head, my upset replaced with guilt. It shouldn't have happened like this. A massive milestone in our relationship only happened because, for a split second, I thought I might lose him. Damien has stood by me no matter what drama or revelation I threw at him, wanting me in spite of all that, and I should've known from the start letting Damien touch me could never have been anything other than everything I want and need.

"I was joking," he adds, probably reading the anguish on my face. Using his finger, he lifts my head to look at him.

"I didn't want it to happen like this."

"I don't care how it happened, Dani." He pulls me in closer and places a chaste kiss on my lips. "Just that it happened."

Always so rational, and the perfect ointment to my forever-open wound of negativity. I kiss him like there's no tomorrow and with every ounce of relief and gratitude pouring through me.

"All right," I hear Paul's voice behind me. "It's not a private room."

I pull away from Damien and grab the curtain, pulling it around and leaving Paul on the opposite side out of view. Damien laughs, but Paul quickly reopens the curtain.

"Very funny," he mocks, taking a seat on the resident chair that sits by the hospital bed. "I did tell you he was okay."

"Excuse me for being happy about that," I say sarcastically, sitting down on the bed next to Damien, his arm wrapping around my waist.

"We're all happy about that, lass," Paul says. "Are they keeping you in?"

"Nah," Damien answers. "My CT's clear. I'm just waiting on the doctor to sign off on my discharge."

"Twats." Paul shakes his head in disgust. "There are some days I wonder what the hell happened to civilisation. The bloody Army is more civilised than the youth of today."

Whilst I totally agree, I can't help but smirk. "Youth of today," I repeat. "You do know how you just sounded, right?"

"Like my dad," Paul admits. "Except now I get where he's coming from."

"It's not just youths, mate," Damien pitches in. "Whoever the pricks were, they were fully grown men."

"That only makes it worse," Paul grumbles. "Did you get a good look at them?"

"Hoodies and scarves, mate." Damien is clearly less than impressed. "Not a clue."

"Have the police been to see you?" I ask.

"I gave a statement at the scene," Damien explains.

"Were there witnesses?" Paul asks.

"Just the two guys who intervened," Damien says. "Saving me from a cracked skull." I shake my head, appalled. "I'm more pissed off the bastards got my phone."

Beating the crap out of someone for the sake of a phone. We really do live in a seriously twisted society, and people wonder why the idea of stepping out my front door is such an anxiety-inducing experience.

"What about your wallet?" Paul asks.

"Safe and sound in my back pocket."

"That's odd," Paul says. "Why would they leave your wallet?"

"Who knows?" Damien shrugs. "But I fucking dare them to take another shot *without* a bat."

I think someone's pride is damaged.

"Just be grateful you're in one piece," I say, shaking my head at him. "I am."

"Dani's right, mate," Paul backs me up. "Two on one with a baseball bat, you're lucky you got a hit in." Damien merely grumbles. "But anyway, I'd stick around, but I'm sure Amy's eager to get in here, and I promised Kayleigh I'd drive over with some more of her stuff."

"Drive where?" I ask.

"My sister's place in Salford," Paul answers, unable to hide the disappointment in his tone. "Kayleigh wanted to get away for a while and school have agreed, given the circumstances, she can study at home for the next couple of weeks whilst the police are still investigating. I'd rather have her at home, but I get she needs the space."

"It won't be forever," I tell him. "And it's not personal against you, remember that. It's not you she's trying to get away from."

"Yeah, I know," Paul sighs. "I just wish I could do more to help her."

"You're doing everything you can, mate," Damien encourages. "Now, go on, get yourself away, and tell Kayleigh we say hi."

Paul rises to his feet and gives Damien a manly handshake, half hug, yet Damien keeps one arm firmly wrapped around me the entire time.

"I'm really glad you're okay, mate," Paul says.

"Thanks."

Paul starts to walk away, but he stops a couple of metres away, turning back with a mischievous smile. "You make sure you take good care of him," he says directly to me, and there's just a little too much suggestion in his tone. "Be gentle though."

"Two words," I reply.

"Fuck off?" Paul answers for me, and I can't help but laugh. At least he can take a hint.

Paul disappears out into the corridor, and I lean my head into Damien's chest, wrapping my arms around his stomach and back, holding on tight. "I should go get Amy."

"No," he says, lying down on the bed. He pulls me along with him, wrapping his arm around my shoulder as I nuzzle my head into his chest. "I want you to stay right here."

"I'm pretty sure visitors ain't supposed to lie on the beds."

"I'm pretty sure I don't give a shit," Damien says bluntly, his hand rhythmically stroking my back.

I lie in Damien's arms, revelling in his warmth and the tingling sensation coursing through me at the feel of his fingers

229

running the length of my spine. It's not quite the way I wanted my anxieties to be lifted, but it'll do, and it's without a doubt the greatest feeling I have ever felt.

"Do you have any idea how amazing this feels?" he asks.

"What's that?"

"Holding you."

"About half as amazing as it feels for me," I state. "I want to lie here forever."

Damien chuckles. "Maybe not in the hospital."

I get that. I've spent far too much time in hospitals too, and I had hoped to avoid one for as long as humanly possible.

"I don't care where I am," I say soppily. "As long as you're with me."

Damien lifts my head, leans in and kisses me with a fiery passion that has my stomach doing backflips.

"This isn't a dream, right?" he suddenly asks. "I haven't hit my head so hard I'm hallucinating?"

"It's real," I say, laughing. "I promise."

I lean in and kiss him once more, as though to prove my reality. Our little moment is interrupted by the arrival of Amy, Jess and Raif. "Not all at once" has clearly gone out of the window.

"Oh, my God." Jess beams, her eyes on me. "You're…" She looks to Raif and Amy. I'm assuming she's realising they have no clue as to my issues surrounding touching, and she quickly remembers herself. "Alive," she says, using Damien as a cover-up, yet looking at me with a proud smile only I understand.

Reluctantly, I force myself to sit up, moving to the edge of the bed. Amy immediately starts fussing over her brother, and Jess takes advantage, luring me away to help her carry the coffees she's conveniently offered to buy. I inwardly shake my head at her inability to wait for the low-down, and the second we're out in the corridor, away from prying ears, Jess pounces.

"Start talking," she orders. "Like right now."

"I have no idea what you're talking about." I don't half get a kick out of winding her up.

"Don't." She points a finger at me.

"Turns out," I say, "my fear of losing Damien, as in *losing* him, losing him, outweighs everything."

Jess squeals. "I can't believe it. I mean, how did it happen? What did you do?"

"I ran and threw my arms around him," I answer.

"Just like that?" The simplicity is not lost on me either.

I nod. "I guess they ain't wrong when they say trauma has a way of putting things into perspective."

Jess squeals again, gaining a few questioning eyes from fellow visitors, and she quickly stops. "I know the circumstances are crap," she says, and I nod in agreement, "but how great is it something unbelievably amazing came out of something that could have been potentially disastrous?"

"Thank God it wasn't."

"But at least now," she gushes, "you can make the most of that personal trainer body Damien's got going on."

I laugh. "Don't ever change, Jess. Ever."

"Of course not," she declares. "Just think how boring life without me would be."

I can't argue with that. Jess and I hunt down some coffee and carry them back to the others. I plonk myself back down beside a frustrated-looking Damien, which I'm assuming is Amy's do-ing, and he wraps his arm around me. I look up at him and smile. I stare into those sky-blue eyes, my gaze lingering even when Amy steals his focus, and I find myself counting my lucky stars.

Damien's patience, beauty and understanding are second to none, and there's no one in this world I'd rather be with right now. Maybe, just maybe, Damien is my chance at happiness. A chance I'm going to grab with both hands and never let go.

Chapter Eighteen

I wake up screaming and covered in sweat. An arm wraps around me, causing my heart to race even faster, if that's possible, until I realise it's just Damien. I sigh with relief, turning over and burrowing my entire body into Damien's warmth as my nightmare sits on replay. With a desperate need to feel safe, I cling to Damien as though letting go would make me crumble into nothing but ashes and dust. Damien holds me tight, running his fingers gently up and down my back.

"You're shaking like a leaf," he says.

"Sorry."

"Don't be sorry," he insists. "Just tell me how to make it better."

"Just hold me," I say quietly, silently rejoicing in the fact he can, despite my current anxious state.

I cannot even begin to describe how amazing it feels to have Damien's arms around me right now, about as amazing as it felt to fall asleep to the sound of his heartbeat last night. It feels like a dream, if I'm honest, like I'm about to wake up at any minute, still the same don't-touch-me mess I was only yesterday, except it's not a dream, and after my usual mind-numbing wake-up call, Damien's touch is all the comfort I need.

Damien insisted on staying at mine last night, mostly to avoid dealing with a freaked-out Amy, but I didn't take much convincing. A combination of wanting to fall asleep in his arms and a desire to keep an eye on him in case any symptoms of a concussion flared was all the motivation I needed to agree.

"Go back to sleep," I urge Damien. "You need to rest."

"I'm getting up for a run anyway," he tells me, and my head

shoots up faster than a speeding bullet.

"Are you kidding?" I ask in disbelief, and Damien irks me further by laughing.

"I'm fine," he insists. "I need to keep my routine up."

"One day won't kill you," I argue. "The doctor said to take it easy for a day or two."

"And I will," he argues back. "I'll only hit four miles instead of eight."

"You're an idiot," I state. "Don't come crying to me when you've got extra aches and pains. You won't get any sympathy from me."

"Yes, ma'am," he mocks, offering an Army-style salute to boot. I ignore his poor attempt at humour by lying back down with my back to him. "Is that how you're gonna play it?"

"Yes."

"You know you're cute when you're pissed, right?" he says, wrapping his arm around my waist and gracing my neck with a few soft kisses.

"You may have mentioned that before," I state, pretending the feel of his lips on my body isn't sending my nerves into a tailspin.

"I promise I'll come back in one piece," he says. "And when I do, I'm taking you out."

"I might not want to go out." I'm not done being arsy just yet, but Damien merely laughs, disappearing off to the bathroom to get sorted for his run.

Within minutes, Damien's back, fully kitted out in the running gear he evidentially packed in the overnight bag we detoured to collect on the way home from the hospital. He squats in front of me, leaning in for a soft, gentle kiss.

"I'll be back in a bit."

Damien leaves. I don't go back to sleep, opting to help myself to a much-needed coffee before showering and heading back into my bedroom to get dressed. I didn't even hear Damien return, but when he enters the bedroom, I'm only half-dressed in my jeans and bra, and I instinctively cover my scars with my top.

"You don't have to hide your scars from me, Dani."

"Why would you want to see them?" I ask. "I don't."

Damien shakes his head, unimpressed by my honesty. Attempting to push my insecurities aside, I don't stop Damien from taking my top and throwing it on the bed.

"Because they are a part of you," he says. "Just like mine are me."

Damien's talking about the surgery scar that sits at the bottom of his spine, and a small, self-defence training, knife-fight-gone-wrong scar that sits upon his shoulder blade. Apparently, there's another that lies underneath his tattoo as a result of a bullet that grazed his arm, but the ink does a good job of making it invisible. Considering the time Damien spent in Afghanistan, his battle scars are pretty minimal.

"You don't have to prove –" Damien puts a finger to my lips to silence me, but I manage to get in a roll of my eyes before he pulls me close and kisses my lips.

Pulling away, his lips graze each scar, one by one. He starts at my shoulder and works his way down to just above my waistline. I can't quite describe how I feel, but it's somewhere between embarrassed and quivery, yet it's not a scared quiver, it's one of desire, which surprises me a little.

Damien makes his way back up my body, one painfully slow kiss at a time, and by the time his lips meet mine, my insecurities have evaporated, replaced with a warmth and longing that overwhelms me.

"You're beautiful," he tells me, adding a few extra kisses to my neck. "Scars included. And when the day comes, whenever that may be, I plan on showing you just how beautiful you are."

My stomach is doing somersaults, but Damien is already pulling away, chucking my top back at me, and I'm even more surprised at how disappointed I feel. My entire body is prickling with excitement, and my bed is suddenly looking highly inviting.

"You okay?" Damien asks.

"Uh-huh," I answer, popping on my top, but I'm not sure I really heard the question. My mind's a little preoccupied. "Just really hoping a drama-free day with my boyfriend is an actual possibility." That's my way of distracting my wandering thoughts with a daily dose of paranoia. Damien's new-found bad luck in the form of a battering has got me a little more nervous than normal, though I've yet to air my concern aloud.

Damien moves close and pulls me into his arms. "You know, that's the first time you've called me your boyfriend."

"Is it?" I act dumb despite knowing he is spot on in his observation. "Well, I don't remember you calling me your girlfriend yet."

"I thought it was a given."

"So did I," I state. I totally didn't, but Damien doesn't need to know that.

"Liar." Apparently, he can see right through me.

"I don't need to put a label on how I feel about you."

"And how *do* you feel about me?"

Well played once again. "That depends," I tease. "Do you mean right his second…?"

Damien laughs. "I'm not gonna bite."

"Wise choice."

One shower for Damien later, and we're heading out the door. I drive given Damien is supposed to be resting, but after listening to Damien moan about how shit my car is for the first thirty minutes, I silence him by threatening to abandon him on the motorway hard shoulder. It's annoying enough having to rely on Damien giving me directions, his refusal to tell me where we're going never-waning, but when he directs me onto the M55, I smirk.

"Blackpool," I state. "Huh."

"What do you mean 'huh'?" Damien asks, lacking a denial.

"I didn't peg you for a Blackpool fan."

"Who doesn't love Blackpool?" Damien scoffs.

"Possibly me," I say. "I wouldn't know, would I?" Have I been? Who knows?

"*Everyone* loves Blackpool," Damien assures me.

Once off the M55, I navigate through the promenade traffic until I find a car park with a space. Despite Damien's chivalrous protest, I get out to pay for an overpriced ticket, and hand in hand, we head to our first destination, Blackpool Pleasure Beach. I have a funny feeling I'm going to learn a lot about myself today. I don't even know if I've ridden a roller coaster before, but I'm intrigued to find out if I enjoy one.

Damien and I nab ourselves a wristband, and we spend the next few hours riding every roller coaster in sight. Damien is a natural thrill-seeker, we all know that, but as it turns out, I love roller coasters. Adrenaline pumped, Damien and I head off for a spot of lunch, and Damien's healthy eating takes a nosedive. He happily indulges in an enormous burger while I finish half of my hot dog, and I make a mental note to wind him up about the calories later in the day. Damien drags me on one last roller coaster, the biggest one, and as the ride plunges downwards, I'm regretting my decision to eat. My food is threatening to resurface, and I think I'm officially done with being spun in every direction.

Next stop is minigolf, and I've finally found something Damien is rubbish at. It's a freaking miracle, and I take the opportunity to wind him up relentlessly. Damien takes it on the chin, but when he accidentally loses his ball to a golf-ball-eating bush, my laughter is uncontrollable. Damien scowls as he rummages around to retrieve it, throwing me an I've-had-enough glance en route back to the windmill designed putt. Luckily for him, we've only one hole left, and it's the best hole yet. I bag myself a hole in one to finish, and Damien shakes his head in disbelief. I've well and truly kicked his arse, and his competitive side is groaning, I can tell.

Damien abandons his sulky demeanour as soon as we reach the arcades. I don't know how long we spend wasting an absolute fortune on ten pence machines, zombie shooting, Mario Kart racing, and every other activity the arcades have to offer, but by the end, we've managed to snag enough tickets for Damien to buy me a plastic love heart bracelet. It probably costs a mere pound to buy, and although it makes me feel about twelve, it's a result of hard work, and it's sweet, so I'm wearing it with pride.

My cheeks hurting from the endless laughter, Damien and I head out on to the promenade, walking hand in hand.

"So, what next?" I ask, but Damien isn't listening. He's too busy looking up ahead at a band playing in the distance.

Damien leads me a little faster, and to my surprise, we join a bunch of couples, mostly of the older generation, for a dance. I can't dance, but it's a slow enough song, so I let Damien lead me, one arm wrapped around my waist, the other cupping my hand. I can't help but laugh. I feel ridiculous, but I don't even care. For once, I'm enjoying the moment, the smile on my face becoming a permanent fixture. At least until Damien, in all his wisdom, decides to spin me around, and I almost squeal in surprise. He pulls me back in and lowers my back towards the ground, flashing me that beautiful smile, and I laugh hard. He silences me by kissing me like there's no one watching, only there's a lot of people watching, and when he pulls me back up, the blush rushes to my cheeks.

Shaking my embarrassment aside, Damien and I head onto the beach, and I'm grateful to take a minute to sit and rest. I know Damien is active, but I'm knackered, and surely, after the attack only yesterday, even Damien's got to be feeling the effects. I sit between Damien's propped-up legs, my back against his chest, Damien's arm wrapped around my waist. I place my arms over his, my hand gently caressing his hand, and as I stare out into the sunset, I smile at how perfect today has been. This, lying in my boyfriend's arms on a beach after a day filled with laughter and fun is exactly what life should be, and I want more. I want to make the most of every second. I close my eyes for a few minutes, letting the breeze fan my face.

"What are you thinking?" Damien asks.

"I'm thinking," I say, "that this is what I want for my future. Endless moments of bliss. No stress. No worries. Just happiness."

Damien caresses my lips with his, and when he pulls away, those sky-blue eyes burn into me with a mesmerising intensity.

"I will spend the rest of my life making you happy," he says, and although things between Damien and me are moving faster than I ever thought they would, his words don't scare me. They excite me in ways I never thought possible. "I love you, Dani."

My breath hitches. "I am madly, crazily, deeply in love with you."

I sit there, paralysed to the spot, eyes wide, jaw dropped, and absolutely floored by Damien's use of the L-word. Love. Such a simple, yet powerful word. The kind of word that can either make a situation or break it into a thousand pieces. A word that can bring comfort and happiness yet a whole new world of pain, a songwriter's paradise. I write songs about love all the time, and I know I loved my family, but do I understand what love really is? I stare into Damien's eyes and smile.

"I can't believe I'm saying this," I answer, "but I love you too."

"I know," he teases, laughing. "I'm a lovable guy."

I roll my eyes. "Way to ruin a moment." He apologises by kissing me, and I accept his apology wholeheartedly. "In all seriousness, I never thought I'd ever be able to feel love, or that anyone *could* love me –"

"That's 'cause you're an idiot," he interrupts, and I slap him on the chest.

"Sorry," I offer, clocking his wince. "Your determination to *not* take it easy is making me forget."

"So, *you* hit *me*," he declares. "And it's *my* fault."

"Yes," I say. "But I am sorry it hurt."

"Everything hurts," he admits.

"And you call me an idiot."

Damien instantly softens, running a finger down my cheek. "You're not an idiot," he assures, yet there's a warmth to his voice that excites me. "You are the most amazing woman I have ever met." Smooth. "To go through what you have, and still be the selfless, kind, beautiful woman you are is mind-blowing. And you can give me all the credit you want, but I know everything you've overcome has got jack shit to do with me."

"That's not true," I argue. "I only pushed myself because you gave me a reason to."

"Why is irrelevant," he argues. "The fact is you did. *You* were the only one who could change things, Dani, and you overcame a shedload before I came along."

That's true. If Damien had shown up a couple of years ago, it wouldn't have mattered what he did. If you think I'm broken now, the anxieties I have today are nothing compared to those I experienced in the months, a year even, after Adrian. I guess Damien showed up exactly when I needed him.

"You should be proud of how far you've come," Damien adds. "I know I am."

"Deep down, I am proud," I admit. "But that doesn't mean you didn't play a part. Therapy helped me to step out of the traumatised mess I was in and gave me the basic tools to survive, but you've given me a reason to actually *live*. You've reminded me happiness is real, and I deserve it just as much as anyone else."

"You deserve it *more* than anyone else," Damien states.

"Well, in the words of this unbelievably amazing and gorgeous guy I know," I tease, gaining me a smirk, "I don't care how we got here. Just that we did." I lift my hand to Damien's cheek. "And I'm done looking back. All I want to do now is look to the future. A future with you." Damien smiles that beautiful smile, and I snuggle back into his chest, staring out at the sea. "I don't want today to end."

"I'm so glad you said that."

Damien doesn't elaborate, rising to his feet and dragging me along with him. I probe him relentlessly during the forty-five-minute drive back to Damien's home, but I'm left none the wiser. Feeling excited, confused and a little dubious about the apparent surprise Damien has in store, I'm letting Damien lead me inside. And when he opens the door, I'm rendered speechless.

I'm standing in the entrance to Damien's home, feeling like I've walked into one of those romantic, chick-flicks Jess makes me watch far too regularly. The entire flat is covered in candlelight, the fake tealight kind, and Damien's coffee table is in the centre covered with a white tablecloth, set for dinner for two. On top sits a beautiful bouquet of roses, and there's a cushion on the floor at each end of the table – Damien's version of table and chairs. It's beautiful, and I can't stop the beaming smile from creeping across my lips.

I'm about to say something when Elton John's "Your Song" fills the room, and that's when I spot Amy over by Damien's music set-up, smiling like the Cheshire cat.

"I will leave you guys to it," Amy says, giving Damien a quick hug before leaving and closing the door behind her.

I stand for a minute, taking in the smell of food coming from the kitchen, not that I'm at all hungry, wondering what I've done to deserve such a romantic setting. I feel Damien's hands on my shoulders as he slides off my jacket, and I turn to face him. He chucks my jacket onto the nearest stool and smiles that beautiful smile.

"What's all this for?" I ask.

"Do I need a reason to have a romantic meal with my girl-friend?" I guess not.

"*When* did you do all this?" I ask, though the answer should be obvious.

"I didn't," he admits. "I got Amy to do it. And Amy will be spending the night at yours tonight. I hope you don't mind."

"Not at all," I say, wrapping my arms around his neck. "If it means we get the place to ourselves."

"If I didn't know any better," he mutters, lifting me, my legs wrapping around his waist, "I'd say you were flirting with me."

"And if I didn't know any better," I tease, as Damien carries me and sits me down on the island, "I'd say *you* were trying to seduce me."

"Do you *want* me to seduce you?" he asks, dropping his playful tone in favour of a soft, yet serious voice.

I bite my lip, that all-too-familiar self-conscious feeling reawakening. Surprisingly though, even though Adrian is always at the back of my mind, it's the fear of not living up to expectation, shall we say, that's got me feeling extra nervous. Let's get realistic here. Damien is hot, and I have no doubt he has plenty of notches on his belt, notches that I could never measure up to. Sex equals pain, that's all I've ever known, and the thought of being a disappointment fills me with a new-found dread that sickens me to my stomach. I feel like a virgin, only I'm not a virgin, I'm worse. I'm damaged goods. My concerns must be evident in my face because Damien is scowling at me.

"I didn't do this," he says, "or tell you I love you to get you into bed, Dani. I did it because you deserve it. You deserve to be treated right."

"It's not…" I hesitate. "It's not what you think."

"Then what?" he asks. "What's going on in that head of yours?"

I sigh. "It's embarrassing."

"Try me."

"I'm scared of…" How to put it. "Not living up to your previous conquests." I'm not sure how else to word it, though saying it out loud only makes my embarrassment levels soar.

BROKEN

"How many women do you think I've had?" he asks, sounding a little offended.

"Are you kidding?" I ask. "Look at you. You've probably had women throwing themselves at you your entire life."

"You're doing wonders for my ego." Damien laughs.

"I'm serious," I say, sighing. "You may be one in a million, but you're still male, and I'm not naïve enough to think you've been as patient and gentlemanly as you are now."

"Not all men are dogs in heat, babe."

I'm not convinced, and it's written all over my face. "It's got to be double figures, right?"

"Three," Damien says bluntly, and I almost fall off the island in surprise. Luckily, Damien is there to keep me rooted.

"Three?" I repeat, loudly and high-pitched. "How is that possible?"

"I spent a lot of time in the Army." Damien shrugs. "And I'm not a one-night stand kind of guy. Never have been."

"Oh, God," I say, the realisation hitting me like a dagger to the heart. "You've been in love before."

Damien doesn't answer, and I don't know why but I suddenly feel sick. I force Damien backwards with my hands and jump down from the island, my insecurity increasing tenfold. I walk further into the living room, close to the makeshift dining table, and wrap my arms around myself. I know I'm overreacting, and I have no right to, but the thought of being compared to someone he used to love is making my anxiety hit the roof. How the hell am I supposed to live up to that?

"I take it that bothers you?" Damien asks.

"Yes," I state bluntly, turning back to face him as he slowly walks towards me. "It shouldn't, but it does."

"Why?"

244

"I don't know," I say. "Jealousy maybe? Insecurity definitely."

"There's nothing be jealous of," he assures. "Or insecure about."

"That's easy for you to say," I argue. "I don't have anyone for you to be jealous of."

"That you know of," he points out.

"I'll never compare," I blurt out.

Damien sighs, moving closer and placing his hands on the tops of my arms. "There is no comparison," he argues. "I have never felt about anyone the way I feel about you, and if you want the God's honest truth, it scares the shit out of me."

That's not what I was expecting to hear, yet it's oddly comforting, and exactly what I didn't know I *needed* to hear.

"I have a past," he adds. "But you do too, and if you take me down off the confident, self-assured pedestal you've got me on, you'll see you're not the only one who's nervous here, Dani."

"What do you have to be nervous about?" I ask, not in a cocky, your-feelings-don't-matter way, but in a genuinely curious way.

"Everything," he answers. "What Adrian did…" He hesitates. "I'm terrified if I make one wrong move or do something a little too rough…" Damien takes a heavy breath. "I'm scared it will send you right back to drowning in your pain, and the thought of being compared to him –"

"Adrian wasn't my boyfriend, Damien," I cut him off. "It's not the same, and you could never do anything to make me compare you to him."

"A part of me believes that but…" He sighs. "You're not the only one who gets insecure sometimes. I have fears and worries just like anyone else." Fair point. "You told me the one thing you're scared of the most is losing me." Never forgets a single thing. "Well, the same goes for me too, and I'm not saying any of this just to make you feel better before your crazy mind goes there. Although, I hope it *does* make you feel better."

I let out a quiet laugh. Damien moves to put a hand on my cheek, those sky-blue eyes staring into mine with a blazing intensity.

"I can't lose you, Dani," he whispers. "I love you more than you will ever know, and no one will ever compare to you."

"You need to tell me," I say.

"What? That I love you?" he asks. "I just did."

"No," I say, chuckling. "Although, I do love to hear that. I mean, you need to tell me what you're feeling. You're on a pedestal because you always seem so together, and you spend so much time making *me* feel better, I never have a clue as to what's going on in your head or what you're *really* feeling. But I need to know. So, the next time you're worried, or scared, or whatever, promise me you'll talk to me."

Damien smiles softly. "I promise."

I lean in and kiss him gently. He drops his lips to graze my neck before pulling away a little and staring deep into my eyes. I can see the desire as if I'm looking into a mirror.

"I don't know what the hell you've done to me," I say softly. "I'm sure people ain't supposed to fall so easily."

"You call the past five weeks easy?" Damien teases. "Dani…" He reaches a hand to my cheek. "I don't care if it takes five *years*, but I need you to know you could never be a disappointment. Nothing I could ever do with you could be anything other than perfect."

"Maybe we should test that theory," I suddenly say, my mind made up.

246

"Dani –"

"Don't," I cut him off. "I want to. If I put my relentless insecurities aside, I don't want to let anything hold me back anymore. I just want you."

Damien stares at me, his eyes searching for any signs of hesitation or deception, I'm assuming, but as I press my lips to his, kissing him with everything I have, Damien lets his reservations go. His hands make their way up my back, sending welcome shivers down my spine. I deepen the kiss, and Damien lifts me, allowing me to wrap my legs around his waist once more. He starts to carry me towards the bedroom, when, at the worst possible moment, Damien's front door slides open, and in comes Amy. Damien almost growls, dropping me down to my feet.

"I'm so sorry," she says, holding her hand in front of her face to prevent her from seeing something she might regret. I refrain from dissuading her assumption purely out of amusement. "I forgot my charger. I'll be out of your hair in a jiffy."

I can't help but laugh, but Damien looks major-league pissed off at his little sister. Amy disappears into the spare bedroom, reappearing seconds later, minus the hand in front of her face this time.

"So sorry," she repeats, yet she's smiling, telling me she's equally amused at the situation.

Damien doesn't say a word, but I offer a little wave as she disappears out of the door, closing it behind her once more.

"Well, that killed the moment," Damien says, sulking, but I'm distracted by…

"Can you smell burning?"

"Oh, shit," Damien says, darting into the kitchen, and I slowly follow. Damien opens the oven, letting out a puff of black smoke and popping a very burnt-looking lasagne on the

247

counter. "And that's dinner out the window." Damien doesn't hide his irritation all that well, and his disappointment is rather entertaining.

I move into the kitchen, kicking the still-open oven door shut. "I don't care about dinner," I tell him, leaning up and popping a gentle kiss on his lips. "What I care about has nothing to do with food." I jump up to sit on the island, dragging Damien close by the hand and wrapping my arms around his neck. "I want you to show me just how beautiful I am."

"Are you sure you want to do this?" he asks, an obvious doubt kicking in.

"I'm sure."

"If at any point it gets too much," he rambles, "or you decide you're not ready –"

"Damien," I interrupt. "I know I told you to tell me what you're feeling, but right now, you need to stop talking."

Damien obliges to my request, kissing me with an urgency that makes my entire body shiver in delight. I pour every ounce of the desire I feel for him into the kiss, and he mirrors my longing perfectly, sliding his hands under my top and feeling his way over my flesh in purposeful motions. I lift his T-shirt over his head, marvelling at him as my hands explore every ripple his gorgeous body has to offer. I run my fingers along his back, tracing the large scar his back surgery left behind and smile. It's a reminder that Damien is human, and as perfect as he is, he's right. He's got battle wounds just like me, and if anything, it only makes me want him more. Unbelievably, Damien's door opens a second time.

"For fuck's sake," Damien curses, walking over to a smirking Paul hovering in the doorway.

"Sorr –" Paul starts, but Damien swiftly cuts him off.

"All due respect, mate," he says. "Fuck off."

Damien closes the door, bolting it shut this time, and I burst into a fit of giggles. Damien makes his way back over, shaking his head and muttering incoherently. He stops to stand between my legs, and I grab his dog tags, unable to stop smiling at his frustration. Pulling him close, our bodies pressing against one another, I run my free hand through his hair.

"If only you bolted the door in the first place," I tease, but instead of biting back, Damien kisses me with a passion that, if I was standing, would make me weak at the knees.

I revel in the feel of his touch, his fingers brushing my skin as he lifts my top over my head. I ignore the pang of self-consciousness as Damien takes a minute to reassure me with his eyes that my scars are irrelevant. I stare at him, smiling, and when he kisses me again, lifting me and carrying me towards the bedroom, I leave my doubt behind, determined to allow myself to enjoy Damien and everything he has to offer.

Thank you, universe, for sending me Damien, and please let the biggest leap I'm about to take go exactly the way I want it to.

Chapter Nineteen

I wake up to a little note on the pillow where Damien should be. I smile, the memory of last night at the forefront of my mind. Before you start thinking I'm moving on from a horror story to a fairy tale though, you should know by now I don't live in a fantasy land, and it wasn't entirely smooth sailing. But then, nothing ever is.

The biggest hiccup was the fact at first, sex hurt. Between my warped brain and its sex-equals-pain theory causing me to in-stinctively tense, plus the fact that it has been almost three years since Adrian, there was pain. Unfortunately, Adrian made a very brief appearance too, but one look into Damien's eyes, re-minding me I was with the man I love, was enough to banish any doubt or fear. If anything, I felt empowered, as though a weight had been lifted from my shoulders, and I realised after so much wasted time, I'd finally taken back control.

Damien took his time, patient as ever, and credit where credit's due, for a guy who's only slept with three women, four now, he knows what he's doing. My smile grows at the thought of Damien's lips on my body, and the way he made me shiver in all the right places. We got off to a rocky start, and we took things extra, extra slow, but by the end of the night… Well, I'll leave it to your imagination.

I turn my attention to the note, which reads: *Morning, sleepy head. You looked too peaceful to wake. Got a full day of PT. Downstairs door code's 1409. Don't worry about locking the front door if you leave, but you're welcome to make yourself at home. I love you xx.* I want to kill him for going back to work so soon, especially a work that involves hours of rigorous exercise, but then I think back to last night, and I'm struggling to stay mad at him.

I look at the time on my phone sitting on Damien's bedside table. Holy shit, it's almost ten o'clock in the morning. I haven't a clue as to what time I drifted off last night wrapped in Damien's arms, but I reckon I must have got a good eight hours' solid sleep. Double holy shit. I didn't have a nightmare. Or if I did, I don't remember waking up because of it, which is highly unlikely, and that means I've just slept through the night for the first time in forever. Okay, if the smile on my face gets any bigger my cheeks are going to start aching.

Elated and feeling a little like I'm still trapped in a dream, an amazing, wonderful dream, I drag myself out of Damien's ridiculously comfy king-size bed and head straight for the shower. After letting the hot water soothe my aching muscles, I wrap myself in a towel and pad back into Damien's bedroom. I'm not entirely sure how Damien pulled it off – I can imagine Jess was involved – but a bag of spare clothes, *my* clothes, is sitting on the bedroom floor. Of course, Damien always thinks of everything, and I'm grateful to be able to change into something clean and fresh.

I meander out to make a brew before resigning myself to a day of job hunting. Amazingly, today is one of the few days I don't need a coffee to keep myself awake, and I rejoice in feeling energised for a change. It's remarkable what a good night's sleep can do for a person. Either that or sex with Damien is a major energy boost. Whichever way, I would like to keep doing both.

After deciding to hang around Damien's rather than go home, I shoot a message to Damien's backup phone – apparently, it's sensible to have one – asking permission to use his laptop. One brew and a go-ahead from Damien later, I set to work.

Hours pass, gruelling mind-numbing hours of application

forms and emails, and by the time Damien strolls through the door, I'm exhausted.

"Hey," I say, closing the laptop and standing to greet sexy, sweaty Damien with a kiss. "Good day?"

"Hard," he admits. "The mugging took more out of me than I thought."

"I'm not gonna comment."

"I'm gonna shower then nip to the Chinese down the street," he says, wisely changing the subject. "Have you eaten?"

Not a single thing all day. Sometimes I wonder how I keep functioning, but I have had several coffees, so maybe it's the sugar that keeps me going.

"No," I answer honestly.

"Why doesn't that surprise me?"

Damien heads off to shower, and I decide a little recreational time is in order, helping myself to his guitar. I wish he owned a keyboard mind. I write better with a keyboard, but regardless, I dig out some paper and a pen and kill time by writing whatever pops into my head. Damien stops for a kiss before leaving, but I'm so lost in my music, I don't hear him return until he sits beside me on the couch, moving my hair to one side to free up my neck for a few gentle kisses.

"New song?" he asks, massaging my shoulders.

Wow. The guitar is soon propped up against the couch as I welcome Damien's magic hands kneading out the many, many knots.

"You can keep playing." Damien laughs.

"What you're doing is too good of a distraction," I state, my relaxation swiftly turning to desire, and yes, I am very surprised by that fact.

"Since when are you so easily distracted from music?"

Damien asks.

"I obviously need to be inspired," I say, Damien's hands stiffening a little in response.

"And is there a way I can help *inspire* you?" Damien asks in a sexy, husky tone that awakens a shiver of delight.

"I might be able to think of something," I tease, forcing Damien backwards and climbing onto his lap. His hands find my waist, and his beaming smile is a welcome confidence boost. "But I'm feeling especially uninspired," I say in my best seductive tone, trailing kisses down his neck. "So, it's gonna take a *lot* of motivation."

"I think I'm up to the challenge," Damien purrs in my ear.

I cover his mouth with mine, and he kisses me back hungrily. My hands are in his hair, his hands sliding up my back, but all too soon, Damien forces himself to pull away. I'm assuming due to the impending arrival of our friends. It's band rehearsal tonight.

"Just lock the door," I state. "They can wait."

Damien laughs. "Who are you and what have you done with Dani?"

"You opened the door," I tell him.

"Last time I checked," he teases. "*We* opened the door *together*."

"Whichever way." I shrug. "It ain't closing any time soon, and when I think about last night, I want more. You should take it as a compliment."

"Oh, I do," he says.

"I never thought sex would be something I would enjoy," I say in all seriousness. "But you proved me wrong last night, and I just want to show you how thankful I am."

"Last night was amazing for me too," he says.

"Just because I'm blowing your trumpet," I say, chuckling, "doesn't mean you need to blow mine. I'm aware I need a little work."

"No, you don't," Damien argues. "Last night was perfect because *you're* perfect, and I love you."

"Actions speak louder than words."

I lean in and kiss him with all the passion I can muster. Despite his reservations, he kisses me back, his arms wrapping around my waist, and pulls me closer until our bodies are pressed together. I feel him harden underneath me as I trail kisses down his neck, and it only spurs my excitement.

"You're making it damn hard to resist."

"That's the idea," I whisper in his ear.

He flips me over, laying me on my back, and lifts my top, sliding his hand over my breasts. His lips slowly make their way down my stomach, and as Damien's fingers trace his kisses, stopping at the waistline of my jeans, I let out a soft moan. He hesitates, looking deep into my eyes, teasing or asking permission, either is possible, and I lean up to kiss him. It's all the confirmation he needs, and he slides his hand down my jeans. Of course, because Damien never bolts the front door and I have the shittiest luck in the world, Damien's door slides open. Before I have a chance to blink, Damien's hand is gone, and I'm left hanging.

"Mother…" I whisper, but Damien merely laughs, moving to sit up, his hands concealing his not yet deflated anatomy.

"I don't even want to know what we just walked in on," Amy states. "In fact, I'm gonna go to the bathroom and vomit. A lot."

Amy does just that as I move to sit and compose myself. Jess and Raif are hovering by the door, smirking like petulant teenagers, when I run a hand through Damien's hair en route to the kitchen.

"Not a single word," I warn the terrible twosome, moving past them to set the kettle to boil.

"You really need to learn to bolt the door, honey," Raif says to Damien, who's back in control of himself and joining us in the kitchen.

"Or you lot could learn to knock," he points out.

They do treat Damien's home like a free-for-all, but I don't think Damien minded too much – he did give them the down-stairs door code – until I came along. Speaking of not knocking, Damien's door is opening for a second time, and in wanders Paul.

"Evening all," he says, heading straight for Damien's fridge.

"All right," I reply, sparking a chorus of hellos around the room as Paul sits at the end of the island, beer now in hand.

"So," Jess says, taking a seat next to Paul, Raif beside her. "Pleasurable afternoon, Dani?"

"It would have been," I state, a little extra honest than normal, "if you hadn't walked in."

"Oh, shit," Paul says as Amy, who's returned from the bath-room, sits opposite him. "What did I miss?"

"Just Damien and Dani getting cosy on the couch," Raif an-swers.

"You really need to learn to bolt the door, mate," Paul re-peats Raif's assessment. "That's the second time you've been interrupted."

"Second time?" Jess asks.

"I walked in on them last night," Paul explains. "Got a nice eyeful."

"You did not get an eyeful," I argue, ignoring the lingering sexual frustration and proceeding to brew up for the crowd, minus Paul, whilst Damien dishes out the takeaway food sitting on the counter. "You saw Damien with his top off. I know that'd float Raif's boat..."

Paul throws me a sarcastic ha-ha face, and I can't help but smile at the giggles coming from the others.

"Oh, I've seen Damien topless before," Raif says, wafting his hand in the air as if witnessing Damien shirtless is a regular occurrence. "You're a lucky lady."

"Yes, I am."

"I really didn't need to hear that come out of your mouth," Damien tells Raif.

"Just saying how it is." Raif shrugs, tucking into his chicken chow mein as I dish out the brews.

"And how is it?" Jess asks, ignoring Damien's heavy sigh.

"Hot," Raif gushes.

"Seriously, mate," Damien scoffs.

"He's not wrong," I say to Damien.

"I think I'm gonna be sick again," Amy groans, pushing her noodles away.

"I'm right there with you," Paul agrees, fake heaving, yet proceeding to eat his food afterwards.

"Green is an ugly colour," I tease Paul more so than Amy.

"You're becoming a cocky bitch, you know that?" Paul exclaims, and I laugh.

"You're rubbing off on her, mate," Damien jokes.

"I am *not* cocky," Paul argues, and both Jess and Raif scoff in eerie unison.

"Pull the other one, honey," Raif says.

"It's called confidence," Paul protests.

"Overconfidence more like," I mock, and Paul replies with a middle finger.

"Well," Jess interjects, her mouth half full, "you're not the only one who got laid last night."

"Who's the lucky bloke?" I ask as Damien hands me a box of food, grabbing one for himself too. "Or didn't you ask?"

"Jeff," she answers defiantly, but when the doubt materialises in her face, I laugh. "I think."

Jess's lack of certainty is not even worth commenting on. It's nothing new. I take a minute out of the conversation to nip to the toilet, and when I return, I opt to make an effort and attempt to eat my food, taking small, forced bites. I'm not sure how I'm not hungry given the severe lack of food in my system, but a few bites are more than enough.

"You seeing Diego again tonight?" Jess asks Raif.

"Who's Diego?" I ask.

Damien pulls me to stand in front of him, my back pressed against his chest as he wraps his arms around my shoulders. Either he's eaten his food ridiculously quickly or he's abandoned it, much like I am right now, depositing it on the counter.

"Raif's latest lay," Paul answers bluntly.

"While you were getting jiggy with lover boy over there," Raif explains further, his jiggy comment gaining him a roll of my eyes, "Jess, Amy and I decided to go out. I managed to bag myself a kick-boxer named Diego, and oh, my word, he's amazing in all the right places."

"Too much information," Paul argues, laying his eyes upon Damien's sister. "Please tell me I'm not the only one around here who's *not* getting laid."

"Mate," Damien scoffs, "that's my sister. I don't want to hear that shit."

"Yeah 'cause listening to this lot prattle on about you and Dani is exactly what *I* want to hear," Amy argues, and I can't help but laugh. "But no, you're not the only one, Paul. Even if there had been any takers, I'm pretty sure Dani wouldn't have appreciated me bringing someone home to *her* flat."

"Damn right she wouldn't," Jess says dramatically. "I stayed at hers once, and she lay down bloody ground rules. No overnight guests."

"That's 'cause I was in the next room," I argue, though I am glad Amy didn't taint my spare bed.

"And Jess is loud," Raif teases, gaining him a punch in the arm from Jess.

"So, this Diego," I say to Raif. "Was it a one-time thing or…?"

"He's taking me out for a late-night romantic meal after rehearsal," Raif gushes.

"Fancy," Jess says, impressed. "Diego could be a keeper."

"We'll see how it goes," Raif says, attempting to be casual and failing miserably; his Cheshire cat smile suggests he's hoping for the best outcome.

"I do believe I've never seen you smitten before," I tease. "It's adorable."

"And I do believe I've never seen you so smug before." Raif never fails to give as much as he gets. "I guess sex with Damien has done you wonders."

"What makes you so sure Damien and I have had sex?" I ask. I haven't technically given anyone a confirmation, and since Damien's been at work all day, I doubt he has either.

"Are you kidding?" Raif asks. "You're practically glowing. You might as well be wearing a sign that says 'I got thoroughly fucked last night'."

I burst out laughing whilst Damien shakes his head, and Amy reverts to looking like she might throw up on the counter.

"Okay, enough," Paul says. "Not all of us have the pleasure…" That only makes me, and everyone bar Paul, laugh harder.

"Poor choice of words there, mate," Damien jokes.

Paul scowls, not bothering to finish his sentence, looking at his watch instead. "Where the hell's Danny anyway?" he asks.

"Dani's right there," Amy states.

"He means the male Danny, our guitarist," Damien tells her, and although she briefly appears embarrassed, she shrugs it off as quickly as it came. "I'll give him a ring," Damien offers, heading off into his bedroom to retrieve his phone, I'm assuming.

"You, me," Jess says, pointing in my direction. "Bathroom, now."

"Why?" I ask, confused.

"Privacy." Code for "I want the gory details".

Reluctantly, I follow her to the bathroom, sitting down on the toilet seat lid as she closes the door behind her.

"Well?" she asks.

I smile, unable to contain it, and Jess squeals. I shush her, not wanting prying ears to be drawn to the door, and she covers her mouth with her hand. I don't mind sharing a little more with Jess, but I'd rather the others didn't have any more ammunition to attack me with. I love banter, I do, but everyone has their limits.

"It was…" How to put it. "Weird at first. I was nervous, and a little shaky."

"Obviously," Jess says casually. "Totally to be expected."

"But Damien took his time, and once we got going…" I feel a little flush at the memory. "It was amazing. *Damien* is amazing."

"Oh, my God," Jess says quietly. "And no unwelcome

flashbacks?"

"Briefly," I admit. "But only because it hurt at first."

"How did Damien take that?"

"I didn't blurt out 'Adrian's in my head'," I scoff. "But Damien could tell there was something. He did the gentlemanly thing and asked if I wanted to stop, but…" I smile. "I love him, Jess."

Jess's face softens into something between sweetness and admiration. "You love him," she repeats, and even though it's not a question, I nod anyway.

"And all I had to do was remind myself that Damien loves me too, and Adrian was long gone. After that, it felt so comfortable like we'd been at it for years. He knew every spot to hit."

"Did you climax?" Jess asks the blunt question, and my smile is all the answer she needs. "Give the man a pat on the back."

"Oh, he deserves more than a pat on the back."

"I'm so happy for you," she says sweetly. "Look at how far you've come."

"I know," I admit. "It's all a little surreal."

"You deserve every second, Dani," she says. "After everything you've been through, you deserve happiness."

That comment means more than Jess will ever know, and randomly, I find myself on my feet, embracing Jess in a hug. She hesitates, probably from the shock, before returning the gesture.

"You're hugging me," she almost sobs. "You're actually hugging me."

"I figured it's the best way to say thank you," I say, pulling away to find a stray tear rolling down Jess's cheek. "For always having my back."

"Are you kidding?" she asks. "You're my sister from another mister. I'll always be there for you." I smile. "And if you want any tips in the bedroom department…"

"I know who to ask."

"Damn straight," Jess says cockily. "Now, hug me again."

After a minute of hugging, Jess and I return to the kitchen and rejoin the chatter – apparently, the other Danny has cancelled tonight, some family emergency. Looks like it's another motley crew night, and I'd bet my life on it turning into a late one. Not that I mind. I'm in far too good a mood, and nothing is going to bring me down.

"Fancy rehearsing without Danny?" Paul asks Damien, obviously eager to make music tonight.

"Or…" Jess says suggestively. "You could still rehearse *with* Dani." I instantly catch her drift and want to slap her.

"Jess, honey," Raif says, patronisingly, "I know you can be a little slow on the upkeep, but Damien's just told us Danny's not coming tonight."

Jess sighs dramatically, but I notice out of the corner of my eye that Paul's cottoned on, his face lighting up and his eyes heading in my direction.

"No," Jess argues, slapping the back of Raif's head. "You're the one slow on the upkeep, 'cause I'm talking about *that* Dani."

As if noticing my annoyance at my supposed best friend, Damien pulls me to stand in front of him again, his arms wrapping around me.

"Oh," Raif says, probably feeling like a prize dope. "But Dani doesn't know the songs."

"Have you met Dani?" Jess asks. "I bet you any money, give that girl half an hour, and she'll have a least –" she ponders "– five songs down pat."

"I am itching to play," Paul muses aloud.

"But Dani doesn't perform in front of people," Amy reminds

261

them, and I'm grateful someone in the room is actually thinking of me in all this. I may be riding the biggest high of my life tonight, but I'm still a nervous wreck underneath. I also don't particularly appreciate being talked about without actually being consulted. Not that anyone seems to care.

"Pfff." Jess wafts a hand for dramatic effect. "Dani's far too loved up and happy to give a shit about that. Besides, we're practically family."

Are we? That's an interesting statement, although, given my lack of blood relatives, I guess my friends are the closest thing I got to a family now. I'm surprised at how warm that makes me feel.

"I wonder who the gobby one is the family is," Paul states, inciting a chorus of laughter.

"Shut it, daddy," Jess bites back.

Surprisingly, Paul shrugs. "I've been called worse."

"That I don't doubt," I tease, gaining me a middle finger.

"All right, so if you're the daddy, and Jess is the gobby one…" Raif repeats. "What's that make me? The beautiful one?"

I laugh a little too hard, gaining me a less-than-impressed glare from dear Raif.

"Sorry, *honey*," Jess says, "but Amy gets that title."

"Me?" Amy can't hide her surprise. "You've got to be kidding. You're way prettier than me."

"Not without make-up," Jess retorts.

"I feel sorry for any bloke that wakes up next to you," Paul utters, hiding behind his beer, which nearly spills all over him when Jess smacks his arm.

"Maybe we should change your title to the violent one," Damien teases Jess, and she throws him a threatening stare.

"Yeah, all right," Jess says. "Not all of us can be the sensible, responsible one." Damien laughs.

"Damien's definitely the glue," Raif says, spot-on in his assessment.

"Raif gets the drama queen title," I pitch in, and when Raif holds his hand to his heart in fake offence, my point is proven. "See?"

"Laugh all you want, missus," Jess says. "You're the crazy one."

"I totally agree with that," I admit.

"How the hell is Dani the crazy one?" Amy asks, reminding me of her blissful ignorance.

"She's not," Damien argues, and as a thank you for coming to my defence, I turn to kiss his cheek. "She's the passionate one."

"We'll take your word for it, honey," Raif teases.

"That's totally not what he meant," I say, gaining me a visual of Raif's childish tongue. "But you are right about one thing."

"What's that?" Damien asks.

"We're dysfunctional enough to be a bloody family."

"Aw," Jess gushes. "We love you too, Dani. Warts and all."

I can't hide my happiness, and I don't want to. "I didn't say anything about love." I'm teasing. "I'd call it more of a tolerable acquaintance."

"You are so full of shit." Paul scoffs.

"All right," Amy intervenes. "Can we go back to the part where I get to hear Dani sing?"

"No one said anything about singing," I remind her. "Danny with a Y plays the guitar, and if Dani with an I is hypothetically considering the idea, singing is not a requirement."

Paul sighs. "Hypothetically? You scared you'll screw up and

fall from the pedestal this lot have got you on?"

"Oh, babe," Damien gushes in my ear. "Paul doesn't believe you can learn the songs quick enough. Do you really want to let him think he's right?"

"You too, huh?" I ask, and upon turning my head to look at him, he flashes me that beautiful smile.

"I'm not entirely convinced either, honey," Raif wades in.

"Well, I am," Jess scoffs. "So, how's about we make things interesting?"

Paul's eyes are the first to light up. "What are the terms?"

"Half an hour," Jess says. "Five songs."

"I'll take that bet," Paul says eagerly.

"Erm, hello?" Again. "I ain't agreed to shit."

"Oh, come on," Amy pleads. "Even *I* hate to see Paul think he's right." Paul merely chuckles at that.

"I'm assuming you're betting against me?" I ask Raif, who annoyingly nods.

"You're gonna regret it." Damien is clearly on my side, and rightly so.

"So, it's game on?" Paul beams.

I sigh. "Do I get the scores or am I expected to learn by ear?"

Paul scoffs. "Learn by ear? Yeah, right."

"Oh, mate," Damien states. "When are you gonna learn to stop underestimating my girlfriend?"

Smiling from ear to ear, I turn in Damien's arms and kiss him, again thanking him for his support. It's only when Amy starts groaning that I pull away, laughing.

"All right," I say, abandoning Damien's grip and moving to retrieve his guitar. "You got two options. Either I get the scores, and I get half an hour to learn five songs, or Damien plays *two* songs twice over, and I learn them by ear. But…" What's realistic for me? "I get twenty minutes solo to give them a run-through."

Paul weighs up the options, but it's all for show. I already know which option Paul's going to choose.

"Two songs, twenty minutes," he answers, awakening my haughty smile. "But after your little practice, you got to run through it with the full band, and if you screw up a single note, you lose."

"And what do *I* get *when* I win?"

Paul smirks at my confidence. "My devoted respect."

I laugh. "Whether you want to admit it or not," I state, "I earned that a while ago, mate."

"Keep telling yourself that, lass."

The challenge is set and accepted, and if that's not a flashing, neon reminder of how far I've come in such a short space of time, the banter-filled room and my boyfriend definitely are. I'm starting to wonder why I let my stupid, irrational fears and paranoia hold me back in the first place. No wait, I remember. I'm still a drama magnet, and it's only a matter of time before something or someone comes along with a shoe to drop. You're probably shaking your head at me right now, and I don't blame you, but rest assured, no matter how good things get, negativity will forever be my friend.

Chapter Twenty

I nail it, and Paul is left eating his words. Eventually, he congratulates me gracefully, but when he reopens the offer of joining the band, especially as he's convinced it's only a matter of time before the other Danny bows out, I swiftly decline. I may be on the right side of my horror story, but I'm not an idiot.

That leads to an interrogation, and to silence them, I make Amy's wish come true by stalking off and having a little singsong. I keep it quiet, as if I'm not trying to be heard, even though I know they are all listening intently, and surprisingly, I feel at ease. In fact, when Damien decides to join me and we end up duetting, I thoroughly enjoy myself. The sound of Damien's husky singing voice is always a delight to hear, even if it does stir a want to get rid of my friends so Damien and I can be alone. Geez, I'm becoming as sex-crazed as the rest of them.

It's now Friday, and since Amy is going home in two days, she's managed to convince me – she a master at the puppy-dog eyes – that going out tonight is a good idea. I tried to wriggle out of it, but since Jess and Raif are off out on a double date with Diego and his mate – his *straight* mate – and Paul is treating Kayleigh to a father-daughter night, I officially have no excuse to avoid Amy's invitation. Thankfully, I have the added security of Damien's company to keep my anxiety at bay. Me and pubs tend to end badly, but I'm trying not to think about it too much. That, and I'm moving on, one step at a time, right?

So here I am, at Damien's, waiting for Amy to get ready, which is taking forever I might add, reminding me of Jess a little too much. I'm sitting sideways on the couch, my legs stretched across Damien's lap, welcoming the little foot massage he's honouring me with as I sip at a coffee. Damien is looking as hot as ever with an open denim shirt sitting over a tank top, the sleeves rolled up, and dark denim jeans. I'm in my usual outfit, although I've swapped my Converse for my dark grey ankle boots as I do in any going-out situation, and it's about as much effort as I'm going to make.

I glance down at my now-empty cup. "Should I make another or is Amy planning on surfacing any time soon?"

Damien glances at his watch and sighs. "Come on, Amy," he shouts. "Today would be nice."

I laugh, but Damien's plea does the trick, and Amy appears from the bedroom. Wow. She looks stunning. She's wearing a tight, strappy black dress that falls to just above her knees, which is more reserved than I was expecting, but then her brother probably wouldn't approve of anything slinkier, and her short brown hair is bone straight, highlighting her slender, elegantly decorated face perfectly. My eyes trail to the six-inch heels with straps that wrap around her ankles and the bottom of her legs, and although I would never be seen dead in a pair of shoes like that, they are very nice.

"Are we good to go?" Damien asks as Amy slides on her fake leather jacket.

I rise from my seat, sliding on my boots and taking a detour to the kitchen to drop my cup in the sink. As we head for the door, I notice Amy smiling from ear to ear a little creepily, and I'm wondering if she doesn't get out much back home. She seems a little *too* excited.

"It's only Stanton," I remind her.

Amy pulls a sarcastic I-know face as we follow Damien out of the door. Damien and I walk hand in hand, Amy walking by my opposite side, and the journey into town is short and sweet.

Damien picks a bar with an eighties theme despite Amy's many, many protests, on the promise we'll head somewhere more Amy's style later. The bar is quiet when we walk inside, but it's early, almost seven, so there's plenty of time to draw a crowd.

The bar itself is quite big with tables around the edge of the large dance floor. It's basically a massive square, with the bar at the far side in a long line against the wall, and a space in the opposite corner for the DJ. It's all very disco, with coloured lights dancing around the room, and a large glitter ball hanging from the ceiling above the middle of the dance floor. I'm suddenly wondering if Damien plans on showing me some dance moves, other than the romantic ballroom style he introduced me to at Blackpool, and the thought tickles me.

We grab a table near the door, one of the few that has a couch, and I happily sink into it. I might as well pick a comfy spot to park myself for the night. Amy sits down on a neighbouring chair, plonking her matching black clutch bag on the table.

"What are you wanting to drink?" Damien asks, remaining standing.

"Usual," I answer first.

"What's the usual?" Amy asks.

"Diet Coke."

"You don't drink?"

"Nope."

"What the hell's wrong with you?"

Ha! Where do I start? Amy shakes her head at me as Damien fake coughs to regain her attention. She hasn't yet answered his question.

"A cocktail," she says, but Damien hovers, seeking a more detailed answer. "Surprise me."

Damien heads off to the bar, and I spot a couple of women

standing to attention when he arrives, ogling him like a piece of meat. His black eye from the attack is almost completely faded, most of his cuts have healed, and he's a stone's throw away from being back to his flawless self, so I'm not surprised the two women find him attractive. Hell, I was attracted *with* the cuts and bruises.

Damien turns his head to look at the women, and they throw him a seductive wave. Damien merely diverts his attention to the now present bartender. Oh, it must be so hard being so beautiful.

One of the women decides to make a bolder move, rising from her seat and moving across the bar to stand next to him. She places her hand on his bicep, obviously flirting, and for a second, my heart rate rises. I let out a silent sigh of relief when Damien increases the distance between them, freeing his arm from her grip, and I give myself a sharp slap.

Damien points at me, and I quickly realise my name has dropped into the conversation. I smile, waving at the severely disappointed woman at the bar.

"Who are you waving at?" Amy asks.

"The woman at the bar hitting on your brother," I say, laughing.

Amy turns to look in Damien's direction. "Doesn't it bother you?"

I shake my head. I have many, many issues, but I don't want jealousy to be one of them. Okay, so maybe I got a little jealous of the mysterious woman Damien loved in the past, but that was completely different. I know for a fact that Damien will spend the rest of his life being ogled and hit on by women, and I need to accept that. Jealousy would be a colossal waste of time and energy. Besides, Damien has given me no reason not to trust him.

"It would me," Amy says as Damien returns carrying a bright pink cocktail for Amy, my usual and a pint of lager, cider or beer, I can't tell the difference, for himself.

"What would what?" he asks, setting the drinks down and sitting next to me, sliding his arm around my shoulders.

"Some other woman hitting on my boyfriend would bother me," Amy explains. "I'd be getting in her face telling her to back off."

"She didn't know Damien's spoken for," I argue. "As far as she's concerned, he's a gorgeous guy in a bar. You can't blame her."

"You're far too nice," Amy says, shaking her head.

"I didn't need to get in her face anyway," I point out. "Damien did it for me."

"Damn straight," he says cockily. "I've only got eyes for the most beautiful woman in the room."

I straighten up and glance around the room for dramatic effect. "I don't see her."

Damien shakes his head, smiling. As I lean back into the sofa, he kisses me softly.

"Seriously, you two," Amy groans. "The whole cute, lovey-dovey crap is getting beyond nauseating." Amy fake heaves in an over-the-top fashion that makes me smile.

"Bathroom is over there." Damien points, then kisses me again, more to wind his sister up than anything else, but I'm not going to complain.

We sit chatting for a while as the bar starts to fill up. It's not crazy busy, but most of the tables are now occupied, and there are quite a few people hovering on the dance floor and at the bar. I notice the DJ setting up in the corner, and it's looking like the party's about to get started.

"All right, boys and girls," the DJ speaks into a microphone. "Are we ready to kick off eighties night?"

The crowd cheers enthusiastically. I have to say, the younger generation is far outweighed by their elders, eighties night drawing a more mature crowd, and it makes me smile. I'm sure their maturity will fly out of the window along with their sobriety, and it's not long before the dance floor is rammed. I'm happily watching, my head resting comfortably against Damien's shoulder, his arm leaning against the back of the couch as his fingers run through my hair when Amy stands. She reaches down and grabs my hand.

"Oh, no." I shake my head.

I pull back, refusing to move as the realisation that Amy wants me to dance sinks in, but Amy is freakishly strong, and she yanks me to my feet, almost taking the table and our drinks along with me.

"Damien can watch the drinks," she practically shouts above the music. "Come on."

"I don't dance," I insist, wriggling out of Amy's grip and looking out at the buzzing crowd. I'm not going out there amongst that, not a chance. That's one step too big.

"Please," she begs, but I shake my head. I know my limits.

I retake my seat, ignoring Amy's pout and snuggling back into the safety of Damien's arms. He offers me a sympathetic smile, but I know he understands. Amy on the other hand, not so much.

"I'm gonna head to the toilet instead then," Amy tells us, and I'm wondering if she'll have a little dance with herself en route to dampen her disappointment.

I watch her shimmy her way through the crowd, and when I

turn back to Damien, he's texting one-handed. "Anyone interesting?" I ask. Damien looks at me, confused, and I point to his phone.

"It's Paul," he answers. "He's in the pub across the road."

"I thought he was having a father-daughter night?"

"Apparently, it's happening tomorrow instead," Damien explains.

"You head over if you want?" I suggest. "I can grab Amy, and we'll meet you there."

"You sure?" he asks nervously, and I'm assuming it's the idea of leaving me alone that's the cause.

"Babe," I say bluntly. "You're not my babysitter, and if I plan on, you know, living, I'd like to think I can manage to make it to the toilets and back again unscathed." Stick that in your pipe and smoke it, anxiety.

"I'm not trying to babysit you, babe," Damien groans. "I just know how you feel about crowded places."

I briefly glance out at the crowd, but there's an unfamiliar resolve stirring inside me. Dancing in the thick of it is a step too far, but I'm not about to let a bunch of people who have no interest in me whatsoever stop me from standing on my own two feet. I refuse to rely on Damien to survive. I've done that far too much already.

"I'm good," I insist. "I can go around the crowd, and I'm hoping I'll surprise myself by staying calm."

"Want to say that with a little more conviction?" Damien teases. "Otherwise, I'm not going anywhere."

"Go," I say. "I'll get Amy."

Damien hesitates a minute longer, a tinge of worry sitting upon his brow, but I plaster on my best smile and rise to my feet. I slide on my jacket and plant a kiss on Damien's lips before heading in search of his sister. I carefully make my way around the growing crowd until I finally reach the ladies' toilet. I'm not surprised to find Amy standing in front of the mirror, spreading fresh lipstick across her lips. No wonder she was taking so long.

"You about done?" I ask, and Amy turns her head to smirk at me. "You'll be happy to hear we're abandoning eighties night." Amy's face lights up like a Christmas tree as she deposits her lipstick in her clutch bag. "Paul's in the pub across the road. Damien's headed over, so, when you're done beautifying..."

Amy rolls her eyes, but when I make a beeline for the door, she follows. We make our way around the bustling crowd and out onto the street. Feeling the night's chill, I pull my jacket a little tighter as I wait for the passing traffic to die down and allow us to cross over. I can see Damien through the window, sitting at a table with Paul, throwing me a little wave.

After what feels like a lifetime, Amy and I step out into the road, but upon hearing a clang and spotting my phone on the floor, I'm forced to bend to retrieve it. A loud screeching sound steals my focus. A speeding car is heading for Amy. Instinct kicks in, and I dive for her. She stumbles onto the path, but I'm knocked off my feet.

Time moves in slow motion. The look of shock upon the driver's face. My head hitting the bonnet. My legs soaring in the air. Landing on the cold tarmac with an almighty thud. I scream at the pain engulfing my senses. I can hear the commotion around me, but I can't respond. It's like I'm paralysed, unable to speak or move, yet there's no panic or fear. There's a calmness I wouldn't have expected, and a peacefulness that's a little disturbing.

All I can think is, *this is it. This is how I'm going to die.* My eyelids are so heavy. I can feel my body going limp, any energy or fight slipping away. The already blurry world starts to fade. I'm in and out of consciousness. My head is spinning. I can hear voices. Damien's here. He's holding me, I think. He's begging me to stay with him, to respond, but every time I try to open my eyes, my lids refuse to cooperate. I open my mouth, but no sound comes out.

I'm inches away from accepting my fate, except… Something's off. That's not right. My eyes are closed but I'm seeing things, random, chaotic images that make no sense. I'm about to put it down to my delirium, but I'm hit with more and more…memories? Am I remembering things?

Holy hell, I *am* remembering things. No, that's not possible. What I'm seeing is not possible. I don't know if I laugh out loud or in my head, but whichever way, I'm laughing. Of course it's possible. My whole life is the making of an Oscar-winning film, or at the very least, I'm a walking, talking soap opera, and I should know by now *anything* is possible. I make a mental note should a bright light appear, to *not* go towards it, just in case.

The confusion is overwhelming, but I force my screwed-up brain to focus on just one memory in a feeble attempt to make sense of the chaos. I'm running through a corridor. College, maybe? Yes, college. I'm carrying books, and I'm obviously running late, but in my haste, I crash into someone. Literally crash, causing the books to scatter across the floor. I'm apologising profusely, scrambling to collect my books, and when I look up at the squatting figure handing me the last paperback, I'm met with the most gorgeous sky-blue eyes I have ever seen, like a cloudless sky on a bright day.

Do you understand now? Well, that's a twist I never, *ever* saw coming. In fact, if I wasn't so close to dying right now, I wouldn't believe it. I'd blame my fucked-up brain playing tricks on me, but there's more. A montage of undeniable images, and the emotion… I can feel the happiness and love embodied in each memory, and holy hell, the feelings I feel for that man are indescribable.

I'll spell it out in case you're not quite with me. Sixteen-year-old me is staring into the eyes of a seventeen-year-old Damien. The same Damien I supposedly met just a few weeks ago, but if the flashes are to be believed – I'm not ruling out my imagination just yet – I didn't meet Damien a few weeks ago, I met him a good few *years* ago. Damien is not a stranger, nor is he a friend or my boyfriend either.

He's my fiancé.

He's the love of my life.

What the royal fuck?

Chapter Twenty-One

My head is in the toilet, vomit flowing out of my mouth in searing waves. Oh God, I feel dizzy, but I think I'm half satisfied I've got nothing left to expel, so I stand and move to wash my hands. I take a few deep breaths before heading back out into the hospital corridor. Damien is waiting by the door, his back leaning against the wall, and I can tell from the less-than-impressed look upon his face, he still disagrees with my decision.

"Are you sure you're ready to go home?" he asks.

"Four days was long enough."

And what an interesting four days it's been. I woke up in the hospital to discover it wasn't a bad dream, and I had indeed been hit by a car. I was dazed and overwhelmed thanks to the added bonus of the whole I-already-know-Damien revelation, but despite the confusion, I wasn't surprised to find Damien sitting by my bed, clinging to my hand for dear life. At that moment, I didn't care about anything other than feeling happy and grateful he was there. That, and I'd yet to really process everything. I was too busy feeling grateful just to be alive.

I have a now-sealed-in-a-cast broken wrist, bruised ribs, plus a thousand other bruises covering my left side, which was apparently the side that hit the ground, and a nasty bump and gash that required stitches to the head. Oh, and a concussion, I got that too, hence the vomiting that's refusing to subside. But after four days consisting of a CT scan, X-rays, neurological tests, and constant checks of my blood pressure and temperature, the doctors have signed off on my discharge, albeit with conditions. I'm not to be left alone for at least forty-eight hours, so I'm off to Damien's home, not mine, and I'm to return to the hospital if I experience one of the many, many possible side effects that come with a head injury and, you know, being hit by a car.

"I'm fine," I insist, taking Damien's outstretched hand and letting him lead me towards the hospital exit. "Feel like I've gone ten rounds with Mike Tyson, but other than that…"

Other than that, I'm in a weird limbo. I've had four days to process the fact that not only didn't I dream the car accident, I also didn't dream the memories that have plagued me ever since, and although there are countless questions still to be answered, I've managed to figure out a few details, here and there. And no, I've yet to discuss the revelation with Damien; one, because I've been in a hospital, a less-than-private place, and two, because I simply haven't had the energy to hash it out yet. The confusion is too much to handle.

Okay, so I'll iron out a few details for you to bring you up to speed. Damien and I met in college. That much I know. We literally crashed into one another, but in my haste, due to my desperation to avoid tardiness, I apologised then took off. I can't lie and say there wasn't an instant attraction because there was, the butterflies in my stomach were proof of that, and I can *feel* it even now, as though I'm reliving it somehow, but I was still surprised when Damien tracked me down in the canteen later that day. Happy, but definitely surprised.

From what I can gather, that's where it all started. A little chit-chat in a canteen and the rest, as they say, is history. I can vaguely remember a couple of trips to the theatre and a far-too-passionate kiss for a public place at the top of Blackpool Tower – turns out I have been to Blackpool – plus a couple of nights cuddled up on the couch watching a scary movie, but my clearest memory is of the day Damien asked me to marry him. We were on a boat, no, a yacht, standing at the front under the moonlight. Damien got down on one knee, and after spouting a highly romantic, well-rehearsed speech, I didn't hesitate in saying yes. My God, I loved that man, and what's terrifying is I can feel the emotion of that day as if it was only yesterday.

The downside is, there's a less-than-cheery memory floating around, and it's the day Damien was deployed overseas. I can see him standing on my doorstep, dressed in his Army uniform as the tears stream down my face. I remember clinging to him for dear life, begging him to come back in one piece. Hell, I begged him to stay, but we both knew going AWOL wasn't a viable option. I was so scared. I don't know for sure, but I doubt Damien hid his intention to join the Army, so I probably knew it was coming, but Afghanistan… Nothing could have prepared me for that, and I'm pretty sure a piece of my heart broke as I stood and watched him walk away that day.

There are a few other memorable moments, like my apparent graduation and some Army promotion thing for Damien's dad and so on, but just to bring back the cheerier side of things, what's truly amazing is the memory of a simple family dinner. Yes, I said family, as in *my* family. I think it's a birthday dinner since I can remember balloons and cheesy party hats, but I have no idea whose, not that it even matters. What matters is that I can see my mum, whom I get my hazel eyes from just by the by – cannot describe the happiness that tiny piece of knowledge has given me – and my dad, plus Pops, Uncle John, Aunt Sharon and even Seth, albeit he's a shedload older. In fact, the tall, skinny, pinnacle of high fashion dude sitting facing me at the table is almost unrecognisable, but it's his cheeky boy smile that gives him away.

Damien's there too, and would you believe it – the icing on the cake – Paul. No, you didn't hear me wrong. That bastard has known who I am all along too, and like Damien, he's kept his mouth shut. That "I know you better than you think" comment at Kayleigh's birthday party is echoing in my ears, and I'm starting to think the whole dragging me on stage to sing stunt or the "learn by ear" challenge were games Paul took far too much enjoyment in playing. If he knows me, then he knows fine well I can sing and learn songs in the blink of an eye. I know, even without any memories, that music has been a massive part of my life since birth.

Although thinking about Paul's involvement only makes me question Amy's innocence. Yes, she was away in Australia, and no, she didn't have any contact with Damien, but surely, she must have seen pictures or something. Or at the very least, heard things from Damien or his dad. Unless he erased my memory to cover his tracks. God only knows at this point.

But anyway, I digress. Back to the party and the wonder that is my family. The smell of homecooked chicken pie is mouth-wateringly good, but what's even better is the laughter coming from the people I hold dear. The smile on my mum's face is priceless, and the pride in my dad's eyes when he looks at me is worth its weight in gold. Even remembering Seth throwing cake at me is a joy to behold, though I doubt it was at the time, and I cannot begin to describe how amazing it feels to have a snippet of my family back. To know that, before the shooting, before Adrian, I was happy is more than I ever could have asked for.

So, by my reckoning, since no matter how hard I've prodded and probed my mind the past four days, I can't seem to remember any form of a break-up, Damien and I were together for close on seven years before the shooting. Although, if Damien and I never actually split up, you could say that we never ceased to be a couple, and if that's the case, technically, Damien is still my fiancé. How bizarre is that? So bizarre. So very, very bizarre.

You have no idea how many questions are running through my mind, but I will kindly enlighten you as to just a few. For example, why hasn't Damien told me the truth? Why has it taken him three years to re-enter my life? Where was he when I was shot and recovering from said shooting? Afghanistan? Or what about before, during and after Adrian? Why did he lie to me? Why has he continued to lie to me the entire time he's been back in my life? Was he hoping I would remember? Was he ever going to tell me the truth?

It's gotten to a point that my head is banging so much, I've given up trying to make sense of the chaos. That being said, so many things about life with Damien Take Two make so much more sense to me now. Damien's eerie ability to read my mind and make me feel instantly comfortable; no wonder I felt like I was talking to an old friend after just a couple of encounters with someone I believed to be a stranger. My subconscious at work, maybe? Not to mention Damien's determination to be with me, despite my scars, my fucked-up-ness, and the short time we'd known each other. He already knew me, and more than that, he was already *in love* with me. My God, I even said to Damien it felt like I'd known him for years, and I told Jess that sex with Damien felt like we'd been *at* it for years. I guess now I know why, and yes, I know how ridiculous all of this sounds. Try bloody living it!

Talk about an emotional whirlwind. I honestly don't know whether to feel ecstatic that the love of my life is *still* the love of my life or insulted that he's practically manipulated his way back in. I can't lie and say I'm not pissed off because I am. Damien's lied to me. There's no two ways about it, he's lied, and is technically *still* lying to me every second we're together. Okay, so officially he's omitting details, but as far as I'm concerned, it's the same thing, and as much as I hate to say it, I feel a little exploited.

Damien's had an unfair advantage, and I can't help thinking the past few weeks have been one big charade. Damien knows me like the back of his hand, and even though I'm a different person from who I was back then, there's no anxiety, scars or shitty experiences in the handful of memories I've been blessed with; I'm still me at my core. I'm still the same woman Damien fell in love with, just a little more broken than I used to be, and he used his knowledge to worm his way into my heart.

And that's where the true issue wades in: how much did Damien know? Did he already know about Adrian? Or my no-touching deal? I mean, there's just no knowing how much information Damien had at his disposal, and it hurts. Telling Damien and reliving the horror I experienced at Adrian's hand was one of the hardest things I have ever had to do, and if it turns out he already knew and had me repeat it for the sake of keeping up the pretence, pissed off will be a massive understatement.

What I will say though, is I one hundred percent applaud Damien *and* Paul for not letting any tiny little detail slip, and I'm genuinely thinking they've missed their calling as actors. I mean, hats off to them. If the shoe was on the other foot, there's no way in hell I'd have been able to spend so much time with the man I love or his closest friend and keep my trap shut. I guess Damien's determination to be with me, no matter what, is a force to be reckoned with, and in a way, it's admirable. I am wondering what Paul's take on the situation was, but something tells me he was all for a game of charades. Looking at it from a positive perspective though, which we all know is a rarity for me, it shows just how much Damien loves me. I mean, the lengths he's gone to are, in a word, insane.

So, all in all, I have reached the following conclusions. One, I love Damien, and apparently, I always have; I just lost a few years. Two, Damien is undoubtedly in love with me, and irrelevant of where the hell he's been the past few years, he's made a tremendous effort to find me, which is arguably commendable. *But* there's a three, and it's not quite so positive: I'm angry. Damien kept me in the dark and lied to me, and whether his intentions were good or not, there are questions that need to be answered and gaps that need to be filled.

Will my love for him outweigh his betrayal? Most likely. But not before I get my explanation. When I find the courage and strength to broach the subject, that is.

"You need to rest," Damien tells me, snapping me back to reality as we climb into his car.

"I've spent the past four days resting." We all know I hate hospitals. "Besides, there's no difference whatsoever between resting in a hospital or resting at home." Damien wisely doesn't argue.

After a far too slow navigation through Manchester's morning traffic, Damien pulls up outside his warehouse home. Maintaining his gentlemanly style, he swings around, opens my door and helps me to my feet. I can't lie and say I'm not grateful because I'm telling you, four days later, and I'm still aching all over. Every movement is hard work, and even breathing too deep makes my ribs hurt. Something tells me my recovery is going to be a little longer than I hoped, and the thought is increasingly infuriating.

Damien opens the main door, and I head inside. I'm about to tackle the stairs when Damien takes my hand and tugs gently, stopping me in my tracks.

"I'll carry you up," he offers.

I laugh until I realise it hurts like hell to laugh, and I quickly shut up. "Last time I checked, my legs are working just fine, thank you."

I don't give Damien a chance to argue, slipping out of his grip and taking one painful step at a time. I can practically hear Damien's scowl behind me, but I manage to make it to the top without passing out. Damien makes sure to move past me to unlock and slide open his front door though, and I step inside. I'm surprised to find an empty flat, if I'm honest. I figured Jess would be here, waiting to go into fussing mode, but I'm going to assume Damien's determination to get me to rest has something to do with her absence. She's not the only one who appears to be elsewhere either.

"Amy not here?" I ask, following Damien into the kitchen.

Thanks to my heroics, something Amy has not stopped thanking me for the two times she visited me, Amy survived the car incident unscathed. She was supposed to go home two days ago but she's decided to stick around a little longer. I have a feeling making sure I'm truly okay is something she needs to do before she returns home, just to ease her conscience. Not that she has anything to feel guilty for. None of what happened was her fault, but I guess there's probably an element of survivor's guilt at play, though thankfully, I'm not dead, just injured.

"She spent the night at Jess and Raif's," Damien explains, pointing a finger to the couch, gaining him a pointed look from me.

"I'm gonna go get in my pyjamas first," I state as Damien sets the kettle to boil. "If that's all right with you?"

Damien scowls. "I'm only –"

"Trying to take care of me," I cut in with a slightly petty tone. "I know."

I let Damien press a kiss to my forehead before making my way to his bedroom. Sliding out of my jacket, I sit on the edge of the bed and reach down into the suitcase Damien retrieved from my flat yesterday in preparation for my homecoming to grab my pyjamas, but when I do, I can't help the yelp that escapes my mouth. Damien is in the bedroom like a shot.

"You okay?"

"Yeah," I groan. "Just hurts to bend."

"Let me help," Damien says, reaching into the suitcase and depositing my pyjamas on the bed.

I stupidly move to take off my shoes, but I'm swiftly back to yelping. Damien takes the reins, sliding off my shoes, and the disdain is written all over my face.

"Just let me help, babe," Damien says softly. "I'd rather that than risk making things worse."

Damien moves to slowly lift off my top, and I let him without argument but with a scowl. Normally, I would enjoy Damien taking my clothes off, but not now. Now, I'm extra angry. I'm angry I'm unable to do basic things because I need to recover from the aftermath of yet another bad experience, an experience that could've quite easily killed me. Some days I'm surprised I have a body left to be broken. I've spent so much time battered and bruised, healing and recovering, and just when I'd managed to heal enough of my *emotional* wounds to feel like a relatively normal human being… Boom. I'm back to being broken.

Damien helps me into my pyjamas, and I slowly make my way back out to the living room. I sit on the couch, but when I move to put my feet up, I stifle yet another yelp. I think the last dose of painkillers I took at the hospital is wearing off because holy hell, my entire body, especially my ribs, is in unspeakable agony.

"Chuck us some painkillers please, babe," I ask Damien, who is in the kitchen.

Damien appears beside me with a freshly made brew and pops two tablets in my hand. Relatively comfortable in a sitting position on the couch, I revel in the sweet aroma of coffee as I swallow the pills.

I take a few more sips before the nausea creeps back up, and I'm yelping in pain to the bathroom. I just about manage to lift the lid before the projectile vomit takes over. Damien's hand brushes my neck, pulling back my hair, and when he rubs a hand up and down my back in a rhythmic motion, I'm warmed by his comfort. I need it. I need *him*. Not in a pathetic take-care-of-me way, although I obviously do if my stubbornness took a back seat, but in a more, I just need to be touched and feel loved kind of way.

Once I'm done vomiting, Damien disappears and reappears with my toothbrush, and I quickly wash my hands and brush my teeth.

"If you keep throwing up," Damien says, hovering in the doorway, watching me like a hawk, "I'm taking you back to the hospital."

I rinse my mouth, turning off the tap before answering. "I'll be fine," I insist. "It's not like I ain't been through this shit before." A bump to the head is nothing new, neither is bruised ribs or broken bones. "I think I'm just gonna lie down for a bit."

Damien follows me into his bedroom and helps me find a non-agonising position before squatting down in front of me, tucking my hair behind my ear. I instinctively close my eyes, revelling in his touch again, but when I do, all I can see is the car screeching towards Amy, and I force my eyes open again.

"You okay?" Damien asks.

"Stay in bed with me," I pathetically plead. "Please."

"Course, baby," Damien says softly, climbing in beside me. "Whatever you need."

I ever so carefully nestle into his chest. His arms wrap around me, and all the emotions I've been holding in the past few days come pouring out in a waterfall of tears.

"Am I hurting you?" Damien asks, loosening his grip a little. I shake my head, and his grip tightens. "It's okay, babe," he soothes. "I got you."

"Why me?" I sob. "Why does bad shit keep happening to me?"

Damien sighs. "Don't do that, babe. This…" He hesitates. "You got hit by that car because you're the most selfless woman I know, and you were too busy thinking about making sure my sister didn't get hurt…" Oh right, yeah. This one is all my own fault. I almost forgot that part. "I'm so sorry, Dani."

I manage to lift my head to look at him, annoyed by the guilt in his eyes. "Don't *you* do that either," I order. "Do not put my shitty luck on your head. You ain't my bodyguard, so pack it in."

"Yes, ma'am." It's a poor attempt at humour.

"I'm serious."

"Okay," Damien says softly, but I glare at him. "Okay," he repeats dramatically.

Half-satisfied, I lay my head back down on his chest and let the sound of Damien's heartbeat soothe me. We lie in silence for a little while before Damien surprises me by breaking it.

"I don't think I've ever been so scared in my entire life," he says, his voice trembling a little. "Seeing that car hit you and being powerless to stop it…" He pauses, and when I look up at him, a stray tear is falling down his cheek and melting my heart. "I ran as fast as I could, but finding you motionless on the ground… I honestly thought I'd lost you for good."

For good. I wouldn't have noticed the significance of those words before the accident, but I do now, and the tears fall from my eyes.

"You stopped breathing, Dani," Damien continues, and my eyes widen in surprise. The doctor gave me a full rundown of the events, but he never mentioned I stopped breathing, or maybe he did, and I switched off, either is possible. I was pretty out of it for a couple of days. "Your heart stopped beating for less than a minute, but…" Damien's voice trails off.

Take a second for that to sink in. My heart stopped beating. I died. For less than a minute, I was gone. My stomach churns at the anguish that must have caused Damien. I hold him tight, reaching a hand to his cheek. Ignoring the pain, I kiss him with everything I have, and when I pull away, I wipe the tears from his eyes.

"I can't lose you, Dani," Damien states.

Why do I get the feeling Damien's just omitted an *again* from that statement? Holy mother of light bulbs. I was dead, and I'm not talking about the car. After the shooting and in an unsuccessful attempt to keep me safe, Ray and the police let the world believe I had died along with my family. In the months I spent in the hospital afterwards, not once did Ray mention Damien or a fiancé, or anyone… Does that mean Damien thought I was dead? Is that what kept him away?

"Oh, my God." I'm talking to myself. "Raymond Jackson, I'm going to kill you."

I bound out of bed in a moment of pure rage, instantly regretting it when my ribs scream in response.

"What?" Damien asks as I hunt down my jacket from the bottom of the bed. "What are you doing?"

"Trying to find my phone."

"Why?"

"Because I need it," I snap.

"Dani." Damien moves to stand in front of me, grabbing a hold of my hands. "Stop. Talk to me. Who's Raymond Jackson?"

"Ray," I spit, Damien's innocent act only managing to enrage me further.

"The police officer?" He doesn't let up. "Your uncle's partner?"

I force myself free of Damien's grip, overwhelmed with emotion and unable to process it. So many lies. So much deceit. I trusted Ray, and I trusted Damien, and both of them have kept things from me, life-altering things that should never have been kept. It's almost funny how quickly I've gone from heart-melting to pure pissed off but add in the discovery that I died and the whirlwind of emotions clouding my judgement, no wonder my head feels like it's about to explode.

"I need air." I dart out of the bedroom, but Damien is hot on my heels, gently grabbing my arm and stopping me just shy of reaching the kitchen.

"Woah, Dani," he pleads. "You need to rest."

"No," I state. "What I need is to clear my head."

"Why?" Damien asks. "What's going on? What are you not telling me?"

I laugh a highly sarcastic laugh. "That's rich coming from you."

I yank my arm free from Damien's grip and try to make my escape, which yes, is idiotic right now, but I don't care. It's also feeble, and I think deep down, I know that. Damien's standing in front of me quicker than I can blink, blocking my path and forcing me to stop once again.

"What the hell are you talking about?" Damien asks. "Do you blame me? Is that it? Because if you're leaving to punish me…"

I scoff. "Yes, because I'm that childish," I say sarcastically, which Damien clearly doesn't appreciate since he's scowling. "You know I don't blame you for the car accident."

"Then what?" Damien pleads. "Why are you trying to run away from me?"

I inwardly laugh. Damien's hit the nail on the proverbial head, and it's downright annoying. I'm doing what I always do when things get rough – I'm running and hiding, or I'm trying to, at least.

"Because since the shooting I have only ever trusted two people more than anyone else," I yell, omitting Jess for dramatic effect. "And it turns out, both of them have kept secrets from me, and it hurts, and I'm pissed and…"

I turn away from Damien, lifting my hands above my head, but when the pain sears through my chest, I opt to wrap them around myself instead.

"Dani –"

"Ray is one," I cut him off. "The other is you." Damien's silence tells me either he's cottoning on or he's genuinely too confused for words, so I turn and face him. "And what I want now is the truth. All of it. Every last detail, right now."

Chapter Twenty-Two

"What truth?" Damien asks, and I honestly can't tell if his dumbfounded tone is genuine or fake.

"Okay," I say slowly. "Let me jog your memory." See what I did there? "Damien *Eugene* Coyle." And yes, I randomly remember Damien's middle name, and the emphasis on that fact has Damien's face dropping to the floor.

"What did you just call me?" he asks as I force myself to the couch, unable to take the pain of standing any longer. "I never told you…"

"That's because you hate your middle name." I remember that fact too. "But I think it's a tribute to a…" I look to Damien, seeking clarification. "Family member?"

"My mum's brother. He died from leukaemia when he was six," Damien explains, his eyes lighting up as the metaphorical light bulb above his head shines so bright it's close to bursting. "You remember?"

"I remember bits," I say quietly.

"About me?" Damien asks, sitting down beside me. "About us?" I nod. "Dani…" Damien leans in, his intention to kiss me evident, but I put a hand up to stop him.

"Oh, no, you don't," I state. "I love you, and you have no idea how happy I am to remember things, and to see you alive, but I am major league pissed off at you for lying to me."

"Dani…" He repeats my name, albeit in a pleading tone this time around, but he makes no further attempts to kiss me, sighing heavily instead. "When?"

"When what?"

"When did you start to remember?"

"The accident," I answer. "I don't know if it was the knock to the head or temporarily dying or what, but things started to come back. Not everything, but enough."

"Why didn't you say something earlier?"

I shrug. "I was in the hospital, and it's a lot to take in. At first, I wasn't convinced my screwed-up brain wasn't making shit up, but then I started to process things and well, I couldn't deny what I was feeling."

"And what were you feeling?"

"The emotion in every memory," I explain. "Like the day you left for Afghanistan." Damien's face softens. "Or the day you asked me to marry you." Despite the current situation, I can't help but smile. "From what I can remember, it was the happiest day of my life."

"Mine too," Damien says, unable to hide his joy.

"But it's not every day you wake up to find your boyfriend is actually your fiancé," I mutter. "And he's been lying his arse off."

Damien sighs. "I didn't... I wasn't..." He brings his hands up to his face before holding them clasped at his chin. "I never wanted to lie."

"Yet you did," I state the obvious. "You manipulated me –"

"Is that what you really think?" Damien cuts me off, clearly hurt and disgusted by my suggestion. "That I manipulated you?"

"I don't know what to think right now," I reply honestly. "You let me believe you were a stranger, Damien. Here's me thinking you were this amazing, intuitive guy who had a re-markable talent for reading me like a book when in reality, you already knew everything about me. You used that to your ad-vantage, and I was suckered in, hook, line and sinker."

I gulp at the sight of Damien's dejected and heartbroken face, but I need to say how I feel if we're going to move past it. I can't keep it all bottled up because we all know that doesn't end well. The last time I let my bottled-up emotions and truths spill out, it ended with Damien walking out the door, and as pissed off as I am, I don't want Damien and me to end.

"I never even thought about it like that," Damien admits quietly.

"But that's not what hurts the most," I add as Damien holds my gaze. "What hurts is you had answers. You saw what not knowing anything about my family did to me, how hard it is having a massive gap in my life, and all right, you couldn't fill in *all* the blanks, but you could've given me something. Instead, you kept it all to yourself, and as much as I want to sweep it under the rug and just be happy you didn't die in the Army, I need you to understand how much that hurts."

"I wanted to tell you," he argues. "But it wasn't that simple, Dani. You have to understand, I never meant to hurt you."

"I know that." And somehow, I do. "But if I hadn't gotten hit by that car, you'd have just carried on with the charade, and I'd have never known any different. And I don't know how I feel about that. I mean, what the hell were you thinking?"

"Honestly," Damien says, lowering his hands to lean his forearms against his thighs, "I didn't *think* much past having you back in my life, no matter what it took. I couldn't lose you again, and if I had to, I'd lie all over again if it meant I got to spend the rest of my life with you."

Always so smooth, but right now, his way with words is infuriating. I feel like I'm reading a romance novel and swooning at the use of such a simple, yet oh-so-powerful statement. Except I don't want to swoon. I want an explanation.

"I didn't lie to manipulate you," Damien says as if reading my mind. "I did it because I was scared." He sighs. "The first time I saw you, you were closing up Lloyd's. You walked straight past me. You even met my gaze for a second, and… Nothing. You had no clue who I was."

Shit. My anger is already dissipating, the guilt soaring. "I don't remember that."

"Why would you?" He sighs. "I was just a stranger walking down the street to you." It's my turn to sigh. "I don't know, I guess it was stupid to hope you'd just remember."

"Hope is never stupid," I offer. Pointless sometimes, but not stupid.

"After that," he says. "I didn't know what to do. Paul…" I snigger. "You remember Paul?"

"He's floating around."

"Paul didn't *want* to lie any more than I did," Damien continues. "But you didn't have a clue, and the last thing either of us wanted was to scare you away and lose you all over again. I knew, deep down, if I told you who I was from the get-go, you'd have run for the hills and never looked back. You weren't exactly great at dealing with emotional situations *before* everything went tits up…"

"Thanks for that," I say sarcastically, and surprisingly, Damien chuckles.

"It's true," he states. "You always went one of two ways. You avoided the situation completely or you lost your shit. There was never any middle ground with you."

"Yeah, I don't remember that either," I say. "But I can believe it, and I guess it's nice to know I ain't completely changed."

"I didn't plan to lie for so long," Damien adds, keeping the conversation on track. "But the closer we got, the harder it got.

I couldn't risk screwing it up. I think a part of me hoped spending enough time with me would –"

"Trigger a memory."

Damien nods. "Do you remember saying the whole daring Army thing?"

"Oh, my God," I say softly. "That's why you looked disappointed." At Lloyd's. There had been a mixture of sadness and disappointment in his eyes. "You didn't realise your dog tags were out, and you thought I remembered…"

"Something," he almost whispers. "But you didn't, and after that, I was playing it by ear, secretly hoping the truth would come out on its own." He got his wish, although probably not the way he'd hoped. "It wasn't easy though, hiding the truth. I need you to know that. I didn't enjoy it. I just…I didn't see any other way. All that mattered was having you back in my life because I love you. I never stopped loving you."

My heart sinks through the floor. I *forgot* Damien. I forgot my fiancé, and even after spending so much time together again, I *still* didn't remember him. He lost me, and although he found me again, I was still never quite here. I can't begin to imagine how that feels. I silently curse my screwed-up brain. And science. And Adrian. And the universe for being so cruel and unfair. In fact, dear universe, since you're determined to play games with my life, I sincerely hope I'm making for good entertainment.

"Walking into the café wasn't an accident though, right?" I ask. "You knew where I worked."

"The café, yeah," Damien says. "But I honestly didn't know you worked at Dave's. That was pure luck."

"Or fate," I mutter. I don't believe in fate, but the surrealness of Damien and my story is a good a reason as any to start. "Did you…" I cringe a little. "Stalk me?"

Damien scoffs, his disgust palpable, but I'm a little creeped out by the thought of someone watching me without my knowledge, even someone who loves me.

"I did not fucking stalk you," Damien spits. "I didn't know where you lived, just where you worked, and I walked past the café twice, that's it. Jesus, Dani. I'm not some sicko with an infatuation."

"I know." And again, somehow, I do. "Sorry."

"The café was the only thing Ray told me," Damien explains, and I'm back to wanting to kill Ray. I take note to make that phone call later and give him an earful for lying to me too. Although, I'm also back to thinking the worst…

"How much did you know?" I ask. "About, well, everything?"

Damien sighs. "At first, I knew nothing. I was out in Afghanistan. My dad called and told me about the shooting." Damien pauses. "He told me you were dead."

I was right. I knew it. "For fuck's sake, Ray," I spit. "When he told me everyone thought I was dead, he never mentioned there was a fiancé who would grieve for me." Damien smiles weakly. "I'm so sorry."

"Don't be," Damien assures, resting his hand on mine. "It's not your fault, babe. I don't even blame Ray. Not anymore. I was pissed off when I learned the truth, but I understand why he did it. Although, he could've skipped the funeral part."

"You went to my funeral?" My voice just reached a new level of high-pitched. "Wait…I had a funeral?" Damien nods.

I know my family did, though I didn't attend on account of being hospital-bound and, you know, dead, so I left Ray to arrange it all. He never mentioned my inclusion, but I guess it makes sense to sell the Dani's-dead story. Not at all eerie.

"Oh, God," I groan. "Is my name on the plaque?" Damien nods again, and I run my hands over my face. "Ray said he'd had one made for my family, but I never visited it." My paranoia was beyond intense back then, and I was convinced visiting would only lead to getting attacked or kidnapped, or killed even, by someone, anyone, related to Adrian, so I never went. I groan a second time. "For fuck's sake."

"You were supposedly cremated along with your family," Damien says softly. "I wanted to visit you in the funeral home and say goodbye, but the supposed fire damage to your body…" My house was set on fire and all those inside burned, which, as far as Damien was obviously concerned, included me. "Ray warned me against it, and I didn't want that to be the last image I had of you."

Nicely played, Ray, using the fire as a cover for the lack of a body. A little twisted, but nicely played nonetheless.

"You went to my funeral," I say extra slowly as the significance of such a thing slams into me like a battering ram. "Just when I thought things couldn't get any more fucked up."

"Of course I went," Damien continues. "I had to say goodbye, but it destroyed me watching that curtain close…"

The pain in Damien's eyes is soul destroying, melting my rage into a pool of regret. As usual, I've been so wrapped up in my own mind and my own feelings, I didn't stop to think about how hard any of this must have been for Damien. He lost the woman he loved, and to think he went to my funeral, said goodbye and mourned, only to discover the whole death scenario was just a charade. It's heartbreaking on an epic level. I take Damien's hand, and he immediately pulls it to his lips, clinging to it as though his life depends on it.

"I was just a month away from retiring from active duty," Damien says regretfully. "Finishing the rest of my contract as a reserve."

"You were?"

Damien nods. "But after you died, the Army was all I knew. I figured if I focused on the Army, I'd find a way to cope. Only I didn't cope at all. I was surrounded by death and suffering and…I started screwing up. I went off the rails for a while, ignoring commanders and looking for trouble. I had a death wish, and I was an inch away from ending up in a casket or dishonourably discharged. If it wasn't for Paul, I probably wouldn't be here right now."

Okay, so that makes me a little less mad at Paul. I'm grateful he was by Damien's side. Can you imagine what it would feel like if I got my memory of Damien back only to find out he'd died in the Army? You know what, it doesn't bear thinking about at all.

"I remember thinking…" The tremble in Damien's voice is gut-wrenching to say the least. "It should've been me. I was the one putting my life on the line, not you. I spent my entire career avoiding death." A stray tear falls from his eye. I use my free hand to wipe it away, my hand lingering on his cheek a little longer. "I just, I couldn't live my life without you."

My heart has officially just shattered to pieces. Even with gaps remaining, I know, without a shadow of a doubt, the love Damien and I shared was a one-of-a-kind type of love, the kind that was meant to last forever. I know because I feel it now. I fell in love with Damien twice, and if I lost him, it would destroy me in ways Adrian never could. The heartache Damien must have felt knowing our life together was over, I can't begin to truly imagine. Only it wasn't over. I was alive, and that only makes it ten times worse.

"Next thing I know," Damien continues as I lower my hand, "I'm getting another call from my dad telling me you're alive. He'd paid a visit to Ray, I can't remember why, but it was *you* that opened the door."

"Holy shit," I suddenly say. "I remember him. He's the guy in the Army uniform that knew my name. It was a couple of months before I moved here, but Ray dragged him away. I saw them arguing outside through the window, but when I asked Ray about it, he said it was a family friend he'd been having a few disagreements with, and I never thought anything of it. I didn't know who he was." Surreal. So very surreal.

"He couldn't believe his eyes at first," Damien says. "He'd never forget your face, but even if he had, he'd have known that tattoo anywhere." I bring a hand to my neck. "He let rip on Ray."

"Can't say I blame him." That's exactly what I'm going to do.

"Ray eventually explained everything."

"I doubt your dad gave him much choice." I don't remember much about Arthur, other than a glimpse here or there, but considering Damien's just told me he was screwing up in the Army because I died, I can imagine Arthur was furious to learn it was all a lie, and Damien's erratic behaviour could have been avoided.

"Talk about a head-fuck." Damien chuckles sadly. "But he never went into detail. I knew the basics – shot, kidnapped, recovery. So no, Dani, I didn't know exactly what you'd been through until you told me."

"Promise me that's not a lie," I ask desperately, and Damien shuffles to sit sideways on the couch, his entire body facing me.

"I promise you," he says. "I didn't know."

"You have no idea how much I needed to hear that," I say, a tear falling down my cheek. "Telling you about Adrian was so hard. I ain't sure how I'd feel if you'd already known and had me repeat it for the sake of keeping up the charade."

Damien sighs. "It wasn't a charade, Dani. Nothing about the past seven weeks has been an act. I just…left a few details out. I'm still me. I'm still –"

"That wasn't a dig," I cut him off, and he nods.

"Hearing what Adrian did to you," Damien says. "I wanted to rip the bastard's throat out." Understandable. "That's the real reason I didn't text from Kent." The twelve days he spent caring for his dad. "I was struggling to deal, and I needed to get my shit together before facing you again."

The impact of what Damien heard is only just dawning on me. Adrian didn't hurt a woman Damien met a few weeks prior, he hurt the woman he loved, and if it wasn't for Adrian, Damien and I would probably be married and living our best life right now. Hiding his pain can't have been easy.

Light bulb. "No wonder Paul pushed me to get in touch," I say, feeling a little like a pawn, yet understanding Paul's honourable intentions. "He was hoping if I made the first move, you'd snap out of it." I'm making assumptions, but it makes sense to me.

"Paul didn't share that with me," Damien says, "but it sounds like something he would do. In his defence, he just wanted to see us happy again. He saw first-hand what losing you did to me." I nod in understanding. "I was on my way to the airfield to hitch a ride home the second my dad called." Damien turns the conversation back on track. "But the convoy was ambushed."

"The bomb," I say softly. Just when I thought I didn't have any pieces of my heart to break, although it explains Damien's absence for the past year. If Damien's dad came to see me a couple of months before leaving London, well, that was roughly fifteen to sixteen months ago, but Damien and I didn't re-meet until just under *two* months ago.

"I was in the hospital for a long time," he says. "I was in a bad way for a while, and then I had to learn to walk all over again, which took longer than I'd hoped, but the only thing that kept me going was hoping that at the end of it, I'd get to see you."

"Hoping?" Interesting choice of word.

Damien sighs. "Ray wouldn't tell me where you were at first, and it took a lot of begging to convince him. Pretty sure my dad won him round in the end, but I don't know how exactly. I never asked, and neither of them ever told."

"Why?" I ask, and I can only hope Damien has already asked Ray that question. "Why keep you away?"

"He was worried me showing up would only cause you more pain," Damien says. "He didn't tell you about me at first because you didn't remember me, and since I thought you were dead, I wasn't going to come looking for you." Yep, so going to kill him. "Then after Adrian, you were going through a tough recovery, and your memories were still gone. He asked me to stay away completely and let you move on and for a second, I wondered if he was right."

"You did?"

Damien nods. "You had no clue who I was, and so much time had passed since the shooting. I didn't want to screw up the life you'd moved to build and..." He pauses. "I was scared you'd found someone else."

"I spent eighteen months on a psych ward," I state bluntly. "Do you honestly think I was ready to move on?"

"You did with me."

"Yeah, well," I say. "If you ask me, my subconscious knew something I didn't."

"Meaning?"

"There was something about you." I shrug. "You made me feel comfortable from the second you opened your mouth, and no matter how many times I told myself to put some distance between us, I couldn't. Even our first conversation was effortless. You learned more about me in two days than Jess had in a year." I chuckle. "I even said to Jess, the night we had sex for the first time, or what I thought was the first time, after the awkward pain part, it felt like we'd been at it for years." Damien smiles softly. "If I'm honest, the effect you had on me in such a short space of time, especially considering everything I'd been through and how long I spent in therapy to get to where I was when you showed up, terrified me. It's almost a relief to able to blame a subconscious pull to the man I already loved. Makes me feel a little less crazy."

"You were never crazy," Damien assures, but I let out a scoff that has Damien smirking. "Okay, maybe a little."

"I guess already knowing me probably helped you get inside my head quicker."

Damien shakes his head. "Please don't do that, Dani. I didn't *use* anything, or if I did, I didn't do it intentionally. I tried to act like it was a fresh start. Why do you think I asked questions about your family? I already knew what happened to them, but it would've have been weirder *not* to ask. Everything I did, I swear, I did it because I love you." I furrow my brow in confusion, and of course, Damien notices. "What?"

301

"I'm just realising I never asked how long you've lived here."

"I moved after Christmas last year," he tells me. "Paul and I kept in contact, and he was a massive support in my recovery, despite having a full-time job *and* a teenager."

"So, you waited just over two months to make a move?"

Damien shakes his head. "First thing I did was drive straight to the café, but…"

"You saw me locking up." I nod in understanding. "And I didn't recognise you."

"It threw me," he admits. "Paul told me to take a step back, focus on getting started up with the PT and getting settled."

I laugh. "You got settled after just two months?"

Damien smiles softly. "No," he admits. "I'm still working on the business side, but I couldn't wait with you. I had to do something."

"You're lucky I didn't move," I say. "I never planned to stay in Stanton as long as I have." Hence the forever packed suitcases.

"I'd follow you anywhere," he says softly, warming my heart. "But I'm not surprised you got too comfortable. You never did like the idea of moving around much."

"I'm assuming we had a conversation about that?"

"We did." Damien nods. "After Army training, I was based in Belfast. You offered to move there to be closer to me after college, but we both knew your dream was to study at King's College and leaving your family behind would've killed you. Not to mention your precious West End."

"Trips to the theatre." I nod, remembering the things I've already remembered, if that makes sense. "That was my doing. So, you really are a festival, concert kind of guy?" Damien nods. "Why don't I remember one of those?"

Damien laughs again. "'Cause you hated festivals with a passion, and you only went for me."

"How can someone so in love with music hate a festival?"

"'Cause you and camping don't mix," he teases.

"Huh." I'm not entirely sure what to say to that, so I decide to steer the conversation back to the point. "But what about after my degree? I mean, I was almost twenty-three when I got shot. I vaguely remember graduating, and that was at twenty-one, right?"

Damien nods. "You did a masters."

"A masters?" I can't hide my surprise.

"I was in and out of Afghanistan, so it made sense to make the most of our time apart," Damien says. "Plus, when I wasn't deployed, I got plenty of leave, and we took turns travelling back and forth."

"That still leaves another ten months unaccounted for," It may seem like a meaningless question, but I'm just trying to make sense of things.

"I was back out in Afghanistan," Damien readily explains. "My last tour before moving to the reserves, and I was gonna come back to London. Like I said, I never could have torn you from your family."

"But what about yours?" I ask. "I already know you miss them."

"I left Belfast for London when I was eight." After social services got involved. I don't need my memories back to remember that part. Interesting Damien's time in London never came up in conversation before. Good job really. I'm pretty sure my paranoid side would have struggled to let that snippet of information slide. "I was used to being away from my lot back home, and your family were good to me, like *really* good. Your parents were everything my parents weren't, loving and close, and they treated me like one of their own."

My heart swells with pride. "I wish I could remember more about them."

"I'll tell you anything you want to know," Damien offers. "As much as I can." I nod. "It's the least I can do after keeping you in the dark…" His voice trails off.

"I get why you did."

I'm not happy he lied, but I understand why he did it. He did it out of fear, the fear of losing me all over again, and if there's one thing I understand, it's fear. It's irrational, and it makes you do crazy things. But he also did it out of love. A love that refused to be extinguished even in fake death, and I'm not the only one who's suffered here, Damien has too.

"Please don't hate me," he almost begs, and my heart bleeds for the vulnerable man sitting beside me.

Feeling any lingering anger dissipate, I lean in and kiss him. I pour every ounce of love and admiration into his lips before forcing myself to pull away, staring into his worried sky-blue eyes.

"I could never hate you," I say softly, my hand on his cheek. "I love you. I have always loved you."

Damien's eyes soften, and I kiss him again, caught up in the elation of knowing I have a second chance with the only person… I pull away.

"You're the only one?" I ask. I'm pretty sure I already know the answer, and I'd like to think I'm right considering I was a mere sixteen when I met Damien, but with my memory, it can't hurt to seek confirmation. "Guy I've loved?"

"As far as I know," he half teases, and I gently slap his chest. We're quickly back to kissing, and I'm back to revelling in the elation of a second chance with the only man I have ever loved. Damien's lips devour mine with an intense need, as though all his fear and heartache are melting into me, relieving him of any pain or guilt, and he wraps his arms around me, pulling me close. It's only when I feel a sharp pain in my chest, I force myself to pull away again.

"You really need to rest, babe."

"I don't want to rest," I groan. "I want you."

Damien laughs. "I want you too." Good to know. "But I'd rather do this when I don't have to worry about hurting you."

I'm not happy, but I grumble, "Fine."

Damien leans back into the sofa, and I lay my head in his lap, letting the feel of his fingers running through my hair comfort me.

"We got all the time in the world, babe," he assures. "All the time in the world."

Chapter Twenty-Three

Since I'm resting, which involves doing absolutely nothing, I'm eagerly listening to Damien filling me in on every detail he can about our past, and the more he enlightens me, the more fascinated I am at how many little things are creeping back. Like my dad not only playing the guitar but working as a violinist in the West End. Or the confirmation my mum was indeed a writer, with a total of two novels and ten children's books to her name. Or Seth being the Bill to my Ben, my right arm, and the closest thing, bar Paul, apparently, I had to a brother.

So many happy memories, but as with any relationship, Damien and I weren't always so smooth sailing, which is oddly refreshing. Although Damien and I didn't argue often, when we did, it was explosive. We could easily go days without speaking to one another out of nothing more than sheer stubbornness, and randomly, I now have a rather vivid memory of one of our make-up sessions. If you ask me, the argument was totally worth it.

Damien, the sensible, routine-loving, guitar-playing teen seemingly took me on a whirlwind of adventures I've yet to remember. Holidays abroad, including a trip to Egypt and a visit to the pyramids, hikes up countless countryside hills, theatre trips, concerts, festivals, romantic meals in fancy restaurants, cinema visits, bowling, minigolf, Blackpool... The list is endless. Yet between college, university, the Army, and my apparent theatre hobby, as in performing not watching – my dream was to star in the West End back in the day – I'm amazed we had any time left to spend together. We found a way to make it work though, and up until Damien enlisting full-time, we rarely spent

a night in bed alone. Damien was my entire world, and I'm beyond grateful to have him back in my life.

I do have a slightly hilarious fact for you that has me feeling
embarrassed yet highly amused. Remember the woman Damien was in love with? Number three? The woman I was jealous
of before I conquered my fears around sex? Yeah, that's me.
Number one is the girl he lost his virginity to at fourteen, number two is a brief six-month relationship he had at sixteen, and
number three is, in Damien's words, the gorgeous, music-loving, fiery teen he met in college otherwise known as me. I cannot
believe I was jealous of myself. And just in case you're wondering, Damien holds all of my firsts, except kissing, I guess. Apparently, I kissed a boy on the lips when I was twelve, or so Damien tells me, but I'm not entirely convinced that counts.

I have to say, Damien's stories and knowledge, shy of getting
all my memories back, is everything I could ask for. I'm laughing, a lot, which has my ribs spending most of the morning
groaning, but it's worth the pain. I've spent three years asking
silent questions with nothing but my imagination for an answer,
but I can honestly say the truth is so much better; it's priceless.
I had a loving family, an honorary brother in Paul, who was
apparently a regular tag along on Damien's trips home, and an
amazing man who loved me enough to follow me even when I
forgot him. What more could a girl ask for?

Okay, so we all know by now I'm physically incapable of remaining positive and eventually, I can't stop the tears from falling down my cheeks. Replaying Ray's vague description of the
shooting in my head doesn't stir any memories, but it is stirring
a whole load of pain.

I had everything I could have ever asked for and it was torn
from me in the blink of an eye. My life, my loved ones, my

memories, and as if that wasn't enough, the bastard who orchestrated the shooting went on to steal my dignity, my sanity, and ultimately, everything that made me *me*. And if it wasn't for a car briefly killing me, I'd still be in the dark, and no, that's not a dig at Damien, honestly. I understand his reasons, but in what world is it right to be grateful for being hit by a car? My world, apparently.

Damien being Damien though, he's reminding me the worst is over, and now we can focus on the rest of our lives – an honest, secret-free life. And he's right. All that matters now is the future, and when I think of the friends I've gained, all of whom made sure to visit me in the hospital whenever they could, and the beautiful man I'm lucky enough to call mine, I'd say the future looks rather bright. If the universe decides to cut me a break, that is.

"You okay?" Damien suddenly asks. He's now in the kitchen, making me a brew, whilst I lie on the couch, replaying today's conversation over and over in my head.

I slowly move to sit up, catching Damien's eye over the back of the couch. "Yeah, why wouldn't I be?"

"Just worried it might be getting to the information overload stage."

I laugh. "Ouch," I groan. "I really need to stop laughing." Damien offers sympathy by sitting beside me and handing over a freshly made brew. "But no, I don't think it will ever be information overload. I just hope I can keep remembering things. Not that I'm not grateful for everything you've filled me in on, I just…" I sigh. "I *want* to remember, you know?"

"Actually." Damien rises to his feet. "I have something that might help with that."

Damien disappears into his bedroom, returning with a

medium-sized cardboard box, setting it down beside me. "What's that?" I ask as Damien sits and opens the box lid.

"That is every letter you ever wrote me while I was away," he says. "It's every keepsake I kept, and everything you left at my dad's old place."

"Oh, my God," I almost squeal, fighting the urge to burst into tears but wasting no time in abandoning my brew to the coffee table and pulling off the box lid. Damien bypasses my hands to retrieve something, dangling it in front of me. "A charm bracelet," I state, drawing a blank, yet taking it from Damien's hand and inspecting the collection of silver charms, my eyes landing on one in particular. "Damien and Dani forever."

"That was the first-ever birthday present I bought you," Damien explains. "You accidentally left it behind on one of your visits to Belfast." Nothing's coming back to me, but rather than dwell on it, I focus on rummaging through the box.

I pull out a few of the letters I wrote and skim through them. I laugh at some of the ridiculous things I wrote about, like my first day at the part-time job I snagged during university as a personal assistant where I managed to spill coffee down my boss's shirt. I guess I had a habit of not paying attention to where I was going and crashing into people.

"Oh, I wish I could remember what you said to that," I say to Damien, pointing to the letter and letting him read the spillage part. Damien laughs.

"I asked if I should be worried," Damien says, yet his tone is playful. "Since that's pretty much how we met."

I laugh, making every effort to ignore the pain. "I have a feeling my boss was probably old."

"Oh, so if it had been some good-looking, twenty-something –" I cut Damien off by kissing him.

"No one could ever come close to you, babe."

Damien smiles. "Nice save."

The next thing I pull out is a photo and unable to hold back, I let a few tears fall down my cheeks. It's a picture of my family, my parents, Uncle John, Aunt Sharon, Pops, Seth, Damien, me, and Paul all cuddled in together, smiling the brightest of smiles.

"We look so happy," I say softly.

"We were," Damien assures me. "That was your twenty-first birthday."

"We, erm…" I start, wracking my brain. "My parents organised a party, right?"

"Yeah." Damien smiles. "Even half of my Northern Ireland lot made the trip over."

"Really?"

"Hell, yeah," Damien states enthusiastically. "They bloody loved you, and my lot never turn down a good party." I laugh, then groan… You know the drill.

Although, come to think of it… "Speaking of family," I say. "Where does Amy fit into all of this?"

Damien sighs. "She's in the dark."

I furrow my brow in confusion. "But how? I mean, I know she was in Australia, but she's been back a year, and you must have talked about me, right?"

Damien shakes his head. "Not to Amy."

"Why the hell not?"

He laughs. "Because I didn't want her getting involved," he says. "She can be a meddling cow when she wants to be."

"Are you serious?" I ask. "You kept me a secret because you were worried about her meddling?"

He sighs. "I guess maybe on some level I knew reconnecting with you wasn't going to be plain sailing, and I didn't want anything or anyone to screw it up. That, and you were shot and kidnapped, babe. Ray refused to go into detail, but for all I knew, you were still in danger. Ray faked your death for crying out loud. That's not exactly an everyday occurrence, and I didn't want to risk the wrong person getting wind you were alive."

Fair point. "But what about pictures? Keepsakes?"

"By the time Amy showed back up," he explains, "Dad had already moved twice. Everything I had was either at the Army base or in this box, which my dad kept in his attic, just in case you were wondering."

Damien smirks, and I shoot him a sarcastic ha-ha face. He can't blame me for wanting a thorough explanation, but I'm pleased to say he's answered my questions to a satisfactory standard.

"You know Amy's gonna kill you, right?"

He laughs. "She'll get over it."

Turning my attention back to the box, I pick out another photo and laugh. Damien is dressed as John Travolta from *Grease*, me as Olivia Newton-John, right down to the skin-tight, black leather catsuit. Paul is beside Damien as Johnny Depp in *Pirates of the Caribbean* and Seth is Lily Savage. Damien leans in to have a closer gander and smiles.

"The veterans costume party," Damien explains, and although I'm amused, I don't remember jack. "Charity thing."

"I can imagine it was a great night,"

"We had a lot of great nights," Damien assures me. "And days, and weekends…" I smile softly. "You looked so damn hot that night." Pretty sure my insides just did a backflip. "And this," Damien says, handing me another picture, "is just after I asked you to marry me."

Okay, I'm crying now. I can't help it. I mean, I remember Damien's proposal, but it's one thing to have the image in my mind and another to see proof sitting in my hand. Damien pulls me into his arms and kisses my forehead.

"You made my dreams come true that night," Damien says softly.

"Okay, if you're trying to get me to stop crying," I tease, "you're doing a shitty job."

Damien laughs. "Just as long as they're tears of happiness."

"Of course they are," I exclaim, pulling away to have another look at the beautiful picture of Damien and me kissing under the moonlight, nothing but a barrier and the ocean as a backdrop.

A thought hits me. "Engagement ring?"

Damien's face saddens. "If you don't have it…" I shake my head. I guess anything could've happened to it.

Once again deciding not to dwell, I continue to sift through the huge pile of photos, smiling away as my tears dry up and revelling in the evidence of a life filled with love and laughter. Until – go ahead and shake your head at me – my insecurities resurface, and my smile fades. Damien, because he never misses a thing, doesn't hesitate in calling me out.

"What?" he asks, but I shake my head. "Babe, I can practically see the cogs turning in your head."

"Just…" I pause, dropping the photos to the couch. "I guess I'm realising you didn't fall in love with the scarred me. You're in love with the memory of me, the me in these pictures –"

"That's not true," Damien interrupts.

"If you hadn't already been in love with me," I continue anyway, "you never would've glanced in my direction as I am now."

"Yes, I would," Damien protests. "You're beautiful, Dani, then and now."

"That's easy to say."

"I'm not lying, babe," Damien insists, but my refusal to believe his words is written all over my face. "Dani, I went into this knowing there was a chance that we'd already lost what we were, that we were both different people now, but I can honestly say I fell in love with you all over again. If it's possible, I fell *more* in love with you."

"I highly doubt that."

Damien sighs. "Dani, don't. Stop letting your insecurities creep back in. I love you, and yeah, I love the old you, but I swear, the Dani who's been through hell and can still make amazing music and melt my heart with the sound of her voice, the Dani who gives Paul a run for his money in the cocky department or endures listening to Raif and Jess bang on about their sex lives twenty-four-seven…" I chuckle. "The same Dani who's willing to do anything and everything for the people she cares about, who talked a kid down off a bridge and risked her life to save my sister…" Yep, I'm going to cry again. "I love *that* Dani with all my heart because that Dani is an inspiration."

"You're giving me too much credit."

"You're selling yourself short," he counters. "You're an amazing person, Dani, and you shouldn't be ashamed of your scars. They are proof of your strength, and what you've overcome to get to where you are now." I sigh. "Everything you've been through —"

"Everything *we've* been through," I correct.

"It brought us back together in the end," he says. "That's all that matters."

Damien's way with words will forever be a tad annoying, yet

they make perfect sense if I slap my insecurities down.

Wobble dealt with, Damien and I continue to rummage through my former possessions until the exhaustion consumes me. One random afternoon nap later, I'm opening my eyes to the faint sound of voices coming from the living room. I wince my way out of bed, but when I hear what sounds like pain in Damien's voice, I find myself stopping shy of making myself known, listening to the conversation through a slightly ajar door.

"I can't get it out of my head," he says. "Every time I close my eyes, I see Dani lying there, not moving –"

"Mate," Paul cuts him off. "Dani's good. Yeah, all right, she's got a few battered limbs, but it's Dani, that's not exactly anything new." I silently chuckle. "And I think you're forgetting the good parts."

"I'm not," Damien protests. "I'm just struggling to let the guilt go, mate." I think it's Paul who sighs. "I wasn't there for her when she needed me. The shooting, Adrian…"

"Mate, we've been over this," Paul says. "We were in Afghanistan. There's jack shit either of us could have done. None of it is on you."

"James is," Damien declares. "And I was right there for the car accident. If I'd just stayed with her –"

"You can't babysit her, mate," Paul points out, sounding a lot like me. "Dani is capable of standing on her own two feet, and even if she doesn't remember it yet, we both know she's a force to be reckoned with when she wants to be." Is that so?

"I never should have lied to her."

"We've been over that before too, mate," Paul states. "Lying was the best option at the time, and chill, I'll make sure Dani knows it was my idea." Why am I not surprised?

"It doesn't matter whose idea it was," Damien protests, followed by a heavy sigh. "I don't know, I guess I'm just realising how fucked up the past few years have been."

"All right," Paul says sternly. "I have held your hand the whole way, mate, but you seriously need to get your head out of the sand." Damien chuckles. "Yes, you two have had a shit time of it, but who cares? It's done. Dani's back, mate. I mean, why the hell are you not shouting hallelujah from the bloody rooftops? Dani remembers you. Hell, she even remembers me, and I'm telling you, I was convinced she'd purposely blocked me out." I silently laugh. "So, what the hell is with the moping?"

"I'm not moping," Damien grumbles.

"Yeah, you are, mate, and you need to bloody well stop," Paul instructs. "Top and bottom of it is, mate, the day Dani died, I lost both of you, and I honestly thought I'd be burying you right alongside her. Until you got that call." The call to say I was alive, I'm assuming. "Everything you did after that was because you love that woman more than I've ever seen anyone love someone, and Dani *knows* that, so whatever the hell it is you're worried about, let it go, mate. Just let it go."

"I just wish things could have been different," Damien says, determined to wallow. "And when the novelty of getting her memories back wears off, I'm scared she's gonna remember I lied to her, that I've done nothing but let her down, and hate me for it."

Okay, that's enough earwigging. As much as I'm appreciating knowing Damien is human and needs to wallow just as much as the rest of us sometimes, I'm not about to let him beat himself into the ground, especially when none of it is his fault. Been there, done that, and it's not pretty.

I slowly walk out into the living room. "You're an idiot."

Damien's head snaps in my direction faster than the chick from *The Exorcist*, forcing me to stifle a giggle. Okay, so it's not the nicest thing to say when someone's wallowing, but I'm taking a leaf out of Damien's book and giving it to him straight.

"I hope you're gonna back that up with a compliment," Paul jokes, rising to his feet.

"Don't worry," I assure him. "I'll sort him out."

"Good," Paul states, heading for the door. "I'll go grab us all some tea and be back in a bit."

"Thanks, mate," Damien says graciously.

As Paul takes his leave, I stand in front of Damien, and he parts his legs to allow me to get a little closer. I run my fingers through his hair and plant a soft kiss on his forehead. He avoids my gaze for a few moments, but eventually, his tired eyes meet mine.

"You should be resting," he says.

"And you should be talking to *me*." I don't begrudge Damien talking to Paul, especially when I now know just how close Paul and Damien really are, but I need to know what's going on inside his head too.

"How much did you hear?"

"Enough."

Damien sighs. "I'm fine."

"Don't do that," I say sternly. "Don't bullshit me. You promised you'd talk to me."

"I promised you a lot of things," Damien says. "That's partly the problem."

It's my turn to sigh. Knowing I probably shouldn't continue to stand as my legs and ribs are groaning, I sink into the couch beside Damien.

"And like I said," I state, "you're an idiot." Damien turns his gaze away from me, staring ahead blankly. "None of what happened is your fault, babe."

"I know that," Damien admits. "But it doesn't stop the guilt. Joining the Army was the stupidest decision I ever made."

"Did you ever stop to think joining the Army *saved* your life?" Damien furrows his brow in confusion. "If you had been with me the night of the shooting, you'd have probably ended up with a bullet to the head like everyone else. In fact, you'd have died making sure I got out, so no, joining the Army was not the wrong decision."

Damien sighs. "And what about every decision after that? Lying? Trying to push you out into the world only to see you get hurt again? I feel like all I've done is bring more pain into your life."

I scoff, and I'm suddenly realising what it must have felt like to be Damien during the past seven weeks, dealing with me and my constant insecurities and negativity; it's infuriating. I make a mental note to apologise profusely for putting him through that, but for now, ignoring the searing pain as I move, I force myself onto Damien's lap to stop him from avoiding eye contact. If I'm going to try to comfort him, I need to know he's hearing me.

"Dani," he protests, but I put a finger to his lips to silence him.

"No," I say. "I need to deal with you before I can rest because I ain't gonna sit back and watch you beat yourself into the ground. Sorry, you don't get to be me."

Damien sighs, remaining determined to avoid my gaze, but I gently grab him by the chin and force him to look at me.

"You need to take your own advice." I'm sure we've just had a similar conversation. "What I've been through," I say. "What *you* have been through –"

"Mine is nothing –"

"Don't," I cut him off. "Do *not* downplay what you've been through." He sighs. "We've both suffered here, Damien, but it's time to stop dwelling on things that were out of our control."

"I want to," he admits. "But after the car shit, I honestly feel like I'm walking on eggshells waiting for the next thing to come along and take you from me. It makes me want to wrap you in cotton wool or lock you in the bedroom for the rest of eternity."

I laugh, yet I can totally understand Damien's fears. The difference is I'm feeling uncharacteristically positive.

"Babe," I say, "I get it, I do, but I have spent the past three years hiding, and I don't give a crap what the universe throws at me next, I'm not just gonna lie down and let my life pass me by. Not anymore. Because if I do that, then all the shit we've been through has been for nothing, and like you said, everything that happened, happened for a reason…" I smile. "To bring me back to you." Damien lifts a hand to my cheek. "And I'd go through the pain ten thousand times over if I had to. That's how much you mean to me."

Damien's entire body softens as he trails his hand from my cheek to the back of my neck. "Dani…"

"You've got nothing to be scared of, babe," I assure him. "Yes, you lied, and yes, I was pissed off at first, but I was never going to let that come between us. I never hated you. I just wanted an explanation, that's all." Damien smiles softly. "Everything you did, you did it out of love, and an optimist would describe it as incredibly romantic."

"You're a natural pessimist," Damien reminds me.

"True," I agree. "But the point still stands."

Damien's hand finds its way to my cheek again. "I'm so

sorry," he says softly. "For the lies. For everything."

"Don't be," I insist. "I'm not."

"I'd follow you to the end of the earth if I had to," he declares. "You know that, right?"

"I know."

Damien kisses me. It starts out slow, but it's not long before I melt into him, every kiss and every touch meaning more to me than ever before, a combination of love and adrenaline fuelling my need to feel a happiness only Damien can give me. Until the front door slides open, and Damien pulls away, laughing.

"When you said you'd sort him out," Paul retorts, dumping a carrier bag on the island, "that's not what I was expecting."

"With your dirty mind," I tease, moving to join Paul in the kitchen, "it should've been."

Paul merely laughs. Damien takes himself off to the bathroom whilst I grab three plates from the cupboard, unsuccessfully hiding my wince.

"Easy," Paul says, followed by an, "Is he all right?"

"He will be." I nod. "We both will."

"Good," Paul states, laying out the takeaway boxes. "I knew you couldn't stay pissed off for long."

"At Damien maybe," I tease. "You…"

Paul laughs, turning his entire body to face me. "Come on then, lass. Get it out of your system."

If I didn't know any better, I'd say there was a hint of guilt in Paul's eyes, but I take a step closer regardless, my best stern face in place. I stand for a minute, making him sweat, before wrapping my arms around him, and when he hugs me tight, he laughs.

"It's good to have you back, Dani," he says, and I smile into his chest. "Especially so close to home."

"I'll have to ask Ray if moving me close to you was intentional." It is one hell of a coincidence I ended up a stone's throw away from Damien's best mate's hometown, but it's not really a priority right now. "Thank you." I pull away to meet his gaze. "For taking care of him."

Paul pulls me back into the hug. "Till the day I die, lass," he declares. "Till the day I die."

"Mate." I hear Damien's voice, and I lift my head to see him standing behind Paul. "Get your hands off my girl."

"For starters," Paul says, releasing me and holding his hands up in a don't shoot fashion as I slowly move to grab some cutlery from a drawer with a smile. "Dani is a woman, and second, she wanted that hug just as much as me." Damien shakes his head, moving to wrap his arms around me from behind as I stand at the island. "Maybe if you showed the lass some real affection…"

I laugh. "And he's back." Paul's cockiness is never far away.

"Would you want me any other way?" Paul asks.

"I don't *want* you at all."

"That she reserves for me," Damien pitches in.

Paul grimaces as though someone just walked over his grave. "Not what I meant."

"I know." I laugh. "But your face is priceless."

At that very moment, Damien's door slides open and in walk Raif, Jess and Amy, laughing away. Paul's eyes turn instantly mischievous.

"I can't wait to see the looks on *their* faces," he mutters. "You do know they're gonna slaughter us, right?"

"Pretty sure I'm a dead man walking," Damien says, and I'd love to say he's wrong, but I already know all three of them are not going to be happy about being kept in the dark. Especially Jess.

"Brace yourself," I warn.

"Brace yourself for what?" Jess pipes up, catching the tail end of the conversation.

"Oh, just you wait, lass," Paul states. "'Cause it's one hell of a story."

Chapter Twenty-Four

One life story later. One gruelling, exhausting life story full of never-ending questions and explanations that left Raif, Jess and Amy in utter shock is probably more accurate, followed by the longest, most detailed interrogation of my life, plus a few emotion-fuelled spats – Jess being the instigator – and the story is told. Everyone knows everything, from the very beginning to the very end, or to present-day anyway. I'd like to think Damien and my story is far from over. In fact, I'd say it's just beginning.

Two and a half weeks of resting drag by, and I'm about half a second from calling it quits and going back to work at Dave's tomorrow when Damien pulls out the surprise of a lifetime in the form of a trip to celebrate the upcoming birthday I'd forgotten about.

Post-Adrian but pre-returned memories, my birthday was just another day in my empty, anxiety-riddled existence, but not anymore. Damien's determined to make my birthday memorable, even inviting the motley crew along too, and arranging whatever it is he's apparently got planned for the duration of the trip. Everyone is keeping tight-lipped on the subject, of course.

As I step out of Paul's van, my eyes widen at the sight of a beautiful mansion-sized house in front of me. I stand for a minute, taking in the white-painted, exterior brickwork, and the Greek-style pillars that form an entrance porch that leads to the front door. The windows have old-style shutters outside, painted a weird light green colour that almost matches the grass, but not much else, and the windows themselves are Victorian rather than the usual PVC double-glazed type.

I follow the others inside and step into a grand hallway, a beautiful Cinderella-style staircase taking centre stage. The floor is hardwood, not cheap laminate, and there are tables at either side of the hallway playing home to a couple of vases full of flowers. The walls are standard magnolia, but there are several pieces of abstract artwork, giving the room a nice colour burst.

"Wow," I whisper.

Raif leads the way through the door to the right, and the rest of us follow into what I'm assuming is the living room, but given the size of the house, I can imagine there's more than one. It's a nice room with three sofas making an N shape, and a large mahogany coffee table in the middle. There's a flat-screen telly, at least sixty inches, hanging above an old-fashioned coal fire and Victorian-style fireplace. Talk about mixing the old with the new.

Craving caffeine, I step through the archway and wow, what a kitchen. All white cupboards and jet-black granite worktops, with a Damien-style island in the middle, albeit twice the size and playing home to eight stools in the same shape as the sofas. Appliances wise, I'm assuming it's all built in, hidden by cupboards, which makes it Damien's idea of a perfect kitchen: neat, tidy, and clutter-free.

Damien intervenes, ushering me back into the living room with a stern reminder of my injuries and brews up for the group. That's when I spot a pile of presents sitting on the coffee table. I hadn't expected gifts, but I'm not going to say no.

"Open mine first," Jess insists, thrusting her gift into my hand as I plonk myself down on the couch.

I rip off the bright pink wrapping paper, opening the box underneath to find a cheesy but sweet bracelet with the word *friend* engraved on a dangling, broken love heart. Jess swiftly reveals a matching bracelet with the word *best* on it.

"I suddenly feel about ten years old," I say. "But thank you."

A joint Jess and Damien gift comes next in the form of a photo album with the words *just in case you forget* written upon the front cover, which is cheeky, but it makes me laugh. Inside the album is a collection of all the photos Damien kept, and a description of who, what, when and where written underneath. Putting aside the worry the two of them obviously think another serious head injury or brain damage or possible dementia is in my future, I'm genuinely touched. It's a heartfelt kind of gift.

A new denim jacket comes from Amy, which is well received since my old one is a little past its expiry date, and dear Paul blesses me with a music voucher and a pile of blank scores. A box of condoms too, because, well, it's Paul, but hey, you can't go wrong with a practical and useful gift. As for Raif... Holy hell, it's a dress.

"Did you make this?" I ask.

"I did indeed, honey," Raif answers.

"It's beautiful," I say, standing and moving to hug Raif. "Thank you."

"Hey," Jess protests. "I didn't get a hug."

I laugh, and before I have time to blink, the entire motley crew get in on the action, throwing their arms around me, and I find myself standing in the centre of a massive group hug.

"Watch the ribs," I remind them, but not one of them pulls away. "Yeah, yeah," I say. "I love you guys too."

Eventually, they let go, and after a reminder from Damien of tonight's plans, minus any specific details, we disperse to get ready.

Damien gathers up my gifts and leads me upstairs to our

designated room. The first thing that catches my eye is the four-poster bed with silky light green bedding and about a thousand matching throw cushions sitting on top. White antique-looking bedside tables, each with their own antique lamp sit either side of the bed, opposite the mirrored wardrobes, and a white dressing table and matching set of drawers sit off to the right, not that I plan on using them.

Dumping my presents on the bed, Damien pops off for a shower, leaving me to get dressed for the evening. Sliding into Raif's dress, I survey my reflection in the mirror and almost gasp. It's a tight, figure-hugging dress that fits perfectly, highlighting the curves of my breasts, the only real curves I have, and my hourglass figure seamlessly. It's tastefully designed, with a fitted bodice and a pencil-style finish, falling to the middle of my thighs, and I'm extra grateful my legs are not an issue.

Starting at just above the bust, the neckline and sleeves are made of a mesh fabric, which would normally be see-through, but this beauty has the added bonus of suede-style rose patterns that trail from front to back and down the length of the long-sleeve arms. Whilst I have undoubtedly grown, I'm still not overly keen on parading my scars to the world, but thanks to Raif's handiwork and attention to detail, everything that should be concealed is hidden faultlessly. And just when I think I'm done being impressed, my heart swells at the sight of thumbholes at the end of each sleeve.

I marvel at my refection, refusing to acknowledge the never-fully-dwindled complex about my face, and I can honestly say, I look like a different person. If I was a little more confident, I'd go as far as to describe myself as beautiful, but I'm not, so I won't.

I spot Damien in the mirror as he exits the en-suite

bathroom, wrapped in nothing but a towel, and I can't help but beam when his eyes widen upon seeing me.

"Wow," he breathes.

"Can you…" Damien is already behind me, his hand grazing my bare flesh as he slowly eases up the rest of the zipper. "Well?" I ask, though I can totally see the heat in his eyes. "What do you think?"

He meets my gaze in the mirror. "I think –" he plants a shiver-inducing kiss on my neck "– that I'm the luckiest man on the planet."

The kisses continue, his hands roaming, and I'm so close to abandoning the dress completely when Damien remembers himself. Damien caved roughly ten days ago, but when I woke up as stiff as a board the next morning, Damien was less than impressed. I'm pretty sure he was more pissed at himself for giving in, which, for me, was a welcome confidence boost, but since then…zilch. Nada. Nothing. And since Damien is pulling away, I'm guessing today is no different.

"Please don't stop," I plead.

"We've been here before."

"Yeah, like over a week ago."

I pull him in for round two, and although he obliges to a long, tantalisingly sexy kiss, annoyingly, he pulls away. Again.

"You're still healing, Dani," he insists. "And you've got a birthday to celebrate."

"It's just another day." I shrug.

"No, it's not," Damien argues. "It's *your* day, and I'll be damned if after all the shit, I'm not gonna make it a special one." I smile at his sweetness.

"Fine," I relent. "I'm sure whatever you've got planned will be just as satisfying as a mind-blowing orgasm."

Damien smirks. "Mind-blowing, huh?"

"It's been so long," I tease. "I can't remember."

Damien sits on the edge of the bed and pulls me close, nestling me between his open legs. "You're relentless, you know that?"

"Jess is rubbing off on me." I shrug.

"Maybe I can find another way to make you happy?" I eye him curiously. "Like with a birthday present?" Not quite an orgasm, but I guess it'll have to do.

Damien leans back and snags a wrapped gift from his bag and I take it from him. I rip open the paper to reveal a small box, and when I open it, I smile.

"A key?" I ask. "To the warehouse?"

"Move in with me." He comes right out with it. "We've lost so much time, I don't want to waste another minute. I want to wake up with you every morning and sleep beside you every night."

My heart swells. "You didn't need to sell it, babe," I say, yet touched by his usual way with words. "I want all that, and more."

"Is that a yes?"

I laugh. "Of course it is." I plant another kiss on his tasty lips, my arms wrapping around his neck. "I can't imagine ever sleeping without you."

"Never again, babe," he says, so softly it's almost a whisper. "Although, you said more. What kind of more are we talking?"

I smile. "Everything. Marriage, kids, the whole shebang." Did I just say kids?

"Kids?" Apparently, I did, and I'm suddenly feeling a little self-conscious.

"Did I not want them before?" I honestly don't remember,

and I've never thought about kids post-shitstorm until literally thirty seconds ago, so I'm not entirely sure where it's come from. Wow, I really have come a long way.

"You did." Damien smiles. "We both did." That's good to hear. "I always said I wanted a family like yours, or like my lot back home, and if I can be half the dad your dad was, I'd be more than happy."

I fight back the pending tears. "Damien Coyle, your way with words will be my undoing." Damien laughs. "You will make an awesome dad, but I'm talking a good five or six years down the line yet, babe." Damien nods in eager agreement. "First, I want to live. I want to go on crazy adventures and make *unforgettable* memories. I just want you, in any way I can have you."

Damien stares at me with a burning intensity that has my stomach fluttering. "Fuck it," he says, and without another word, he kisses me with a fierce and overwhelming yearning that consumes me. When we fall to the bed, I melt into him, getting lost in the man I love.

Two mind-blowing orgasms later, and I'm watching post-second-shower Damien dry himself off. Already back in my dress and ready to go, I decide to tear myself away before we end up abandoning tonight's events completely. Heading downstairs into the kitchen, craving a caffeine fix, and a couple of painkillers in case my usual headache decides to make an unwelcome appearance, I find Paul sitting at the kitchen island wearing a suit, minus the jacket and tie, nursing a coffee.

"Well, if that smile's anything to go by," Paul says as I move to boil the kettle, "I'd say Damien's lifted his no-sex ban." I merely smile even wider. "You look gorgeous by the way."

"Thanks," I say awkwardly. I'm not convinced Paul's ever

called me gorgeous before, and for some reason, it feels a little weird. "You scrub up pretty well too."

"I'm sorry," he says, holding a hand to his ear. "For a second there, I thought you were giving me a compliment."

"Don't get used to it."

"Oh, believe me," he says, "I won't."

I laugh, preparing my brew and downing my painkillers. Damien appears looking as hot as hell in a black shirt and trousers combo, and wow, shoes instead of his usual trainers. He slides his arms around me from behind and kisses my neck. My smile reawakens, and I abandon my coffee to the counter, covering his arms with my own.

"Please stop," Paul pleads. "As happy I am you two are back to your old selves, I'd rather not spend the whole night heaving."

"Better get yourself some anti-sickness pills then, mate," Damien suggests. "'Cause I don't ever plan on stopping."

It's not long before Raif, Jess and Amy appear, giggling away like a trio of teenagers, each carrying a glass of wine. Raif looks as trendy as ever in his usual curved edge shirt, a blue one, a pair of tighter than tight black leather trousers, and a casual black jacket. Amy is rocking a beautiful, skin-tight, light blue pencil dress sitting under a matching bolero, and Jess... Well, colour me stunned.

I've always known Jess is a beautiful woman, but tonight, she is every inch the picture of elegance. She's wearing a conservative black, rose-patterned strap dress that falls to just above her knees paired with strapped heels, her blonde hair is up, dangling down over her shoulders and neck, and even her make-up is tasteful and natural, highlighting her lightly tanned glow. In a word, she looks radiant.

"Well, someone stole my thunder," I tease, not that I care. "Look at you." Jess smiles. "That's got to be Raif's handiwork."

"Thanks, Dani," she replies sarcastically. "Are you saying I can't look this good without help?"

"That's exactly what I'm saying." I can't resist winding her up. "Am I wrong?"

"I've had fun playing Barbie," Raif says. "It's your turn next, Dani."

"Not on your life, mate." I laugh. "Although, thank you again for the dress. It really is beautiful."

"You look absolutely stunning," he compliments.

Damien releases his hold on me and moves to wrap an arm around his sister's shoulder. "You took beautiful too, sis."

"Amy always does," Jess retorts, unable to hide the sting of jealousy.

Amy looks up at her big brother. "Thanks."

Damien graces Amy with a peck on the top of her head, to which I smile. There's something endearing about watching Damien's obvious love for his kid sister.

I'm distracted by a beep, followed by Paul's, "Taxi's here." And with Paul taking the lead, we head for the door. "Now, Dani," he adds, "for all of our sanities, try not to get hurt, yeah?"

"I was doing so well keeping my anxiety in check," I retort. "Until you opened your big mouth."

"It's all right," Damien assures, taking up the rear, locking the door behind us before wrapping an arm around my shoulder. "She's not leaving my arms tonight." If that's not something to be excited about, I don't know what is.

The journey to our destination is short and sweet, but I'm surprised when we pull up to a harbour. I let Damien take my hand and lead me down a small pier towards a large, glorious yacht. It's a rich man's kind of yacht, and it's beautiful. Although, I'm suddenly wondering if Damien's come into some serious money during our time apart. A trip out on a yacht like this can't come cheap.

Surprise overload, a man is walking off the boat and handing Paul the keys.

"Wait," I say to Damien. "Paul is driving?" All I get is that beautiful smile and a nod.

I didn't know Paul was into boats, and I definitely didn't know he could drive one, not now, not ever. Unless that little detail is lost in the black hole, never to be remembered. Not that I mind not remembering, nor that Paul is driving. In fact, I'm chuffed. It would appear we're getting all the privacy I could wish for. Good old Damien. He knows both the old me and new me far too well.

Paul leads us on board, and the first thing I notice is the fairy lights streaming above the open deck at the front. There are several loungers and a couple of tables, each playing home to a tealight candle, and I can't help but smile when I see the sound system, a guitar sitting beside it. The thought of Damien singing the night away makes me brim with excitement. Unless the guitar is meant for me, and the motley crew are expecting a birthday performance.

Paul disappears to the top deck, whilst Jess and Raif disappear down below. I let Damien lead me onto the open deck, and I stare out at the ocean. I can feel the chill of the impending night's air, but Damien's arms are all the warmth I need.

Jess and Raif reappear carrying drinks, and Amy, whom I hadn't notice join them downstairs, sets down a few trays of food. I'll admit, for a change, my stomach is rumbling. Damien laughs, obviously hearing my hunger, and when Amy disappears and reappears carrying a handful of plates, Damien wastes no time in dishing out the freshly cooked – I take a glance at the plate Damien thrusts in my direction – bangers and mash. I laugh, probably a little too dramatically, but I can't help it. Bangers and mash on a fancy yacht in fancy clothes; there has to be a reason, I just have no clue what it is.

"Significance?" I ask.

"It's what you were eating in the canteen the first day we met," Damien explains, smiling. "The day I knew I'd met my soulmate."

Swoon alert. "You knew from one conversation I was your soulmate?" I shake my head, taking a seat on a lounger as Jess hands me a knife and fork. "I highly doubt that."

"Yeah, all right," he admits. "That might have been an exaggeration, but I knew you were special, and I was gonna do whatever it took to get to know you."

"Now, *that* I can believe."

Paul reappears, and Damien moves to hand him a plate. "I'll quickly eat this, and we'll be on our way."

"Is there a destination?" I ask, noticing Jess handing out drinks, myself not included.

"Not really." Paul shrugs. "But far out enough to party the night away without being heard."

Damien raises his glass. "To Dani." And the rest follow suit, echoing him. I smile, yet I'm witnessing the return of the blush I haven't experienced since my first few encounters with Damien, this time around, of course. I'm not sure I'll ever be completely comfortable with being the centre of attention.

"The most sarcastic, utterly infuriating person I have ever known," Jess says, making me smile. "With a heart of pure gold, loyal to a fault, and the best friend a girl could ask for."

"Hear, hear," Paul cheers, and I'm met with a chorus, and by chorus, I mean singing, of "Happy Birthday".

"Oh," Jess adds, once the singing has ceased. "And thank you to Damien for inviting us along this weekend. This is freaking amazing." Jess moves to sit on the lounger beside me and leans into my ear. "Is he a secret millionaire?"

I shrug. "Not that I know of." I look to the entire group. "But I'm glad you're all here."

"You might not think so by the end of the night, honey," Raif says. "'Cause I plan on making the most of Damien's wallet tonight." He takes a large gulp of his drink for dramatic effect.

"Me too," Amy says, beaming.

"Just don't fall overboard, yeah?" I joke. "I don't fancy ruining your dress saving your drunken arse." Raif draws a cross over his chest where his heart lies underneath.

"Do you even remember if you can swim?" Paul asks, and I genuinely have to stop and think, which has the others laughing.

"You know what," I say, suddenly a little conscious I'm on a boat, soon to be out in the middle of the ocean, "that's a point."

"Don't worry, babe," Damien assures. "I'll save you from drowning."

"Her hero," Jess taunts.

"Actually, let's not tempt fate," I say. "With my history, I wouldn't be surprised if the universe threw in another freak accident."

"That's a point too," Paul agrees, but I can tell from his amused face it's only in jest.

"Hey," I protest. "I ain't joking."

The food is soon eaten, and while the drinks flow, Paul sets sail. I sit curled in Damien's lap as the music starts, and I don't know how much time passes, but I'm soon acutely aware of a lack of movement, and Paul rejoining the party. It's not long before my friends, including Paul, are dancing the night away, well on the way to being way over the legal limit. Not Paul, just for the record. Drinking and driving, even if it is a boat and not a car, is a definite no-no.

I don't want the night to end. I'm wrapped in Damien's arms, surrounded by the people I hold dear, my cheeks hurting from the continuous laughter. I can't think of a better way of celebrating my birthday, and I'm immensely grateful. I still don't believe in perfect, but I have to say, this moment, right now, it's pretty damn close.

I'm not overly happy when Damien taps my leg, silently asking to be let out from underneath me, but I sink straight back down into the lounger the second he's gone. My happiness quickly returns when I spot Damien plugging the guitar into the sound system, and the rowdy dancers take a seat, equally excited. Or maybe that's the booze. Probably the booze.

"For those of you who don't know," Damien speaks, sliding the guitar strap across his body, "which with your big gobs is probably none of you…" Short laughter. "I suck at writing lyrics, but −" his eyes find mine "− I've been a little extra inspired lately, so I want to share a song for the birthday girl, and the love of my life." I hear Jess squeal, but Raif quickly shushes her. "It's called 'You and I'."

I find myself sitting a little straighter in my seat, eagerly awaiting. I clock Paul's wink, before turning my full attention to Damien, and when he starts to sing, I'm a goner. I barely register the end, tears streaming down my face like waterfalls of sheer amazement. Every word, every note… Beautiful, heartfelt, sincere and everything in between. Screw it. I do believe in perfect, and I just witnessed it. Hell, I'm in love with it.

The motley crew cheer and clap, but when Damien abandons the guitar and heads my way, I throw my arms around him. I kiss him, telling him just how much his song meant to me through my lips, and when I pull away, I stare deep into those gorgeous sky-blue eyes.

"That was..." No words can live up to what I'm feeling. "The best birthday present ever. I knew you had it in you." I'm referring to the writing lyrics part there.

"I have a good muse," he says, as smooth as ever.

"Just good?" I tease.

The pre-recorded music returns, and I find myself locked in a slow dance with Damien. Until Paul goes and ruins the moment by turning the music off, which gains him a rather loud protest from Jess, Amy and Raif. Those three are so far past drunk, I'm surprised they're still standing upright.

"Pretty sure it's time for my birthday present," Paul says. I thought I'd already had my presents from Paul, but hey, I won't say no to another.

Paul looks to Damien, who nods, leading me to the very edge of the deck at the front of the yacht. Paul moves along with us, instructing me to close my eyes. I'm not overly at ease with that idea, but after a pointed just-do-it stare from Paul, I oblige.

"I'm gonna talk," he says, "but you better keep those eyes closed until I say otherwise, you hear me?"

I laugh at his authoritarian tone. "Yes, sir."

"Save the submission for Damien," he jokes, and I slap a hand to his chest, or at least, I'm hoping it was his chest. I can't actually see. "Okay." He takes a deep breath. "Roughly three years ago, I lost my kid sister..." That's me, I'm assuming. "And not long after, I lost my brother." That'd be Damien. "Until I got the happiest phone call of my life. My kid sister was back from the dead, and I sat back and watched as my brother came back to life, his only goal to find the woman he loved. Luckily, he got his wish, and even though she just had to make the road so much harder than it needed to be…"

I can hear the quiet laughter coming from the others, and I'm forced to resist the urge to slap him a second time.

"Two of the most important people in my life were reunited," Paul continues. "So, I decided, should the time come that I got to share their happiness, I wanted to give them something extra special."

I feel Paul slide something small but cold into my hand, but I'm still awaiting the order to open my eyes, so I merely close my hand around it.

"It was a long shot," Paul admits. "And most of the credit goes to Ray…" Ray? I turn my head in the direction of Paul's voice to portray my surprise. "Turns out, he's a stickler for holding on to things." Okay, now I'm confused. "I doubt Dani's given much thought to this, and I know Damien thought it was lost…" What the… "Open your eyes, lass."

I do as I'm told, and I look down to find a ring sitting in my palm. A beautiful three-diamond band that somehow, I instantly recognise: my engagement ring. The same engagement ring Damien gave to me all those years ago. I can't believe it. I look to Paul, but he nods his head to… Oh, my God. Damien's down on one knee in front of me, and I instinctively bring my cast-covered hand to my mouth to cover my gasp. The yacht, the moonlight, the ocean backdrop… Damien's recreating his first proposal and I'm as stunned, yet unbelievably happy, as I was then.

"It's been one hell of a road to get here, babe," Damien says. "But for me, this is just the beginning of the amazing life I want for us, filled with passion, laughter, and more love than I ever thought possible." The tears are refusing to be fought, but I don't even care. "I love you more than life itself, and after experiencing how it felt to try and live a life without you, I never want that to happen again. I want to stay by your side for eternity. I want to hold you, make love to you…"

That gains him a whoop, from Raif, I think, and Damien can't help but laugh. I would laugh, but I'm too busy crying.

"You are my heart, my inspiration, and my strength," Damien continues. "I promise you, if you want me, I'm all yours, babe, and I will do anything and everything to make you happy for the rest of your life. So…" Damien takes the ring from my hand and holds it at the edge of my finger. "I'm asking you…"

"Again," I hear someone say.

"Daniella *Blake* —" he overemphasises my newer surname purely for the fun of it, I think "— will you do me the honour of making me the luckiest and happiest man alive by marrying me?"

"Yes," I say without hesitation. "Of course it's a yes!"

Damien's slides the ring onto my right-hand finger. Wrong one, yes, but the other is a little cast hindered. He stands, and when his lips meet mine, time stands still, the entire world fading away. All I can see is the beautiful man I love.

The cheers erupt, and I'm forced to tear my lips away. Jess is the first to drag me from Damien's grip, pulling me into a tight hug that swiftly reminds me I'm not entirely healed, not that I complain aloud. When she pulls back, her tears are flowing as freely as my own.

"I'd better be maid of honour," she says, jabbing a finger at me. "Congratulations, Dani."

Amy's next, and again, I'm fighting the urge to groan under

her intense grip. Surprisingly, she kisses my cheek before pulling away. "Welcome to the family, sister-in-law."

Raif follows suit, albeit gentler, for which I'm silently grateful. "That was the most beautiful scene I have ever witnessed," he gushes, wiping away tears. "If that's not the fairy-tale ending you both deserve, honey, I don't know what is."

Words are eluding me. I'm far too emotional to speak. No one seems to be minding much, and when Paul wraps his arms around me, I'm back to sobbing. He merely laughs, letting me cry into his chest for a minute before pulling away.

"What you just did…" I manage to say.

"Like I say," he insists. "Thank Ray."

"Oh, I will." I nod. "But to even think about trying to track down my old engagement ring…" I think I'm beyond stunned. "You're gonna make some woman a very happy lady one day with sentiment like that."

"I can only hope, lass," he says before joining the excited chatter coming from the others.

Damien wraps his arms around me, and I bury myself in his warmth. It's a clink of a glass that has me lifting my head to find my friends standing around us, holding their drinks high.

"To the happy couple," Paul says. "May their nauseating love for one another never end. I want to wish you both all the happiness in the world. After the seriously fucked-up shit you've been through, you had better make it worth it."

"Congratulations," everyone yells, and yep, the tears are never going to stop. I know I'm an emotional wreck at the best of times, but this takes the biscuit.

I'm soon bombarded by Raif, Amy and Jess chatting all things wedding, and as Paul retakes his driver's seat, I let the gentle rocking of the boat bring me back down to earth.

The yacht reaches the harbour, and Damien and I walk hand in hand, the others walking a little ahead, unable to wipe the smile from my face.

"Did they know you were gonna propose?" I ask Damien, and his grin is all the answer I need. I take my hat off to them for managing to keep their mouths shut for a change. "So, what now?"

"Now," Damien replies, pulling me into his arms, "*we* are gonna do a little celebrating on our own." The sexy, husky tone of his voice has my insides screaming in delight.

"We're going out," Jess pipes up. "Give you guys some privacy."

Paul turns to look at us, walking backwards. "Although, if you're still at it when we get back –" I roll my eyes "– my room is next to yours so please, do me a solid and keep it down, yeah?"

Damien calls a taxi, and we're soon arriving back at the house. The second the door is closed, my hands find Damien, and in a whirlwind of emotion, I make love to my beautiful fiancé until my eyes refuse to be kept open, and I blissfully fall asleep.

It's the sound of my phone vibrating that has me opening my eyes to the first signs of sunlight. Groaning, I fumble until I feel the cold exterior on the bedside table and press it to my ear.

"Hello?"

"Hello, Daniella." A menacing, gruff tone penetrates my ear.

I bolt upright, my heart jumping to my throat, the colour draining from my face.

"Adrian."

Chapter Twenty-Five

Time stands still. This can't be happening. It's not real. It has to be a nightmare. Pathetically, I pinch myself, silently pleading with the universe to wake me the fuck up, but it's useless. I'm not dreaming.

"It's good to hear your voice," he says.

"How…" I falter, my voice trembling. "How did you get my number?"

"I have my ways."

"What do you want?"

"Isn't that obvious, Daniella?"

"There ain't no way I'm visiting you, Adrian."

Adrian laughs that arrogant cackle I remember all too well, sending a screaming shiver down my spine. "Which is why I've come to you."

My heart stops. "Wh –"

The phone slips from my hand, hitting the bed with a bounce. With teary eyes, I instinctively glance beside me, but the side of the bed where Damien should be is empty. I jump to my feet and race into the bathroom. Nothing.

"No, no, no, no," I mutter, pacing the bedroom in a daze.

"Daniella." I hear Adrian's gravely tone, and with shaky hands, I force the phone back to my ear. "If you're looking for your beloved," he taunts, "I'm afraid he's otherwise detained. His early morning run took a turn for the worse."

I fall to the floor in a heap, my head spinning. I can't see straight. The panic-laced fog is taking me under, and my chest is tightening. I can't breathe. I sit, gasping for air. The flash-backs are coming thick and fast. My head is going to explode.

Any confidence I've gained over the past couple of months evaporates into a cloud of dust, and I'm the same broken shell I always was, every instinct in my body telling me to run, run as fast as my feet can carry me and never look back. Only I can't, because Adrian is here, and he has Damien. My past is well and truly back to haunt me, and my fiancé's life is hanging in the balance.

"Here's how it's gonna go, Daniella," Adrian says, but I'm barely listening. "Daniella?" His stern voice cuts through me. "Pay attention," he barks. "There's a car waiting at the end of the drive." I move to the window and peel back the curtain just enough to see a black car sitting outside. "Get in it, Daniella."

I blink repeatedly, forcing my brain to think rationally. "Where's Damien?" My anger awakens, and Adrian's condescending chuckle sickens me. "How do I know you ain't already killed him?"

"You don't," he replies calmly, "but if you don't come quietly, I can assure you Damien will be dead before the day is done."

I fight back the pending nausea. I don't have a choice. It's me Adrian wants, and if there's a chance Damien's still alive, there's a chance I can bargain for his life with my own. I let the tears flow silently yet relentlessly.

Composing myself as best I can, I ask, "Can I at least put on some clothes first?"

"Of course," Adrian says. "But don't even think about waking your friends, Daniella. It won't end well."

I huff sarcastically. I couldn't wake them even if I wanted to. There's no way they'd let me go, sacrificing myself like a pig to the slaughter, not even for Damien.

After being instructed to stay on the line, I quickly chuck on a top and some jeans. I hear a creak from the hallway, and my heart skips a beat, but when I peer out through the door to find the coast clear, I let out a sigh of relief. Tiptoeing downstairs, I hover in the hallway for a second, questioning my sanity and the reality of what I'm about to walk into.

"Time's ticking," Adrian urges, and it takes all my strength not to scream "Fuck you!" down the phone.

Without further hesitation, yet shaking like a leaf in a hurricane, I head outside. Before I even reach the car, a figure appears behind me, and a needle punctures my neck.

I wake up feeling groggy. My head hurts, my ribs are screaming in agony, and... I look at my hand, unsurprised to find it cuffed to a radiator. I yank at it until common sense kicks in and reminds me that escape is futile. There's no way it's coming off. I rub my eyes with my free hand, and once the blurriness subsides, I scan my surroundings.

I'm in what used to be a living room but is now a dilapidated space that's falling down around me. An abandoned house, no doubt. I scramble to my feet, my hand remaining close to the floor, thanks to the bastard cuffs, and I stretch as far as I can to glance through the crack in the boarded-up window. Nothing but countryside and out in the middle of nowhere. Of course. Horror movie, take two.

I sink back down, and that's when I see him. Damien. He's on the floor at the far end of the room opposite me, both his hands cuffed to a second radiator, tape plastered across his mouth. My heart sinks into another wave of panic. His eyes are closed, and he's not moving. I'm about to burst into a flood of tears, assuming the worst, when I see his chest rise and fall, and although the tears still descend, I let out a sigh of relief. He's still alive. Battered black and blue, but alive.

I instinctively pat myself down in search of my phone, despite already knowing it's probably lying on the driveway or smashed to pieces by now, leaving no trace or breadcrumbs to our location. I could scream, but from what I briefly saw through the window, there are no neighbours close enough to hear. The car Adrian's lacky used to bring me here will be burnt out no doubt, all evidence erased, and it'll be hours before my hungover friends wake and realise Damien and I are gone. Fuck. I yank at my cuffs again out of nothing more than pure frustration.

Let's face it. Adrian's managed to escape prison and make it all the way here without being caught. He's a clever, manipulative bastard who thinks a thousand steps ahead and won't make the same mistake twice. I'm not going to be rescued, not this time. I'm the only one who can save Damien and me, but as someone who's spent so much time ruled by fear, a fear Adrian will no doubt reinstall at the earliest opportunity, I'm not liking my odds.

My eyes drift to Damien. We were so close. So close to putting everything behind us and moving on to the future, a bright, happy future with marriage and kids, and all the love a person could ever need. So fucking close. At least I'll get to say goodbye this time, but my heart is already breaking because even though it's me Adrian will physically hurt, emotionally, we'll both spend the rest of our lives in pain.

It will kill Damien knowing he's lost me to Adrian – again. Damien and I have been through so much already, neither of us deserves any more suffering, but Damien will drown in guilt and blame anyway, and it only makes me hate Adrian more. Adrian is the one who should be suffering, not us, but I guess the only comfort I have is knowing the motley crew will do their best to keep Damien afloat, and he'll at least be alive. That's all that matters now, and I'll do everything I can to keep it that way, even if it means resigning myself to a life of endless torture.

It's the sound of footsteps that drags me out of my thoughts, and when Adrian wanders into the room, my entire body instinctively tenses. I lift my head to stare into the cold, piercing brown eyes of the one man I despise more than anyone or anything else on this planet, and the sight of that smug smirk on his face is enough to make the nausea hit the back of my throat.

For an escaped convict, he looks awfully well kept. He's ditched the curls for a shaved do, and in true Adrian style, he's clean-shaven. Wearing a black suit with a white shirt and matching black tie, topped off with a few extra muscles since the last time I saw him, he screams power and dominance, and it sickens me. Prison clearly suited him, the bastard.

"You look well, Daniella," he compliments. "As beautiful as ever."

I dry heave. I'm not in the mood for small talk, funnily enough, and there's only one thing on my mind. "Let Damien go."

Adrian cackles. "Why would I want to go and do that?"

"Because you've got what you want."

"Except we both know he'll never stop searching for you."

"Does it matter?" I ask. "Since I'm guessing this shithole is just a pit stop, it's not like he'll find me."

Adrian nods. "True."

"He doesn't need to die," I state.

"I have no intention of killing Damien, Daniella." I let out a sigh of relief. "Death would be a kindness but living…" Adrian's face fills with contempt. "The guilt of losing you, of knowing I have reclaimed what is rightfully mine, will eat him alive, and I'll take great pleasure knowing he will spend the rest of his measly existence suffering."

The tears well in my eyes. Silence falls as Adrian pulls a rickety old, wooden chair from the corner of the room and places it in front of me – just out of reach – before taking a pew, and casually crossing one leg over the other with a smile.

"How did you do it?" I ask, curiosity getting the better of me. "Escape."

"Good old-fashioned manipulation and bribery," Adrian declares. "I doubt you'll be overly surprised to hear I kept a few loyal names out of the extensive list I provided the police." The list that gained him a lesser sentence. "Nor that police corruption is not limited to a cinema screen." Unfortunately, not.

"Are you getting to the point?"

Adrian scowls but continues. "I was temporarily released from prison to aid a drug trafficking investigation." He smirks. "It took months and months of planning, but with the help of two particularly money-minded police officers, the prison reluctantly agreed, and I disappeared before fulfilling my role." I shake my head in dismay as Adrian glances at his watch. "Although, I should imagine the second watch has arrived by now to take over babysitting duties."

"And your accomplices?"

"I'm sure they've devised a suitable story that doesn't implicate them."

"Of course," I say sarcastically. "My God, I really am living a soap opera life."

Adrian merely laughs, but at least it explains Ray's lack of contact. I doubt he was told about Adrian's temporary release in the first place. Ray no longer handles drug cases, switching out to delve into the world of murder, and although I don't remember if my uncle told me much about life on the force, I have watched a crime show or two in my time, and I could imagine communication between departments isn't always open. That, and Adrian's corrupt buddies probably made sure Ray was kept in the dark.

"I've had a lot of time to prepare for this day, Daniella," Adrian says. "I'm a man of my word. I told you I'd be back."

"Yes, you did." I nod, before tilting my head to one side. "You never heard of moving on?"

Adrian scowls, clearly unimpressed by my cockiness. The old Dani didn't talk back.

"What can I say?" Adrian shrugs. "I'm a passionate guy. When I want something, I stop at nothing to get it, and when I do, I never let it go."

"You got issues, mate."

"My, my," he says, uncrossing his legs and leaning forward in his chair. "You've gained a cocky mouth in my absence."

"I've gained a lot since you've been gone."

"I can see that." His eyes trail to a still-unconscious Damien. "It appears I'm not the only one willing to follow you to the end of the earth."

I let out a weak laugh. "I bet you knew who Damien was before I did."

"The Belfast-based Army soldier fiancé," Adrian states. "I'm assuming you regained your memories." I nod. "Well, that explains the swift re-engagement."

His words hit me like an avalanche, and I force myself to meet his piercing gaze. "How do you…" I gasp. "You never lost me, did you?"

Adrian sneers. "Of course not," he declares, as if I've just suggested something highly outrageous. "I've had eyes on you the entire time, Daniella."

"Wh —" My face drops to the floor. The needle-wielding lacky. I shake my head in disgust. I'm about to spit out my loathing when my breath hitches, another blatant realisation sinking in. His face. I briefly saw his face when he jabbed the needle into my neck, but I put his familiarity down to a drug-induced delirium. It's the same face I caught a glimpse of before my head slammed against the bonnet. Oh, for fuck's sake. "The car accident wasn't an accident, was it?" Adrian shakes his head. "But why? It nearly killed me."

"It wasn't meant for you," Adrian states, and for a second, I don't understand, until…

"Amy," I whisper, and Adrian nods. "Why?"

"It's petty, really," he admits. "Damien took something from me. He took what was mine, and in return, I wanted to take something from him, other than you, of course."

Is he having a laugh? "Hurting an innocent woman for the sake of getting one up on Damien." I scoff. "That's a new low, even for you."

Adrian's lips curl into a conceited smirk. "Amy wasn't my only victim, Daniella."

My eyes widen. "What?" Adrian glances towards Damien, and the light bulbs just keep on coming. "The mugging." Oh, how could I be so blind? "That's why Damien's wallet was left behind." I let out a groan, pissed off that my paranoid side decided to take a rare day off and overlook that precious little detail.

"I knew I'd be needing to contact you," Adrian explains. "Orchestrating the theft of Damien's phone was the simplest method of obtaining your number, and of course, the opportunity to hurt Damien was far too good to miss."

"You sick son of a bitch," I spit, my anger soaring to levels I never knew existed.

"You came very close to ruining my reunion plans," he says icily, reminding me of the hit I took on Amy's behalf.

"Not close enough."

Adrian merely laughs, but I turn my gaze away with a heavy sigh. It doesn't matter where I am, I'll never be free. That's what I told Damien, and boy, was I right. I was never free.

"Don't look so defeated, Daniella," Adrian says cockily. "I'm sure it was fun while it lasted."

I turn to glare at him defiantly. "Yes, it was," I state. "It was worth every second, and Damien…" My eyes find my fiancé. "He gave me a happiness most spend their entire lives dreaming about." Adrian scoffs, and I chuckle at his evident jealousy. "Sorry to disappoint, Adrian, but Damien is a thousand times the man you'll ever be, and it really doesn't matter what you to do me because my heart will always belong to him. Not even death will stop me from loving *him.*"

The flash of anger that creeps across Adrian's face doesn't go unnoticed, yet for the first time, I don't flinch. Not even when he kneels in front of me, running a hand through my loose hair. It's a desire not to gag on the nauseating smell of his aftershave that has me turning my face away.

"Careful, Daniella," Adrian warns. "Or I might just test that theory."

My eyes meet his again, and my heart stops. Shit, that's what I get for mentioning death. My love for Damien has made him just another tool hanging from Adrian's belt, and I'm perfectly aware of the lengths Adrian is prepared to go to. He killed my family after all, albeit not with his bare hands, and I give myself a sharp mental slap. I'm supposed to be sacrificing myself to *save* Damien, not to let my mouth get him killed. If Damien dies, his blood will be on my hands. Unfortunately, my anger is refusing to be dampened, and it's making me act irrationally.

"You're wanted, you idiot," I state. "You think it's gonna help your case if Damien shows up dead?"

Adrian shrugs. "I don't plan on getting caught."

"You can't run forever."

"We'll see about that." Adrian sniggers. "But just in case, I'd better make the most of our time together."

It's a threat hidden amongst a poor attempt at wit. Unfortunately, I have an inkling into how Adrian's brain works, and something tells me when Adrian's clock finally stops ticking, he won't be leaving in handcuffs. He'll end it this time, and he'll take me down with him. That's fine. My own death I can handle, but I won't let him take Damien too.

"You kill him," I warn, "I'll kill myself."

Adrian laughs. "Sorry, Daniella," he says, rising to his feet. "There'll be no coward's way out this time."

It's my turn to laugh. "Oh, Adrian," I taunt. "It wouldn't be the coward's way out. Not this time. It'd be revenge."

"Revenge?"

"If Damien lives, he suffers, right? That's what you said?" Adrian remains silent, but I can see the intrigue in his eyes. "Because he loves me, right?" Adrian tenses. "Well, in your sick head, you love me too, more than anything else in the world, and that makes me your only weakness. You *need* me. I'm like a drug to you. Hell, you escaped prison especially for me. So, what do you think losing me a second time will do to you?" Silence. "Give me an excuse, Adrian. I will take great pleasure in knowing *you* will be the one in pain, and me, I'll finally be free."

That gains me a smack across the face, and I'm forced to spit blood onto the floor.

"I promise you," I say, "if he dies, I will find a way to end my life, even if it's the last thing I ever do."

I stare at him, my eyes burning with rage and determination, and I can only hope it's enough to keep Damien alive.

"I look forward to beating that new-found confidence out of you, Daniella." That, I don't doubt for a second. "I'll remind you who you really are."

I let my curiosity get the better of me again. "And who's that?"

"The willing submissive." I choke on air. Is he for real?

"Willing?" I scoff.

"You can't deny our connection, Daniella," he continues anyway. "You can play the victim to the outside world, but I *know* the real you. The beautiful, compliant little damsel who underneath the presence of fear, secretly begs and yearns for a thrill that can only be achieved through force and pain. You and I are made for each other."

I burst out laughing. "Wow, I always knew you were delusional, but now you're just taking the piss." New-found confidence indeed. "If you honestly believe…" A sudden realisation descends, and my eyes widen. "Oh, my God, you actually think I love you, don't you?"

Adrian says nothing, showing a rare weak moment, and it's all answer I need. If I didn't already know Adrian needs psychological help, I do now. I think I'm borderline delirious, teetering on the edge of suicidal because all I do is laugh harder.

"I don't love *you*," I spit. "I could never love *you*. There's no feeling…" That's a lie. "No, I do have feelings for you, Adrian. They're called hate and disgust. You repulse me. Rationalise your sick, twisted impulses all you want, but I'm telling you now, I will never, *ever* love you."

I watch as the darkness in Adrian's eyes takes over, and despite my apparent bravado, I involuntarily start to shiver. Pulling a key from his pocket, he unties the handcuffs and drags me across the floor. He kicks me hard in the chest, and I'm quickly reminded that my ribs are already battered. The searing pain is excruciating, yet I make no sound. He drags me to my feet, slamming my back against the wall.

I should be afraid, but I'm not. I'm serenely calm, which I'll admit is a little disturbing. Maybe it's because I've been here before. Or maybe it's because, with every minute that passes, I'm forcing myself to become numb, determined to block out the memories and the darkness I'm being dragged back into. Or maybe it's because I *know* the only reason why I'm giving in to him now, why I gave into him then, is because there's nothing else I can do.

Light bulb bursting, shattered glass everywhere... Maybe there is something I can do. Upon pissing Adrian off, I've granted myself a golden opportunity – I'm not cuffed anymore. Holy shit. I need to find a way out of this, and if not for me, for Damien. If nothing else, he didn't go down without a fight, clawing his way back to me despite the obstacles in his way, and he deserves the same effort in return.

That's the difference between now and then. As Daniella Thompson, as far as I knew, I had no one. I was alone with nothing to live for, but I'm not her anymore. I'm Daniella Blake, and I have *everything* to live for.

I lift my knee and ram it into Adrian's groin. He stumbles backwards, releasing his grip. Knowing I can't leave without Damien, I go to grab the key Adrian resigned to the floor, but Adrian recovers fast. He yanks me by the hair and throws me to the ground. I desperately try to regain my feet, but he's raining

351

kicks to my chest again, and it's taking all my strength not to scream in agony. I kick out, but it's fruitless.

"Keep resisting," he begs. "You know how much it turns me on."

He climbs on top of me, pinning my hands to the ground with his knees. An arm rests heavily across my chest. A knife I had no idea he had presses against my throat. I'm forced to push back the mind-numbing fear seeping in.

"Do it," I spit. "Put me out of my misery."

Adrian laughs. Pressing down harder on my hands with his legs, he uses the knife to slice open my top in one swift motion. He trails a finger down my middle, and I cringe at the feel of his cold touch. He brings the knife down to my chest. A whimper escapes as I bite down on my lip to stop my screams.

The blade slices through my skin. Once… Twice… I catch Adrian's gaze, and the nausea burns the back of my throat. The release pouring through his breath is toe-curling. I watch as his tension dissolves into sheer bliss, his eyes glazed over, and his lips parted. Tearing into my flesh is Adrian's high, but all the blood and tears in the world will never be enough to quench his thirst for pain.

"I've waited so long for this," he says, and when his hands trail to his trousers, my heart stops.

No, no, no. I thrash with all my might, but his overwhelming strength, the pain from his weight pressing on my not-yet-healed wrist, and the dwindling sting from my wounds are stirring an unavoidable dizziness. It's the sound of groaning that distracts us both, and I turn my head to see Damien waking up.

"Perfect timing," Adrian says with a highly amused tone laced with arrogance, and I lie there watching as the man I love widens his eyes.

Damien's fury takes over. He yanks hard on the cuffs keeping him in place with so much force that, for a second, I think he might rip the radiator right off the wall. Adrian merely laughs, and when his hand finds the button of my jeans, I let out a frustrated scream. I can't, I *won't* let that monster rape me. I refuse to let him break me again, but the more I fight, the more powerless I feel. Damn it. For fuck's sake, universe, give me something. Anything!

And that's when I see it − a plank of wood lying on the floor within arm's reach. I can use that. Now, all I have to do is find a way to free my hands. I need to loosen his iron-cast weight, but… I look to Damien fighting tooth and nail to free himself to no avail, and when his eyes meet mine, the anguish I see is intolerable. I'm only going to make it worse, but what I'm about to do is all I can think of.

Pinned, desperate, and out of options, I mouth *I'm sorry* in Damien's direction before leaning up and pressing my lips to Adrian's. Fighting the urge to gag, I feel Adrian's entire body freeze, but when he deepens the kiss, clearly getting lost in the moment, his newly relaxed state allows me to free my hands from under his legs. I run a hand through his hair to keep him distracted, and he moans appreciatively. The nausea hits me, but I swallow it down. I need Adrian to think I want this. I need his entire focus on my kiss.

Slowly, I use my free hand to reach for the wood, and the second my fingers grasp it, I slam it into the side of his head as hard as I can. It's enough to disorientate him, and the knife crashes to the floor. Bucking underneath him, I scramble for the blade, but Adrian clocks my movement far too quickly. Grabbing my uninjured wrist, he snaps it like a twig, and an ear-piercing scream escapes my mouth.

"Oh, how I love to hear you scream," Adrian says, beaming, and the sound of Damien's desperate tape-covered protests is deafening.

Keeping a tight hold of my newly broken wrist, Adrian drags me towards the radiator. Oh, hell no. He gets me back in those cuffs and I'm screwed. With all the strength I can muster, biting my lip to brace myself for the searing pain, I yank my wrist hard, taking Adrian by surprise. I slam my foot into the back of his leg. He buckles and drops down to a knee, his grip on my wrist evaporating. I crawl for the knife, but it's almost as if the universe is with me one minute then against me the next. Adrian grabs my ankle before my fingers can clamp around the only weapon in sight.

I look around the floor, searching for something, anything else I can use. I fight the urge to scream in delight when I spot a nail. I grab it, thankful it's long enough for my grip not to be hindered by my cast and plunge it into his thigh. He screams in pain, and it's all the distraction I need to clamber to my feet.

Damien's protests only get louder. One look into his eyes tells me he wants me to run without looking back, but there's a fat chance of that happening. There's no way I'm leaving Damien behind to die. I finally grasp the knife, but Adrian grabs my cast-free broken wrist and twists it. I let out another ear-piercing yelp, and the throbbing pain has me falling to my knees. Adrian crouches down in front of me, continuing to twist my wrist back and forth to keep me doubled over in mind-numbing agony.

"Did you honestly think you could escape me?" he yells, his free hand finding my neck. "You are mine! You will always be mine!"

I can hear Damien's muffled protests, but all I can see is the darkness in Adrian's eyes. His breath is ragged, his teeth clenched. His grip around my throat tightens, and I gasp for air. He's losing control.

"If I can't have you…" he roars, and for the first time, I honestly believe Adrian wants to kill me.

Unfortunately for him but lucky for me, his arrogance has led him to forget one vital detail that could potentially save my life – I didn't drop the knife. I plunge the cold steel into Adrian's neck and watch as something I never thought I'd see materialises in those cold, dead eyes of his, something I am all too familiar with: pure, unmistakable fear.

"You always did talk too fucking much," I spit before yanking the knife back out and letting the blood flow free.

Stumbling backwards, Adrian releases my wrist. His hands close around the seeping, bloody hole in his neck as I climb to my feet. Fighting the dizziness threatening to drag me back down, I stagger over to Damien and rip the tape from his mouth. He gasps for air whilst I hunt down the key, and once uncuffed, Damien wastes no time in wrapping his arms around me, pulling me close, the relief pouring from him in waves.

"We need to go," he says. Probably best *not* to wait for Adrian's lacky to resurface.

"Daniella," Adrian rasps, and I don't know why, but I force myself to look at him.

He's lying on the floor, the blood oozing through his fingers to form a pool beneath him. I should feel…I don't even know. Remorse? Guilt? Adrian's going to die. He's bleeding out, but even if I wanted to help, I have no clue where we are, and by the time I figure it out and the paramedics get here, he'll already be dead. I've killed him. I've taken a life, and the humanity inside me should be wrecked, yet all I feel is relief.

Damien pulls me to my feet, and I stare down at the pathetic man who instilled fear into my very soul for so long, feeling lighter than I have in years. I took on the most dangerous, vicious monster I have even known and won. I fought for my freedom, and I survived. An epic way to say "Fuck you, Adrian" if ever there was one.

Carefully bending down and ignoring Damien's loud protests, I pick up the knife – you never know when the universe will turn on you – and take a few tentative steps closer to Adrian. I squat down in front of him, his drooping eyes finding mine. The desperation as what little life he has left drains away is palpable. I never thought I'd care about giving Adrian a taste of his own medicine, but watching him now, vulnerable and defeated, his silent pleas falling upon deaf ears, I can't lie and say it doesn't bring me a semblance of comfort, as sick as that may sound.

Fumbling in his pockets and finding a phone, I rise back up to my feet, his eyes trailing my movement, and with one last breath, I say the words I never thought I'd get to say and unequivocally, without a single shadow of a doubt, believe are nothing but the truth.

"Goodbye, Adrian."

Chapter Twenty-Six

One Month Later

Standing in the empty space of what was my former living room, I smile. I've just handed the keys over to my ex-landlord, and even though Damien wasted no time in moving what little possessions I own – my music set-up being the most important – as soon as we got back from our life-changing trip away, I still had to give the necessary one month's notice.

As overjoyed as I am to be sharing a home with Damien, I can't help but think about the memories I made here. Late-night music sessions, movie nights filled with laughter and home-cooked food, the birth of Jess and my everlasting friendship and of course, Damien and my first kiss, sequel style. So many ups and downs in such a terrifyingly short space of time, but I don't regret any of it, not even the bad times. I'm still here, against all odds, living to see another day with the man I love, so I can safely say it was all worth it in the end.

Entwining my fingers with Damien's, I say a final goodbye before stepping out into the crisp fresh air. I take a deep breath and turn to plant a soft kiss on my fiancé's lips.

"Let's go home," I say.

One short journey later, and I'm crossing the warehouse's threshold. Damien's shushing me, reminding me of our guests camped out on the two couches I brought with me when I moved in, sitting either side of Damien's L-shaped sofa. I smirk, unbelievably tempted to make noise just for the fun of it, because it's *my* home, and I can do whatever the hell I want when

I want, but I wisely decide against it. Hangovers and early mornings are not a good mix, and my brief kick of amusement would be severely outweighed by the extra crabbiness I'd endure. Sensibly, Damien and I quietly head into our bedroom, closing the door behind us.

Feeling ridiculously energised and in desperate need of a release, I ease my gorgeous fiancé onto the bed and straddle him, trailing my lips along his neck.

"Do you think I can't feel you tensing?" he asks, and I stop kissing him, leaning back so he can see the disdain on my face.

"I'm fine," I groan.

Adrian's excessive attacks to my already battered ribs resulted in a fracture, ultimately delaying my already long recovery time, and I reckon I've got another couple of weeks before I'm feeling one hundred percent. Having two cast-bound wrists isn't helping any, and it's been far too long since I made any music, which is highly annoying, but thankfully, Damien escaped without any broken or seriously injured limbs. Just an uncountable number of bruises that took a good couple of weeks to die down.

"Lazy day for you today," he urges.

"If you had your way," I say, "*every* day would be a lazy day for me."

Damien's incessant need to take care of me skyrocketed in the first couple of weeks after Adrian, but I knew it was his way of easing his guilt. Not that he had anything to feel guilty for. If anything, since it was *my* psychotic kidnapper who beat Damien to a pulp, the guilt was all mine, but I'm pleased to say that after many, many mini-breakdowns and heartfelt conversations, Damien and I have officially moved on. We've accepted the only person to blame for the shitstorm that was our life was Adrian.

Not Damien. Not me. Adrian.

"Well, the quicker you heal," Damien says in a butterfly-inducing, smoky tone, "the quicker neither of us needs to hold back. At the very least, I want you at full strength for our wedding night."

Damien and I aren't wasting time, and our wedding date is in just two months. I've left the entirety of the planning to Jess, my maid of honour, who is having an absolute field day, and Raif has been honoured with the task of designing and making my wedding dress. Amy and Kayleigh are going to be bridesmaids, and dear old Paul is, of course, Damien's best man. I've made it clear it's not to be a lavish event, but with Damien's Northern Ireland lot making the trip over, it sure as hell isn't going to be quiet.

"What are you thinking?" Damien asks.

"That I want to marry you." It's only half a lie. I know fine well my mind wandered beyond our upcoming wedding.

Damien laughs. "I figured, given you said yes when I asked you to."

"Funny," I mock.

"Seriously, babe," Damien says, tucking my hair behind my ear. "What's going on in that head of yours?"

"Such a dangerous question," I tease, but Damien's no-nonsense stare has me dropping the act. "I've just been doing a little thinking…about what I might want to do with my life, other than marriage and kids."

"Yeah?" Damien says in an encouraging tone.

"Yeah," I say. "I mean, I've never given it much thought, but things are different now. Adrian's dead, and thanks to Ray, I'm not rotting in prison for murder…"

"It was self-defence, babe," Damien insists. "It was you or

him, and you did what you had to do to survive." I nod. "You saved *both* our lives, Dani. Don't ever forget that."

Doesn't make taking a life any easier. There was no coming back from a severed artery though, even if my humanity did win out in the end. He was dead before the paramedics arrived, as predicted, but the guilt soon surfaced. Adrian doesn't deserve my guilt, but that's what makes me better than him. It makes me human, a good one with a real live, beating heart, and whilst I don't regret Adrian's death, a part of me will never forget the blood on my hands, no matter how justified, and that's okay. It's just another experience to dump in the acceptance pile.

"Point is," I say, "I don't want to waste my life in a meaningless job. I want to do something, *be* something."

Damien smiles. "You have no idea how happy it makes me to hear you say that."

"Why?"

"Because you're ridiculously talented," he praises. "And talent like that should not be kept hidden." That's not exactly what I had in mind. "And I love seeing you happy."

"I love *being* happy," I admit, smiling afterwards. "That's all I ever wanted. To feel something more than just fucked up and broken."

"You were never broken, babe," Damien insists, and I let out a short, hearty laugh.

"I'm totally broken," I argue, holding up both of my cast-covered wrists. "See?" Damien laughs. "But in all seriousness, I don't need to look over my shoulder anymore. I have a real future now." I smile softly. "And if there's one thing the whole Adrian Take Two shit taught me, it's that I *am* strong. I'd have to be to go through all the shit we have, take on my biggest fear head-on and not be the one buried in a casket, *and* end up ridiculously happy, right?" Damien smiles softly. "And with you, and the motley crew, there's nothing I can't do."

Damien kisses me, but it's not passionate or sensual, it's more like a kiss of pure relief, and when he pulls away, I laugh.

"Finally," he practically yells.

I give him a gentle slap to the chest. "There's just one last thing I think I *need* to do." Now I feel it's safe to do so. "And I'm hoping you'll come with me."

"Anything, anywhere, babe."

"I want to visit my parents," I say. "I want to visit the plaque, lay some flowers or something…" I fight back the tears. "With everything that happened, and my memories long gone, I never really got a chance to say goodbye, not really." Damien smiles warmly. "Do you think it's a bad idea?"

Damien shakes his head softly. "It's a great idea."

Make room for the return of a small, yet significant insecurity. "Do you think my parents –"

"They'd be nothing but proud of you." Never have I been more grateful for Damien's ability to read my mind. "So, damn proud."

I nod, partially satisfied. "I figured we could combine it with a trip to see your dad."

"You want to see my dad?" Damien laughs.

"Why wouldn't I?" I shrug. "I know he can be a dick, but he's still your dad, and this whole estranged relationship you two got going on, your mum too, needs to come to an end. Family is precious."

"I got all the family I need right here."

"Sweet, but a cop out."

Damien laughs. "All right, I'll make a little more effort with my parents… For you."

"Thank you."

"Anything for the future Mrs Coyle," Damien says, drawing a smile to my face.

"Mrs Daniella Coyle," I say aloud, noticing a flicker of heat shining in Damien's eyes.

"You have no idea how sexy that sounds," he says.

"Oh, really?" I ask, sensing an opportunity. "How sexy?"

"So sexy, I'm questioning my restraint."

My eyes light up with an eager hunger, yet I can't help but wind him up just a little, adding, "I need to rest and heal," in a poor imitation of Damien's voice.

"Oh, don't worry, baby," he says in a hot-as-hell, almost animal-like tone that makes me quiver with delight. "I plan on taking things very, *very* slow."

If only Damien was kidding. Agonisingly, painfully slow is still an understatement, but my God, it's worth it. I'm revelling in the orgasmic high when Damien eventually abandons me to do a food shop, but I've been so busy daydreaming, I have no idea how long ago that was. I glance at the bedside clock, and holy hell, it's almost lunchtime.

Dragging myself out of bed and heading into the living room, I smirk at the sight of a still-passed-out, couch-hogging Raif, assuming Jess decided to bunk in with Amy in the spare room. In true motley crew style, last night was a late one. Damien and I called it quits around two in the morning, but the rest of them were showing zero signs of packing up and going home. I figured I'd wake up to guests this morning, and my dear friends didn't disappoint.

Paul is up and about though, standing fully dressed in front of the cooker, making what looks like scrambled eggs, and looking surprisingly fresh considering the terrifying amount of alcohol the motley crew consumed last night.

"Good morning," he says.

"*Very* good morning."

Paul groans, sensing my sexual happiness. "Spare me the details."

I laugh as I make my brew. Taking a seat at the island, a moan draws me to the attention of Raif's staggered approach, sporting a pair of what look like Damien's checked flannel pyjamas, and since they're at least three sizes too big, they look extremely odd on his usually so-stylish self. The bags under his eyes are the size of America, and his usually perfectly styled hair is a definite unintentional bedhead do, giving him a death-barely-warmed-up look. He's ridiculously pale too, even rivalling me, and as he sits next to me at the island, I'm not entirely convinced he's not going to defile the counter with the return of last night's booze.

"How you doing, Raif?" I ask.

"It was the shots," Raif groans, his hands rubbing his temples. "So, so many shots. Jess is such a bad influence."

"You're only just figuring that out?" I mock. "Looks like it's a lazy day for *everyone* today."

"Ha!" Raif scoffs. "I'll believe that when I see it."

"Oh, Raif, now I'm gonna be extra lazy just to prove you wrong," I tease.

"Damien will be so proud," Paul mocks, sliding a plate of breakfast toward Raif, who merely pushes it away in disgust. When Paul hands me mine though, I happily accept it. For a change, I'm starving, and I'm intrigued to see if Paul can cook. I don't remember eating a Paul-made meal in the past.

"I think we could all use a night in," Raif admits, rubbing his eyes. "*Without* alcohol."

"Wow," I say, never thinking I'd see the day. "Just how much did you drink?"

"Enough to know it's gonna take me at least a week to recover," Raif groans. "Besides, Jess told me she wants to cook for everyone tonight."

Worst time in the world to take a sip of my coffee, and I'm now wearing half of it. Raif, of course, laughs at me. "Please tell me you're joking?" I beg.

Raif laughs again. "She can't be that bad."

"You live with her," I remind him.

"She's never cooked for me."

"There's a reason," I state. Jess has only ever cooked for me once, the first time I agreed to her relentlessness after moving in, and there's a reason beyond preferring the comforts of my former flat why *I* hosted all future movie nights. "Last and *only* time Jess cooked for me, she served me raw chicken." Paul's looking at me like I'm overreacting, but I swear, Jess is a terrible cook. "Just you wait."

Speak of the devil and he – or she, in this case – shall appear. Jess is sitting herself down at the end of the island next to Raif, still fully dressed in last night's sweater and jeans combo yet looking remarkably bright-eyed and bushy-tailed, as they say.

"Just you wait for what?" she asks.

"Your food," I say bluntly.

"Have you been slagging me off?" she asks, without a hint of surprise.

"You, no," I say bluntly. "Your cooking skills, definitely."

"I've been practicing," she argues. "I had no choice when the chef next door moved into her boyfriend's."

"Fiancé's," I correct with a smile that doesn't come anywhere near close to Jess's beaming grin when Paul pops her breakfast down in front of her, reminding me of Jess's healthy appetite. Although, I'm managing to polish off more than normal, and I'm pleased to say Paul's a decent cook.

"Thank you," she says gratefully, wasting zero time in tucking in. "Where is the fiancé anyway?" Jess asks between bites.

"Right here," Damien calls from the doorway, carrying several carrier bags. Sliding the door closed with his elbow, he detours to plant a soft kiss on my lips.

Raif groans loudly. "How's about you take your nauseating public displays of affection elsewhere?" he suggests, wafting a hand for dramatic effect. "The smell of pheromones is making me want to heave."

"That'll be the shots, mate," Paul says, thoroughly amused. Raif doesn't argue, burying his head in his arms and resting against the island.

"Poor Raif," I only half mock as Damien dumps the carrier bags on the kitchen counter.

"So," Jess says. "What's today's plan?"

"Absolutely naff all," I'm the first to answer. "I'm gonna lie on that couch and not move."

"Now you're getting it," Damien teases, proceeding to unpack the shopping.

"Told you he'd be proud," Paul pipes up.

"I'm with Dani," Raif mumbles into his arms.

"Oh, come on," Jess pleads. "That's so boring. We should do something. Go somewhere."

"Where?" Paul asks, giving Damien a hand.

"I don't know." Jess shrugs. "Somewhere fun. Other than Dani's birthday, we've never gone out as a group, and since Dani is *finally* borderline normal –" I smirk "– we might as well make the most of it before something comes along and sinks her back into her bottomless pit of negativity."

"Erm, excuse me," I protest. "My bottomless pit of negativity has been sealed, thank you very much."

"Prove it," Jess goads.

"Who's proving what?" Amy asks, appearing from the spare bedroom and joining the conversation, stopping to stand beside Damien near the fridge.

"No one's *proving* anything," I state.

"Chicken shit," Paul says.

"Sorry," I say, "but my mind-blowing wake-up call this morning was more than enough exercise for one day." Amy groans, and I mouth a *sorry* in her direction.

"Remind me why I decided to stick around?" Amy asks.

Amy's abandoned the idea of going home completely and has officially accepted a spot at the University of Manchester for September. Amy's slid into the motley crew with about as much ease as I have, and if she cares as much as I do about the people in this very room, I think she knows they'd be hard to leave behind.

"Because life would be severely boring without us," Jess answers Amy's question, and never has a truer statement been spoken. Life is anything but boring with this lot around, or me for that matter, although I am hoping the universe plans to finally let me live out my days in peace.

"I'm with Jess," Paul says, steering the conversation back on track. Jess gapes dramatically, but Paul merely shrugs. "There's a first time for everything, lass."

"You know what," I say, and the light that beams from Jess's eyes is blinding. "Screw it. We all know I won't last five minutes lying around anyway. I'm in. Let's do something."

"Now, we're talking." Jess's voice dances in delight. "Any

ideas on what to do?"

"Something…" I think for a minute. "Crazy."

"Did I just hear that right?" Raif makes the effort to raise his head. "Daniella Blake wants to do something crazy?"

"Why not?" I shrug.

There's a sudden buzz about the room, especially from Jess, who's practically dancing in her seat. Poor Raif is back to snuggling the counter, mind.

"How crazy are we talking?" Amy asks, her excitement evident.

"I got an idea," Paul cuts in. "But with your injuries, I'm not sure Damien will like it."

"Screw my injuries," I state. "And screw Damien." I offer Damien a sweet smile, and he smirks in return.

"Dani wants crazy," Jess states. "So, let's give her crazy."

"Dani's already crazy," Paul utters, gaining him a middle finger from me.

"Just spit it out already," Jess pleads.

"It'd be easier to show you," Paul declares.

"Oh, chill out," Jess says to a heavily sighing Damien. "Unlike you, I've yet to see Dani's adventurous side, and as her best friend, I'm sorry, but I'm not going to let your wonderful, devoted need to take care of her deny me the opportunity."

Damien laughs. "Your ability to slide a compliment in there is appreciated." Jess smiles proudly. "But I already know whatever Paul has in mind is gonna piss me off…royally."

"You know me so well, mate." Paul slaps Damien on the arm in a manly, yet reassuring kind of way that has Damien rolling his eyes.

"Are we doing this or what?" I ask, feeling the urge to make good on my random burst of determination before I chicken out. It's time to take that wacky thing called life and give it a good shake.

Paul proceeds to give Raif a slap on the back of the head, triggering Raif's loud groan. "Come on, mate," Paul says. "We're going on a road trip."

I glance at Damien, but all credit to him, he merely shrugs, and after finishing packing away the shopping, followed by a few showers and a change into something more appropriate for those of us in pyjamas, we head outside.

"Maybe I should stick Raif in the back." I'm assuming Paul's referring to the seatless section of his van, though I'm not sure which one of us he's talking to. "I don't fancy cleaning sick out of my seats."

"I heard that," Raif pipes up as Damien and I climb in the back of the van, letting Amy and Jess climb into the front. "And I'm more than happy to be left behind."

"Trust me," Paul says, climbing into the driver's seat as Raif slides in beside me. "If Dani decides to participate, and it's a massive if, you're not gonna want to miss it, mate." Oh, hell, what have I gotten myself into?

The journey is roughly a couple of hours or so in length, and when Paul pulls up to some random coastline, parking up beside the beach, I'm clueless. We let Paul lead the way, and after one hell of a hill climb that has me mimicking Damien and my second attempt at a first date by jumping on for a piggyback, we find ourselves standing at the top of a cliff.

"Are you insane?" I ask Paul.

"Hey," he protests. "You wanted crazy, and I chose the smallest cliff."

"No way," Damien states.

"Mate," Paul argues. "I've made this jump a thousand times.

It's one of the few places it's relatively safe. No rocks waiting at the bottom, just the water."

"*Relatively* safe," Jess murmurs, staring down at the vast drop. "That sounds comforting." If I didn't know any better, I'd say Jess was a little nervous *for* me. Her excitement faded fast.

"Come on," Paul protests. "I wouldn't let Dani jump if I honestly thought it would end badly. That'd be a little too close to home, don't you think?" There's a brief awkward tension to which Paul scowls. "Moving on…"

"I'm game even if Dani isn't," Amy pipes up, stripping down to her bra and underwear faster than I can blink. Damien's uncomfortable shuffle doesn't go unnoticed.

"And I thought Damien was the adventurous one of the family," I tease Amy, but she merely shrugs, pumped and ready to go.

"Babe," Damien pleads, but I ignore him, moving closer to the edge and looking down. It's not as far as I thought, but there is one issue I should probably address.

"I don't know if I can swim."

"Pretty sure if you jump," Paul says cockily, "Damien will be right behind you to play hero."

This is absolute insanity, yet I'm totally intrigued. Like Paul said, I asked for crazy, and I definitely got it. I stand for a few minutes, contemplating. Damien is behind me, and I can hear him reminding me of my injuries, but to be honest, he's sounding a lot like a broken record.

I'm standing in one of those rare moments of life where I can either run away or take the plunge. Running away is my default mode, the safest option, but there's something inside me, probably the same something that saved me from Adrian, urging me to just let loose and, well, throw myself off a cliff. You only live once, right?

And that's exactly what I want to do. I want to live my best life. I want to do stupid things and laugh more than ever before. I want to experience everything this crazy-ass world has to offer and make the most of the future. I want unforgettable stories to tell my kids and grandkids, stories that outshine my shitstorm past a million to one. I want to feel the thrill of an excitement-fuelled adrenaline so I can erase the only adrenaline I have ever known, one that comes from anger and fear.

Fear. Once my best friend, and my strongest emotion. Irrational, controlling and relentless to a fault, I never thought I'd ever be free of the fear that consumed my existence. Until I found them. I turn to face my family with a smile.

My eyes find Damien's. His worry is evident, but that only makes me smile harder. Damien has been a massive part of my life for longer than I first realised, and his unconditional, undying love for me has given me nothing but hope for a future I never dreamed could be a possibility, let alone full of love and happiness. My beautiful, amazing Damien, he's the light in my darkness, the strength in my heart, and he's taught me something I will be forever grateful for.

I'm a survivor. I've been to hell and back, and I've come out the other side – I would say unscathed, but that would be a humongous stretch – stronger, and maybe even a little wiser. I'm a victim, and I always will be, but with my family beside me, I'll be damned if I don't make the most of my freedom. Adrian is burning in hell, or at least he better be, and I can finally look to the future without the fear of my past haunting me later down the line. Adrian is gone, and he's not coming back. If that's not something to celebrate with a little craziness, I don't know what it is.

"Fuck it," I say, stripping out of my jeans.

Damien protests, igniting a rather loud group argument I opt to ignore. Amusingly though, when I pull my long-sleeved, thumbholed top over my head and drop it to the ground, the group fall eerily silent.

I stand, in nothing but my bra and underwear, and the eyes-wide, jaw-dropped expressions upon my friend's faces are highly entertaining. Amy's and Raif's are a little more shocked than the others, but it is the first time either of them are seeing a glimpse of my scars.

"For people who tell me I shouldn't be insecure about my scars," I tease, taking off my socks and ignoring the twinge of pain in my ribs, "you're doing an awful lot of staring."

"I just…" Jess starts. "I never thought I'd see the day…"

"Yeah, well," I say, moving further onto dry land in preparation for a run and jump kind of manoeuvre. "I'm about to jump off a bloody cliff. Something tells me my scars are the least of my worries."

Underneath the fierce disapproval of my intention to jump, Damien is staring at me in awe, and I know without hearing the words that he's proud of me. Hell, I'm proud of me. Damien's right, my scars are a reminder not of what I've been through but what I've overcome, and that's not something I need to hide, least of all from the people I love.

"You're serious about doing this?" Damien asks.

"Yes, I am," I reply firmly. "And if I die, at least I'll die happy."

"Not fucking funny, Dani," Damien scolds.

I sigh. "Don't you get it yet?" I ask rhetorically. "This is an unbelievably stupid, reckless, yet exhilarating way to say one last fuck you to Adrian." Damien shakes his head, but I think it's more at the name drop than my little rant. "I'm finally free. Free to live my life, to do whatever the hell I want, whenever I want without being held back by fear, and it's all thanks to you bunch of misfits." Smiles all around. "So yeah, I'm gonna jump off that cliff, and I'm hoping you'll be right behind me, because as determined as I'm feeling, there's a distinct possibility of drowning, and I'd rather not *actually* die." It would be sod's law on an epic level if I did.

Damien stares me down for a minute longer, before stripping down to his boxers.

"I said I'd follow you to the end of the earth if I had to," he declares, moving to stand beside me. "And I meant it."

I smile brightly. "On three?"

Damien scowls, highlighting his continued disapproval and reluctance, but with a grit of his teeth he says, "On three."

"One," Paul starts the count.

"Two," the rest of my family pitch in, kick starting my adrenaline rush. "Three."

I take off running, Damien beside me, and when my feet leave the edge of the cliff, my entire body hurling feet first towards the water, the excitement brimming through me is like nothing I could have imagined. My heart pounding, my palms sweaty, any lingering fear dissipates, and I'm overwhelmed by a strange serenity that warms my heart.

This is where I belong, knee-deep in craziness, my past buried in the deepest, darkest corner of my mind, my family cheering me on, and my future happiness jumping right alongside me. I'm free, and nothing could make me happier. Unless, you know, the universe decides to kill me off for my new-found cockiness and obvious disregard for my life right now.

Shake your head all you want, but I'll always be me. Even

with Adrian gone, the anxiety, the lurking paranoia, and the relentless insecurities will be just as much a part of me as any other emotion, and you know what, I can live with that. If I wobble, I'll find my balance. If I panic, I'll find my breath. If I need help, I won't run or hide or bottle it up out of fear or the misunderstood notion that needing help is a sign of weakness; I'm past that. If I need help, I'll ask for it, and the best part is, I'll get it from a group of amazing, relentless, quirky individuals. And when the anxiety or insecurity hiccup passes, I'll remember who I really am. It's amazing how utterly life-affirming plummeting down hundreds of feet can be.

The cold water engulfs me, and as I kick my way back to the surface, pleased to discover I can indeed swim, the relief in Damien's face as he swims towards me echoes my own. The pain radiating through my limbs dulled by an adrenaline high, I burst out laughing. Shaking his head, Damien pulls me close, pressing my body to his, and when his urgent lips meet mine, it's the perfect way to celebrate being alive.

So, here I am, in all my dysfunctional, disfigured glory.

A victim, yet a survivor.

Afraid, yet fearless.

Scarred, yet healed.

Broken, yet... Let's not get *too* cocky, yeah?

Acknowledgements

My husband, Andy
Thank you for your patience (you've needed it!), understanding, dedication & the amazing cover design! But more importantly, thank you for being my rock, my sanity, for believing in me even when I didn't believe in myself & for relentlessly pushing me to make my dream come true. You are my right arm, my inspiration & my strength. I couldn't have done any of it without you & your support. You deserve more credit than I can give!

My kids
Now you know what mum does when you go to bed every night & why I'm always tired :) Dreams can come true, never forget that. Everything I do is for you!

My best friend, Claire
Thank you for being the first person to finish reading my book, for listening to me bang on & on about all things writing & for always being just a message or phone call away. But mostly, thank you for walking this incredible journey with me & for loving *Broken* as much as I do!

My mum, Cathy
Thank you for always being honest, for believing in me & picking me up whenever I doubted myself & for always being on the other end of the phone. Extra big thank you for reading more books than anyone else I know. Your knowledge, insight & opinions are worth their weight in gold.

Steve & Dale
Thank you for always answering my messages, for sharing your honest opinions & your unwavering support.

Emily & Matt
Thank you so much for bringing Dani & Damien to life.

Denise & Jim
Thank you for letting Claire repeatedly put you on the spot & for providing a fresh point of view.

Sandra
Thank you for your friendship & support.

Kath
Thank you for liking, sharing & shouting about my book. You did what I was too embarrassed to do & I'm extremely grateful for your support.

Blanche
Thank you for always being the first to like & share my posts & for your words of encouragement & support.

Our dog & bearded dragon
If I didn't include you, my son would never forgive me!

My readers
Broken would be nothing without you. I am beyond grateful (more than words can describe) to every single person who is willing to give my book a shot. Any honest feedback & reviews are greatly appreciated & I can only hope you enjoy Dani's journey. Thank you so much!

About the Author

Born in Burnley, Lancashire, K.M. Harding is a part-time NHS worker and lover of all things fiction, now living in Cumbria with her husband and two kids. An avid reader, she went on to study Creative Writing at Staffordshire University before embarking on the exciting journey to becoming an author. When not busy entertaining temper tantrums or fighting through traffic on the school run, she can be found buried in a good book or typing away on her laptop with a pair of headphones blaring her favourite songs.

You can follow K.M. Harding on:
Facebook –
https://www.facebook.com/kmhardingauthor
Twitter – **@KMHardingAuthor**
Instagram – **@k.m.harding_author**
Or contact directly via email –
kmhardingauthor@outlook.com

Printed in Great Britain
by Amazon